GENTLE LOVING

The world outside the wagon ceased to exist as Nigh's mouth claimed Brianna's, taking, inciting, absorbing. His mouth worked magic on hers, teasing and tantalizing.

"You taste like the moon," he murmured against her lips while his fingers tangled in her hair.

Brianna's laugh was brief and throaty. "How does the moon taste?"

"Soft, mysterious, elusive." His tongue traced the outline of her ear. Then he grazed her lobe with his teeth, smiling when she shivered.

His mouth blazed a trail along the senstive skin under her jaw, then down the slender column of her neck where he dipped his tongue into the fragrant hollow at the base of her throat. She moaned and Nigh kissed her again, ignoring the aching need of his body as he strove to gentle her. To teach her to trust. To give. To love.

* * *

Praise for Charlene Raddon's TAMING JENNA:

". . . Charlene Raddon keeps the sexual tension high, the characters appealing and the western flavor authentic throughout this sensual novel."

—*Romantic Times*

TODAY'S HOTTEST READS
ARE TOMORROW'S SUPERSTARS

TENDER TOUCH

CHARLENE RADDON

For
Andrea—
A good friend
is like a book I
would forever keep.
Love
Char

ZEBRA BOOKS
KENSINGTON PUBLISHING CORP.

This one is for my family: my sister Janyce for always being there when I need her; my mother Velda for her loving support; my stepdaughter Jenny for eagerly proofing each new book for me; my son-in-law Kevin for knowing when not to tease; my grandson Cody for all the hugs and sticky kisses; and, mostly, for my husband Darrell for being my *Columbus Nigh.*

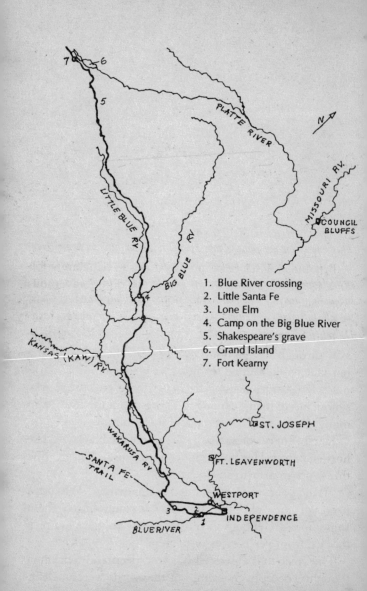

1. Blue River crossing
2. Little Santa Fe
3. Lone Elm
4. Camp on the Big Blue River
5. Shakespeare's grave
6. Grand Island
7. Fort Kearny

Chapter One

St. Louis, Missouri, April 1849

Brianna Wight's heart pounded as she reluctantly followed her housekeeper's son inside the dingy, cavernous livery stable. She felt as though she were entering the very bowels of hell.

Heat from the blacksmith's shop blasted her delicate skin through her clothes and fluttered the veil covering her face as she waited for her eyes to adjust to the darkness. The flames leaping from the forge and the murky silhouettes of men, seeming to dance about the fire like so many devils, were all she could make out.

Harsh, angry voices flew at her out of the blackness, like hurtled knives. Her body stiffened with instant terror. She threw up an arm to shield her face.

"Wait your turn, you stinkin' squawman. Whaddya need yer horse shod for anyways? It's only one o' them Injun horses. Get back to yer slut squaw an' have her pick the lice from yer hair, why doncha?"

The voice that answered was soft, deep and—Brianna thought—deceptively calm, but the words were unclear.

"Why, you bastard!" the first voice yelled.

The sound of flesh and bone striking flesh and bone froze Brianna to the spot. Her heart stopped. That sound was entirely too familiar to her, as was the pain that always followed. She tensed, waiting for the expected blow.

Instead, a man came sailing toward her out of the smithy. Brianna screamed in the instant before he slammed into her. Together, they tumbled to the straw-littered floor in a tangle of arms and legs and skirts.

"You blasted squawman!" someone bellowed. "Look what ya done now. Get up, damn you! That's a lady you're laying on."

Brianna fought for air and shoved frantically at the heavy man weighing down her already bruised and battered body. Pain from a hundred places threatened to rend her unconscious. Inside her head, a voice was saying *"It's not Barret! It's not Barret!"* But the fear had her in its grip and she could not stop battling for her life, as she had been forced to battle so many times before.

Close to her ear a low rumbling voice muttered, "Hell-fire! Give it up, woman, I ain't gonna hurt you."

Hands like steel bands pinned her wrists to the hay-and-horseshit-strewn dirt floor. His panted breath warmed her cheek, smelling of tobacco, and, oddly enough, apples. Brianna could feel her breasts flatten against his hard chest, could feel that same hard chest expand and deflate along with hers, as they each gasped for air. Something stirred inside her, something she had never felt when Barret held her this way, something that left her feeling confused, as well as scared.

"All right," the low voice rumbled. "I'm gonna get up now."

The weight lifted from her body. He towered above

her, ten feet tall and at least three across. As she lay there staring up at him through her veil, still fighting off the fear, he reached down to offer her a hand up. She could see better now, well enough to note that his palm was dirty and callused, the smallest of the long, slender fingers missing a joint.

"You all right?" he asked, not unkindly.

Before she could gather enough sense, and wind, to answer, Sean and his mother were there, bending over her. Brianna groaned as they hauled her to her feet. Every bone in her body ached. It was all she could do to stay upright while Mrs. O'Casey brushed the dirt and straw from her rumpled skirts. She refused to give way to the tears and the pain and the terror that threatened to engulf her. If she couldn't even survive one day of freedom without knuckling under, how would she live long enough to start a new life?

The stranger, glowering now at something said behind him, turned away. Muttering what sounded like a vile curse in a foreign language, he launched himself at his antagonist. Brianna and the O'Caseys barely made it out of the way before both men came hurtling toward them again, locked in a death grip, grunting, cursing, sweating. Sean shouted for the liveryman.

Big enough to pull a wagon to Oregon by himself, Moses Longmire shoved one brawler up against the wall. The other he restrained with only a gentle hand on the man's heaving chest. To the latter he said, "Calm down, Nigh. Ain't nothing but a Kentucky farm boy, not worth bruising your knuckles on."

Now that she was standing, Brianna saw that the man, Nigh, who had knocked her down, was tall—though ten feet was an exaggeration—and lean and lanky, all sinew and muscle without an ounce of fat to spare. His shoulders were broad, his hips slim, his legs muscular and slightly bowed from too many years horseback. She blushed at the sight of his naked shoulder protruding from the neck of his buckskin hunting shirt where it had been half torn off him. As though aware of her reaction, he shrugged back into the thigh-length garment with easy grace.

Never had she seen a man like him. Half the whangs were missing from the fringed seams of his shirt and there was enough grease and ground-in dirt on it to bury a horse. If not for the lightness of his long, shaggy hair and the darker stubble on his face, she would have taken him for a savage.

"Sorry, Longmire." Nigh wiped his bloodied mouth on his sleeve. "Bastard insulted my wife."

There was arrogance as well as defiance in the way he flung his dirty, matted hair from his eyes. Brianna cringed at the idea that he might be throwing lice on everyone. When he picked up a wide-brimmed felt hat decorated with feathers and snake skin, and slapped it against his knee, she sneezed at the dust.

"Now why'd he go an' insult Little Beaver?" Longmire was asking him. The Kentuckian, still pinned to the wall, answered for himself.

"She's a squaw, ain't she? I heard you askin' about her. If you ask me, anybody who'd lie with a whorin', lice-infected squaw ain't got no right walking the same streets as decent folk. Them red heathens wouldn't hesitate to slit the throat of a white man. And I say whites as who mates up with 'em ain't no better."

Longmire glared at the man. "You know, Nigh, I'm wondering now why I tried to save that scum's life." With a wink he stepped away.

Swift as an arrow, Nigh let fly with a blow that knocked the air from the young Kentuckian's lungs with a whoosh. A right cross finished the man. His eyes eased shut and he slid to the ground in an undignified heap. Nigh straightened and dusted off his hands, while Longmire cackled gleefully.

"Goshdangit, Nigh, you ain't lost none of your sap, have you, old hoss? That big mouth's been hanging 'round here for days, haranguing me about the price of my oxen. You know dang well I'm cheaper than anybody else in town."

For the first time, Longmire noticed Sean O'Casey standing with his mother and a woman in widow's weeds. He hurried over and spoke to the widow: "Ma'am, you must be Sean's friend, the one what needs to get to Independence. I hope you'll overlook my friend's rough-house behavior here." He jerked a thumb at Nigh. " 'Twas the Kentuckian's fault. Believe me, ordinarily, Nigh here's as calm an' reliable as an old granny."

Even in the dim light Brianna could see the outraged pride still simmering in the plainsman's stormy gray eyes, putting the lie to the liveryman's words.

Stepping closer, Nigh squinted at her as though trying to see beneath the concealing veil. "Meant ya no harm, ma'am."

Beside her, Sean coughed and cleared his voice. "Er, Mrs. Wight? This here's the man I told you about, Columbus Nigh. He's the one Ma and me hired to guide you to Independence."

Brianna's mouth opened but no sound came out. In horror, she stared at the crude and dirty man standing before her, while her stomach heaved and the room began to spin. A man with lice in his hair who lived with a squaw. A man every bit as violent as the one she was running away from.

Chapter Two

Columbus Nigh squatted with his back against the outer wall of the livery and began to whittle a small piece of wood. His hands flashed as he deftly turned the stick into a tiny, lifelike cougar. From under his hat brim, as he worked, he studied the widow he had agreed to escort to Independence. She was picking her way across the livery yard, careful as sin to avoid each aromatic puddle and suspicious looking pile of muck.

If he could have guessed her age, his blood might have raced a bit at the sight of the white lacy petticoats and trim, black-stockinged ankles peeking out from under her cautiously raised skirts. Truth was, she could be eighty and ugly as a pock-faced whore for all he knew.

So far he hadn't glimpsed a square inch of bare skin on the woman. Even her hands were covered with gloves—white ones, of all the fool things. His only certainty was the slenderness of her body which the black dress and cloak failed to hide. Her voice sounded youngish, but he didn't reckon that proved much.

Seventeen years in the wilderness—which had honed his senses to a fine edge, particularly his sense of judgment—told him she was hiding more than her age under those black garments and the thickly veiled hat she wore.

A man didn't live long in the wild unless he learned to make instantaneous decisions based on nothing more than the sudden flight of a robin or a glint of light where it oughtn't to be. The right decisions. Then, of course, he had to be able to move fast enough to escape whatever form of death was about to descend on him, be it grizzly or a Blackfoot warrior in full war paint.

Columbus Nigh had learned his lessons so well that the Indians called him Man Without Fear.

They were wrong about that; there were plenty of things scared him plumb silly. Such as dealing with "ladies" that likely didn't even speak the same sort of English he did.

Right now, as he watched the O'Casey boy introduce the widow to the horse she was to ride, Nigh's instincts told him she was the one who was scared. And of more than being alone on the trail with a filthy old squawman like him.

Normally Nigh wasn't a curious man, but he found himself wondering who the woman was, and what, or who, she was running from. More than likely, that was why he'd decided to take the job of getting her to Independence so she could join her sister on a wagon train to Oregon. Not a purely sensible reason, he'd admit, but then a purely sensible man never would have left the comfort and safety of the States to roam a savage wilderness in the first place.

Not having known much comfort and safety as a young'un on the docks and crib streets of St. Louis, Nigh hadn't had much difficulty learning to survive out there in the West. He felt a lot less confidence about the woman introduced to him as Mrs. Brianna Villard.

There was another odd thing, because Nigh was positive he'd heard Sean O'Casey call her Mrs. Wight when the boy informed her who was to be her guide.

The woman likely came from money. She was greener than the spring grass poking up through last year's leaves. Simply getting on that horse would be a triumph for her; she'd obviously never been on one before. Her face under the veil was likely as pale as the tatted white collar on her prissy black dress, and he'd be willing to bet that her knees were knocking something fierce under her skirts.

When the boy fetched a sidesaddle and plopped it on her mare's back, Nigh almost ran over to snatch it off. But he'd discovered long ago that experience was the best teacher, and the harder the lesson, the better it was learned. Chances were that she'd get tossed off that worthless scrap of leather before they even got out of the livery yard. No self-respecting horse would be caught dead wearing a sidesaddle.

"She's ready, ma'am," Nigh heard Sean say as the boy finished tying a basket and satchel on behind the bedroll his mother had brought from their buggy.

Mrs. Villard, or whoever she was, peered at Nigh over her shoulder, looking nervous as a sparrow in a tree full of cats.

The boy placed a wooden crate on the ground next to the horse. "Climb up here, take hold of the pommel, and put your left foot in the stirrup." The words were soft, meant only for the widow to hear, but like a hawk high in the sky, Nigh could detect the whisper of a mouse creeping through damp grass. He missed none of the exchange.

"Which is the stirrup? No, don't point," the widow

whispered back. Sensing her rider's nervousness, the mare shied, nearly dumping the woman before she could hook her knee over the pommel. Only Sean's steadying hand kept her in the saddle.

Columbus Nigh put away his knife and rose to his feet in one fluid motion. He swung into his saddle with as little effort as most men used stepping onto a sidewalk. Warily he eyed the satchel and basket on the rump of the widow's mount. "That all you're taking?"

Her abrupt nod was a disappointment. He'd wanted to hear her voice again. Earlier, it had been soft as the downy breath feathers of an eagle's breast, and tremulous, like an aspen leaf on a summer morn.

"Write to me," the old woman said, placing a hand on Mrs. Villard's knee.

The widow looked back at the boy and his mother. Nigh sensed her sudden panic at the thought of leaving her friends, and felt respect bud inside him as she tucked the fear away and told the couple, "Watch out for yourselves, I worry . . ." The way she cut her words off and glanced at Nigh told him she didn't want him to hear the rest.

Turning back to the old woman, she said instead, "Goodbye, dear Mrs. O'Casey. I'll never forget you, you've been far more than a housekeeper to me. Someday I'll repay the enormous kindness you've done me today."

" 'Twas nothing, child. Just you be happy now, that'll be our reward."

Nigh gave a silent nod to the couple, then nudged his dappled gray gelding toward the street. The widow woman clucked her tongue at her mare, and followed. She sat ramrod stiff, hanging on to her dignity and her courage as though they were all she had left. He slowed so that she could ride beside him, hoping to lend her some measure of security with his presence.

Eventually the traffic on the road leading out of St. Louis diminished. Businesses gave way to houses. Then those too became scarce. The smells of kitchen garbage, backyard privies and horse manure faded and Nigh gratefully breathed in the fresh scents of budding green growth and fresh-turned earth. As always, his spirits soared as he left civilization behind and entered a stretch of forest.

The time would never come, he supposed, when he could be content for long within the confines of a town. The noises, the smells, and the sight of so many structures blocking out the sun and fouling the sky with their fumes, bowed him down. Only the taste of the whiskey seemed to improve, until he found himself three-quarters of the way to a good drunk most of the day and night.

Even the whores repelled him, their sore-riddled bodies making him yearn for the sweet, cleanliness of his Snake wife. The thought of lying again with a soft, giving woman created an ache in his groin. It had been so long.

His mind began to speculate once more as to the age and looks of the woman he would be spending the next five or six days—and nights—with. Suddenly, he realized there was no sound of hooves plodding the road behind him. He cursed as he reined in, pivoting the gelding about at the same time. No black-garbed widow on a buckskin mare filled his sight.

She was gone.

Cursing again, Nigh kicked his horse and galloped back toward St. Louis.

He spotted her around the next bend, ranting at her mare as it nibbled contentedly at the new grass alongside the road. His scowl changed to a smile and he slowed to a silent approach.

"You awful beast," she was crying, "don't you know that man will leave us here? He won't care if we get lost. Come on, go, go!"

"Thinking 'bout farming that spot?" he asked.

She nearly jumped out of her saddle. Her hand flew to her heart. "Must you be so quiet? You frightened me half to death."

He eyed her coolly for a long time before answering. "Smart man don't make no more noise than he has to, 'less'n he knows what's about. You ready to go on now?"

"No, I can't. . . . She won't—" She cut her whining short, drew herself up and faced him square on. "Yes, now that you mention it, this does seem a likely spot to settle. It's close to town, there's plenty of wood and a stream nearby."

His mouth quirked in a lopsided smile and she grew even more stiff.

"The truth, sir, is that the horse and I are having a difference of opinion as to the rate of speed we should travel. Perhaps you'd care to add your view?"

The tremor in her voice was plain, though she'd tried to sound calm, even imperious. She reminded him of a lizard, rearing on hind legs to enhance its size and hopefully scare its enemy away. He was tempted to call her bluff. Instead, he took a wooden sliver from a pouch tucked inside his shirt and stuck it in his mouth. It bobbed up and down as he talked.

"Got to show 'er who her master is, ma'am. Right now she reckons it's herself. Pull her head up and poke 'er in the ribs with your heels. Be firm, she'll get the idea."

After a moment's pause, the widow attempted to follow

his advice. Nigh winced at the sharp jerk she gave the reins, but she didn't knuckle under to the mare's whinnied protest. She kept the animal's head high, prodded with her knees and clucked her tongue. When the horse returned obediently to the road, Nigh hid a smile at Mrs. Villard's gasp of surprise, edged with pleasure and pride.

Sheltered by the dense shade of oaks, cottonwoods, maples, and hickory trees, bursting with bright new growth, Nigh and the widow forded creek after creek, until the warmth of sunny, flower-scented meadows and plowed fields was a welcome change.

The widow kept a close watch on their back trail. At the sound of approaching hoofbeats she urged her horse closer to Nigh. Before long, he could see that the strain and unaccustomed exercise of horseback riding was taking its toll on her. He stiffled a smile, knowing how her bottom must be rubbed raw and every muscle probably ached like the dickens. She could barely keep her seat in the awkward sidesaddle, yet she refused to ask for a rest. Taking pity on her at last, he spoke.

"We'll eat here, unless you want to stop at the inn up the road."

The woman's head snapped up, telling him she had indeed dozed off as he'd suspected. Her sudden movement nearly caused her to fall out of the saddle. To save herself, she jerked backwards, inadvertently yanking the reins. With a loud whinny the buckskin reared, almost trampling Nigh, who had dropped back to ride beside her.

He cursed as something flew at him out of the basket on the mare's back. The critter leaped onto his chest, clawed its way up his shoulders, and launched itself into a tree. "What the hell?"

There wasn't time to see what had attacked him. The woman was screaming and clinging desperately to the rearing horse. He grabbed the bridle and brought the mare under control, then pulled the widow from her saddle. In spite of his anger, he was instantly aware of the thinness of her waist and the soft, feminine feel of her.

Her knees buckled the instant her feet touched ground. With a small cry, she clutched at his thighs to keep from falling. Bracing her with his hands on her arms, Nigh slid from his saddle and felt a strong, sudden burst of pleasure inflame his body as her breasts and thighs brushed the entire length of him.

Her scent filled his nostrils. She didn't smell of sweat and sex and cheap ale as the whores did, but of fear and damp wool and roses. At once, his body hardened. The widow tensed. Before she could jerk herself away, he set her from him with gentle hands, wanting her to know she had nothing to fear. She quickly turned her back to him, while he silently cursed the veil that hid her face from him.

"Now what in hell was it jumped outta that basket at me?" he said, resisting the urge to snatch off her hat.

"Out of the basket? Oh—" She glanced about frantically. "Shakespeare, my poor cat. He must be terrified. Where did he go?"

"A cat? What in tarnation are you doing bringing a cat on a trip like this? Don't you have no sense at all?"

She flinched, threw a protective arm over her face, and backed away.

"Gawdamighty!" It angered him that she believed he would strike her. He took a deep breath and forced himself to speak calmly. "Your fool cat's somewhere up that tree. Reckon he'll come down when he gets hungry. Now, you want to stop at the inn or eat here?"

Her reply was slow in coming. Finally, she lowered her arm and looked at him. "Here, p-please. I'd as soon avoid crowded inns, and strangers."

"Suits me."

He led the horses into the trees, leaving the widow Villard behind to search for her pet. Her voice vibrated with timid emotion as she called the cat to her.

Nigh was hobbling her horse with a length of hemp when she found him in the small clearing. Out of the side of his eye, he saw her wince as she sat on a log beside the stream, a grey tabby held securely in her arms. He shook his head ruefully as he wondered how a helpless female like the widow expected to survive a gruelling trek such as it took to get to Oregon. She'd be doing good to live long enough to see Fort Kearny on the Platte River.

"You want somethin' in your belly, you're gonna have to pitch in," Nigh said, uncertain why he was so irritated with her. It meant nothing to him if she died on the trail. "I hired on as your guide, not your servant. For starters, you can tend your own horse."

"The beast is already grazing, and there's water nearby. What else does it need?" Her tone was defensive, as well as weary.

Nigh moved to fetch supplies from the pack lying near his saddle. "What would you want after haulin' some idiot greenhorn around all day?"

Drawing herself up, she retorted, "I may be what you derisively refer to as a greenhorn, Mr. Nigh, but I am not an idiot."

"Reckon you can figure things out for yourself then."

Taken aback, she stood there, probably glaring at him

as he busied himself with a fire. Then she turned and walked to her horse. He noticed her careful effort to keep a safe distance and didn't bother to hide his smirk.

"Well, Beast," she said softly to the horse, "what is it you'd like? Your saddle off? That would feel better, wouldn't it?"

With her chin in her hand, she studied the saddle. Trying to remember how Sean O'Casey had put the thing on, he reckoned. She glanced at him as he filled a pot with water from the stream. He pretended not to see. Saddling and unsaddling her own horse was something she needed to learn, and he had no intention of interfering.

"All right," she whispered, inching closer to the horse. "I'm only trying to make you more comfortable so don't do anything nasty like biting me."

After removing the basket, satchel, and bedroll she looked about, then carried them to a flat, clear spot near the fire. Next, she attempted to loosen the saddle girth, all the while keeping a wary eye on the animal's head in case it decided to become hostile. When she finally had the girth undone and tried to lift off the saddle, she found its weight more than she could handle. She struggled hopelessly to hang onto it, then, giving up, she let go and hopped out of the way, allowing it to fall to the ground.

"Reckon that's one way of doing it," Nigh said, not bothering to hide his disgust. "That bit of leather ain't worth much, but it won't be easy to replace where you're going, so you'd best take care of it."

Taking the gnawed toothpick out of his mouth, he tossed it into the fire. "You bring any riding clothes?"

"I fail to see what possible business it could be of yours what my wardrobe contains," she retorted.

He shrugged and turned back to his cooking. The

woman had spunk, and courage, he'd give her that. But she'd need a whole lot more where she was going.

The meal was simple: boiled coffee so thick it almost needed to be eaten with a spoon, fried bacon and pan bread generously dipped in bacon fat. Nigh had expected the widow to claim that she was too weary to eat, but instead, she dug into the grub with gusto, tossing frequent tidbits to the cat.

From across the fire, Nigh watched her try to eat and keep the veil over her face at the same time, and his curiosity grew. The fool woman hadn't even taken off her gloves. When she finished, she played with the cat, throwing a piece of knotted rawhide for him to catch. He stalked the toy and pounced on it as though it were a mouse, which he then carried proudly back to her. She cooed over the animal and petted it until it purred loudly enough for the man to hear several feet away.

Nigh shook his head. The woman was the perfect image of an old spinster, with nothing and nobody to care about except for a sneaky cat. It arched its sleek back to reach her stroking hand, and butted her leg with its head. What did she look like under the bulky padded cloak and ridiculous veil? Thin, he knew that much. The fabric of her clothing was good quality, and she sounded educated. In spite of the youthful quality of her voice, she moved with the stiffness of an old woman. The longer he watched her, the more he wanted to see her, and learn her story.

What was she running from? A cruel husband? The law? Or a past that might not have been as refined as she tried to make out? The only fact he was sure of was that she had lived in or near St. Louis. One of thousands, and therefore of little help.

The evening grew cold. The widow hugged her cloak

closer about her. She raised a delicate, gloved hand to her mouth, as though to hide a yawn, and asked if he would soon be setting up the tent.

"What tent?" he replied.

"You don't expect me to sleep on the ground, do you?"

"Expected a lady like you to insist on sleepin' in a bed. Myself, I'm used to the open air, ain't done me no harm."

Again she drew herself up to face him. "I am a woman, sir, not some trail-hardened man unused to the comforts of a home. Why, it's barely spring. Look at the sky, it could easily rain tonight."

Nigh glanced up at the pink-tinged clouds. "All right, I'll build you a shelter when we camp for the night. Meanwhile, there's dishes need washed. We'll trade off. I cook, you wash. You cook, I wash."

With barely contained fury, she said, "I take it, Mr. Nigh, that you do not feel your wages sufficient to cover all your services?"

"Oh, they're plenty—for the services I intend to provide." He crossed his ankles and grinned crookedly. "Tell you what, take a five minute nap while I wash up. In the morning, you can cook and wash."

"What do you mean, a five minute nap?"

"Smart man never camps where he cooks. Attracts company you ain't liable to like."

"Company?" She peered nervously into the deepening shadows that danced beneath the sheltering boughs.

"Wolves." He hid the twinkle in his eye.

The widow leaped to her feet, tucked the cat into its basket, then hurried to the stream with the cookware and tin plates. Following Nigh's instructions, she scoured them with sand, shook off the water, and carried them back for him to pack away. Minutes later they were saddled and heading up the road.

At least she knew how to get the work done, once she took a notion to do it, he admitted grudgingly, as he watched her ride ahead of him, her body swaying gracefully in her awkward sidesaddle. That was more than he'd give most "ladies."

Columbus Nigh's experience with white women of quality had not endeared them to him. Oh, they were beautiful enough, and generous, if a young man was willing to enslave himself to them. But he wanted more than to be a rich woman's sexual toy. He wanted respect, and found it was too much to ask.

On the streets near the wharves, among prostitutes and thieves and poor folks simply trying to survive, a man was respected for how much money he flashed about, or for the fear he was able to engender. Nigh wasn't sure which was worse, the pimps, the footpads, or the rich women in their guarded coaches who toured the streets in search of a man who could made them feel brave, adventurous and wicked.

At seventeen, he had felt flattered by the enthusiasm such women felt for him, and proud. Until the night he realized he'd left his knife in the bedroom of a shipping magnet's wife and returned to get it, in time to hear her explaining to her maid the pleasure she found bedding a dangerous man of the streets, "in spite of his crassness and stupidity," while she scrubbed vigorously to rid herself of his smell.

Lost in his bitter memories, Nigh's first hint of the widow Villard's danger was her piercing scream of terror.

Chapter Three

Brianna's scream ended and she woke abruptly as she landed with a splat on the dark muddy road. How something as soft and squishy as mud could feel so hard, she didn't know. She had no breath to moan. Surely she had broken every bone, she thought.

"What in thunder you doin' now?"

The sarcastic voice of her guide jolted her further. Still, she could do nothing but lay there and wheeze, her bonnet half-covering her face, while pain stabbed through her whole body.

"You dead, woman?"

His voice was closer now. With extreme effort she struggled to sit up before he assumed the worst and buried her so he could get on his way.

"No, I'm not dead," she said. "I merely fell asleep and slid out of my saddle."

"If you'd been riding astride the way any sensible person would, you'd a had a better chance of staying on."

"I am a lady, sir! Not some backwoods drab, and I'll thank you to remember that!"

Nigh only laughed. He watched her try to right her hat and said, "Why don't you take that fool thing off?"

"It keeps away the insects." She strove to give her tone hauteur, while yearning for the courage to ignore her fine training in manners and swear at the man.

Mud oozed between her fingers as she attempted to push herself to her feet. Her hands slid out from under her and she found herself on her back again, expecting to hear the man's laughter once more. There was only the whistling of leaves in the wind and the heavy plop of muddy water as it dripped off of her.

The second time she tried to stand neither her hands nor her feet stayed put. The man snickered, leaning against a tree as though he'd nothing better to do than watch her make a fool of herself. Fury tempered her limbs and she came instantly to her feet.

"Reckon, since you got outta that puddle by yourself, you won't need help gettin' back on your horse," he said.

Brianna glanced nervously at the mare, certain the animal had enjoyed dumping her on the road and would do so again the first chance it got. "Please, can't we camp here for tonight?"

"Can, but you still have to get back on that horse. Tomorrow'll be worse. If you can't get on that horse, you'll find yourself walking to Independence alone."

"Alone! But . . . you took my money. You agreed—"

He pushed away from the tree and shoved his face in hers so fast she didn't have time to step back. "I didn't agree to walk you there. You want to go with me, gonna have to show you've got at least as much brains as a halfgrowed Indian. Even a four-year-old Shoshone knows to get right back on or the fear'll defeat him and he'll never ride again."

He stepped back, his gaze raking the length of her as he wrinkled his nose at her smell. "Ought to throw you in the river. You're a mess."

Her mouth opened, closed, and opened again as she glowered at him.

"In fact, you stink of horse piss," he added, the darkness hiding the glint in his eye.

"I'm a mess?" This time she poked her nose in his face. "Let me assure you, Mr. Nigh—if I may correctly call you thus—you smell no better, nor look any cleaner than I. Not only are you the filthiest specimen of manhood it has ever been my misfortune to know, but you are also the most discourteous, most impudent, ignorant, ill-bred, ill-mannered, uncivil—"

"Whoa there, ma'am." He put up a hand, then placed it on his chest. "I'm a simple man, unused to such fine, high-toned compliments. Why, I might get swell-headed listenin' to all that."

Too flabbergasted to speak, Brianna stood there, stiff with anger while mud dribbled from her hands and clothing. The dim light nearly hid the lopsided curve of his smile; she itched to knock it from his insolent face.

"Reckon Mr. Nigh would be proper, all right," he said. "But since we'll be laying our bedrolls next to each other for awhile, it'd be more friendly to use Columbus or Col."

Brianna gritted her teeth so hard she could barely talk. "I have no intention of laying my bed next to yours—*ever!* I've never had lice in my life, and I don't intend to get any now."

"Me neither." His voice was hard and emotionless, like a rock. "At least my clothes are a damned sight more sensible than yours."

"I'll thank you to mind your language in front of me.

I happen to be a lady, not one of the tarts you undoubtedly associate with."

He tucked his thumbs in the back of the wide beaded belt he wore low about his hips, his mouth slowly lifting in that one-sided smile she was becoming familiar with. His gaze roamed the length of her cloaked figure so suggestively she felt as though he had touched her naked body. She blushed, fists clenched at her sides.

"No, ma'am, reckon not," he drawled, "though it's a bit hard to tell from where I stand. Don't know how you come up with that outfit, it's about as attractive as a pig in slop."

"*Came* up with. Oh—" She resisted the urge to stamp her feet. "—I don't know why I bother to continue this conversation. You obviously haven't the education for intelligent intercourse."

Nigh's smile broadened to an open-mouthed grin. "Now there you're wrong, ma'am. When it comes to intercourse, I'm as educated as the next man. More'n some."

Brianna's jaw dropped. Her face flamed hot as an overheated baking oven. She whirled away from him, picked up her muddied skirts and slogged down the road after her horse.

If it hadn't been for the clink of metal as Nigh unsaddled his horse, Brianna might never have found the camp. It had taken her some time to work up courage enough to climb back into her saddle. Now she wanted nothing more than to get back off the horse and lay her chafed and battered body down to rest. She stifled a groan as she dismounted on a rock, clinging to the saddle for a few seconds to gather strength before trying to walk.

The dappled gray blew softly and stamped his hooves, impatient to be free, but Nigh ignored him as he rubbed him down with a handful of grass. With a weary sigh, Brianna unloaded the saddlebags, her valise, and Shakespeare's basket. The cat jumped out and stretched the moment he was free. Even the sight of her pet failed to take her mind from her aches and pains. Her entire being was one enormous misery. Every movement was an effort. She didn't even attempt to lift the saddle, but let it drop to the ground, hoping the man would say something sarcastic so she could tell him how despicable she found him.

When Nigh finished with the gray he built a small fire. Then he gathered poles and leafy branches and went to work constructing a three-sided structure with a sloping roof that also served as the rear wall, placing it so it would block the wind. Branches were piled on top and against the sides. The fourth side was left open to the heat of the fire. Brianna inspected the structure with a skeptical eye, doubtful it would keep out the rain. But she laid her bed inside, knowing it was the best she could expect that night.

A wolf howled in the distance and she whirled toward Nigh. At her feet, the cat emitted a low growl and the hair lifted along his back.

"Fire'll keep away the wolves," Nigh told her.

She felt little convinced. She had hoped to wash up in the creek and put on her one clean change of clothing. Now she was afraid to leave the safety of the fire. She made do by brushing the mud from her clothes as it dried.

Amused as well as irritated, Nigh watched her turn her back to him while she took off her shoes. For him to see her black stockinged feet would be a grave breach of propriety, he supposed. She was so prim and proper he wondered how she would ever lower herself enough to sleep on the ground. But she did not hesitate. Calling the cat to her side, she crawled into bed, cloak, hat, and all. He spat into the fire. The only sensible thing about the woman was her sturdy leather boots.

He watched her curl up on her side, her fist tucked beneath her chin, as a child might sleep. Even with her face hidden by the veil on her hat, she looked defenseless and vulnerable. The cat nestled in the curve of her warm body and her hand came out from under the blanket to stroke the velvety gray head. She scratched behind his ears and under his chin, and the cat purred, licking now and then at her hand. With a sigh, the woman snuggled deeper into her blankets. Her breathing slowed and she slept.

Nigh knew he had witnessed a nightly ritual between the woman and her cat, one so deeply ingrained in her that even exhaustion could not keep it from taking place. She loved the cat the way only a childless woman could. Loneliness, he thought. It touched him in a way that disturbed him.

Giving himself a mental shake, he took out his knife and began to whittle. Not since he was a young'un had he allowed himself to feel the empty ache of loneliness. As a man he had reveled in the freedom of a solitary existence, unshackled by the responsibilities of civilization. But something about the woman and her cat made him look at his life in a new light.

Aimlessness was the word that came to mind. He had gone where he wanted, done whatever he felt a notion of doing, ate when he was hungry, slept when he was tired.

A good life for a young man. He grunted at the thought. He must be getting old to be wondering if he shouldn't have some purpose in life, some justification for his existence. Then, letting his mind delve deeper into his soul, he knew it wasn't the widow that had brought about the change. It was Little Beaver.

Little Beaver had brought softness to his life, the kind only a woman can bring, with a word, a touch, a smile. He felt guilty for a moment, realizing it was more the softness that he missed, rather than Little Beaver herself. She had been a good wife and he had cared for her, but he doubted there had been any real love between them, not on his part, anyway.

Someday he might find himself another Little Beaver, a woman to ease his physical needs and maybe give him children. An Indian woman who would ask nothing more from him than meat in the pot and a little foofuraw now and then. He didn't try to fool himself about finding love. That was for romantics, women and children who hadn't learned the harsh realities of life. Nigh knew, though. He knew the closest he would ever get to love was the respect of an Indian woman who appreciated the food, shelter, and protection he provided in return for her warm body in his bed. That was reality.

Across the fire the cat lifted his head at the loud crackling of a log. The luminescent feline gaze settled on the man, narrowing to golden slits that seemed to warn him to keep his distance. Holding the cat's gaze with his own, Nigh smiled wistfully. Overhead, thunder rolled across the dark sky. The woman was right; they were in for a storm.

But Nigh had known it long before they stopped to eat. He had smelled it on the wind, heard it in the howl of the wolf. The cat knew it too, and snuggled closer to his mistress beneath the brush shelter.

It was then Nigh realized that the hand still peeking from under the woman's blanket was gloveless. It was also smooth and slender and young.

The first thing Barret Wight noticed when he arrived home that evening was the absence of cooking smells emanating from the kitchen. Odd, he thought.

His voice, as he shouted for his wife, echoed ominously in the long empty vestibule. He raced up the stairs two at a time to find the master bedroom empty. The wardrobe and her dresser still held her clothes. Nothing seemed to be missing. She had probably fallen asleep in the garden again.

Splay-footed, he posed before the serpentine-fronted chiffonnier and surveyed his image in the beveled mirror. His face was as perfect as ever except for the lock of hair that drooped obstinately onto his forehead. He spit on his fingers, plastered the unruly lock back in place, and hollered again out the bedroom doorway.

"Brianna, where the hell are you?"

Built something like an upended boxcar, Wight shook the floor with his heavy-footed gait as he strode down the curved staircase. In his mother's native German his given name meant "mighty as a bear" and he was proud to have a body that fit the bill. At the foot of the stairs he glanced into the empty parlor. Then he headed for the kitchen. "Damned woman," he mumbled. "What does she mean, ignoring my call?"

The corners of his mouth curled toward his feet in a

vicious snarl as he kicked open the kitchen door, ready to chew his young wife's head off.

The scene that met his gaze not only brought him up short, but wiped the frown from his face as well.

"What the blue devil . . . ?"

Words failed him. For the first time in his life Barret Wight was at a loss to know what to say or do or think. But a distinct tightening of his innards warned of the terror that soon struck him full force in the belly.

Cupboard doors hung open, their contents strewn about. Chairs lay toppled across a rag rug littered with broken pottery, cooking utensils, embroidered tea towels, a single low-heeled slipper—Brianna's—and blood.

Blood was everywhere.

He sidestepped a chair as he made his way into the room, brushed against the wall and tore his shirt on a nail where a decorative plaque once hung. At the table he picked up a small crock Brianna used to hold her household money. It was empty. He righted two chairs and bent to gather up the remains of Brianna's favorite tea pot, its shiny surface marred with flecks of dried blood.

Dropping the shard, he stared at the smooth, plump flesh of his hands while an image formed in his mind, Brianna with her eyes swollen shut, her lip split. Brianna lying on the floor, so still, so very still.

"Ah Jesus," he muttered.

But she had been all right this morning, he was sure of it. Where was she? Was it her blood on the kitchen floor? Dread twisted his bowels as he barreled from the room. He searched the entire house before rushing outside. The barn was empty except for the matching pair of sorrels that Brianna called Maisy and Marve. A multi-colored barn cat curled around his leg and mewed hungrily. She'd probably named it, too. He kicked it out of his way, then ran from stall to stall, up the ladder to the loft, and back down. He kicked the cat again, then lurched out into the yard. His breathing became ragged before he made it completely around the house, searching in and around the bushes, but he didn't stop.

He raced through the budding orchards, tromped across the freshly plowed vegetable garden. A bit of cloth the color of her dress was snagged on the fence. On a bush he found another swatch. The trail led to the river. He tore down the hill, oblivious of the bloody slipper he still carried in his scrunched fist.

Bent from the waist, his clammy hands braced on his knees, Barret Wight blinked to clear his eyes of sweat and stared at the muddy Mississippi. The river churned within its swollen banks, as brown as Brianna's tea with its full dollop of cream. Its depths were known to hide more than one body. It seemed to mutter her name, ending with a chuckle.

Wight had passed the ripe age of forty-six some months back—twenty years his wife's senior. His strong body was not as tight and smoothly muscled as when he'd married her. Could she have run away? Fear was a vile stench in his nostrils.

She'd grown thin but was still handsome in her way, especially in the pastel colors he picked out for her— colors she seemed terrified to wear, but wore for him anyway. And when she smiled, then, by thunder, she was almost beautiful. It shocked him to realize how much he hated to lose her.

Brianna wouldn't have had the courage to leave him voluntarily. Of course, someone could have helped her run away. He frowned, considering the possibility. Who?

Snoopy old Mrs. O'Casey who came every day to clean and cook for them? Or—even more absurd—a man? No, she was too skinny and drab to attract a man.

Yet someone had ransacked his home. And Brianna was gone. He had no choice but to believe she was dead.

Who would have dared to enter his home and lay hands on what belonged to Barret Gunther Wight? Anger roared in his ears. His chest expanded as he sucked in air and flexed his sagging muscles, ready to fight. Where was the skunk-breathed, belly-crawling snake of a sonuvabitch who'd violated his home and . . . ? He didn't want to say what else, didn't even want to think it. Yet it was there, burning his brain the way prime Scotch whiskey burned his throat.

"Where is she?" he ranted. "Where the hell is my wife?"

An hour later Barret Wight stood beside a seated Mrs. O'Casey, watching Marshal Will Rainey examine his ransacked kitchen. The marshal looked harmless enough, with his big ears and sleepy hound dog eyes, but Barret knew that underneath, the man was a bulldog.

"What time did you leave, Mrs. O'Casey?" Will asked.

"Oh, 'twas nigh on to two o'clock, me usual hour. I'd prepared lunch for Mrs. Wight, then did the laundry and tidied up. She liked to prepare supper herself. Tonight it was fricasseed chicken, Mr. Wight's favorite."

Rainey looked at the overturned pan on the stove. "Smells like burnt chicken to me. Some of it must have spilled into the firebox." He bent to peek inside the cold firebox, then reached in to draw out a wad of scorched fabric. As he shook it out, Mrs. O'Casey leaped to her feet.

"Mrs. Wight's dress!" she cried. "My lands, it's all bloody and torn."

Wight collapsed onto a chair. He ran a hand over his face, his eyes wide with shock. "My God, she's dead. She really is dead."

"Can't be sure of that till we find her body," Rainey said. "Is this the only room that was ransacked, Wight?"

"Yes."

"Why, 'tisn't true!" Mrs. O'Casey said. "The silver's missing from the dining room and the tea service as well."

"That's right. I forgot." Wight mopped his forehead with his kerchief. He'd been a fool to fetch the marshal. It shamed him that he'd let panic rule him instead of smarts. "Her jewelry is gone, too, and my money stash, nearly seven hundred dollars. Had a good week at the poker tables. But none of that matters. All I care about is my wife."

The man's slick, Rainey thought. Too slick—like the underbelly of a snake. He'd always hoped someday to see Wight behind bars permanently, if not hanging from a rope. He picked up the soft doeskin slipper, still damp from the man's sweaty hands. "You know of anyone who might have wanted to harm her?"

"Who, for Chrissake? She didn't know anybody, never left the property," Wight said.

"Humph!"

The men turned to stare at Mrs. O'Casey and Wight felt a moment of panic at the hate she directed at him.

"I don't like to speak ill of an employer, but—" the woman said, "—him there, Mr. High and Mighty, he could answer that, if he had the gumption. Why, I can't count the times I've come in to find the poor missus all bruised up, eyes blackened and all, like she'd been in a drunken brawl. This morning, for instance. Clumsiness, she claims. Bah!"

"Is this true?" Marshal Rainey peered speculatively at the man. "Were you in the habit of striking your wife?"

Wight cursed wordlessly. He'd fire that blinking busybody the moment this was over with. "There might have been a time or two when I'd had too much to drink and slapped her around a bit. Never more than she deserved, though. And I swear she was alive when I left for the brewery this morning."

Rainey's eyes narrowed. "Seems to me I've seen you around town with a certain little redhead. Fact is, I'm surprised to learn you still live here at the old place. I was under the impression you owned that house Glory lives in on Locust Street."

Before Wight could answer, Mrs. O'Casey shouted, "You philandering blackguard. 'Twasn't enough that you beat her every chance you got. Why, you aren't fit to walk the same ground she does, the poor child."

The marshal's eyebrows rode up his forehead as he noted the murderous glint in Barret Wight's eyes as the man glared at his housekeeper. "Go on home, Mrs. O'Casey. I appreciate you coming over here with us. If I need anything more from you, I know where you live."

At that moment they heard the marshal's name called from outside. Wight and Mrs. O'Casey followed him into the yard. They stood on the porch, frozen by curiosity as a policeman handed a shoe to the marshal. Another policeman came from the barn carrying a shovel and a dirty, bulging flour sack. He handed the sack to Rainey.

"Found this here buried in the barn, in one of the stalls. I think you'll find it interesting."

A gasp brought Mrs. O'Casey's gaze around to Wight, his face as pale as the flour sack had been when new. He swallowed and erased his expression.

"Here's your wife's other shoe." Rainey tossed it to him. "It was down by the river, along with a slew of prints and a piece of her dress."

Wight fumbled and nearly lost the shoe. His gaze was glued to the sack in Rainey's hand. He struggled to contain his panic as he watched the marshal set the dirty sack on the wooden porch, then slowly open it. Inside was the missing silver.

"Know anything about this, Wight?" Rainey said.

Wight shook his head. His mouth opened but nothing came out. He had to clear his throat before he could say, "Is that all they found?"

"Why? You bury something else out there?"

"Me? No." Wight let his eyes widen as if the full implication of the marshal's tone had just struck him. "You think I killed Brianna? Jesus, maybe I did slap my wife around a bit. What man doesn't? I think she even liked it. But kill her? You—" His voice hardened. "—I want you to find the bastard who did this, you hear me?"

"I hear, Wight, and I'll find him, if I haven't already."

"How'd you tear your shirt?" a policemen asked. "Get in a fight or something?"

A thousand years had passed since Wight caught his shirt on the nail in the kitchen. He'd barely noticed it then and was a long way from remembering it now. Rainey stepped over to inspect the tear.

"Seems you've some questions to answer, Wight."

Wight's head pounded as his guts twisted and writhed.

Think, man, think. His throat seemed to close in on him. He didn't see the satisfied gleam in Mrs. O'Casey's eyes.

"Nothing to say?" Rainey pursed his lips and gave a slight nod. "All right, what do you say we go down to the river and see how close those prints come to matching yours? If that doesn't loosen your tongue, maybe a few nights in jail will."

Golden Heart Finalist

Tender Touch

Brianna Wight fled her
wealthy but abusive husband,
harboring terrible secrets.
She found safety and much more
in the arms of another--
mountain man Columbus Nigh.

Zebra Lovegram Dec. '94
ISBN 0-8217-4777-0

Other Books By
Award Winning Author

Charlene Raddon

Taming Jenna
June '94

Forever Mine
Jan. '96

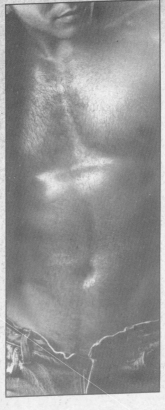

Tender
Touch
by
Charlene Raddon

Chapter Four

Shortly before dawn Brianna awoke to a dreadful sense of unease. Instinct warned her the cause was not the drizzling rain soaking her bedding. She felt for the old pistol Mrs. O'Casey had packed in her saddlebag. In spite of her doubts about being able to use it, the presence of Columbus Nigh sleeping so close to her was enough to make Brianna hide the gun under her blanket before going to bed.

Fortified by the weight of the cold steel in her hand, she eased her eyes open. Even though the eastern skyline had begun to lighten, the veil of her hat kept the night dark as pitch. Still, she was able to make out the three pairs of muddy boots silhouetted against the fire. Her heart crept into her throat as her gaze inched up the boots to see dirty pantaloons, poncho-covered torsos, and finally, dark leering faces crowned by broad, flat-topped hats. Each man held a rifle. An arsenal of knives and pistols protruded from their belts.

"Look, Jose, the señora ees awake."

"Sí."

"Get up, señora, let us see what you look like, eh?"

The men's laughter was coarse. Brianna was too frightened to move.

"Come on, woman, move it!"

This voice held no Spanish accent, or patience.

Brianna crawled from the shelter as modestly as possible, the gun concealed in a fold of her rain-dampened skirt as she rose to her feet. A quick glance told her Columbus Nigh was gone. And so were the horses.

Even in the dim light she could see that the third man was not Mexican like the others, but fair and lanky.

"Ahh, so tall." The Mexican's smile was missing teeth. "You weel need a ladder for thees one, Jose."

"Ees *bueno*," said Jose. "Can hump and kiss titties at same time, no?"

They laughed.

Brianna blushed. She wondered if the pistol hidden in her skirt was loaded and ready to fire. Never before had she even held a gun, though Barret kept a collection of weapons in the gun cabinet in his study.

"What do you want?" She tried to keep her voice steady. "My . . . husband will be back any moment."

The blond man glanced around the clearing.

"What husband? 'Pears to me you're all alone. Get that hat off and let us take a look at you."

With one hand she pulled out the long hat pin, then took off the bonnet and let it fall to her feet. At least she could see better now.

"Eet ees the widow, Jose, the one we see in town, remember?"

"Ai-yi-yi, someone punch her up good, no?"

The blond American shushed the others. He seemed nervous, his gaze darting around every few moments. "What are you doin' out here alone?"

"I told you, my husband is here somewhere."

Her hand was shaking so hard she feared she would shoot off her own toes, or stab herself with the sharp hat pin she still held in her other hand. Where was Shakespeare? And Nigh? Anger shafted through her at the thought of her paid guide abandoning her there to the mercies of scoundrels like these three.

"We waste time, *gringo*. Tell her to take off the clothes. I grow eager." Jose rubbed himself.

The American gave one last look around, then motioned for her to disrobe.

Brianna tried to back away and came up against the brush shelter. Her feet in the damp stockings were so stiff and cold she doubted she could run if given the chance. She tried to breathe in only the fresh smell of the rain but the stench of the three unwashed men was too strong. Their breath stank of onions, chili peppers, and whiskey. The jingle of harnesses and the braying of a mule out on the road told her they were probably Santa Fe traders. Would they take her with them, or merely use her and leave her there like unwanted refuse?

She could shoot only one of them with the old pistol before the others would be on top of her; time would not allow for reloading. It would be better to stall and pray someone came along to help her.

"Please, you can see I'm already injured. Don't—"

"That's real sad, lady, but you're wasting your breath. Get undressed—now!"

"No, I . . ." Her eyes widened as Jose drew a knife and tested the long slender blade on a thumbnail. Her mouth was too dry to speak any more. It didn't matter; she was out of time. She was about to be raped. Could she expect them to be gentler or kinder than her own husband? Not likely. Determination darkened her eyes as she raised the gun from the folds of her skirt and pointed it at the big man.

"Go, or I'll shoot." She spit the words through clenched teeth to keep from stammering. Without moisture in her mouth, they sounded slurred. The nose of the long, heavy pistol wavered. She clamped the hat pin between her teeth as if it were a rose and gripped the gun with both hands to keep it steady. Her hoarse, dry voice rose to a shriek. "I mean it, get out of here."

"I'd do what she says, boys. She looks a bit wobbly. Gun's liable to go off any second."

The voice came from somewhere behind her, a low, even drawl that seemed placid until one noticed the menacing undertone. It sent shudders down Brianna's back, though she knew its owner was on her side.

"You get the big one, ma'am. I'll get the other two. Don't try to get fancy, aim for the heart. Dead men can't shoot back."

With a nervous laugh Jose made a show of putting away his knife. "Hell, we were only funning with her, señor. She ees ugly, anyhow."

The eyes of the three traders sifted shadows in a desperate search for the newcomer, their hands edging toward their weapons.

"Hawken's gettin' heavy, boys. Makes my hand tired holding it so long. Might accidentally squeeze the trigger 'fore I'm ready, if ya know what I mean."

The American jerked his head at his partners. They scurried for the wagon and he followed.

Even after they were gone, Brianna stayed where she was, so rigid with cold and fear she couldn't move if she wanted to. The wagons clattered down the road, and still she stood there.

"Put that gun away now, ma'am."

She looked down at the weapon clenched in her half frozen hands. How proud Mrs. O'Casey would have been at the way she'd faced up to the men. Hysteria bubbled inside her at the thought of how Barret might have reacted. Laughter burst from her like thistledown from a ripe pod.

Nigh closed the distance between them with long urgent strides. "You going crazy on me, woman?"

She covered her face with her hands, pistol in one hand, hat pin in the other.

"Dang fool, give me those before you put your eye out or shoot one of us." He grabbed for the weapons and she ducked in the instinctive manner of a woman used to being hit. "I wasn't going to hit you."

Her head came up and she peered at him anxiously, one eye discolored, the other swollen shut.

"Ah Jesus," he muttered. "Did those bastards do that?"

She bowed her head, shaking it slightly. He took the pistol from her and set it aside. Then, with one finger under her chin, he forced her to look at him. His gentle hands tested her torn lip and the swelling along her cheek and jaw.

"Who did, then?" His voice was soft but with an edge to it.

"I fell."

"Like hell you did."

His hands dropped to his hips as he stared at her, disgust plain on his face. She refused to meet his gaze. He stalked off into the trees, returning with the horses. She watched him hobble them, then rebuild the fire with quick, angry movements, and thought about the gentle way he had examined her face. Her guilt was heavy, knowing now that he had only meant to help her. Had Barret's cruelty rendered her incapable of recognizing kindness? The silence grew tense and unbearable as she debated how to make it up to him. "It was my husband," she said softly.

Nigh swiveled on the balls of his feet as he crouched by the fire, looking up at her. "Thought you were a widow."

"I am," she blurted, flustered now. "He . . . he was older and . . . and he suffered a seizure while he was hitting me. He was buried yesterday morning before Mrs. O'Casey drove me into St. Louis."

"Weren't in any hurry, were you." It was a comment, not a question.

Brianna's face flushed with heat. "There was nothing to keep me there. I have to reach my sister in Independence before she leaves for Oregon Territory. There was no time to lose."

"No house or property to take care of?"

"My solicitor will see to that." She wondered when she had learned to think so quickly and lie so well.

Nigh rose to his feet and went to the packs for bacon and coffee, certain she was lying. When he brought the food back to the fire, she held out her hands.

"I believe it's my turn to cook." He handed over the food and went to sit with his back to the tree where he had spent the night.

"I thought you had abandoned me," she said as she knelt by the fire and began to slice the bacon on a piece of tough rawhide with the knife he had left there.

"Confounded horse of yours decided she wanted to go home." He took out one of his homemade toothpicks and stuck it between his teeth. It was good, having a woman cook for him again. "Amazing how much ground a horse can cover, hoppin' along, hobbled like that. Would a-been funny if I hadn't been so damn angry."

"I see your language has not improved."

Nigh grunted. Damn but she was a prissy one. "Never felt no need to improve it before."

As on the previous day, the smell of bacon sizzling brought Shakespeare running. She snatched him to her and hugged him until he complained. "You're going to have to learn to stay near or you'll be left behind, you naughty cat."

Nigh admired her long, graceful fingers as she stroked the cat. Tendrils of hair had escaped her bun during the night and fluffed out about her face. His hands itched to touch them. "How long were you married?"

Brianna released the cat, wiped her hands on her skirt, and bent to turn the bacon strips. "Three years."

"No children?"

She shook her head, with sadness, he thought.

"Why'd you stay with him?"

One thin shoulder lifted and fell. "I was twenty-three when Barret came along and asked me to marry him. You've heard the expression, 'Beggars can't be choosers.'"

It bothered him that he felt her pain so keenly. His sudden need to protect her bothered him even more.

She sat back on her heels and stared into the fire. "The first time he hit me was on our wedding night. When I threatened to leave him, he destroyed every stitch I owned. I wore one of his shirts for three weeks until he was satisfied I would stay put. That was before Mrs. O'Casey came to work for us."

Nigh spit out bits of toothpick. He had gnawed it until there was little left but splinters.

As if just realizing she had spoken aloud, she colored and said, "I'm sorry. I-I don't know why I told you that. I've never told anyone that before."

There was nothing he could say so he changed the subject. "You know how to shoot that gun of yours?"

"No, it was Mrs. O'Casey's. She insisted I take it."

"Better learn 'fore you try to use it again. Damp as it is, that old pistol likely woulda misfired or blown up in your face. Caplocks are more reliable than flintlocks, but not by much."

The silence that followed lasted through the meal. While Brianna gathered up the plates and cookware to scrub in the stream, Nigh fetched a clean set of buckskins from his pack. Then he yanked off his dirty shirt and stuffed it inside.

Brianna blushed at the sight of his broad naked chest and the curly hair that angled down over his hard flat stomach to vanish beneath the waist of his trousers. When he turned, she saw they weren't trousers at all, but Indian leggings tied to the drawstring of a breechclout, leaving his naked buttock exposed to her view. She knew she should rebuke him for taking such liberty in front of her, but couldn't stop staring at him.

He saw her standing there as if turned to stone, the dishes forgotten in her hands.

"Stay upstream if you're heading for the creek," he said, hiding his smile. "Someone pointed out recently that I needed a bath." He tossed a bar of soap in the air and caught it deftly in his palm. "Might consider trying the water out yourself."

At the creek she scooped up fine sand and scoured the skillet while she considered his suggestion. The water was neither deep nor swift and looked wonderfully inviting. She glanced downstream. How long would his bath detain him? She drew her lower lip between her teeth and studied the water again. Then she gathered up the dishes and raced back to camp for her valise. Minutes later, she was wading into the creek, her clothes neatly folded on the bank.

The water reached only to her upper thighs. She sank down until it touched her chin and the sandy bottom grated against her bare bottom. Water boiled about her shoulders, the backwash pooling between her breasts. She sat on the bottom a long time, enjoying the tug of the current at her body, before she washed the dirt from her skin with sand, wishing she had Columbus Nigh's bar of soap.

As if her wish were magic, the soap landed in front of her, splashing her face. She nearly lost her balance as she grabbed to keep it from floating away. Then she saw him.

On the bank, Columbus Nigh hunkered on the balls of his feet, shockingly naked, dressed only in his clout. His lips quirked up on one side as he watched her flounder.

"What do you think you're doing?" She huddled under the water, praying he could not see through the swirling current. "How dare you come here and spy on me like this. Go, at once, or I'll . . . I'll—"

He laughed, a blade of grass dangling from his teeth. "Or you'll what? Reckon I'm the one with the advantage here. How 'bout I scrub your back?"

"How 'bout you drop dead!" she hissed.

Chapter Five

The smile left Columbus Nigh's lips. He scowled, hating himself for using her fear of men against her, but knowing she would never let him examine her injuries otherwise. "You placed yourself in my care, woman, so you're just gonna have to put up with me. I figure, bad as your face looks, you likely have other injuries I can't see under your clothes." He paused for effect. "And I intend to see."

Her mouth fell open. "Why, you're nothing but a filthy, licentious old lecher."

The smile returned. "There you go, complimentin' me again. You through washing?"

"No! And I'm not coming out until you go away."

Nigh stood slowly. "Reckon I'll just have to help you finish up then. Ain't got all day."

Brianna gasped, unable to believe the man's nerve. At the edge of the water he stopped to pull off his moccasins. He was so close she could see the hair on his arms, the veins standing out on the backs of his large hands—and more.

Nigh relished the way her blush spread down her neck onto her chest, but his gaze didn't stop there. It dove beneath the surface of the water, past the arms crossed over her breasts, to the shadowed vee at the apex of her slender legs. When his eyes darted back to her face and he saw her blanch with fear, his amusement died.

She was beautiful, in spite of the bruises and her thinness. Beautiful, brave, and cruelly abused.

Once again, he felt sick with himself for the way he had to treat her, but his need to make sure she wasn't too badly injured was too strong to ignore. He gentled his voice when he spoke: "No reason to fear me, woman. Seen a hundred women bathing naked in the Indian villages I've lived in. Don't reckon you're put together any different than them. And I ain't so hungry I got to stoop to spying on you, either."

He slipped his moccasins back on his feet, knowing he was trying as hard to convince himself as he was her. The truth was, he was hungry. Hell, he was starved. But that wasn't why he was there. He'd put two and two together and had come up with cracked ribs. How fast they traveled would depend partly on how much she could take, which wouldn't be much with cracked ribs. He hadn't expected the sight of her body to tie his insides in knots, then send his blood racing hot and wild so he had to sit down to hide the evidence of his desire.

But he should've known. Like he knew right now that the honorable thing to do would be to leave.

Brianna shivered in the chilly water. "If you didn't come here to spy on me, why won't you go away?"

The very question he had been asking himself. "Are your ribs broke?"

"I . . . I'm not sure."

"That's why I'm not leaving till you let me check you over. Now, are you coming out, or do I come in after you?"

She wanted to defy him, but Barret had done his work too well. Man commanded, and she obeyed. First, she drew the pins from her hair and let it tumble into the water. As she stood, she pulled the thigh-length mass in front of her so it hid her breasts and abdomen like a fur cape.

The sight tightened the knot in his gut. Her hair was the color of pine bark, brown with a hint of red, thick and glossy with gentle waves that ruffled about her upper thighs. Hair a man could get lost in.

She started toward him and his breath caught. His stomach contracted in pain, as though Longmire had just punched him with one of his ham-sized fists.

The moment she reached shore she snatched up her drawers and pulled them on over her wet skin beneath her shield of hair. The strands parted as she worked, teasing him with tantalizing glimpses of bare skin. The fine muslin of the garment clung and became transparent, adding to, rather than detracting from, her allure, in spite of the bruises it failed to hide. When she picked up her chemise he said, "If you've got broken ribs, they'll need to be bound up 'fore you put that on."

"I've no intention of allowing you to put your hands on my bare. . . . If you must check my ribs, it will have to be through my chemise."

"Fine, let's get to it so we can get out of here."

Before he could object, she pulled on her petticoats. Then she turned her back to him so he could get on with his examination.

"The first chance I get," she said, "I shall write Mr. Longmire a scathing letter about the type of men he recommends as trustworthy guides for unprotected females."

Nigh chuckled. "Longmire'll get a good laugh out of

that, probably nail the letter to the livery wall for every-body to read."

Beads of water trailed from her neck down the smooth flesh of her back to soak into the lacy edge of her chemise. His gaze followed the droplets as he slid his hands around her waist and gently tested each rib. When his thumbs brushed the undersides of her breasts, she sucked in her breath, and he froze. Her heart thudded wildly in time with his own until the sound filled his ears.

The need to cup her breasts with his hands and bury his face in her hair was overwhelming. He wanted to put his lips to her soft skin and drink the moisture beaded there. He wanted to erase her pain and show her not all men were like her husband. His jaw worked as he struggled for control. Easy, squawman, she'll bolt like a half-broke filly, he told himself, purposely using the hateful name to help cool his ardor. Still, a year's worth of seconds passed before he could drop his hands, a month's worth before he could speak. "Nothing cracked, near as I can tell. Get dressed. We're wasting time."

Letting out the breath she had been holding, she bent to take up her dress and corset.

"Damn fool woman!" He grabbed away the corset. "No wonder you almost passed out at the livery. Your body hasn't suffered enough, you got to torture it more? Lord save me from greenhorns! First a damned sidesad-dle, now a corset. Trail's no place for wearing foofuraw like this. I ought to— No, by hell, I will!"

With that he flung the garment far out into the creek. The current carried it away. She seemed so timid he didn't expect her to jump him, fists flailing.

"You had no right to do that," she screamed.

He seized her wrists and pinned them behind her to

stop her from hitting him, bringing her body against his.

Mortification filled her as her thinly clad breasts flattened against the hard wall of his chest and her thighs brushed his. She writhed against him, struggling to break free. His hands tangled in her hair, pulling her head up so she had to look at him.

For one long moment he stared down at her, at the thick brown lashes that lined the one startlingly blue topaz eye that was able to glare back at him, at the finely etched curves of her upper lip and the cracked and swollen lower one that made her look as though she were pouting. At the storm-dark bruises that failed to hide her beauty. His hands clenched at the feel of the silky hair they held. His body reacted to her wiggling body. He longed to rip away her garments and taste her warm flesh, to feel himself inside her. It was insane, yet he knew if he didn't walk away soon, she would find herself on the ground beneath him. Without a word, he let go and stalked away.

Left alone, Brianna gulped in air and ordered her body to stop shaking. She felt chilled after the heat of his embrace and wrapped her arms about herself. Gradually the fear receded and her pulse slowed. What had he thought as he stared at her? As he held her? She had felt his hardness pressing against her belly and knew he could easily have forced her to submit to him. Was it honor that made him walk away? Or revulsion?

By the time Brianna returned to camp, Columbus Nigh had put out their fire and stored away their gear. The dappled gray stood patiently while Nigh smoothed out the saddle blanket, then swung the saddle onto the horse's back. Nigh knew the instant she walked back into the camp. He felt her presence with every nerve ending, every muscle, every pore.

Her skirts rustled slightly as she went to the brush shelter to ready her own things. Nigh adjusted the cinch. He heard the cat complain as she ousted him from her bed, heard the blankets snap as she shook them. He caught the clean, woman smell of her and gritted his teeth, trying to concentrate on his work and ignore the way his body reacted to her, like a bull elk in rut. She was a complication he didn't need. Even if he were looking for a woman to take into his life, it wouldn't be a bluenose like her. Not that he was fool enough to think she might accept him, not an illiterate old fur trapper like him—not a squawman.

Brianna hurried to saddle Beast and tie on her bedroll and valise. Though she had not looked at him once since entering the camp, she was well aware that Nigh was mounted and waiting for her. She glanced over at him as she tucked Shakespeare into his basket and was surprised to see that he was clean-shaven now. Cleaned up and dressed in his new buckskins, he was almost handsome. Not sinister at all. Even his hair was clean.

The leather squeaked as she lifted herself into the saddle. She squirmed to seat herself more comfortable. Suddenly the saddle gave. She yelped as she slid to the ground.

Nigh was beside her in the flash of a horse's tail. "You all right? What happened?"

"I'm fine, just a bit shaken. I don't know what went wrong. The saddle slipped." She stared at the saddle hanging upside down under the horse's belly while the pain slowly receded.

Anger surged through Nigh. He had expected too much of her, insisting she take care of her own horse. Her fall was his fault. Twice in one day he had endangered her life, first by leaving her alone when he went after her horse, then by not double-checking her saddle before she mounted. No, by damn, it wasn't all his fault. "It's that damn sidesaddle!" He pulled her to her feet. "Asinine female nonsense ain't worth a pocketful of buffalo piss on a dry day."

He didn't notice her grimace of pain at his rough handling. He undid the girth, yanked off the sidesaddle and pitched it into the creek. Brianna watched the tiny bubbles rise to the surface where her saddle sank out of sight, taking her heart with it.

"You'll use my saddle the rest of the way." His tone brooked no argument. "And you'll ride astride. This ain't no Sunday ride in the city. Anything, a coon or a flock of birds taking flight, could spook your horse. In that damned sidesaddle, you wouldn't have a chance of keeping your seat."

"But my skirts will bunch up and let my . . ." She couldn't bring herself to mention a part of her anatomy to a man. It simply wasn't done.

He stared at her, his eyes as cold and piercing as a winter wind. "Let your what?"

A lancet of fear sliced through her. She could not get out a single word.

"Fallin' outta that fool sidesaddle and breakin' your neck is better than lettin' me see a bit of your ankles? Hell, woman, I watched you bathe. You're likely wearing thick black stockings anyway."

Her blush told him he was right.

Tossing the saddle into the creek had done little to stem his anger and frustration. Her foolish display of modesty was like tossing lamp oil on a fire. "Go on, then, get your damn saddle back. You know where it is." His arm shot past her head, pointing to the creek.

Brianna ducked, shielding her face with her hands.

Nigh groaned. He thrust his thumbs into his belt behind his waist to keep from reaching for her and stared at the ground. "Told you I'd never hurt you."

He hadn't, not really. She was trembling and knew she looked like a doe poised for flight, but she forced her shoulders back and faced him. "I'm sorry, I couldn't help it. And I don't mean to make things difficult. It's not easy to let go of tenets drilled into you almost from the moment you were born and do something you've always believed would be contemplated only by a . . . a strumpet."

Nigh heaved a sigh and let his shoulders slump while he mulled the problem over. "I've got a new pair of trousers. You can wear them."

"But that would be almost as bad as—"

His fists clenched. "Woman, you got two choices. Either ride with your skirts hiked up or wear my trousers. No, I lied. There's a third choice. Fetch yourself back to St. Louie and find some other idiot to get you to Independence."

He didn't wait for her decision, but marched to the dappled gray and proceeded to remove his saddle. She watched him switch the saddle to the buckskin's back and loosely do up the girth. Then he slugged the mare in the belly. Beast blew out a rush of air. The mare's stomach contracted and Nigh quickly tightened the girth. That was what Brianna had forgotten to do with the sidesaddle, she told herself. The mare had been holding her breath so the strap couldn't be tightened enough. It was as clear now as the blue sky overhead, but Brianna didn't bother to explain to Columbus Nigh. He was right, she was a fool.

"I will accept your generous offer of the trousers," she told him.

Without comment he fetched them from his pack. "Need a shirt, too."

The shirt was the typical thigh-length tunic farmers and tradesmen wore, made of slate blue linsey-woolsey with smocking at the shoulder seams and the tops of the long sleeves. She looked doubtfully at the slit-neck opening, knowing it would probably reach nearly to her waist, but didn't dare complain. Folding the garments over her arm, she waded into the bushes.

Nigh shook his head as he watched her go. She acted as if she were going to her own execution. White women were more troublesome than buffalo gnats or skeeters. He thought of the young Snake wife he had lost barely a year ago. Little Beaver had been as practical as they came, cooperative and helpful. No inhibitions and no righteous morals to get in the way. Not once had he regretted taking her—until the day he found her dead.

The iron bars were cold and clammy beneath Barret Wight's moist hands. The stench of urine and dried vomit brought up his gorge. He swallowed it down, then hollered once more for the deputy sheriff. "Hey you, Pratt, come here, will you?"

Pratt stuck his ruddy face around the corner and peered through the gloom at his prisoner. There were four cells, two on each side of the aisle leading to the marshal's office where Pratt drank coffee and studied wanted posters with his boots propped on a scarred old desk. Wight was the only prisoner, but tomorrow being Saturday, Pratt expected there'd be a few drunks to give the man company along about midnight. Maybe then the sniveling bastard would leave a man in peace. "Waddya want?"

"Get me out of here so I can use the privy."

"Use the damned bucket. Waddya think it's in there for, bathing?"

"It's full, hasn't been dumped for days. When's that brat get here? This stinking hole isn't fit for hogs, let alone men."

"He gets here when he gets here. Soon's we got a man needing one of them cells, we'll worry 'bout cleaning 'em."

Wight growled and rattled the bars with his thick fists. "Blast your vermin-ridden hide, Pratt, when I get out of here, I'll . . ."

"Hold onto yer balls. Boy just got here."

For several seconds Wight listened to the murmur of voices from the office as the cleaning boy received his instructions. Annoyed, Wight rattled the bars again. "Hey! Do I have to piss my pants?"

A squatty fourteen-year-old with pimples and lank blond hair falling over his face, sidled around the open door into the large room. He set his mop bucket on the floor before entering the unused cells to haul out the pee buckets that needed emptying. Not once did he lift his eyes to the prisoner in the far corner. With barely contained patience, Wight waited until the boy came close enough to hear his whisper, "Come here, kid."

The boy looked at him insolently. "I ain't talking to no woman killer."

"I didn't kill anyone and I'm not going to hurt you either. Just want you to do something for me." Wight growled with frustration as the boy hung back, eyes full of distrust. "You'll be paid."

The boy jerked his head, clearing the hair from his eyes. "How much?"

"Two bits. You know the tavern at Wight's Brewery?"

"Yeah."

"Find Stinky Harris, tell him to get over here or I'm calling in his marker. You got that?"

The boy scratched under one armpit, then his crotch, peering warily at Wight while his hair drifted back over his eyes. "That's all?"

"That's all, now get."

"Soon's I finish my job."

As soon as the boy was gone, Barret threw himself down on the filthy bunk. He folded his arms behind his head, crossed his feet, and smiled. Brianna must have thought herself clever, sneaking off on him that way and making it look like he'd done her in. But he wasn't as stupid as she thought. His smile spread to a wide grin. The silver had clued him in. No thief would leave something valuable like that behind, especially buried where it was. Yeah, that was what really told on her—and what troubled him most—the silver being buried in that particular horse stall.

Wight's smile faded. How had she known? Had she randomly chosen that spot to bury the silver, or had she figured it out ahead of time? And what had she done with the original contents of the hole?

The slut, the great big Amazon of a slut. She'd left him a message, burying the silver there, that's what she'd done. But she'd find out it took more than a veiled threat to keep him off her trail. She belonged to him, and what Barret Wight owned, Barret Wight kept. He'd deal with her when he got her back, by Christ! She'd rue the day she ever thought of trying to pull one over on him. Maybe he wouldn't kill her—killing was too good for the likes of her—but she'd damn well wish he had.

* * *

Stinky Harris sauntered into the jail about supper time. He wrinkled his nose at the acrid odor of urine that clung to the place like maggots on putrid flesh, then headed for the rear cell where Barret Wight waited.

"Good thing you know what's good for you." Wight greeted him with a sneer. He sat on the edge of his cot using the tip of a thumbnail to scrape the other nails clean. The boredom of sitting idle in a jail cell had him desperate for something to do. He'd even come to look forward to the lousy meals they fed him. At least then he could exchange insults with the deputy sheriff while the tray was slid under the bars.

"Don't threaten me, Wight," said Stinky.

"Then listen up. I've got a proposition for you."

"I'm listening."

Barret moved over near the cell door. His stubby fingers curled around the thick bars. "You heard why I'm in here?"

"Yeah, you finally done in your wife. Glory thinks you did it so you could marry her."

"Sure," Barret snorted. "When hell becomes heaven and they make me king. The whole thing was a set-up. She's run off and you're going to help me find her."

Stinky tugged thoughtfully on his scroungy tuft of a beard and decided he believed Wight. "What do you want me to do?"

"She probably beat it out of here by the most expedient means available, any direction she could go. Check passenger rosters for steamships and stage coaches starting with yesterday morning. Check hotels and boarding houses, too. But first, go to my house and find the daguerreotype I had done of her. It's in my study. Show it around."

Barret's voice filled with venom. He gripped the bars so tightly his knuckles turned white. "I'm gonna find that bitch if it's the last thing I do. She'll learn she can't dump on me like this and get away with it."

"Yeah?" The sun filtering through a tiny barred window cast shadow-stripes across Stinky's sallow face as he studied Wight. "What's in this for me?"

"You do as I ask and I'll tear up your marker. That ought to make it worth your while. Is it a deal?"

Stinky thought it over. It would be good to get out of debt and out from under this man's thumb. Barret Wight was known for his ugly temper. Stinky could refuse and hope they hung the bastard, but that would be risky since he understood they hadn't even found Mrs. Wight's body yet. Besides, life had been dull lately and the challenge of finding a runaway wife appealed to him.

"Yeah, all right," he said. "It's a deal."

"One more thing. She has a sister in Louisville, Kentucky. Julia Somerville, I think. She might have gone there."

"This ain't gonna do you much good if they hang you."

Barret snorted. "Rainey hasn't got shit for evidence. He'll have to let me go eventually. And when he does, I'm gonna teach that bitch of a wife of mine a lesson she won't ever forget."

Chapter Six

The day passed so slowly Brianna thought it would never end. At first the stiffness in her body had been eased by her bath and a few miles of riding, but as the day wore on, she began to ache worse than ever. Her only comfort was that riding astride rubbed new spots raw instead of the same old ones. Her cloak helped to disguise her outlandish outfit, but the veil was missing from her hat—thanks to Mr. Nigh. She ducked her head whenever they passed other travelers and tried to take comfort in the thought that anyone noticing her bruises would probably blame him for them.

To make up for their late start, they ate dry jerked beef and leftover breakfast biscuits while they rode and stopped barely long enough to water and feed the horses. They avoided the inns and villages along the way. Nigh spoke only to give orders and never so much as glanced at her. He appeared so ill-tempered, she gladly kept her distance and reserved her conversation for the cat. It was long after dark before he led the way from the road to seek a place to camp.

Brianna was too exhausted to eat. She fell into her bed

the moment Nigh finished building her shelter and was instantly asleep. Once she awoke during the night and saw him huddled under his buffalo robe, leaning against a tree as usual. His eyes were open and watching her, as cool and unfeeling as when she had first met him. She wondered what his life had been like up till now, but she was too sleepy to give much thought to the matter and was soon fast asleep again. The sky was still dark and dawn far away yet when they got back on the road the next day.

Though Brianna still cringed and had to school herself not to dash off into the woods every time she heard a rider approaching from behind, her fear of Barret catching her had lessened. Surely he would have caught up with her by now if he were going to. But, as they rode into Jefferson City, she noticed a steamboat letting off passengers. She was wondering if Barret could have beat her there coming by steamboat when Nigh informed her they needed to stop for supplies.

"Please, that isn't truly necessary, is it?"

He drew up in front of a store and dismounted. "It is if you want coffee and anything but fresh meat the next couple of days."

He wrapped the reins around the hitching rail, then moved to her side to help her down. Motioning to the dry goods store, he said, "Get us coffee and whatever else you think we need. I won't be long."

"Where are you going? You're not leaving me alone, are you?" Her eyes were wide with alarm.

Nigh frowned. "It'll save time if you get the dry goods while I hunt up grain for the horses."

After he had walked away, Brianna glanced about at the people crowding the street and the plank walk in front of the buildings. Silently she cursed Nigh for tearing the veil off her hat. She pulled the bonnet forward as much as she could and kept her head bowed, her eyes beneath the brim darting everywhere as she made her way into the store.

A long counter lined the back of the building where purchases were tallied and paid for. Several people milled about, looking over the merchandise or waiting to be served. Brianna edged her way into an unoccupied corner while she scanned the faces. A bell jangled as someone opened the door and she bent over a pickle barrel, as if sniffing the briny contents, until she could see who had entered. Slowly she worked her way toward the counter where a short man with a long, scruffy beard was measuring out beans for a plump, garrulous woman in a black mantle trimmed with mink. The bell jangled again as a tall gentleman left.

Brianna waited until the woman had paid for her purchase and headed for the door, then slipped into line behind a farmer in homespun pants and knee-length boots. The bell jangled as the woman went out. While the shopkeeper took care of the next customer, Brianna pretended to study the selection of fabrics stacked in bolts on the counter, one hand fidgeting with the button hanging inside her bodice. She was debating buying new veiling to sew onto her bonnet when a man took hold of her arm.

"What's taking so long?"

She gasped as she spun about, her hand going to her thundering heart. "Mr. Nigh! You startled me."

"Noticed."

Before he could ask her why she was so nervous, the shopkeeper stepped up. Nigh ordered the coffee and a pound of pilot bread. By the time they had packed the food in the saddlebags and ridden out of the town, her shoulders and head were aching with tension. She welcomed the brief noon stop, bathing her face in the cool waters of a stream while Beast drank noisily beside her.

Crouched on the bank, Nigh watched her. If she didn't watch out, she'd lose all her prim and proper ways. His mouth quirked up in one of his half-smiles at the thought. Then he frowned, remembering her fear in Jefferson City.

As they drew closer to Independence they met more and more traffic on the road, young men mostly, rushing to join the thousands of others eager to face the Elephant on the California Trail—the Elephant that was the end of their own endurance. Often the twang of a fiddle or mouth organ came from one of the wagons, along with men's voices lifted in bawdy song. Many called out friendly greetings, taking the couple for man and wife. She left it to Nigh to correct them if he wished.

On the evening of the fifth day, she noticed Nigh setting a more leisurely pace and knew they were getting close to Independence. Her excitement grew as the miles slowly passed. Soon she would see Julia and John and their sweet children. She prayed they would not be unhappy about her unannounced arrival, and that they would not refuse to take her with them to Oregon Territory.

After crossing a shallow creek, Columbus Nigh called over his shoulder that they would camp on its banks. Brianna followed him to a small glade where flowers nodded in the patchy sunshine. A pretty spot.

Nigh cut green poles for her shelter while she gathered firewood. Shakespeare found a mouse hole under a tree root and waited patiently for his prey to emerge. When the chores were finished and the camp made ready for the night, Nigh sat down under a tree. He took out his knife and worked on one of the little animal figures he was always carving out of the apple wood that lent its scent to his clothes and person. Brianna gathered her cloak tighter about her neck, sat on a dry log and watched.

His hands were quick and agile. Yet she knew they could be tender as well. She remembered his gentleness in checking her ribs and the feel of his thumbs brushing her breasts. She also recalled the strange sensations that had shot through her body, pleasant sensations she'd never experienced before. Somewhere in the long days, the long miles, she had lost her fear of Columbus Nigh. He was so strong and self-assured, being with him gave her a feeling of peace and safety.

"What will you do after we get to Independence?" she asked.

He glanced up, then back at his work. "Got a job guiding pilgrims to Oregon."

Pleased, she said, "Maybe it will be the same company my sister and I will be with."

"Mebbe."

Shakespeare chased a wind-blown leaf across the clearing, nearly ending up in the small campfire. Brianna smiled at the easy way he dodged the hot coals and captured the leaf. When she looked up, Nigh was gazing at her, his gray eyes as enigmatic as ever.

"What if you miss your sister?" he asked.

Brianna shook her head. Her eyes filled with fear and uncertainty as they so often did. "I don't know. I-I haven't dared think that far ahead. Tell me what Oregon is like."

His eyes lifted, staring off toward the northwest as though he could see the land in question. "There's plains flat as a table top where nothing grows but grass, mountains so high and rugged you'll wish you never heard of Oregon 'fore you're over them, and valleys like the Willamette, lush as any I've seen."

"The Willamette," she repeated, her voice nearly as reverent as his. "I've heard of it. Isn't the Whitmore mission there?"

"Was. At Waiilatpu. Cayuse massacred just about everybody there couple of years ago."

Her eyes filled with alarm, but he didn't notice. She had moved closer to the fire for warmth and he was watching the light play over her face. They could have made Independence before midnight if they'd pushed it. He didn't want to. They'd been pushing hard enough— sixteen hours in the saddle, forty miles a day. The pace showed in the dark circles under her eyes and in the slump of her shoulders.

There were things he wanted to know about this woman before she passed out of his life. Like why she turned as fidgety as a frog in a frying pan every time someone rode up behind them, and why she'd tensed up like a cat ready to spring in Jefferson City. He'd had a gut feeling ever since they left St. Louis that she was running away from someone. He intended to find out who.

Brianna walked to the edge of the stream, enjoying the changing colors of the western sky through the branches of the trees. "I never thought about the danger of traveling to a place as wild and isolated as Oregon. Surely it can't be too bad, though, if John is taking Julia there."

"It's quiet enough there now."

His mocassined feet had approached so quietly in the soft grass, she had not heard him coming and jumped at the sound of his voice so close behind her. He put his hands on her shoulders and turned her to face him. Her blood iced over at the coldness in his eyes. Her stomach churned and she felt an urge to flee.

"Who are you running away from?" he asked.

The urge became a need.

"No one. I told you, I just want to reach my sister before she leaves on the wagon train."

"Then why do you panic every time someone passes us?"

She lowered her eyes to hide her expression. "I don't. Why are you asking all these questions? What would it matter to you if someone were after me?"

Because I feel responsible for you, damn my foolish hide. Aloud he said, "If you're in danger, that puts me in danger too, so I have a right to know."

Brianna's gaze refused to meet his until he took her chin in his hand and forced her to look at him, a habit she was beginning to detest. "Tell me."

Silence.

"Damn it, woman! How can I help you if you won't talk to me?"

"Help me?" Her brow furrowed. "Why would you want to help me? You don't even like me."

Didn't like her? Every day he had come to admire her courage more. Under all her fear and uncertainty was the strength of a young oak. All she need to make her flower was confidence.

She had grown more beautiful, too, as the bruises faded and the swelling subsided to expose the delicate lines of her face. Her generous mouth was balanced by enormous, startlingly blue topaz eyes and wide cheekbones. Her body was long and willowy, moving with a sensuous grace of which she seemed unaware. Something natural, almost innocent, about her, made him want to shield her from everything that might harm her. But he wanted more than to protect her; he wanted to possess her. And it did no good to tell himself it was only out of sympathy because she'd been abused. Or because he needed a woman.

The ferocity in his eyes seared her. His gaze dipped to her lips. She tried to move away, but could not break his hold. Slowly he drew her against him. Her heart thundered in her ears and she grew light-headed as she watched his mouth draw closer and closer to hers. Surely she would float away if he let go of her. But he didn't. His lips whispered over hers and the churning sensation in her stomach became a tornado.

There had been no time to throw up her defenses, physically or emotionally. His tongue insinuated itself between her lips, and her body quivered. Her heart would surely blister and her bones melt until there was nothing left of her but a shapeless lump, like the river clay she had played with as a child. She stiffened herself against his attack.

Nigh raised his head to look at her, and nearly lost control. He'd expected the fear, but not the banked fire deep in her eyes. "Go." His voice was shaky. "Go on, get to bed."

She was trembling, holding her body so rigid she could barely move. Nigh held onto her arm, the other hand at her waist as he guided her to the brush shelter. It was all he could do not to lay her down and take her as his body demanded. Instead, he shoved the cat in her arms, knowing the feel of something familiar would calm her. Then he strode off into the woods.

Brianna buried her face in the cat's silky fur and

watched Nigh hurry away. She filled her nostrils with the cat's familiar odor and let the rumble of his purr lull her emotions into a semblance of calm. Then she hurried to get into bed.

Even with her eyes closed she could still see him. She felt the smoothness of his lips, the faint prickle of his mustache, the textured moistness of the tongue that forced its way into her mouth. His breath had been sweet, his scent smoky and rich with the flavors of earth and horse and apple wood. She tried to force him from her mind by wondering where Barret was that moment and what he was doing, but found herself instead comparing Barret's kisses with Nigh's, Barret's touch, Barret's whiskey stink.

From the deeply shadowed woods Nigh watched her scramble into bed and cursed himself. He'd asked for trouble, kissing her like that. Insane. Every night he'd struggled to banish the memory of her naked body from his mind. His palms itched to touch her each time he looked at her until he thought he'd go crazy with wanting. But a woman like her would never want a man like him, even if she hadn't been made to fear men and sex.

One kiss, he had told himself, a taste to carry with him in the pocket of his heart. That was all he'd intended to take. He'd expected her fear, and he knew he could use that fear to make her submit to him. He didn't want her that way. But that hint of passion in her eyes had been like a promise of hope, of something that might have been— had life not destined them for different roads and made a match between them impossible.

Tomorrow he would help her find her sister, then walk out of her life. That simply. He would make it be that simple. There was no place in her life for him, and none in his life for her.

Chapter Seven

Independence, Missouri sat on a high point of land overlooking the surrounding country. At the landing on the Missouri River, six miles away, emigrants reconstructed the wagons they had dismantled for the steamboat trip up river. Then they struggled up the steep bluffs to the camps at the outskirts of town.

A pall of smoke hung low over the town from the cook fires of thousands of emigrants. The camps were so close together Brianna couldn't tell where one ended and another began. The press of humanity suffocated her and she longed for the quiet, open country they had left behind. She craned her neck, twisting this way and that, hoping to spot Julia and half-expecting to find Barret instead.

The noise and confusion in the camps were horrendous. Never had Brianna seen so many people, and from so many different walks of life. Farmers and professional men camped side by side, sharing whiskey bottles along with the daily news, trail advice, recipes, and dreams. Here and there were herds of oxen, horses, mules, even pigs, whose droppings lay scattered over the meadows, as plentiful as spring wildflowers, making Brianna thankful to be on horseback.

Nigh led her through the chaos to a spring where a crowd of people waited to fill cookpots or to water their animals. He slipped easily from the gray's back, then reached for Brianna. She was so busy studying the people, she barely noticed how close he stood or the way his hands lingered at her waist after lifting her down. It was good to feel her feet on solid ground again and to give her aching backside a rest.

Columbus had let her stop and change back into her dress before entering town. Still, she felt dirty in front of the women chatting amiably while they waited their turn at the spring. They seemed to be having such fun. Mrs. O'Casey had been the only woman Brianna had had to talk with in the last three years. She'd missed having friends her own age.

Nigh noticed the direction of her gaze. "Them women might know where to find your sister."

Her eyes swung to his tanned face, so familiar and comforting to her now, then back to the clutch of women.

" 'Fraid they'll bite you?" he said.

"No, but they might be rude."

"Seems to me you've lived through worse than that."

He was right. Taking a deep breath, she straightened her shoulders the way she always did when seeking courage, and edged closer to them.

At the fringe of the small circle, she stopped to glance back uncertainly at Nigh. With a jerk of his head, he motioned for her to go on. She cleared her throat, brushed at the dust on her dress, then cleared her throat again. Automatically her hand went to the button beneath her bodice. "Excuse me."

The women went right on talking. Only a short round woman, with graying hair and the rosiest cheeks Brianna had ever seen, noticed her.

"Hello, there," the woman said in a voice Brianna was sure must carry at least a mile. "You a new arrival?"

The other women turned to look at Brianna as the rosycheeked one thrust out a worn, callused hand, saying, "I'm Lavinia Decker. My husband and I hail from Indiana. You headed for Oregon or Californy?"

"Or-Oregon," Brianna stammered. "Provided I can find my sister and her family. They should be here somewhere, getting ready to leave. John and Julia Somerville. Do any of you know them, by any chance?" She scanned each face, hope and dread in her eyes.

The women looked at one another and shook their heads.

"Well, now, dearie," Lavinia Decker said. "We don't know your sister. Ain't many headed Oregon way this year. Me and this bunch are joining up tomorrow with a company what's headed for Oregon. If you don't find your sister here, you look us up on the Santa Fe Trail t'other side of town. We'll ask around for you, see if we can scare up this sister of yours, all right?"

"Oh, yes. Thank you, thank you so much."

"Think nothing of it. Got a difficult journey ahead of us. We'll all be needing to rely on each other for help. It's what neighbors are for."

Brianna returned to Nigh wearing a radiant smile that made his heart skip. Her fear and anxiety were gone, making her look young and passionately alive. It took all his control not to pull her to him there in front of the whole passel of strangers and kiss her.

"Reckon that wasn't so bad, was it?" he said, smiling.

"No, not bad at all."

Brianna saw the heat in his eyes and blushed. The last time he'd looked at her like that, he'd kissed her. It had taken all morning to wipe the memory from her mind. Now it rushed back, bringing with it heat and anticipation. When he merely lifted her onto the buckskin's back and mounted his own horse, she felt oddly disappointed.

Mud sucked hungrily at the horses' hooves as they skirted wagons and herds of oxen and mules offered for sale to emigrants. Slowly they made their way to the center of town where a large parklike square housed a brick courthouse with a conical roof. Houses and stores surrounded the square. The town's permanent population of barely more than a thousand people had swelled overnight to several thousand, mostly argonauts bound for the California gold fields discovered the year before.

Temporary shacks and hastily thrown up tents offered a variety of goods meant to capture a share of the wealth to be gleaned from emigrants who must travel hundreds of miles before reaching another chance to restock for the long journey. The camps themselves spilled in every direction over the undulating and wooded countryside outside Independence and its smaller neighbors, Westport and Wayne City.

In front of the Noland House Nigh paid a boy to hold the horses because there was no room at the hitching rails. He carried Brianna through the thick loblolly of the street to the muddied boardwalk. Then they went inside the hotel to inquire after the Somervilles. The middle-aged clerk shook his head regretfully at their questions and directed them to the next hotel.

Back out on the street, they walked past a gambling house where a fiddle rasped and drunken customers sang offkey. At Wilson's and Clark's General Store they stopped long enough for Brianna to buy a bottle of rose water, and a few other personal items. Farther down the street they passed a gunsmith's shop and a newly set-up daguerreotype gallery where Nigh shook his head in wonder at display photos set on small easels in the window. The post office was the size of a postage stamp, with a couple dozen emigrants trying to wedge themselves inside. Brianna noted its location so she could post a letter to the O'Caseys' before leaving town.

"Keep close," Nigh told her. "Easy to get separated in all this confusion."

In spite of his calm, easy manner and self-assurance, he obviously cared no more for crowds than she did.

At the Independence House, they had no better luck in locating the Somervilles, but the thin, balding owner, recognizing Brianna as gentry and fed up with the riffraff traipsing through his establishment, offered her a small room on the second floor which had just been vacated. Nigh frowned at the signature she wrote in the register. It wasn't the same name he had heard the O'Caseys' use when addressing Brianna, but he said nothing.

Since she was alone and the town was crawling with men, a cot was set up in the hallway outside her door for Nigh. The clerk pointed out the public dining room to the right of the registration desk, then gave them directions to several homes which rented rooms at a dollar a day where they could inquire after her sister.

Nigh put their gear in her room. Then, grumbling, he went to find a box he could fill with dirt so the cat could see to its needs. After stabling the horses, he returned for Brianna and they went to check out the boarding houses. On the boardwalk in front of them a woman was strug-

gling in the grasp of a man who was apparently drunk.
Brianna's steps slowed and Nigh felt her tremble with
fear. He slid his arm about her waist and said, "Has
nothing to do with you. Come on, we'll just slip past
them."

A man shouted somewhere behind them: "Hey you!
Get your hands off my wife!"

Brianna cringed. Then she felt herself shoved into
Nigh's arms as a man pushed past. The husband knocked
the drunk into the mud and traffic along the boardwalk
began to move again. All but Brianna and Columbus
Nigh. He held her close until she stopped shaking, one
hand stroking her back while she buried her face in his
chest. When she calmed down, she drew away, embarrassed to have been seen embracing a man in public.

The first of the boarding houses was of brick in the old
Federal style. A maid answered the door. She denied
knowing the Somervilles. The next two homes were small
frame affairs, and no more help than the first. At last they
came to a fine old home of Spanish flavor where a middle-
aged woman of French extraction welcomed them into
her parlor.

"But of course," she said after hearing Brianna out.
"The Somervilles were a lovely family. They stayed with
us about six weeks before they left to join the wagon
company. That was eight days ago, however." She sighed
wistfully. "I miss Julia and the children. Such a sweet boy
she had, and little Genevieve was as pretty and petite as
her mama. You are fortunate to have such a fine sister."

Brianna managed an appropriate reply though her
spirits, which had begun to soar at the beginning of the
interview, lay now at her feet.

Without thinking, Nigh put a comforting hand on her

back. "Forming a wagon company takes a lot of organizing. That means a slow start. We'll find them." Looking up at their hostess, he asked, "Do you happen to know which company they joined up with?"

"No, I regret I do not."

Brianna was too distraught to notice the way Nigh helped her to her feet and guided her from the house. She felt faint and wondered if she were becoming ill.

"You need food in you," Nigh said. "We'll go back to the hotel and have something to eat."

She looked up at him with dazed eyes.

"You truly think we'll still be able to find Julia?"

"If they left only a week ago, chances are they ain't gone more'n sixty miles. I'll find 'em."

It was then she realized his arm was around her, his hand at her waist. She knew it wasn't proper, that she should reprove him for his boldness, but her legs felt no more substantial than the mud that made up the street and she feared she might fall if he removed his support.

After a solemn meal of venison, greens, bread, and apple pie, they made their way back to the hotel and Nigh went in search of the man who had sent for him to guide a wagon company, promising to ask after her sister as well.

Time passed slowly. Brianna felt too agitated to lay down. She ordered up a bath and soaked in the rose-scented water until it grew cold. Then she wrote a letter to Mrs. O'Casey. After that, there was nothing to do but sit beside the window with Shakespeare curled in her lap and watch the people come and go on the street below. Always she kept her eye out for Barret as well as Julia.

Nigh's earlier question came back again and again to plague her. What would she do if they couldn't catch up with Julia? Did Brianna have the courage to join a wagon train by herself and travel all that long way, hoping to find Julia when she got there? How could she be certain John hadn't decided to go to California instead? There seemed to be no answers. Except that she would not return to St. Louis. There was no question of that. Even Independence was too close to Barret Wight for her to feel safe.

Shakespeare butted against her hand as she scratched behind his ears and she bent to kiss the top of his silky head. The cat looked up at her, his green, slanted eyes half-closed in an expression of love that expanded her heart and filled her with warmth. He was all she had now. How would she keep him safe all those miles to Oregon? She couldn't keep him in a basket for months on end, yet there was no way to make sure he stayed in the wagon and if he got out, he could easily be lost.

In a way, Nigh, too, was all she had now. A cat and a man she knew nothing about. It wasn't much to inspire confidence. But the truth was, she had no choice; she had to go on, to Oregon or to California, anywhere to get away from Barret. And with Nigh going to Oregon, there was no question about her preference.

It was mid-afternoon when Brianna answered a knock on her door to find Nigh leaning against the wall, twirling his hat in his hands. When he saw her he straightened and stuck his thumbs in the back of his beaded belt, letting the hat dangle behind him from his fingertips.

"Thought you might like to ride out to see that woman you talked to at the spring. I rented a buggy."

"Yes, I'd like that very much," she said. "I'll get my bonnet."

The glances tossed Nigh by the women they passed as he drove the rented buggy toward the outskirts of town did not escape Brianna. She studied him out of the corner of her eye and decided he did make an imposing figure in his rugged, form-fitting buckskins. There was something almost primitive about him, a feral sort of wildness she found sensuous as well as frightening. With his stormy gray eyes squinting from under his hat brim, so cool and indifferent, he again put her in mind of the romantic savages she had read of in Francis Parkman's book on the Oregon Trail. But now she realized that beneath her fear of Columbus Nigh lay an undercurrent of excitement and yearning that left her bewildered and dismayed.

"Did you find the people you were hired to guide to Oregon?" she asked, trying to get her mind off the sensations he aroused in her.

He took out a wooden pick and stuck it in his mouth. "Found the man who sent for me."

Brianna waited for him to continue, but he remained silent. Confound the man! Did she have to drag everything from him? "Your journey is all arranged, then?"

Pushing the words past the toothpick clamped between his teeth, he said, "Cholera wiped out most of the company. What few lived, joined other trains."

"Oh, how dreadful."

Fear iced her veins. Nigh would not be going to Oregon. Was he trying to find the words to tell her he was leaving, going back to St. Louis or wherever he had come from? Is that why she sensed the uneasiness in him? Licking her lips, she steadied herself and asked, "What will you do now?"

"Ain't decided."

They were silent for some time while he skillfully drove the buggy toward the prairie west of town. Finally Brianna cleared her voice and said, "It's kind of you to help me look for Julia and her husband. I feel guilty to be taking up your time this way, and I'm very grateful."

"Ain't doin' it for gratitude. Or money."

"*Aren't* doing it . . ." Surprised at her own nerve, her voice trailed off.

He pulled his hat lower and stared straight ahead. Could he tell her he was doing it because her vulnerability had gotten to him? That he wanted to protect her almost as much as he wanted to bed her? Would she feel safer knowing, or more scared?

Feeling rebuked by his silence for her boldness in correcting his grammar, Brianna changed the subject. "I can't wait to see Julia. It's been so long. We wrote to each other—that's how I knew she was going to Oregon—but writing's not the same as visiting, is it? The children will have grown so much. It will be good to hear childish laughter and feel their squirmy little bodies in my arms again."

She sensed Nigh's gaze on her and shut up, blushing as she stared at her gloved hands folded primly in her lap. Well, he already thought her a foolish, worthless female. What did it matter if he also thought her a chatterbox? He would be going out of her life soon enough, and it was for the best. In fact, the sooner the better.

"Think this is it," he said, pulling to a stop.

Forty wagons formed a circle on a grassy meadow near a creek. Oxen and horses grazed peacefully nearby, watched over by barefoot children wielding willow switches. Smoke rose from several cook fires tended by women and older children. Along the creek women were spreading laundry to dry over the bushes. As Brianna stepped down from the buggy Mrs. Decker rushed over to greet her.

"Got news for you, dearie," the woman said. "One of the men here met a Mr. Somerville who left a few days ago with a company headed up by a man named Hatfield."

In her effort to suppress her disappointment, Brianna didn't see Nigh's stricken expression. He quickly cleared his face as she turned to him. "Do you think we could catch up with them?"

Others gathered to stare at the newcomers. One, a thin, chinless man with the dark-eyed look of a weasel, pushed to the front of the crowd.

"You could," he said. "But you'd have to go some to do it and you ain't likely to enjoy what you find when you get there." His gaze rested on Brianna's breasts and he licked his lips before moving on to the man standing next to her. "Howdy, Nigh, been a year or so, hasn't it?"

Columbus Nigh's eyes narrowed. "Goin' to Oregon, Magrudge? Californy gold fields seem more your style."

Edward Magrudge chuckled. "Might wander down thataway eventually, after I see these pilgrims safe to Oregon."

"You piloting this bunch?"

"Naw, got Jeb Hanks for that. I'm the wagon captain."

Nigh nodded. "Jeb's a good man, he'll do you right."

Brianna watched the exchange with interest. Obviously the men knew each other and she had the distinct impression there was no affection between them. She had thought Nigh hard and dangerous, but the way Magrudge's gaze roamed her body made her feel dirtier than when she fell into the mud puddle. Her voice trembled when she forced herself to speak to the man. "Please, can you tell me something about my sister and her family? Their name is Somerville, John and Julia Somerville. The way you spoke a moment ago, I assume you know something about them."

The man shifted his gaze back to her. He studied her face, then her body from head to toes, coming to rest once more on her breasts. Licking his lips, he said, "Don't know any Somervilles, but if they were with Hatfield's company, you'll likely find them about thirty miles up the road. Just look for the wooden crosses."

Brianna looked up at Nigh. "What does he mean?"

Taking her by the shoulders, he drew her aside. There was pain in his voice. "Hatfield's was the company I was supposed to pilot."

"But you said cholera—"

"That's right," Magrudge butted in, his dark feral eyes gleaming. " 'Most every man and woman in Hatfield's company is dead."

"Here's your supper, Wight." Marshal Rainey slid the tray under the cell door.

"Shit! Swill is what you mean." Barret Wight ignored the cloth-covered tray. He rose from his bunk and moved to the bars that separated him from the marshal. "How long are you going to keep me here, on suspicion, as you call it? Why don't you get out there and find my wife instead of locking up honest citizens?"

Rainey shrugged, unperturbed. It wasn't the first time he'd had Wight in his jail, though it had been awhile. Once for roughing up the serving girl at the Gill and Fin near the levee. Three times for brawling. The man was a natural bully, the same as his father. Always had been, always would be. If old Doc Thomas hadn't pulled a couple of Wight's victims through, chances were he'd have hung already. For Brianna Wight's sake, it was too bad he hadn't.

"Figure if I hold you here long enough, something will turn up that will clue me in on what really happened to your wife." Rainey's eyes narrowed speculatively as he stared at the man. "What bothers me is that she stuck with you for three years, in spite of the way you treated her, and you say she was pretty much a recluse."

"That's right. Mrs. O'Casey backed me up on that, you'll recall."

Rainey leaned back against the bars across the aisle from Wight's cell. He folded his arms against his chest and crossed one ankle over the other in a relaxed pose. "So, why would she leave now? Can you answer that? After three years, why would a woman shy of strangers, short on friends, and with no relatives closer than Kentucky, up and take off?"

Wight laid down on the bunk, propped his head on his arms and stared at the cobwebbed ceiling. "I admitted hitting her that last night. Maybe it was the straw that broke the camel's back, how do I know?"

"No one saw her leave town," the marshal continued. "Her name appears on no hotel register, no stage or steamship roster. Fact is, no one answering her description was seen leaving town that day by any means."

Wight came off the bed in a leap. "Damn your execrable hide! I told you her sister must have come and gotten her. Why don't you check it out?"

Rainey pushed himself away from the bars and strolled toward the door that divided the cells from the office. "As a matter of fact, I did. I went to her sister's house, talked to the neighbors and John Somerville's relatives."

"Yeah? Then what the hell did you find out?"

"Obviously, I didn't find your wife." Rainey grinned as he reached for the handle on the door. "By the way, Mrs. O'Casey asked me to let you know she took your wife's cat home to take care of it. Oh, and you have a visitor." He pulled the door open and vanished into the office.

"Hey, wait a minute, you bastard! Aren't you going to tell me what you did find out?" Barret pounded his fists on the thick steel bars. When there was no answer, he threw himself back down on the thin mattress, coughing as dust rose to fill his lungs. Through the dust cloud came a sultry voice:

"Don't you worry, sugar. I hired the best lawyer this two-bit town has. We'll get you out of here soon." The pretty young woman wrinkled her nose at the stink of the place. "I only hope you can last that long."

"Glory!" Barret jumped to his feet. Glory stood in the aisle between the cells, wearing a low-cut dress of emerald and gold-striped silk that played up her catlike green eyes and intensified the red of her ringleted hair. "God, Glory, do you look good."

"Ooh, have you missed me, sugar?" Glory smiled, showing one crooked incisor. It was her most seductive smile, meant to tease and arouse. But she could smell Barret from where she stood and wasn't eager to get any closer.

"Damn right I missed you. Show you just how much as soon as you get me out of here. Now get over here and tell me about this lawyer."

The quick breath she sucked in didn't help much; the entire place stunk. She stepped up to the cell. He slid his hands around her waist and down her back to cup her buttocks while he kissed her through the bars.

There'd never been another woman like her, not his

mother and certainly not Brianna. Glory was small and warm and so deliciously prurient his blood pounded just looking at her.

Only once had he ever struck her, the second time he went to her at a bordello called The Gentlemen's Club. High class, with high prices, the best booze, and the classiest women. Glory had been only seventeen, but she'd been raised with several brothers in a family where violence was a way of life. Instead of bawling when he hit her, like most females would have, Glory laughed.

"If you want to play nasty, sugar, you've come to the right place," she'd said as she snatched a whip off her dresser.

In a split-second, Wight lay on the floor at her feet, his arms bound to his body by the coiled leather. Blood seeped from his thick bicep where the tip of the whip had bitten, but Wight didn't notice. His eyes were on Glory. She straddled his legs, opened his pantaloons and curled her sharp-nailed fingers about him. "They say I can snap the lit end off a cigar, clean as a whistle, without hardly looking," she purred. "So you hit me any time you like, sugar, I like to play rough, too."

Remembering had Barret hard as nails. The very next day he had taken her from The Gentlemen's Club and set her up in the big house on Locust Street. She'd taught him wonderful things since then, tantalizing little games that drove him wild. Oh, she was no tame pussy cat, his Glory. He never got enough of her.

"Ralston," she said, squirming as his bristly chin scratched her tender skin.

"Huh?" His breathing was quick and raspy. He pressed closer to the bars and drew her against him as tightly as he could so she could feel what she did to him.

"Clinton Ray Ralston, the lawyer. What is it, sugar? Something distract you?" She laughed throatily and reached down to caress him. "He'll be around this afternoon to talk to you and get the marshal to set bail. Then Mama will come and take her baby home."

Barret stiffened and went cold. His blue eyes darkened like a night sky and he ground out, "You're not my mama, Glory. You're my whore and don't you ever forget it."

Glory knew, she always knew, when he had reached that thin edge she was careful never to push him over. Fun was fun but the good times ended when they planted you six feet under, and Glory wasn't ready to go yet. "Hey, all right, sugar, you got your point across."

"Yeah, I better have," he muttered, shoving her away.

Chapter Eight

Brianna blanched and swayed at the sound of Edward Magrudge's harsh words telling her of the death of her sister. Instantly Nigh's arms slid about her, supporting her with the considerable strength of his own body. She had the crazy feeling that she was no longer inside her body, that she was outside the scene, a separate entity merely looking on. It eased the pain.

"Brianna."

Her name came to her as from a long distance. She looked up into Nigh's face and saw his lips move as he said her name again. How pretty it sounded in that slow drawl of his. It felt so warm and safe in his arms, she didn't want to move. Someone called for smelling salts, and Nigh asked if she was all right, but to answer, she would have to return to her body and that meant returning to the pain as well.

A hand waved something under her nose. The sharp bite of ammonia filled her nostrils and forced her back to reality.

"There, she'll be fine now," a woman said.

Brianna found herself gazing at the lovely face of a woman about her own age with sable brown hair half-hidden by a flat, derby-shaped hat decorated with ribbon poufs and feathers in the latest French fashion. Her brown eyes were the liveliest Brianna had ever seen.

"Hello, I'm Lilith Beaudouin. Are you feeling better now?"

"Yes, thank you, I'm fine." Brianna glanced up at Nigh, and the pain returned. "Is it true? Julia's dead?"

"Wouldn't take Magrudge's word, if I was you. We'll do some checking and find out for ourselves." The look Nigh sent the man as he helped her to her feet was nothing short of murderous.

Well, well, Magrudge thought, eyeing the couple. He gave Brianna a short bow and a condescending smile meant to pass as sympathy. "Sorry for the shock I gave you, ma'am. It was thoughtless of me, but I didn't realize Mrs. Somerville was your sister."

"Did you know her?"

"Afraid not. All I know is what I told you. Most of the folks with Hatfield's company died of cholera and are buried near the campground at Blue River."

"Are the graves marked?"

He shrugged. "Some likely are, some not."

Turning back to Nigh, she asked, "Will you take me, so I can look for Julia? Please, I have to know for sure."

As Nigh helped her into the buggy, he tried to put aside his doubts about the wisdom of taking her there. She might be in for more than she bargained for. But he'd seen the determination in her eyes and figured if he refused her, she'd find someone else to take her, maybe even Edward Magrudge.

There was no way he would allow Magrudge anywhere near her. He'd met the man several years ago while trapping the Rocky Mountains and never had trusted him.

Twice Nigh had seen the man ride a good horse to death for no reason, yet the man treated his animals better than he treated women.

The road followed along Blue Ridge to the old Red Bridge Crossing of the Blue River near "the line," the unmarked border between The States and Indian land. Directly on the line, with half the building on one side, half on the other, sat a tavern called the House of Refuge, popular with scoundrels. Whenever the Jackson County marshal dropped by, those running from the law simply stepped to the Indian side of the building, out of the marshal's jurisdiction.

Also on the Missouri side was Fitzhugh's Mill and Little Santa Fe where trains camped to recruit and reorganize before starting off across wide open prairie, leaving behind such civilized spots as the House of Refuge.

Nigh was so lost in thought about the woman who sat beside him in the jouncing buggy and what would happen to her if her sister truly were dead, that it took the sound of her voice to bring him back to the present and notice they had reached their destination.

"There are the camps up ahead, Mr. Nigh."

There was nothing unusual about the first camp they passed. It was a pleasant scene, campfire smoke spiraling lazily into the sky, children racing about barefoot and carefree, their laughter as shrill and pleasant as bird song. Farther up, the camps were jumbled and disorganized. Tents were pitched helter skelter, some no more than a tarpaulin pegged to the ground on one side and tied to poles on the opposite side.

Children huddled in somber little knots, unsmiling and unclean while the adults who hadn't yet been stricken by the cholera moved like automatons between soiled pallets and writhing victims. Nigh drove the buggy slowly through the maze of wagons and tents, searching for the burial ground while Brianna stared in horror at the scenes of sickness and death they passed along the way.

The cemetery was larger than they had expected. Some of the graves were the size of a wagon, entire families sharing the same hole. Or worse, total strangers lumped together to ease the grave digger's burden. Most of the graves were unmarked.

Three bodies, partially wrapped in foul blankets thick with flies, lay on the damp earth awaiting burial. Beside them a large man with a raw-boned face devoid of emotion stood in a oblong hole two feet deep, his shovel steadily thrusting into the wet earth, then flinging the rich black soil over his shoulder. He was oblivious to the couple who alighted from the buggy and wandered silently among the freshly mounded graves.

Crows lined the branches of a tree, their raucous cries gruesomely cheerful compared to the agonized moans of the sick and the mournful wails of the bereaved that drifted out from the camps. One of the braver of the flock flew down to land near the putrid bodies. A few hops at a time he ventured closer until he reached a partially exposed head covered with grimy short blond hair. Brianna swallowed the bile that rose to her throat as the bird began to peck at the defenseless face.

"Here," Nigh said, crouching beside a crudely carved wooden cross.

Brianna hurried over to him. The grave was one of few covered with sod rather than plain dirt. She knelt on the damp grass beside the grave and read the inscription cut into the wooden marker: Julia Ann Somerville, age 31, died 20 April 1849. Brianna clapped both hands over her mouth, her voice a choked whisper. "It's true. Oh God, it's true."

Nigh rose to his feet and walked away to allow her to grieve privately. She didn't cry, merely sat there staring at a single yellow daisy growing in the transplanted grass near the cross. Finally, she stood and came to him.

"I'm ready to go back now," was all she said.

He studied her for a moment. She appeared calm and composed, as stiff and emotionless as the clumsily made cross. Too calm. He resisted an urge to pull her into his arms and turned instead to lead the way to the buggy, his hand at her waist.

Wordlessly they retraced their route through the scattered wagons and tents. More than once Brianna's gaze was caught by the arresting sight of a mother comforting her fatherless children, a father carrying the lifeless body of a half-grown son to the graveyard, a dying man dictating to a friend his final words to his family back home.

They had almost passed the last of the wagons when Brianna noticed one sitting off by itself. A toddler stood outside, filthy, half-naked and crying, not another soul in sight.

Brianna put her hand on Nigh's arm. "Stop, something must be wrong there. That baby seems to be abandoned."

"I'll take a look," he said, halting the buggy. But she jumped down before he could fasten off the reins.

The child wore only a woolen undershirt. Her naked bottom and legs were wet and soiled with urine and feces. Brianna cringed as the pathetic little girl came to her with upraised arms, her hands as filthy as her bottom. The stench that emanated from the wagon was too strong to blame on one messy child. It smelled of death. Brianna's gorge rose again to her throat. Dreading what she might find, she forced her feet toward the end of the wagon.

"Anyone here?" she called.

Before she could peek inside, Nigh pulled her away. "See to the little one," he said, his eyes dark and grim. "I'll look inside."

With a kerchief over his mouth to filter out the odor, he thrust his head inside the wagon and waited for his eyes to adjust to the dim light. Gradually he was able to make out the form of a young woman in a nightdress lying on the bed, her eyes staring sightlessly at the man beside her. The man lay on his side facing his wife, his hand on hers. He was naked from the waist down. Both bodies were covered with flies.

"Is anyone in there, Mr. Nigh?" Brianna brushed against him as she moved up to peer into the wagon. He tried to shield her from the ugly scene, but he was too late.

Brianna couldn't take her eyes off the couple inside the wagon, lying in their own filth, so helpless, and so humiliatingly exposed. This was what Julia suffered, she thought with a horror that threatened her hard-won control.

Nigh drew her away. For one second she lifted her horror-stricken eyes to his. Then she shoved him aside and ran several feet before bending over to empty her stomach. When she tried to stand up after it was over, she grew dizzy. Nigh carried her to the buggy, then went to find someone to take care of the little girl. He came back with a bottle of brandy, three-quarters empty, and insisted she take several sips. Halfway back to town, she nodded off, leaning against his shoulder. He eased her down with her head in his lap and let her sleep.

The following morning Brianna awoke to the scent of apple trees and a soft scraping sound. A long way away a dog was barking and she heard the muffled sounds of voices. Through the blanket she could feel the firm

warmth of Shakespeare curled up beside her. For a long
time, she kept her eyes shut, reluctant to leave the safe
world of slumber, though she didn't know why. Then it
came back to her.

Julia was dead.

Brianna moaned at the thought, her head turning back
and forth on the pillow.

Her eyes flew open as a hand touched her face. It was
callused and as rough as pine bark, yet gentle, and she
opened her eyes to see Columbus Nigh gazing down at
her, a look of tenderness in his eyes.

"Julia," she whispered, her throat constricting as she
tried to block the tears. The grief she had been unable to
give vent to the previous day now filled her whole being.
Despite her effort to contain them, the sobs escaped her
in choking gasps while tears laved her face. Without a
word Nigh gathered her into his arms. Trying to calm her
was like trying to stop a waterfall with only a hand.

"Oh God, why?" Brianna said, brokenly. "She was all
the kin I had left in the world. Now there's no one. I've
no where to turn. What's going to happen to me?"

"Shh, it'll be all right," Nigh crooned, his face buried
in her loose hair. She wore only drawers and a thin
chemise with a low, gathered neck. Beneath his hands as
he held her, her skin was soft and smooth and smelled
faintly of roses.

Brianna put her hands on his arms and drew away
from him. "John, and the children . . . I don't remember.
Were they there, too?"

He shook his head. "I spoke to the sheriff. He's tried to
keep a record of those who've died. Your brother-in-law
recovered and took the children home to his family in
Louisville a few days ago."

Though calmer, Brianna felt little comforted. When she lay back down she realized she was practically naked. Worse, she was alone in a hotel room with a man. A man who had kissed her. Two bright spots of rose colored her cheeks as she yanked the covers up to her chin.

"How did I . . . get undressed?"

"You fell asleep on the way back last night. Hotel clerk sent for a doctor. He said you were in shock and just needed rest. It's mornin' now, you slept through the night."

Nigh let her assume it was the doctor who had disrobed her. But he couldn't prevent the heat that speared his groin at the memory of his hands removing her clothing and bathing her skin with cool water. She was sapling-thin, so thin he could count her ribs. He could also have counted scars, if he'd had a notion to, pale blemishes that read like the trail of a wounded deer, telling of the beatings she must have suffered at the hands of her dead husband.

Her husband. God, how Nigh hoped the man were still alive as he was beginning to suspect he was, so he could kill him with his own bare hands.

The only thing that pained Nigh more was the thought of the bastard touching her intimately, touching those places Nigh so longed to touch himself.

Brianna didn't see the fevered look that came into his eyes. She had closed her eyes against the dull throb in her temples. Her mouth felt stuffed with moldy cotton. When she opened her eyes again, Columbus was still there, crouched on one knee beside her bed.

"Did you stay with me . . . all night?"

Nigh shrugged, unwilling to tell her how badly she had scared him. "Somebody needed to keep an eye on you."

"I'm fine, really. You shouldn't be here. I dread to think what people must be thinking."

Nigh frowned as he rose to his feet. Her words were like cold water doused over him. He picked up a knife and a half-carved chunk of wood from the chair by the window and stepped to the door. "I'll be down at the restaurant if you feel up to some breakfast."

Then he was gone.

Brianna sighed as she wiped her eyes. Beneath the chair where Nigh had been sitting, the floor was littered with wood shavings. Such a curious man, she thought. He was as hard as stone, crude, and illiterate. Yet he could be so gentle. He had taken better care of her than her own husband ever would have.

Would he help her get to Oregon? She had to ask. It was the only thing she could do. She eased Shakespeare aside, got up and walked to the chair. Filling her hands with yellow wood shavings, she sniffed. They smelled like apple trees—like Columbus Nigh himself.

Columbus Nigh looked up in surprise as Brianna sat down across the small table from him. As usual she wore her somber widow's weeds, covered by the voluminous black cloak. The restaurant was crowded and smelled of fried ham, bacon, and freshly baked biscuits. He washed down the bite of eggs he had just taken with a slug of hot coffee and asked if she wanted something to eat.

"No." Her stomach lurched at the sight of the greasy food on his plate. "Only tea, please, cream, no lemon."

Lifting his hand, Nigh motioned to a pudgy waitress. When the tea was placed before her, Brianna removed her gloves, added a large dollop of cream and stirred it in without a word. All around them were the sounds of silverware clinking against china, of laughter, and of cheerful conversation punctuated with a few curse words. Nigh's mouth quirked in his half-smile as Brianna winced at the loud belches indulged in by the roomful of men. Except for the waitress, there were only three other women present. He waited patiently for Brianna to tell him what was on her mind.

"Please, finish your breakfast," she said.

Taking her at her word, he stuffed a large helping of ham into his mouth, his eyes still on her. She sipped daintily at her tea, her eyes darting uncertainly about the room. Above the wainscoting the walls were papered in a scroll-like pattern of green and white. Framed etchings of Parisian scenes hung from the molding at the top of the walls. Green oilcloth covered each table. Only after Nigh had taken his last bite did she speak: "What happened to the little girl?"

"Found a couple who'd lost their girl. They seemed real glad to take her."

She nodded, stirred her tea, and straightened the napkin on her lap. "I must ask for your help one last time, Mr. Nigh." She took a deep breath to fortify herself. "I've decided to go on to Oregon if Mr. Magrudge's company will take me. I'm hoping you'll drive me out there today so I can see about arrangements."

Nigh laid down his knife and fork, leaned back in his chair, and studied her. "Why?"

"Why what?"

"Why do you still want to go to Oregon?"

Brianna looked down at her hands, folded primly in her lap. The man's scrutiny made her feel like a specimen under a botanist's magnifying glass. Her chin lifted. Her back was as stiff as a chair leg. "I've nothing to return to in St. Louis. The idea of traveling to a new country appeals to me."

He scooted back in his chair, legs sprawled half-under the table, one arm slung over the back of his chair. "Got any idea how difficult a trip you're talkin' about? Four, five months, camping in the wilderness. Snakes, wolves, Injuns . . . cholera. Dust blowing in your face sunup to sundown, and no privacy for calls of nature. You ready for that?"

Her cheeks reddened at his plain speaking. "I-I have to be, I have no other choice."

Nigh could see she was close to tears, but he wasn't about to let up. "Why? Who are you running from?"

Panic-stricken eyes stared back at him. Unconsciously she began to toy with the plain gold band on her left hand. "N-no one. I don't understand what you're getting at."

The raised voices of two men at a nearby table caught Nigh's attention. Jumping to his feet, he tossed down a few coins to pay for his meal. Then he hauled Brianna from her chair, barely giving her time to snatch up her gloves as he headed for the door. Behind them dishes crashed to the floor as the two men began to fight. Shocked, she turned to watch, but Nigh jerked her roughly through the doorway into the hotel lobby.

"Where are we going?" she asked as he dragged her through the crowded room.

"Somewhere where we can talk."

At the foot of the stairs she balked, but he towed her up the stairs behind him, then down the hall to her room.

He held out his hand. "The key."

"I thought we were going to talk."

"We are, in there. Now give me the key."

She glanced up and down the hall, her words a harsh whisper. "We can't. It would cause a scandal!"

Nigh thrust his face close to hers, his slitted eyes as cold and unbending as the metal key he demanded she give him. "You know one single soul in this town?"

"No, but—"

"But nothing! You intend to live here?"

"No."

"Then why in thunder should you care what these folks think? I could force you into that room, screaming, and have my way with you, and no one would lift a finger. They have their own problems, ain't going to pay no mind to yours."

Blushing from head to toe and bristling with anger, Brianna drew herself up and glared at him eye to eye. "Whether or not anyone else cares how I conduct myself, I do!"

"Fine. Behave as proper as you want, just give me that key. I said we were going to have a talk and I meant it, but not out here where every saddle bum with an itch for gold can hear us."

"No. I-I have no way of knowing what may have happened while I lay unconscious last night, Mr. Nigh, but I don't intend to tempt fate by allowing you to be alone in my room with me again."

Damn the woman! It wasn't fate that had suffered the temptation of hell last night, and won—for her benefit.

Before she could make a move to resist him, he flipped open her cloak and felt at her waist for a hidden pocket or purse. His face was so close to hers, she could smell the coffee on his breath.

"Stop it! You hear me?" she said, struggling to free herself.

"You always this stubborn?" He pushed away her

protesting hands. "Ain't no surprise to me some man found it necessary to beat you. Been tempted to do the same more'n once since I met you and, dammit, I might yet!"

Chapter Nine

Terrorized by Nigh's anger, Brianna froze. It gave him the time he needed to plunge his fingers deep into a side pocket of her skirt and withdraw the key he had felt through the fabric. He ignored the self-loathing he felt for using her fear against her. Throwing the door open, he shoved her inside.

"Now start talking," he said, leaning against the closed door.

Afraid to go near the bed, even to calm the cat whose hair had risen on his back at the tension charging the air, Brianna sat down in the chair by the window. She kept her eyes on her lap, smoothing her skirts, and arranging the folds, hoping to give some semblance of calm. "I thought you wanted to talk to me."

"You know what it is I want to hear. Get to it."

Refusing to look up at him, she continued fussing with her skirts. Then she drew the cloak tightly closed over her bosom and folded her hands demurely in her lap.

Nigh was across the room in a flash. He grabbed her by the arms, lifting her to her feet to face him. "Blast your proper manners all to hell, *madam*. How can I help you if you won't talk to me? Tell me who you're running away from!"

Blue-green eyes stared back at him, large as tea cups and filled with fear. Her full, finely etched lips were parted and quivering. Her rose scent wafted up to him and something snapped inside him. White heat blazed a trail to his brain, obliterating everything except her lips and the desire they awakened in him. With a groan, he folded his arms around her and hugged her tight against his body so she could feel the warmth she had ignited in him.

Then, with a shock, he realized it was more than physical lust he felt. More than frustration and concern. More even than passion. He wanted to protect this woman, to keep her safe, and warm, and forever at his side.

Brianna saw the tumultuous gray of his eyes soften to a warm violet. When his lips touched hers, she stood very still, barely breathing. She reminded herself that this was the man who had saved her from the Santa Fe traders, who had slept within feet of her for days without touching her. Yes, he often infuriated her and sometimes he terrified her—like now. But surely, if he were going to hurt her, he would have done it by now. He had even said he would never hit her. Still, she could not relax, could not banish the fear. And in the back of her mind her conscience was at work, too, telling her that to let this man take what he wanted would be a sin. She was still a married woman; running away hadn't changed that.

His lips were moving lightly over hers, testing, tasting, trying in vain to get some sort of reaction out of her. The feel of her frozen in his arms was more than he could bear. He opened his eyes. As he had feared, her face was white, her eyes wild with panic.

Anger surged in his veins; anger at himself, anger at

her. He shoved her back down into the chair, then leaned toward her, his palms braced on the arms of the chair.

"Dammit, woman, why don't you fight me? If you don't want me to kiss you, say so, stand up for yourself."

Her eyes went blank for a second, the fear turning to confusion. "You were angry."

He flung himself away from her and stomped across the room. "What the hell's that got to do with anything?" He turned and came back to her. For a long moment he stared at her while he sought control. Then he knelt by her chair. His voice was low and smooth. "Brianna, just because I'm angry doesn't mean you have to knuckle under to me. You have a right to get mad, too."

She looked at him as though he'd spoken a foreign tongue. Her delicately arched brows drew together, creating furrows between her eyes. Her long eyelashes blinked. She cocked her head as though contemplating his words, and finding them incomprehensible.

Nigh took her slender hand in his. "Most men aren't like your husband. They don't beat their wives, no matter what their wives do."

"You never hit your wife?"

"No." His mouth quirked up in a lopsided smile. "But she whacked me with a parfleche once when I tracked mud into her tipi."

The softness that came into his face shocked her. It was as though he took pleasure in the memory of his wife striking him, as though it amused him. "And you didn't hit her back?"

"It was her tipi—the lodge always belongs to the woman—and I got it dirty. Reckon she was right to cuff me one, don't you?"

Brianna's smile was small and sad. "I would never dare yell at my husband, let alone hit him."

"You don't have to worry 'bout that no more. And you don't have to be afraid of me, understand?"

She nodded, but he saw the reservation in her eyes. She still wasn't sure she could trust him. He sighed and vowed not to let it bother him. She was like a filly he'd bought once just to keep her previous owner from flogging her to death. It had taken him a long time to win the filly over. Patience, tenderness, a gentle hand. Eventually, the filly had grown into a fine mare. Brianna was worth the effort, the same as the filly had been.

In the meantime, there were other matters to settle. This close to her he couldn't think clearly. He moved away to stand with his back to the door and reached inside his shirt for the pouch that held his toothpicks. The taste of the wood was sharp and slightly acrid after the honey of her lips. Damn! What had she done to him?

"You ready to answer me now?" he said.

"Answer you?"

"Tell me who's after you."

Her frustration was nearly as palpable as his. "What makes you think I'm running away from someone?"

"Could be the way you keep looking over your shoulder," he said, gnawing his toothpick. "Or the way you were slinking round that store in Jefferson City and almost jumped outta your skin when I came up behind you. Then again, might be the way you looked yesterday when you thought that man was telling me to get my hands off you."

She stood and began to pace the room like a caged cougar. "Since you can read my mind so well, it's hardly necessary for me to tell you anything, is it? Who could I be running away from?"

Nigh shrugged. "Looking at you, it'd be mighty hard to swallow, but the law comes first to mind. You rob a bank maybe? Or leave a few unhappy creditors behind? Reckon the sheriff here might have some ideas, been enough time for word to reach him from St. Louie. If not, he could send out some inquiries of his own."

Her restless feet stilled. Panic thrummed in her ears. She could not let him go to the sheriff. Barret may have sent out inquiries about a missing wife. Somehow she had to make Columbus Nigh back down. Drawing herself up to full height, she took a deep breath and tightened her hands into fists at her sides.

"By what right do you make such vile accusations against me, Mr. Nigh? Or even question me? Do I look like a thief to you? Or a welsher?"

The sight of her chin thrust in the air and her eyes pinioning him to the door like a Blackfoot lance pleased him to no end. She was magnificent. He swallowed the grin that crept to his lips. In his slow drawl, he said, "No, don't reckon you do."

His words stunned her. Her bluff had worked. Pride hummed along her veins as she turned and haughtily walked to the window. "Then I suggest you keep in mind that I hired you to see me to Independence, not to run my life. You have been my employee, nothing more." Here she faltered, her voice losing some of its hauteur as she added, "Though I had hoped we were becoming friends."

She paused and Nigh knew she was waiting, hoping, for him to assure her they were indeed friends. But he was still suffering the sting of her earlier comment on the status of their relationship.

After a moment of silence, she stumbled on, "If you are unwilling to escort me to Oregon Territory, I will understand. Independence seems fairly bursting at the seams with men eager to take to the trail. I'm sure I can find one desperate enough for a stake to take the job."

Since she hadn't the courage to face him, she did not see his eyes narrow and harden, but she heard the low, deadly calm of his voice.

"Reckon you can at that."

He opened the door and the click of the latch was like a cannon shot in the silent room, riddling her heart as he stomped from the room.

For a long time Brianna stood by the window, seeing nothing, and hearing only the faint echoing click of the door closing behind him. Closing her out of his life. Enclosing her in her own private hell. Finally, she took off her cloak and laid it neatly over the back of the chair. She untied her bonnet and set it on top of the cloak. Then she lay down on the bed next to Shakespeare. Drawing the cat into her arms, she buried her face in his warm, pungent fur, and cried.

Columbus Nigh stormed into the first tavern he came to. The bar was mahogany, so highly polished he could see his image in the dark surface. The whiskers he hadn't bothered to shave off that morning failed to hide the flush of anger in his lean, angular cheeks. He scowled at the reflection and shouted for a whiskey. The barman was an ordinary-looking fellow with a full red beard and pale skin covered with freckles. Nigh watched while the man set a glass on the bar and filled it with golden brown liquid.

"Two bits," the barman said. "Less'n you want me to leave the bottle. Then it's a dollar."

"Leave it."

Nigh dug in his pocket and slapped down some coins. The first drink vanished down his gullet like rainwater through a crack. He refilled the glass and turned to stand with his side to the bar, one elbow resting next to the waiting glass.

The tavern wasn't as crowded as it would be later when a man could call it quits to a day's work with a clear conscience and let himself relax. Five men sat at a round table playing euchre. They looked as though they'd been at it since yesterday. Others stood at the bar, along with a woman.

Nigh studied her. There was enough rouge on her face to paint an entire tipi, but she wasn't bad looking and the cleavage showing above the low neckline of her dress was more than inviting. A woman was exactly what he needed, Nigh told himself. If he could ease the ache in his loins, maybe he could untangle himself from the infuriating female he'd left at the hotel.

The whore caught his look. Her painted lips spread in a seductive smile as she sashayed over to him.

"You look like a man who needs someone to talk to." Her voice was low and silky. "Maybe someone who can ease your troubles for a little while, hmm?"

Her perfume had proceeded her, a heavy, cloying scent as different from Brianna's rose water as sparrows are to hawks. He was glad. Her breath was sweet enough and she appeared cleaner than most; likely she'd had a bath sometime in the past week.

"I'm Angel." Her painted fingers toyed with the fringe on his sleeve. "Gonna share that bottle with me?"

Angel. Sure you are, he thought. She licked her lips suggestively. He watched her small pink tongue trace the full circle of her heart-shaped mouth and looked down at the plump flesh bulging from the dress front. A half-inch more and her breasts would be rubbing his chest. He swallowed and waited for his body to respond.

"Why not?" He filled the glass and handed it to her. She turned it until she found the moist imprint of his own mouth on its rim, then licked it while she gazed up at him. Nigh shifted, knowing any minute now he'd feel his blood begin to hum.

"You a trapper?" She closed the half-inch gap.

"Among other things."

"Um, like what other things?" She reached for his hand where it hung limp at his side and set it on her waist. Her voice was like a July afternoon on the North Platte, sultry and suffocatingly hot.

He let his hand squeeze her waist, then wander upward. "Hunter, emigrant guide, army scout, translator." The latter brought a half-smile to his face. "Got a reputation for conversin' real well with Indians, specially squaws."

"Is that so?" she grinned as his hand moved between them to enclose a ripe breast. Raising her knee beneath her dress, she rubbed her thigh against his crotch. "You do just as well with us white women?"

"What do you think?" He lowered his head and kissed her full on the lips. Her tongue stabbed into his mouth in a parody of the sex act, designed to inflame him.

"Um, I'd say you communicate real good, honey," she purred. "How about we go upstairs and talk some more?"

Dropping his hand to her buttocks, he pulled her close enough to flatten her breasts against his chest and grind his pelvis into hers while he kissed her savagely. Then he drew back. He looked at her a long moment, waiting. Nothing happened. Her breathing was quick and uneven; his was calm. She rubbed herself against him, begging for more. He felt nothing.

"Maybe later, Angel." He pushed her away gently and picked up the whiskey bottle. "Got other matters to see to right now."

The coin he tossed down for the bartender spun for a moment, then wobbled and clattered to a halt as he headed for the door. The woman gaped after him, her eyes full of disappointment.

Hell, there was something wrong with him. He wasn't so old a whore shouldn't be able to get an arousal out of him. Yet he had to admit that even with Angel's lush body pressed to his, he'd felt nothing. It was Brianna. He could still feel the widow's generous lips beneath his, could still taste her flavor. Damn the woman!

Her employee! The words were like a fresh buffalo chip he couldn't get off his moccasin. Well, if that was the way she wanted things, it was fine with him. Let her find someone else to nursemaid her all the way to Oregon Territory. He didn't need her, that was sure.

Lost in his fury and frustration, he headed for the livery where he figured to find some privacy. If he couldn't ease himself with a woman, he'd have to settle for getting good and drunk. Maybe later he'd go back and give Angel another try.

It was mid-afternoon before Brianna dragged herself off the bed. She bathed her red, swollen eyes with cool water from the ceramic pitcher on the washstand and

dried them on the towel hanging on the rack. There was
no time to indulge in self-pity. Unless she wanted to go
back and face Barret, she had to get herself signed up with
the Magrudge wagon company.

That meant hiring a buggy and driving herself out to
the camp to talk with the wagon captain. The memory of
the man's dark ferret eyes on her bosom, and the sun
glinting off the spittle on his thin lips, made her shudder.
Perhaps she could ask around to see if there were any
other parties heading for Oregon. She hoped the money
she had taken from Barret's study would be enough to see
her there and pay for housing until she could find work.
She would have to be very careful how she spent her
hoard; it might have to last a very long time.

Her skirt was wrinkled from lying on the bed. She
smoothed it as well as she could, then donned her cloak
and put on her bonnet. Stepping out into the hall, she
glanced up and down, glad to find it empty. Carefully she
locked the door behind her and slipped the key into her
pocket. Her steps on the uncarpeted stairs seemed loud
enough to be heard all the way to Jefferson City, but no
one looked her way as she descended to the hotel lobby
and walked sedately to the registration desk.

After receiving directions to the livery stable, she left
the hotel and headed up the boardwalk. Dried clumps of
mud crunched beneath her boots as she walked. Now that
her mind was not caught up in the worry of finding her
sister, she took more notice of the town—and of the lack
of women on its streets. What few she saw were escorted
by men. Her mind drifted back to the incident she had
witnessed the day before, the woman struggling in the
grasp of a drunken stranger until her husband rescued
her.

Almost at once Brianna became aware of the way men were looking at her, their eyes running over her body as if curious about what they might find beneath her cloak. Hoping to bluff her way through this predicament the way she had with Columbus Nigh, she straightened her shoulders, lifted her chin, and forged briskly forward. She ignored the attempts to engage her in conversation, refusing even to blush at the lewd suggestions tossed her way. When she spied a large sign arching over the boardwalk with the name of the livery in bright red paint, she quickened her pace.

Brianna ran down the steps at the end of the walkway, lifted her skirts to maneuver the narrow plank stretched across the muddy alley, and scurried up the stairs on the other side. A man in striped pantaloons tucked into knee-length boots and a faded homespun shirt emerged from a doorway in front of her. His tread was unsteady, his laughter raucous, as he turned to make a bawdy crack to someone behind him. Just as she tried to step past the man, his unseen cohort gave him a push, and Brianna found herself locked in his arms while he regained his balance.

"Well hey, what do we got here?" he said.

Brianna shoved him away and ran for the open doors of the livery, followed by coarse laughter and crude comments. Inside the smelly barn, she threw herself against the wall, panting until she caught her breath. Stalls lined both sides of the big room. Feed buckets, rakes, pitchforks, and coils of rope hung from walls or lay on the straw-covered floor. A wooden ladder led to a loft. To her right, through a wide opening, she could see buggies and wagons. Pushing away from the wall, she took a few halting steps toward the second room, reluctant to penetrate its gloomy depths. Then she heard a voice coming from one of the stalls and the soft whicker of a horse.

"Hello." Her voice sounded thin and reedy. "Is anyone here?"

Three-quarters of the way down the broad aisle between the two rows of stalls, a man's voice answered. "Yeah, whaddya want?"

She walked toward the sound. "I-I need to rent a buggy, please."

The man grumbled something she could not make out. A bucket clanged to the floor and the horse whickered again. Brianna took two more steps. Then the man came out of the stall. He wiped his hands on his dirty trousers as he strode toward her. When he was only a little more than arm's length away, he stopped to look her over.

"Well," he said, "what can I do for you, little lady?"

Little! she thought. Was the man blind? Actually he was quite tall himself, with thick arms sticking out of sleeveless one-piece underwear that must have once been red, but were now a faded, dingy gray. Several buttons were missing down the front. Between the galluses holding up his baggy trousers, the man's hairy paunch protruded from the gaping underwear. He scratched the smudged skin above his naval and grinned as she blushed.

"I need a buggy," she said, "and a horse."

"Yeah?" He scratched under his arm this time. "You gonna drive it all by yourself?"

"Yes, I-I have business at a wagon camp west of town."

He stepped closer and she backed away. "Tell ya what, honey, why don't I drive ya out there? Pretty little thing like you don't want to get herself all dirty now, does she? And if you're nice to me, why, I won't even charge ya nothing. Whaddya say?"

"She says, no."

Bits of straw rained onto her head as Brianna gazed up at the sound of the voice. She blinked to clear the chaff from her eyes and saw two mocassined feet appear on the second rung of the ladder from the loft. The feet were followed by fringed, leather-clad legs. A good four feet from the bottom, Columbus Nigh kicked off and jumped lithely to the floor.

"What business is this of yours, mister?"

Nigh spared the liveryman no glance. "Lady's with me. Finish your shoeing, smithy."

"Now, look—"

Nigh swung toward the man, his eyes glinting steel. "You got a problem?"

The two men glared at each other for one long moment before the smithy backed off. "Lemme know when you make up your mind about the buggy, lady." He lumbered back to the stall where he had been working, grumbling all the way. When he was gone, Nigh pinched his eyes closed with thumb and forefinger. "What the hell are you doing here, woman?"

"I need a buggy so I can go out to talk with Mr. Magrudge."

Hands on his hips, he hung his head as if too tired, or too disgusted, to hold it up. "Be a waste of time. Magrudge ain't gonna let no widow woman in his train unless she's got a man with her who can protect her."

"Then I'll speak with Mrs. Decker. Perhaps she or one of the other families will let me travel with them."

"Dead set on going, are you?"

He was looking at her now and she swallowed nervously under his intense scrutiny.

"I told you, there's nothing left for me in Missouri except bad memories. I want more."

"Only way you can travel with that wagon train without invitin' trouble is with a man, perferably a husband, legal or not. Just how bad do you want to go?"

Her eyes widened. "Exactly what are you suggesting?"

His lips quirked up on one side as he leaned closer, his weight on one leg, thumbs hooked in the back of his belt. "Don't reckon anyone needs to know we ain't hitched proper."

Brianna's mouth fell open. "You are despicable! How dare you suggest such a thing, I—"

"Now hold on." He held up his hands. "Ain't said nothing 'bout living married, only 'bout letting folks think we're married. I'll sleep under the wagon. Is it a deal?"

She chewed her lower lip, pondering his words. The man certainly had nerve. Exactly what was it he wanted from her? Why would he be willing to do this? "Won't people think it strange if my 'husband' sleeps under the wagon every night?"

He shrugged. "Who cares what they think, long as the men leave you alone and the women see you as respectable?"

"Wouldn't it be equally as acceptable if they thought you were my brother?"

Again he shrugged. The idea didn't appeal to him as much, but he could think of no objection to it that she would accept. "Reckon. Do we have a deal, or not?"

For one breathless moment, she stared deep into his cold, stormy eyes. Did she have a choice? "Yes, Mr. Nigh, I *reckon* we have a deal."

* * *

"Hey, Will?"

United States Marshal Will Rainey swung his long legs off the desk and sat upright in the battered old swivel chair. "H'lo, George, what are you up to this afternoon?"

The tow-headed boy grinned as he tossed a dirt-smeared envelope on the marshal's cluttered desk. "Mr. Birch asked me to deliver this letter. It's marked 'Rush.' See?"

Rainey picked up the envelope and sniffed the orange smear across the address. "Been into your ma's apricot jam again, George? How come you didn't bring me any?"

"I will next time, promise, Will."

"All right, thanks." Rainey pulled a penny from his vest pocket and flipped it to the boy.

"Hey!" Rainey shouted as George bolted for the door. "Thank Sam Birch for me, too, will you?"

Alone now, the marshal ripped open the envelope and quickly scanned the scrawled handwriting on the single piece of folded paper it held. He was reading it a second time when Glory wiggled into the office.

"Hey there, Will, how's that man of mine you're keeping locked up back there?"

"If you're talking about Barret, he's gone."

Glory glared at the marshal with all the fire her Irish temper could muster.

"What do you mean, he's gone?"

"Just that." Will Rainey propped his feet on the scarred desk and rifled through the wanted posters brought in with the day's mail. "Your fancy lawyer, what's his name? Rawlings?"

"Ralston, Clinton Ray Ralston."

"Yeah, well, he got Judge Hanley to order me to show cause or release that lover of yours." Dropping the wanted posters into his lap, Rainey grinned up at her. "What's the matter, Glory? Did Wight forget to hustle his plump, hungry body straight over to your little love nest?"

With a final glare that should have seared his eyebrows, Glory stormed out the door.

That evening as Marshal Rainey walked down to the Roast Goose Cafe for his supper, Glory burst out of Ralston's legal office like popcorn out of a hot skillet, nearly knocking Rainey off his feet.

"Hey, slow down there, woman." He latched onto her, as much to catch his balance as to stop her. "I'll have to incite you for horse racing on the boardwalk if you don't slow down."

"I haven't got a horse and you know it, you . . . mule's hind end!" She pried at his fingers which held firmly to her arm. "Let go of me, I've got a snake to run down."

Rainey laughed. "I surely do pity the poor thing if you're after him."

He'd let go of her and started to step past her when the significance of her statement penetrated his brain. Swinging around, he barely managed to grab onto her again. "Wait a minute. What snake is this you're after? Wouldn't be that pimp of yours, would it?"

Glory slapped at his hands. "He's not my pimp."

"You're a whore, aren't you? He owns you, doesn't he? That makes him your pimp in my book."

"Well, your book is made out of privy contents. Now let go of me. Or are you going to arrest me?"

Rainey chuckled. "That can be arranged. Who's the snake?"

"Barret Wight, of course. Why didn't you put a tail on him, if you were so all-fired sure he killed his wife? Now he's gone. Run off after that frigid scarecrow he's married

to. And Ralston says there's not a thing I can do about it."
She poked him with her finger, her eyes blazing with
anger. "But I'll find him, and when I do, you won't have
to worry about building any gallows for him, because I'll
kill the fat bastard myself."

"I'd head for Independence, then, if I were you."

"Why Independence?"

"Because I received word from Mrs. Wight's brother-
in-law today. Seems he and his family were barely outside
Independence with a wagon train when cholera struck.
His wife died, so he brought the children back for his folks
to raise. But if Brianna Wight is still alive, she won't know
that until she gets there."

The marshal leaned back against the wall of the law
office and gave Glory a smirking grin. "My bet is that
Barret's hot on her trail right now. Or maybe he's only
running from that noose I promised him."

She stabbed him in the chest with her finger again.
"Then go after him. You're the marshal, bring him
back."

The laughter leached from his eyes and his mouth
became grim, letting her see how he truly felt about losing
his chance to see Wight hung. "My jurisdiction ends at
the border to Indian Territory, Glory. Once he crosses
that, there's not a damn thing I can do."

Chapter Ten

Dear Mrs. O'Casey

I shall write only a few minutes as Mr. Nigh is waiting to take this to town. The wagon company departs at dawn. Our only problem thus far has been the rain which seems determined to keep us mired here, only forty miles west of Independence.

Our company numbers forty-eight wagons, divided into platoons of four wagons each, which rotate every day so that everyone gets a chance to ride up front out of the dust (if it ever dries out enough for dust). The men number sixty-two, the women thirty, children fifty-five. The greater majority of companies are headed for California and are comprised almost entirely of men, thousands of them.

The cholera is very bad here. There are sick in nearly every camp but ours, and graves everywhere you look.

The next opportunity to post a letter may be weeks away so do not worry if you don't hear from me for awhile. I wish you well, and remain your grateful friend,

Brianna Villard

P.S. Villard is my mother's maiden name. I add one other note; one of the men in our company is the Kentuckian with *whom Mr. Nigh fought that day at Longmire's. His name is Jack Moulton but everyone calls him Punch because he is always fighting with someone—a little like Barret when he was younger. How I wish I knew what is happening back home and if Barret is pursuing me.*

* * *

Stinky Harris cocked his head to one side and spat in the brass spittoon on the sawdust-littered floor at his feet. He propped a muddy boot on the scratched foot rail, leaned his forearms on the whiskey-stained bar, and shouted for another drink. Being only mid-morning, there were few customers yet. In the mirror behind the surly, square-faced bartender, Stinky watched a short, boxy-built fellow enter the tavern and pause to scan the crowd. Barret Wight didn't look quite as cocky as the last time they'd met. Grinning, Stinky turned and waved the man over.

"Didn't expect you till tonight," he said when Wight reached him. "You afraid they'd go ahead and hang you if you stuck around too long?"

Barret ordered a beer and growled, "I told you they didn't have enough evidence to pin that rap on me. Soon the whole world will know that Amazon I'm married to wasn't murdered by anyone. I rode night and day to get here. Damn horse went lame five miles out of town. Had to hitch a ride in a wagon full of brats."

The bartender poured, Barret emptied the glass, and passed it back to be filled again.

"Could've been worse," Stinky said, still grinning.

"Huh! One more thing that bitch is going to have to pay for."

Barret downed the second glass. The brew wasn't as good as what his own brewery produced, but after the

long, dry trek, it would do. He glanced around at the
other patrons of the tavern: greasy-looking Spaniards
from Santa Fe, long haired fur trappers from the Rockies,
eager-faced argonauts bound for the gold fields of California. Damn, but it was fine to be free again, he thought.
"Well, I assume, since you dragged me clear across Missouri to this mudhole, that she's headed west."

"That's right." Stinky dipped a finger in the whiskey
the bartender had spilled filling his glass, and sucked it
dry. "She wasn't registered anywhere under her own
name, but the Independence House had a widow named
Villard there until a week ago, who fits her description.
There was a man with her, a paid guide or something,
who slept outside her door. They joined one of the wagon
companies."

"Villard . . . don't mean nothing to me. Where's she
headed, Oregon or California?"

"Couldn't find out. Going after her?"

Barret pounded his fist on the bar to catch the bartender's attention, then pointed to his empty glass. "You
bet I'm going after her. She seems to have forgotten she
belongs to me, but she'll never forget it again once I get
my hands on her."

"What about this fellow she was with? Mountain man
type, the clerk said. Tough as rawhide and mean as a
bulldog with his balls slit open. Don't think I want to go
up against him."

Wight gave Stinky a look over the rim of his glass that
wiped the grin from the man's face and put worms in his
belly. Wight's tone when he spoke, was deadly soft.

"You aren't me. Now get out of here and buy us some
mules and supplies so we can get our asses on the road.
Whatever headstart she's got on us, we'll be able to make

up easily enough. A bunch of wagons move a lot slower than two men with mules."

"All right, Barret, I'll get right on it." Stinky downed his drink and turned toward the door. Wight stopped him with a hand on his arm.

"Make sure you get a shovel. If she is with a man, there'll be a grave to dig. Maybe two.

By midmorning Nigh knew it wasn't going to be an easy day. Or a quiet one.

"Coover, get them goldanged critters of yours moving, dagnabit! Ain't gonna reach Oregon afore Christmas the rate we're going." Magrudge's deep baritone boomed nearly to the rear wagons, over two miles down the line.

Five days had passed while they waited out the rain and the flooded creeks. Five days of dealing with contrary oxen, runaway horses, and bogged down wagons. But each day they had managed to advance a few miles. Now before them lay the open prairie, as vast and sweeping as the endless sky, as undulating as the washboards the women lugged to the creek on wash day. At last, the sun had banished the clouds. Bedding and clothes were dry and the road was manageable. Nigh figured they were too far from the States to turn back, and that made today the caravan's first full day of travel.

Yet, already, trouble was brewing.

"Hellfire! Go around that mud hole, ya blasted idjet! Think we need more broken wheels?" Magrudge hollered. "Woody, ain't you learned yet how to yoke up your dang oxen? Get Shorthill over there to show you. He drives no better'n a hog on Sunday, but at least his critters stay yoked. And you, Beaudouin, this ain't no Easter parade. Maybe you could drive that fancy rig of yours better if you changed them elegant duds to something more sensible. You know, like work clothes. Ever hear of them?"

By the time they stopped for the noon meal, Nigh reckoned mutiny was a sure bet. Men stood about in small clutches, kicking the ground and shaking their heads. Nigh sat on a wagon tongue, off by himself as usual, whittling creamy yellow curls from a chunk of apple wood to form a two-inch grizzly bear, his eyes flicking every minute or so to his "employer," a term which still rankled.

As usual, Brianna hovered on the sidelines while the other women gossiped and traded recipes. It wasn't shyness on her part, he thought, but plain lack of self-confidence. The loneliness and yearning in her eyes made his insides knot in frustration because he didn't know how to help.

Marc Beaudouin and Tom Coover were walking toward him. The hesitancy of their pace and the careful way they avoided his gaze warned him they wanted something. Nigh tongued his homegrown toothpick from one corner of his mouth to the other and went on working. He knew the men would get to whatever was on their minds eventually.

"What do you think, Col?" Marc's hands were stuffed in the pockets of his wool pants, making knuckle-bulges at each hip.

Nigh lifted one sardonic eye. "What about?"

"Some of the members are talking about breaking off and forming a company of their own. They're tired of being bullied by Magrudge."

Tom Coover squatted down and scooped up the yellow curls of applewood at Nigh's feet, like a farmer sifting soil between his fingers. "The women are all worked up over Magrudge's language, too. Say they won't move another inch till someone talks to him."

Nigh could well believe that. Every time he let slip with a cussword or what Brianna called a "profanity," she bristled up worse than a porcupine. The other women weren't as fine bred as Brianna, but he supposed they had their standards as well.

From beneath lowered eyes, Nigh studied Coover's red, freckled face and young rangy body. He was agile and strong and rarely stayed still for long, as though he feared the young sap in his veins would harden and turn old before he could use it all up.

"Bound to happen sooner or later, folks choosing to go their own way," Nigh drawled. "The women'll be wishing soon enough that a few cusswords was all they had to deal with."

"We were hoping you might talk to Magrudge," Beaudouin said, looking slightly abashed.

Nigh thought that over a moment. "Why me?"

"This is a matter which requires diplomacy as well as composure." Beaudouin nodded toward the men who were still kicking dirt, though their anxious gazes rested now on Nigh. "Some of them are afraid of Magrudge. Others fear they'll lose their tempers and kill the man. As for me, well, Magrudge has made it plain he thinks little of men of my standing, so I doubt he would listen to anything I have to say."

That was usually how it went, Nigh thought. Folks wanted things their way, but they wanted someone else to get it for them. As for Marc, he was dressed and equipped better than any other family in the company. His wagons looked like most of the others, with their blue bodies and bright red wheels. But the heavy white covering bore no catchy sayings, like "Oregon's where we're going, Ohio's where we been."

One of the Beaudouin wagons carried personal items needed on the trail, a tent for Marc and the oldest boy, beds in the wagon for Lilith and Jean Louis. There was a made-to-order collapsible table and three camp chairs— with backs, not just stools!—as well as a sheet iron cook-stove with a detachable bake oven. The second wagon held household goods and furniture. Marc even had a pen full of live chickens beneath the wagon bed. At each stop the hens were let out to forage in the grass, when they weren't defending themselves against Shakespeare. Each morning the boys herded them back up the little ramp into the pen for traveling.

Most folks had to make do with one wagon, leaving behind all their prized possessions. Nigh wasn't surprised some of them had their noses out of joint. For himself, all he needed was a buffalo robe to roll up in at night, his Hawken, his horse, and his possibles sack. At least, that was all he'd needed before he'd met Brianna Villard.

"Well?" Coover prompted, getting restless.

Nigh was scrounging for an answer when Jeb Hanks rode up. From a distance the pilot looked like a boy playing grown-up; he wasn't any bigger than a good-sized hound.

"Hou, Col. Heard you was with this bunch. How's that pretty little squaw you tied up with?"

"Gone under, Jeb."

Hanks wagged his head sorrowfully. "Dead? Too bad, she was a good 'un. How come ever'body's standing 'round with their thumbs up their noses? We got wagons to move."

Not bothering to answer, Nigh said, "Jeb Hanks, boys. Injuns call him No Scalp."

The sun glinted on Hanks's bald pate as he doffed his wolf skin hat to show how he'd earned his Indian sobriquet.

"Ah yes, our famous pilot." Beaudouin was quick to offer his hand. "Your reputation has added greatly to our confidence in making this journey, sir."

Jeb Hanks plunked the hat back on his sleek dome and took the hand, always glad to meet a man willing to accept him at face value, in spite of his size. "Thank-ee fer saying so, even if it don't make much sense."

At Beaudouin's look of confusion the pilot chuckled. "Don't you know what you got here in the form o' Columbus Nigh? Why, he could lead you to Oregon riding backwards and wearing a blindfold."

Beaudouin's eyes widened. Coover broke out in a full-bellied Coover laugh.

"Quit your yarning, Jeb." Nigh sat down and calmly plied his knife to the wood he held. "These boys're as green as that grass you're standing on and likely to believe a wily old coyote like you."

"Jest as they ought to. Now, you gonna answer my question? Why ain't these wagons moving out?"

Nigh did.

When Hanks heard the part about the women, he slapped his knee and chortled. "Bless my flea-bit hide, if that don't beat all! Well, let me handle it. Need to talk to Magrudge anyhoo an' he might take it better from me since I ain't got no stake in the matter."

"You heard him," Nigh said as the pint-sized man rode off. "Tell the women to find something new to fret over."

At the trumpet call thirty minutes later, all forty-eight

wagons uncoiled and began a meandering route across the grassy plain. Sometimes they rode single file, slow and twisty like a cumbersome snake slithering out to seek the sun. More often they branched out, as many as five riding side by side over the broad prairie. Mourning doves rose from their path like puffs of smoke, their soft coos lost to the rumble of wheels, the rattle of chains, and the lowing of cattle.

Jeb Hanks rode ahead to seek out the next stopping place, leaving Magrudge to lead the wagons, smug and stiff-backed in his pride. Coming along behind with the others, Nigh felt a rush of exhilaration as he gazed across the rolling green prairie toward the shining mountains, invisible still except in his heart. Grudgingly he allowed himself a moment of optimism; he was going home.

The only thing that would have made Nigh happier was riding his dappled gray mare off by himself, instead of driving a slow wagon with a slower team of oxen that made him feel as out of place as a bull elk in a dry goods store. Out in the open spaces with a good horse under him, the reins secure in his work-toughened hands, Nigh could feel whole again. He'd feel relaxed and competent the way he had when he and Jeb Hanks and Edward Magrudge roamed the untracked lands, sinking beaver traps in ponds only Indians had known before.

In Oregon territory, islands of civilization were already springing up everywhere, like those left behind in the States. Stores at first, a smithy, a livery, and the inevitable taverns with their smoke and spittoons and ungodly noise. Then the preachers and the teachers and the lawmen, taming the men who had come to tame the land. By then the game would be gone, the trees felled, the wild grasses plowed, and the red men dead or wishing they were.

Nigh felt his eagerness ebb away, thinking about it. Like the old trappers who still haunted the unsettled West, he dreaded the changes, the losses. And he doubted the rightness of it all. But the fact that he had long ago recognized its inevitability didn't detract from the surprise of finding himself thinking of making a place for himself before all the good land was gone. Before he was too old to force himself into the mold civilization demanded of a man.

Or maybe it was something else that had his thoughts taking that direction. Something tall and soft with blue topaz eyes and hair the color of pine bark, with a hint of red in it. He glanced over at the boss lady, treading the tall grasses a couple hundred yards from the wagon, and felt a hunger no amount of good stew could satisfy.

It wouldn't be easy living tame, but he had no hankering to spend the rest of his life existing from one day to the next, guiding pilgrims or helping the army chase down Indians who had once been friends, the way most of the old fur trappers were doing now.

As a boy, struggling to survive on the rat-infested levees of St. Louis, he had yearned for a home and family. Later, he convinced himself he didn't want anything that permanent. With Little Beaver the old longing had returned and when she died, he'd had to put it behind him again. He didn't fool himself about the chances of an old squawman like him hooking up with the likes of Brianna Villard. In fact, he didn't expect to find any woman who'd be willing to take him on, except a squaw. Still, he could get a piece of ground, build a cabin, and whittle away his old age, even if he had to do it alone.

Yep, the more he thought about it, the better it sounded, and Oregon Territory was as good a place as any to settle down. If things didn't work out, he could always get him a squaw with a tipi and go back to following the buffalo. Indian life wasn't a bad way of living, after all. It simply wasn't what he'd found himself thinking about lately.

Long after sundown that night, after the fiddles had fallen silent and snores filled the air like the buzz of drunken bees, two men fumbled in the darkness, setting up camp a short distance from the Magrudge Company.

"Damn it, Stinky!" Barret stumbled over a bedroll. "Why'd you put that there?"

"It's cold. I wanted to be close to the fire."

"Well, move it to the other side. This is where I planned to spread my blankets."

After midnight Columbus Nigh woke to the muffled sound of a woman's cry. He lay still, listening. When the cry came again, he crept to the foot of the wagon and climbed inside. Brianna was thrashing about in her bed, mumbling and sobbing, "No, Barret, please. . . ."

Nigh sat beside her on the bed and gathered her into his arms. "Hush, it's all right," he whispered. "Just a bad dream."

Brianna struggled against him until she fully woke and saw who held her. Relief flooded through her and she relaxed. Nigh stroked her hair and murmured strange words in a lyrical tongue she'd never heard before. She felt warm and safe, almost cherished, in a way she hadn't felt in a long time. To send him away was not what she wanted, but his being in her wagon—in her bed, for heaven's sake!—was too scandalous to be allowed.

"No one knows I'm here," he said, as if reading her mind. "I'll leave as soon as you're asleep again."

The day had been long and the terror of the nightmare

had drained her. She knew she should insist he leave immediately, but the words wouldn't come. It felt so good to be held that way. No hands grabbing at her body, no repulsive demands, no threats. Only a few more minutes, she told herself. Then she'd make him go. Gradually, she drifted into a dreamless sleep.

With an unerring sense of timing, Nigh woke himself an hour before the sentinels would fire their pistols to wake the train. He hadn't intended to break his promise to her. A hundred times during the long hours he had lain awake beside her, he had told himself it was stupid to stay there fighting his need for her, when all he had to do was go back to his own bed. But it was an opportunity that might never come again, one too good for an old squaw-man to pass up.

Brianna never knew when he left her. She awoke to the sound of the sentinel's shot, feeling safe and strangely content, and wondering why.

Later, as she tramped the dew-wet grass while the wagons rumbled over the plain nearby, she remembered the nightmare. To awaken in Columbus Nigh's arms, his deep sensual voice in her ear as he stroked her hair, seemed a wonderful dream in comparison. She wondered if it had truly happened.

The nightmare had been of that last night she had slept beside her husband, the night she had learned his terrifying secret. The memory reinforced her need to escape, and as she watched the ground slide away beneath the slow-turning wagon wheels, she wanted to shout, "Hurry. Hurry faster." Make the wheels roll, make the miles roll, faster and faster, until she didn't have to feel afraid anymore. Until the dreadful days of waiting, of expecting every moment for Barret to thunder down upon them and snatch her back home, ended and she could feel free. Until she could feel safe all the time, the way she had last night, in Columbus Nigh's warm embrace.

A glint of sunlight caught Brianna's eye, a reflection from Lilith Beaudouin's needle as it darted in and out of the linen she embroidered while she rode, and Brianna willed it, too, to quicken the pace.

At the top of a rise a gust of ever-present wind lifted her sunbonnet an inch off her head, drawing its bow snug beneath her chin. She held the bonnet in place and gazed in awe at the measureless sky, blue like the petals of the wild flax waving on the hilltops. Never had she seen so much sky.

Back on the damp, wooded Mississippi, a person felt closed in. But here everything seemed open, free. It was more than the endless expanse of blue sky, more than the land that rolled forever toward the mysterious West. It was . . . oh, she didn't know what it was, except that it made her feel wonderful, free and safe.

The wind tore the bonnet from her head as she stooped to pluck an armful of flax. She felt it flap from its ribbon against her back as though it, too, enjoyed being free. A woman her age going hatless was hardly proper, but the sun on her head was too wonderful to resist. She lifted her face and drank in the warmth, heedless of propriety and the damage the sun's rays might do her complexion.

Two hundred yards to her right the wagon train inched over the land, too slow to leave her behind. The shouts of the drivers and the snap of their whips drifted on the wind, sharp and clear like the crackle of summer lightning. Children played King of the Mountain, the gaiety in their high-pitched voices infectious as they chased one another, screeching and giggling.

Beside their wagon Tom and Betsy Coover walked hand in hand, Tom gazing down into Betsy's upturned face. Brianna didn't need to see his expression to know it was soft and full of love. Then Betsy reached up and brushed the hair off his forehead, reminding Brianna of the way she had brushed the stubborn lock from Barret's forehead, and cradled him in her arms while he whimpered like a child after one of his dreams.

Reality struck her like a physical blow; she might never see her husband again, but neither would she ever know the love of any other man. She was only twenty-six and would spend the rest of her life alone. Her heart squeezed inside her breast as though clenched in Barret's vengeful fist. Had she been wrong to leave him? If she went back, would he forgive her? At least she had known what to expect from Barret.

Turning, she stared across the undulating swells of the prairie toward Missouri and home, the wildflowers and the wide open reaches of freedom forgotten. Her yearning for love and a family of her own was so strong it rocked the very core of her being, filling her with loneliness and dread.

That was how Columbus Nigh saw her, the wind wrapping her black skirts about her thin legs, her bonnet flapping wildly. She looked every bit the scarecrow he had once thought her, except for the bouquet of flax clutched in her arms, the blue flowers so bright against her black dress, it appeared as though she had captured her own piece of the sky. Wisps of hair torn loose from her bun flailed at her cheeks and eyes. She didn't tuck them away like a prim and proper matron, only stood there transfixed, like a mouse mesmerized by the eyes of a snake. If not for her height and her widow's weeds, Nigh might have thought her a girl and ridden on by.

Instead he watched, intrigued. It occurred to him as he snapped the whip above the backs of the plodding oxen, that there were two women standing on that hill. The Brianna who picked flowers and let her bonnet flap freely in the wind, and the stiff and somber widow terrified the world would notice she was alive. She was the Brianna that brought a cat on a two thousand mile trek through the wilderness, the Brianna whose dour face could light up with a smile that seared his heart. Which one of them was it staring now with such longing at the world she had left behind?

If there was one person in this entire passel of sorefooted emigrants who had reason to look ahead rather than behind, it should be her. The bruises on her face and body had faded, the swelling was gone. But he hadn't forgotten them, and he was all-fired sure she hadn't either.

Ordinary homesickness, he reckoned. It was hard on women, leaving their homes behind, as if they had to leave the memories along with them.

Glancing back at her one more time as the wagon moved on, Nigh saw her pull up her bonnet and retie the ribbons under her chin. Her head was bowed and he wished he could let the wagon go on by itself so he could go to comfort her.

Had it occurred to him that she might be questioning her decision to leave her husband, he would have flung down the whip—oxen be damned!—and flown to her. As it was, he eyed the dark clouds gathering in the north and thought only of the drenching she might get if she tarried too long on the prairie.

Chapter Eleven

As fast as her long legs could carry her, Brianna ran up one rise after another until her calves ached and her breath came in ragged gasps.

Exhausted, she flung herself down on the warm grassy earth. Her pulse was racing and her flesh tingled beneath a sheen of sweat. She lay there a long time, watching the birds and the insects and the gracefully nodding flowers while peace once more invaded her being.

Everything would work out somehow. She knew it. All she had to do was wait.

Rested, she heaved herself to her feet and started back toward the wagons, away from the lowering sun. She had just topped a rise when she saw a rider coming in her direction. When he saw her, he put the horse to a gallop. Her thoughts went instantly to Columbus and her heart soared with gladness. But a quick study told her it was not Columbus. This man was short and boxy and alarmingly familiar.

Barret!

For an instant she considered the idea that she may have misjudged his feelings for her; he must love her to come so far to fetch her back. Then the sun glinted off his frigid blue eyes and she knew she was wrong. She recalled the pain his hands could inflict so well, recalled the pleasure it gave him. She wanted to run, to hide, to scream for Columbus Nigh. Her heart pounded so hard she thought it would burst and kill her before Barret could lay a hand on her.

But her feet had grown roots.

"Brianna!" he shouted as he threw himself from his saddle. "Damn! I can hardly believe my luck, finding you so quick."

Her fists balled at her sides as she stared at him. Why had she come out here alone where he could get to her? Why hadn't she run? Would the sight of him always hold this power over her? To make her heart crawl up into her throat, her body to tighten and draw in on itself as though trying to disappear? She deserved whatever he did to her. Anyone as stupid and worthless as she deserved a beating.

"You've put on weight," he said. "Christ, you look almost as good as you did when I married you." The same eyes that had so often stared at her with icy contempt now smiled with arrogance and the cocksure gleam of triumph.

Had he figured out that she knew his secret? That was the key. It wouldn't matter what she said; if he knew what had finally driven her away, he wouldn't dare let her live. She tried to steel herself against what she knew would come, while refusing at the same time to give in.

"I won't allow you to hurt me anymore, Barret. Let me go with the wagons. I've never meant anything to you, not really."

His eyes glittered like shattered ice, the smile gone now. "You're my property. I'll do anything I please with you."

His thick hands flexed, then balled, and she held up a restraining hand as she backed away.

"Please, Barret, you don't realize how much you hurt me when you hit me. I know you don't mean to, but you're stronger than you realize and—"

"You think I've hurt you before?" His breathing became ragged, his words hard and clipped. "I suppose that's your reason for running away? Because I slapped you once or twice? Maybe it's time you learned what hurt really is."

She tried to run. He moved like summer lightning. Grabbing her by the arm, he spun her about and backhanded her across the cheek. She reeled, then caught her balance. When he reared back to hit her again, she kicked him hard in the shin. He cursed, letting go of her arm to clutch at his leg. Brianna ran.

Before she made a dozen yards he knocked her to the ground. Then he straddled her and slapped her again, the sound like a crack of thunder. "You damned bitch," he muttered. "You need a lesson in respect."

She lay beneath him submissively, her chest heaving. Aroused by his own violence, he grabbed at her breasts, squeezing and pinching.

"I've been in jail, did you know that? I rode night and day to catch up with you." He gave an ugly, panting laugh. "That upstart Will Rainey was so sure I'd killed you. I ought to. Maybe I will yet. But first, you're going to make me feel good. It's been too long since I had a woman."

His mouth left a trail of wetness over her face and down the slender column of her neck. Like slug slime, she thought. *Oh, Col, please come and find me.*

Delicate bone buttons snapped in two as he ripped open her dress. His fingers raked her tender skin as he clawed the bodice down off her shoulders.

"Please," she said. "I'll take the dress off, don't tear it."

Barret laughed and yanked harder on the fabric. A groan issued from his throat as his mouth seared her flesh like a hot brand. He adjusted his position while he dug beneath her skirts, pulling at her drawers. The feel of his touch on the warm skin of her inner thigh, once he had freed her legs, felt like spiders on her flesh. She clawed at his face and kicked at his legs.

"Stop it, bitch, or I'll beat you unconscious," he muttered, hitting her again. "I'm only taking what's mine."

Her skirts were up around her waist and Barret was fumbling with his trousers. Like something wild, Brianna scratched and bit and kicked. His hands found her neck and circled it. She tore at his fingers and tried to scream. His thumbs closed off her throat. She could get no sound out, and no air in. Tighter and tighter he squeezed. She struggled for breath, too weak now to fight. A sound like galloping hooves filled her ears and fireflies danced before her eyes as darkness closed in on her.

When she came to, she felt light, free. A cool breeze blew across her face and bare legs. Nearby, she heard the whisper of grass and the thud of feet and fists as bodies rolled over one another, grunting and groaning. Memory returned and her eyes flew open.

Columbus Nigh and Barret were wrestling on the ground, all cusswords and flailing arms and legs. Nigh was on top, his hands around Barret's thick neck while Barret shoved against Nigh's chin with all his might. Nigh let go with one hand to gouge Barret's eyes. When the man let go, Nigh slammed a crushing blow to Barret's ribs and another in his soft stomach. Then Nigh finished him off with an upper cross to his jaw that left the man unconscious.

An instant later Col was kneeling beside Brianna, murmuring reassurances and promising to get her back to the wagon as quick as possible. He pulled her skirts down over her legs and covered her breasts with the remnants of her bodice. Gently, he scooped her up in his arms and set her on his horse. There had been no time to saddle the horse, and he reckoned it a good thing since a saddle would have made riding double more awkward. The dappled gray stood quietly until Nigh leaped up behind, settling the woman comfortably in his lap. Then they were off.

Now that Brianna was safe in his arms and he could relax, Nigh's fear for her turned to anger. "What in thunder were you doing so far from the wagons?"

His voice was harsh. She didn't dare tell him the truth, that she had been wishing for home, and that, like an answered prayer turned nightmare, Barret had appeared suddenly before her.

"I just wanted to be alone. I only meant to get out of sight for awhile, to find some privacy."

"Now you know what privacy can get you out here."

"Did . . . did you kill him?"

"Ought to've. He'll think twice 'fore he tries to rape another woman, but I'll warn the other wagon companies about him."

Brianna's head bowed and she was quiet for some time. "You shouldn't have interfered, Col. He was my husband. He had a right to treat me that way."

"Your what!"

Nigh pulled the dappled gray to a halt and turned her so he could see her face.

"That was Barret Wight, my husband." She looked away. "And he was only giving me what I deserved."

"Giving you . . . dammit, woman, he woulda choked you to death if Tobias Woody hadn't seen you bolt like a blinded buffalo, and some stranger sneakin' after you. No man has the right to beat and rape a woman. Any woman."

They started off again. In the stony silence, he became aware of the way their bodies jogged along together, his hard chest pressed close to her bare shoulder and back, her buttocks neatly fitted within the vee of his legs.

"I shouldn't have run away," she murmured. "He was accused of murdering me and spent a week in jail. I've put him to a lot of trouble, it's no wonder he's angry."

The wind picked up. It whipped her loosened hair against his face and a strand caught on his mustache. It felt like fine silk when he pulled it loose. The scent lingered in his nostrils long after he tucked the hair behind her shoulder. It reminded him of roses after a thunder shower, sweet and clean, earthy, natural. He had a hunch she smelled that way all over, every inch, but he was too angry to be aroused.

"That don't give him the right to hit you."

"I'm his wi—"

"Even a wife."

The silence between them lasted until they rode down into the last hollow before reaching the wagons. Brianna sensed his anger and knew she had some explaining to do. First, she needed to do something about her dress. Her torn bodice exposed almost as much as it hid. "Col, I . . . I can't ride into camp like this."

"Why not?"

Nigh had been concentrating all his senses on their back-trail, in case Barret Wight came after them. The man might be older and his muscle turning to fat, but Nigh knew the fight wouldn't have ended so quickly if he hadn't had such an advantage over Wight. No man fought well when taken by surprise—especially with his trousers down around his rear. For the first time he took a good look at her. And his anger fled.

The front of her dress had been torn clear to her waist. She was clutching the remnants over her breasts but the lacy edges of her chemise showed. In a flash of memory he saw her sprawled on the ground after he'd torn the man off her. He saw her full, firm breasts, and long slender legs. It came to him then that she was naked under her torn skirt. Nothing but the thin black cloth of her skirt and his own leather leggings kept his flesh from touching hers. It was a heady thought. He prayed she wouldn't notice the effect it had on him. The urge to reach up and cup the rounded flesh she was trying to hide was almost irresistible.

Instead he yanked off his shirt and ordered her to raise her arms. Then he drew the shirt on over her head and pulled it down to cover her body, flinching when his fingers brushed the satiny skin of a soft, round breast.

He froze. She froze.

His gaze met hers. Their lips were only inches apart. "Bri—"

Desire whipped through Nigh like a cyclone, wrecking havoc on his control. It would have taken every ounce of strength he could summon not to devour her like he wanted to, if it hadn't been for the haunted look in her eyes and the knowledge of all she'd just suffered.

Minutes later the Magrudge cavalcade came into view. Voices drifted up to them along with the lowing of cattle and the cracking of whips. Thunderheads were building in the north, bringing the scent of rain and fresh manure. No one but Tobias Woody paid them any attention as Nigh walked the dappled gray to the wagon.

Nigh lifted Brianna directly into the back of the slow

moving wagon. At the sight of her, Shakespeare uncurled himself from the bed, stretched and came to greet her. Gladly she enfolded the small furry body in her arms. She buried her face in his warm fur and let his familiar scent comfort her. Outside, Tobias Woody was asking if she was all right, and she heard Col assure him she was fine.

Lying on the bed with the cat cradled in her arms, she ignored the tears that streamed from her eyes, and thought about the way Col had taken off his own shirt to cover her nakedness. How could such a rough and uneducated man be so gentle while her supposedly high-born husband was evil as sin. Obviously background and social position had nothing to do with goodness. A man either had it or he didn't, and beneath Columbus Nigh's rough exterior he was all good.

Col's voice came to her through the wagon cover, asking Tobias to drive the team a little longer while he went to check on something. She knew the "something" was Barret. The thought that Barret might kill him horrified her. She found herself wishing for Barret's death instead, and hard as she tried, she could feel no guilt.

The sounds of the shouting came to Nigh before he topped the rise. He reined in to listen, then dismounted and crawled the rest of the way up. Lying on his belly he peered down the other side. Barret Wight was on his feet, but Nigh had a feeling it would be some time before the man could catch up to Brianna again. A Kansa warrior was relieving him of his clothes. Not surprising actually; no mile of the trail was safe if a man let himself get caught alone and unarmed too far from help. Always the Indians were waiting to take advantage where they could.

Nigh chuckled softly. Wight was ranting at the warrior while he stripped off his trousers. The Kansa took them, looked them over, then started pulling at Wight's woolen underwear. When the man refused to turn them over, the Indian drew a knife. Wight quickly peeled off the one-piece garment. Satisfied, the Kansa warrior tied the underwear to his lance like a tattered banner. Then, yodeling a fierce war cry, he leaped onto his pony, grabbed up the reins to Wight's horse and galloped away.

Wight cursed and stomped his bare feet like a child in a tantrum until a rumble of thunder caused him to look up at the sky. Dark clouds were boiling in from the west, promising a storm. He put his hands on his hips, kicked once more at the trampled grass and stalked off toward the south, the direction he figured would take him to Stinky.

Easing back off the crest of the hill, Nigh grinned. He leaped on his horse and headed for the wagons, humming while he gnawed on a sliver of wood. Nature had its own way of cooling off hotheads like Barret Wight, he reckoned, and it suited him fine.

The storm struck an hour later, forcing the Magrudge Company into an early camp. The wind whipped viciously at the canvas wagon covers and lashed the men's faces with icy rain. Nigh was grateful for the storm; it gave him a chance to talk with Brianna privately.

As soon as the animals had been taken care of, he climbed into the wagon. She was sitting on the bed, her legs drawn up under her skirt, one arm around her knees. The cat was dancing on his toes, back arched, a contented rumble deep in his chest, as she scratched him just above his tail. Nigh sat down on the supply box that extended from the head of the wagon to the foot, along one side.

At the head, the box was four feet wide, divided into two foot sections with hinged lids. Supplies were stored inside and Brianna's bed lay on top. The box that ran the rest of the way to the foot of the wagon was only two feet wide. In some wagons this box was also used as a bed, but since Nigh slept under the wagon, Brianna's was used only for storage space.

When he entered, she glanced up, then away, an expression of dread on her face. His voice was calm. "Want to tell me about it?"

Her shoulders lifted and fell. "What is there to tell? I lied to you."

"Reckoned you were lying a long time ago. Question is, why?"

She peeked over at him. He sat hunched forward, his forearms resting on his spread knees. His shoulders and head were wet and she felt an urge to get out a towel and dry his hair. "If I had told you in St. Louis that I was running away from my husband, would you have agreed to escort me to Independence?"

"No."

"And when I asked you to take me to Oregon, would you have said yes if you'd known the truth?"

"Dammit, woman! That don't excuse you from lying."

"I'm sorry." She folded her legs under her and leaned toward him. "Please try to see this from my point of view. I lived with that man for three years. I left because I was afraid he would kill me if he knew. . . ." She straightened and looked away. "I hated lying to you, Col, it's not my way ordinarily. But I was more terrified of him catching me than of what you'd do if you found out."

"Simple as that, huh?"

"Yes, as simple as that."

Nigh leaned back against the side of the wagon and stared into space while he gnawed on a toothpick as well as her words. Had he been in her place, he'd likely have done the same. And when it came right down to it, what hurt most was knowing she belonged to someone else.

Slowly he turned to gaze at her. She was hugging her knees again, looking so forlorn he wanted to pull her into his arms and show her not all men were like Barret Wight. He wanted to kiss those startling blue eyes of hers, her straight nose and proud chin. To cover her with kisses instead of bruises. To show her how love could be with a man who would worship her body too much to abuse it, cherish her too much to hurt her.

The image of her struggling beneath that madman, his hands around her throat, her face a mottled purple, brought a rush of anger that made him clench his fists and nearly bite the toothpick in two. Then he remembered the shy way she had called his attention to her half-naked state as they rode back to the wagons, and his anger melted in a flood of desire. Her breasts had been barely hidden by her torn dress, and so close he could have kissed them merely by bending his head.

God, how he'd wanted to touch them, to stroke them until the nipples grew taut with desire. To run his hands over her gently rounded hips and her flat stomach, down her thighs, her calves, her ankles, and back up between her legs. He wanted to taste her, smell her, explore every inch of her body with his hands, his lips, his tongue. He wanted to feel himself inside her and give her the pleasure he was sure that bastard she'd been married to had never given her.

Was married to.

Nigh squirmed against the hard wooden box and

leaned forward again to hide the evidence of his desire. He could not have her, would never have her, and he may as well clear his head of fantasies now and for good. He'd have to become in his mind the "brother" he pretended to be around others, and content himself with making certain Barret Wight never touched her again.

After a time, his pulse slowed to normal again. When he spoke, only the huskiness of his voice hinted of the passion he held under tight rein. "What now?"

"What do you mean?"

"What are you going to do? Go back to that bas . . . to your husband? Or go on to Oregon?"

How could he even ask? "I'm going on. Barret will have to kill me to get me back."

Nigh nodded, scolding himself silently for the joy he felt. The rain had stopped. Outside, kettles clanked and hatchets ka-thunked into wood as folks built fires and started their suppers.

"Well then—" He stood and moved to the tailgate. "Reckon I'd best make sure the man don't find you again."

He balanced himself on the edge of the raised tailgate, then hopped to the ground. Brianna poked out her head and he reached up to put his hands around her waist and lift her down. Her hands were on his shoulders, but she didn't let go once her feet touched ground. She gazed up at him with an expression so soft and charged with emotion that it gave him gooseflesh.

"Thank you, Col," she whispered. Then she raised up on her toes and kissed him. It was a quick kiss, a mere brushing of her lips over his, but it was enough to ignite the coals of passion inside him and test his willpower as he resisted the urge to haul her back inside the wagon.

Chapter Twelve

With a canvas tarp and green poles cut from trees growing along the Wakarusa, Nigh erected an awning for Brianna to cook under. They were still uneasy with each other. He figured that was why she had invited the Beaudouins to share their fire, as well as their meal. That and the hunch that Lilith wouldn't have thought to gather wood from the creeks they'd crossed that day.

Lilith brought French wine and crystal stemware and Marc contributed two plump chickens. While the women cooked, the boys, Francois and Jean Louis, perched on each side of Nigh to watch him transform a block of wood into a screaming mountain lion.

"Golly, Mr. Nigh, that's really something," Francois said. "I wish I could learn to do that."

"Got a knife?"

"No."

"How old are you?" Nigh asked.

"I'll be ten come August."

"Boy your age oughta have his own knife." At Marc's nod, Nigh fished a small knife from one of his pouches.

"Here, boy. It's sharp so don't cut yourself. Later I'll help you make a sheath for it to wear on your belt."

Francois's small chest puffed out in pride as he took the knife. "Thank you, sir. I'll take good care of it."

Nigh smiled and tousled the boy's hair. No one had ever called him "sir" before.

"Hey, what about me?" Jean Louis's cherubic face scrunched up as though about to cry.

"You're too young, son," said Marc.

"Here." Nigh handed the boy the fist-sized panther. "Francois can make his own carvings now, so you can have this one."

With a grin Jean Louis ran off to show his treasure to the other boys, the figurine clutched carefully in his small hands.

Nigh was halfway inside the wagon, fetching a piece of rawhide from his pack for Francois's sheath when Edward Magrudge walked up.

The man sidled up to Brianna like a snake looking for a warm spot to snooze. He ignored the cat on the stool beside her and dropped his gaze to her breasts, licking his thin lips. Her bosom had been tempting as hell when she was skinny, but she'd put on weight in the last week or so, and all in the right places. Widows made prime pickings, he thought, as he gave her a wink. "Nice to see some color in those cheeks of yours, Missus Villard. Saw you out walking today."

Brianna recognized the look in his eye; it reminded her of Barret. She backed away, two tin plates held in front of her like twin shields. Her cheeks matched the vermillion clouds fading from the evening sky and her eyes were wide with alarm. Shakespeare growled.

"Good evening, Edward." Marc Beaudouin rose from

his chair and stepped over to put his arm around Lilith's waist where she stood behind Brianna. Setting the plates quickly inside the tableware box, Brianna scurried away.

"Hope I didn't scare her off," Magrudge said, watching her go. He resisted the urge to swat the spitting cat.

Nigh climbed down from the wagon and faced the man. "Want something, Magrudge?"

A leering smile settled on the wagon captain's lips as he wondered what Nigh would say if he told him he wanted to tumble his sister. Then he caught the murderous glint in Nigh's eye. Clearing his throat, he motioned to a young couple waiting off to the side. "Brung some folks to meet Beaudouin here."

He turned to Marc. "Said you was from Bowling Green, Kentucky, didn't you?"

"My family owns the mercantile there."

"Oh, Beaudouin's Dry Goods," the young woman said. "You had the best selection in town. I hope you'll be opening a new store in Oregon."

"Actually, I plan to raise horses and Herefords."

The woman pursed her bow-shaped mouth as though disappointed. "Herefords. You mean those pretty white-faced cows I saw you driving?"

Marc nodded and smiled.

Magrudge drew the man forward. "This here's Punch Moulton. And his wife Dulcie."

Punch Moulton was a swarthy, heavy-jawed man in his late twenties with small eyes and a jutting chin that looked as though it had been gnawed by an angry polecat. It was obvious the man remembered his run-in with Nigh at Longmire's Livery. The hostility between them was thicker than buffalo hoof glue.

His wife was a tiny thing with tiny hands, tiny feet, and

a button of a nose that wiggled when she became excited. Columbus Nigh tagged her as a clever, fluttery little moth that oozed sexuality without even knowing she had any.

"My wife and I were about to return to our wagon," Marc said into the jarring silence. "Why don't you join us, Mr. Moulton? We may find we have mutual friends back in Bowling Green."

Moulton glanced at the crystal wine goblets Lilith was gathering up and the collapsible table covered by a white linen cloth. "Ain't too likely," he said in a surly tone.

When Brianna still hadn't returned an hour after the Beaudouins had left, Columbus went searching for her. The grass was wet from the afternoon's storm and felt cool to his moccasined feet. Already the night breeze had a bite to it. Though the days were warm, the nights were always cold. Out on the prairie where the horse herd still grazed, a night guard was singing a lonely dirge, accompanied by the melancholy howl of a wolf.

Nigh saw Brianna the same moment he heard the cracking sound of Punch Moulton's open palm striking his wife's fine-boned face. Brianna covered her mouth with her hands and froze in terror, cringing behind one of the wagons.

"Please, Punch," Dulcie cried. "I didn't mean to be forward with Mr. Beaudouin."

"Don't tell me that." Punch shook his finger close enough to his wife's face she could have bitten it, if she'd been foolish enough. "I saw ya smiling at him the way you do at other men when you think I ain't looking. Damnation! Why'd I think it'ud be any different away from

Bowlin' Green? Men are men no matter where they are. And sluts is sluts. Even pregnant ones."

"Don't you call me that. I'm no slut."

"Quit yer sniveling." Punch began to walk away as though he couldn't bear the sight of her. Then he swung back and, without warning, his fist landed square on her jaw. The blow sent Dulcie flying three feet. She hit the wagon with a resounding thump and slid to the ground where she stayed, hugging her belly protectively.

"Don't you c-care what these people are gonna think, seeing me all b-bruised up?" she sobbed.

"Ya worried what they think?" He knelt down in front of her. "Hey, sugar, I know how to solve that." With the backs of his fingertips he slapped her across the face. "See? Hurts, don't it? Don't leave no marks, though. I learned that from old Swampy. Remember him?"

"Swampy never hit Mary. She'd of told me if he had."

"He never had to hit her once we knowed them, 'cause by then she'd learned to keep her eyes in her head and her mouth shut. She learned how to please her man, in every way. And this is how he taught her." He pulled her hands from her face and slapped her again.

"Oww, please, Punch. I won't go near Mr. Beaudouin again, I promise. Please don't hit me anymore."

"All right then, get my supper ready. And you be thinking 'bout all the ways ya can make me feel good when I come to bed tonight."

"But, Punch, the . . . the baby."

"You ain't due for three months yet. Expect me to go wanting all that time, ya selfish little slut? Ain't gonna hurt the baby nohow, now get my meat cooking."

Dulcie pulled herself up as he walked away, hanging onto the side of the wagon, one hand still cupped around her belly. Her mouth had already started to swell. With her tongue she probed her teeth to see if any were loose. She wiped away the blood with the back of her hand, then went to stoke up the fire.

Brianna, her hand over her mouth, raced onto the plain. She dropped to her knees, braced her palms on the ground and vomited. When her stomach was empty, she slumped to the damp earth and gave way to the tears streaming down her face.

Never had Brianna seen anyone beaten like that before. For a moment, watching, it had seemed to be her receiving those blows. Punch took on the features of Barret Wight, and Brianna felt her flesh give beneath his knuckles the way she had before, oh, so many times. It was ghastly.

She thought about the melancholy she'd felt earlier that day because she would never have a chance to know love, and the way her knees had turned to water at the sight of Barret bearing down on her. It had taken everything she had to stand up to him. And look at what it got her. What was it about women like her and Dulcie that allowed them to love men like Barret and Punch? Was there something wrong with them?

No, it wasn't that at all. Not for her, she was sure of that. It was simply that she needed someone so badly. She hated being alone, hated knowing people had pitied her as the poor spinster who was too tall and too intelligent to catch a husband. She still hated it.

The breeze wafted the stink of her vomit beneath her nose, making her gag. She didn't hear Columbus Nigh's quiet approach. At the first touch of his warm hands on her shuddering shoulders, she instinctively jerked herself away. But the motion only made her retch again. There was nothing left in her stomach except clear liquid and then, finally, not even that. Still she heaved, humiliated that he should see her this way, but helpless to do anything about it. The convulsions racked her body so violently she thought surely the next heave would bring up her insides, stomach and all.

"Easy," Nigh crooned, worried that his presence was making things worse instead of better. "Take a couple of deep breaths, try to relax."

Her hair had come loose from its bun. He steadied her with one hand and stroked the hair from her face with the other. "Don't look at me," she whispered.

Nigh watched the liquid drip from her lips and chin and saw her tremble. "Don't worry about me, just relax and let your stomach get hold of itself."

He put his hand on her back and ran it gently down her spine to her waist and back up. He massaged her shoulders and neck, then her back again. Never had anything felt so good, she thought. Gradually her stomach calmed and she knew she was done vomiting. She crumpled then, as though the convulsions that had racked her body were all that had kept her upright until now.

Nigh drew her aside to keep her out of the mess she'd made and laid her gently on the ground. Her hand lay on her stomach, the other flung over her eyes. Shivering violently, she struggled to reclaim her dignity. "Thank you, I'll be fine now. You don't need to stay."

He ignored her uppity employer-to-employee dismissal. Taking hold of the neck of his shirt, he whipped it off over his head. Then he pulled her to a sitting position and wrapped the shirt around her shoulders. In the patchy moonlight she could see the light covering of hair on his chest, and the way his nipples puckered in the cool air.

The supple leather cut off the wind, warming her instantly. She drew a deep breath, inhaling the special odors that were his alone, and felt wild sensations dance down her spine. How would the wind feel on her own naked skin? Would he feel the same sensations seeing her naked as she did seeing him?

But he had already seen her naked, in the river the day after they left St. Louis, and there had been no indication then that the sight affected him at all. Of course, that was before he kissed her. The idea that he might try to kiss her again, there in the darkness with no one around to prevent things from getting out of hand, made her stomach flip-flop.

"It isn't proper, our being alone out here like this and you only half dressed," she said, holding out the shirt. "Please put it on."

Nigh chuckled but there was no humor to it. "I'm your brother, remember?"

He wrapped the shirt around her again. Then he lifted her in his arms and rose to his feet. She had no strength to resist. Her arm automatically anchored itself around his neck. One hand was against his bare chest, the hair curling about her fingers. She snatched the hand away, praying he couldn't see her blush in the darkness.

Still holding her, he sat down on the bank of a small creek that flowed into the Wakarusa River near the encampment. She watched him dip his kerchief in the water, feeling awkward, yet strangely at home in his arms. His large callused hands were surprisingly gentle as he bathed her face. When he offered her a drink from his cupped hand, she was too eager to rinse her mouth to refuse. At the touch of her lips on his palm, she felt him tremble.

"Better?" he asked in that brief way of his.

Brianna had never been babied this way before and she found it pleasant. She never wanted it to end.

"Want to talk about it?" he asked.

Heat suffused her face as she wondered if he had read her mind. "Talk? About what?"

"The Moultons."

She shuddered, remembering. "It was dreadful."

Her voice was so low Nigh had to lean closer to hear. He sat with one leg stretched out, the other bent with his foot flat on the ground, Brianna nestled in between. His arm was around her, her shoulder and arm pressed against his bare chest. The intimacy of the pose struck him and it was all he could do not to kiss her. He knew he should move away, but he couldn't.

"No one will ever hurt you again," he said hoarsely. "Not as long as I'm around."

She looked at him, doubting he could care so much what happened to her. "If there are men like you who don't believe in hitting women, what causes men like Barret and Punch Moulton to do it?"

"Makes 'em feel bigger and more powerful, I reckon. Men like that are cowards underneath. They're scum. Shoulda left him the first time he belted you."

"I know." She sighed. "But it isn't as easy as it seems. The money I inherited from my father became Barret's the moment we married. I had nothing of my own except my jewelry and clothing. How would I have lived? I knew I'd never find another man who would want to marry me and I didn't want to be a burden to my sister."

"You were running to your sister when I met you. What happened to change your mind?"

She shrugged. Her hands shook as she plucked a hand-ful of grass only to toss it back down again.

"All right," he said, "if you don't want to answer that, tell me what made you think no other man would want to marry you."

She gave an indelicate snort and said, "I know what I am, Col. An ugly giant of a woman with nothing to offer but a head so stuffed full of knowledge no man can feel comfortable with me unless I keep my mouth shut."

"Dammit, woman, if you ain't the biggest fool I ever met, I don't know who is!" He lifted her chin and forced her to look him in the eye. "What do I have to do to convince you all men ain't the same?"

She gave him a sad smile. "You could marry me, if I wasn't already married."

Chills snaked down his spine as he realized that was exactly what he'd like to do. Marry her and love her and protect her from scum like Barret Wight. All he could do instead was show her how precious she was. That and teach her to stand up for herself.

"Ain't nobody on this earth who isn't special in one way or another, Brianna. Everybody has something to offer the world, same as buffalo and hawks and skeeters, though I ain't figured out yet what skeeters is good for. It's the way God planned it. Marc Beaudouin has a special way with horses. That's why he's going to Oregon so he can do what he's best at instead of living off his family's name. Lilith, well, she's a bit buffler-witted at times, but dang if she don't cheer a body up, just being around her. Tom Coover can charm the rattles off a rattlesnake. Lavinia Decker, loud and bossy as she is, is a deft hand at healing." He chuckled. "Even old Magrudge has his own way of bringing joy to folks."

"Huh! I doubt that," Brianna muttered.

"That's 'cause you haven't heard him sing. Magrudge

has a voice that could lull the devil hisself into turning in his pitchfork for a prayer book."

"And me? What is my special talent, Col?"

"You? Said yourself you got a head full of knowledge. How many folks on this wagon train you reckon can read? I bet when they get to Oregon, these farmers'll be looking for someone to teach their young'uns the things they'll need to know in order to better themselves, like reading and ciphering and such. As for being tall, maybe God made you that way 'cause he knew children learn best from people they can look up to." He chuckled, then sobered. "Maybe he just figured you'd need to be big to deal with all life was going to put in your way."

Mosquitoes hummed in the silence until she said, "Do you truly believe all that?"

"Yep. One more thing—" He stroked one finger down a cheek that felt like the inside of a rose petal. "—ain't never known a more beautiful woman than you."

Moisture gathered at the backs of her eyes. She swallowed hard and blinked to clear her vision. There was no doubt in her mind what Columbus Nigh's special talent was. He had a gentle sensitivity more rare than rubies or gold, and much more valuable. "I didn't even know men like you existed."

He chuckled but there was no humor in it. "You can find plenty of men like me in any back alley of any town big enough to have one."

"That's not true. Why do you say such things?"

"Because right now you're looking at me like I was a saint. I'm not. I'm just a man who's been around a bit and knows how to judge people." He rose to his feet, taking her with him.

"One more thing you'd best keep in mind," he said. "I

agreed to see you to Oregon and I will, but I won't be staying there. Reckon I been a wanderer too long to settle down now."

He glanced up at the sky where storm clouds had obliterated the moon, creating total darkness except for the vivid streaks of lightning jabbing at the earth in the distance. "More rain coming. Best we get back."

Confused by the intense emotions battling inside her, Brianna followed him back to the wagon. The rain struck the moment they arrived. He helped her climb in, tied the cover tightly closed behind her, and dove under the wagon, grateful for the India rubber sheet she had insisted on buying to protect his bed from the dampness.

Rain pelted the taut wagon cover like a thousand fingers on distant drums. For a long time he lay awake, listening to the storm and wondering if Brianna lay above him in the wagon as sleepless as he.

How long had it been since he'd lain with a woman? Long enough that it wasn't any wonder Brianna Villard felt so good in his arms. There was more to his attraction to her than that, but at the moment, he needed to convince himself differently. He tried to switch his thoughts away from her and found himself remembering Little Beaver's young and trusting eyes the first night she had come to him.

Most of the tribe including her family had gone buffalo hunting, leaving behind only women, children, a few old men, and Columbus Nigh. He lay abed in the family tipi, staring at the stars through the smoke hole and thinking he should be leaving soon. His wound was nearly healed.

The only light came from the small central fire and at first he thought her part of the flickering shadows as she rose, silkily naked, from her bed like a bronzed Phoenix, and moved slowly toward him. Halfway there she stopped, letting his gaze drink its fill of her firm body, licked by the dancing flames until she looked sleek and shiny wet, ethereally sensuous and physically undeniable.

When Little Beaver knelt beside him, Nigh found his heart knocking inside his chest as though he were fourteen again, when a young whore had taught his virgin body all it needed to know about pleasing females.

Little Beaver's smooth youthful face had smiled down at him, firelight glinting from the moist fullness of her parted lips and he remembered wondering if she'd ever been kissed. Between her arms, braced on the floor beside him, her breasts dangled like apples sweetened by the first frost, close enough for him to pluck. The buffalo robe covering him had become suffocatingly hot. Every nerve tingled with lightning flashes of heated anticipation. She crawled under his robe and he felt her breasts like soft fire on his chest. When her uninhibited fingers encircled his throbbing core, he was more than ready to take her and less than able to resist.

Even now, as Nigh lay in his bed beneath Brianna Villard's wagon on the wet open prairie, he found himself fully ready. Only this time it wasn't Little Beaver he wanted.

To wake up to the sound of Brianna crying out in another nightmare that night came as no surprise to Nigh. When he went to put his arms around her, she fought him.

"It's all right, Bri, you're just dreaming." He gave her a gentle shake. "Come on, wake up now."

Her eyes opened. With a small cry she crumpled against him.

"Same nightmare?" he asked.

She shuddered. "No. Spiders."

"In the wagon, or in your dream?"

"In the old fruit cellar."

He suspected she was still dreaming, until she went on.

"It was dug into a knoll down by the barn. Dirt walls, floor, everything. When Barret's father had the new house built, a cellar was dug underneath, so the old one wasn't used anymore." She shuddered again. "When Barret learned I couldn't abide spiders, he started catching them in the garden and letting them go in the old fruit cellar. It was his favorite punishment. He'd throw me in there and lock the door."

She was crying now, tears slipping silently down her cheeks. He drew her tighter within the circle of his arms and tried to shush her. Her voice, when she went on, held an edge of hysteria.

"I tried not to cry or scream, but when I didn't, he'd start talking about the spiders through the door, describing how they'd . . . how they'd crawl under my clothes, into my most . . . private places and bite and bite—"

"Shh, it's over. He won't ever put you in there again." He kissed her forehead and stroked her back in soft soothing circles with his gentle hands. "Go back to sleep now. I'll keep the spiders away."

She snuggled against him as he caressed her back and arm, and wished he could be beside her every night to banish all her nightmares.

Nigh leaned his head against the wagon and closed his eyes, trying not to imagine what it would feel like to sleep with her body entwined with his, naked flesh to naked flesh. Then he felt her hair brush against him as she lifted her head to look up at him. Her eyes appeared pale in the dim light and he thought he detected a quiver in her lips.

"Thank you, Col. Will . . . will you stay till I go to sleep?"

He cradled her face in his palm. "I'll stay."

Then he lightly kissed her. She didn't pull away, merely gazed up at him with those big blue-green eyes. He longed to kiss her again but knew he might not be able to stop there. So he contented himself with running his finger over her moist lips. "Go to sleep now."

When she was nestled against him again, her breathing slow and even, he leaned his head back, licked his finger and pretended he could taste the sweetness of her lips on his skin.

Chapter Thirteen

1 May 1849, Big Blue River

Dear Mrs. O'Casey;

We have reached the Big Blue. Storms have left the river too swollen to ford so we have free time on our hands for a change. I take advantage by writing this letter to you.

You won't believe what has happened. We had a visit from Kansa Indians, a pitiful people, thin and dirty and unkempt. Their chief, however, was unusually tall, with a powerful build and eyes that were frightfully fierce and penetrating. He offered my "brother" two ponies for me. I was so shocked I dropped a loaf of bread I was taking from the oven into the mud. Some Indian children snatched up the bread, wiped off the mud and gobbled it as though it were sugar.

Columbus refused the chief's offer, of course, but Punch Moulton took advantage of the incident to cause more trouble about Mr. Nigh being a squawman. I find it extremely distressing to think of Columbus being married to one of those filthy women.

Three families here from another company have decided to return home. I send this letter with them to be mailed when

they reach civilization again. Until next time, I remain your
faithful friend,

Brianna Villard

Brianna hadn't intended to go anywhere near the dancing, but the lively strains of a fiddle, a Jew's harp, and a mouth organ enticed her from her hiding place. Those on the sidelines clapped their hands and stomped their feet as the dancers swirled past, amidst flashing petticoats. The gaiety and laughter were infectious. Brianna couldn't help wanting to join in.

She hovered on the fringes of the crowd, arms folded beneath her breasts, one finger unconsciously tapping out the beat of the music on her elbow. Then, in the middle of the twirling dancers she spotted Marc and Lilith, laughing into each other's faces. Envy stabbed through her and the pleasure she had been feeling fled like mist in the rain.

Ever since the night Punch Moulton had beaten his wife, Col had found one excuse after another to stay away from camp. At first it was his need to take his turn at herding the loose stock, which he used as a means to force Brianna to learn to handle the team and drive the wagon. Then it was hunting, or scouting up ahead with Jeb Hanks. Other times she was certain he had ridden back to check on Barret.

Three days after Barret had attacked Brianna, a man visiting from a wagon company behind them had passed along a story about a man found deathly ill after being robbed by an Indian and left naked on the prairie during a storm. When Brianna questioned Col, he confessed that the man was Barret and that she wouldn't have to worry for some time about her husband catching up with her, if the man survived at all.

Brianna knew Barret Wight was too mean to die merely from exposure. Her fear, knowing he would come after her again, only made her loneliness more intense.

Now, when she felt someone's eyes on her, she turned in joyful anticipation, hoping it was Col coming to ask her to dance. Instead, she saw Magrudge weaving his way toward her through the throng. The wagonmaster was the last man she wanted touching her, even to dance. She ducked behind two wagons and came upon Dulcie Moulton standing alone, her extended abdomen lifting the hem of her oversized dress above her shoes in front while dragging in back. Beneath the ragged hem, the girl's foot kept time with the music.

The two women smiled shyly at each other.

"I'm too awkward to dance now," Dulcie said, with lowered eyes. "But I can feel the rhythm and pretend it's me out there. That's almost as good, don't you think?"

Brianna watched the dancers for a moment in silence. "Every bit as good."

"How come you aren't out there? I bet you dance real elegant."

"Not really. I doubt I even remember how, I haven't been to a dance since I was fourteen."

Dulcie's mouth dropped open. "Aw, a fine lady like you? I would've thought you'd been to plenty of fancy balls and such." A look of horror flashed through her eyes. "Oh, I didn't mean to be rude or nothing. I just meant, well, I thought all rich people. . . . I mean—"

Brianna laughed. It felt good. "Money doesn't guarantee happiness, or even knowing how to dance."

"No, I guess it can't."

A moment of silence fell between them while they

turned their attention back to the dancers and their minds raced for something new to say.

"Evening, ladies." Magrudge tipped his mangy top hat and bowed slightly from the waist. "Having fun, are you?"

The ladies kept silent.

Magrudge drew in a deep breath, puffed out his spindly chest and decided to brave it. "Would you care to dance, Missus Villard? I'm light on my feet, promise not to trample your toes."

"Thank you, but . . ."

Pouting prettily, Dulcie came to her rescue. "You promised to keep me company for a bit."

"Yes, yes." Brianna jumped at the excuse. "I'm sorry, Mr. Magrudge. I did promise, and I've only been here a moment or two."

"Of course, another time."

"Yes, later . . . perhaps." He rewarded them with an oily smile, tipped his hat again and left.

"Thank you," Brianna said when he was gone.

"Think nothing of it. Don't know any woman who'd want to dance with that. He always makes me think of lizards or snakes." Dulcie affected a shudder, hugging herself. "I bet if you touched him, your hand 'ud come away all slick and gooey like bacon drippin's, only not as good smelling."

Brianna laughed. After a while, she found herself studying Dulcie's pretty profile. Although it was the first time she had spoken to the girl, she had felt a kinship with her since the night she'd seen Punch Moulton beat her. She longed to let the girl know she wasn't alone in her situation, but didn't know how. The more she thought about it, the more straightforwardness seemed the answer. "Dulcie, there's something I want you to know."

"Sure, Missus Villard, what is it?"

"You and I share something in common. You see, my husband was often very brutal with me, too."

Bowing her head, Dulcie said, "You must have noticed my bruises. Punch ain't all bad. He's good to me mostly. It's just that he's got a bad temper and, well—"

Brianna took the girl's hands in hers and gave them a reassuring squeeze. "I know. My husband had his good side, too. Look, I didn't bring this up to embarrass you. I only wanted you to know you weren't alone, that you have a friend who understands."

"You mean that, Missus Villard?"

"Yes. And please, call me Brianna."

"Thank you. I'm so glad. Oh, not that you got beat up, too." Dulcie flapped her hands, feeling rattled but happy. "I just meant it's good to know I'm not the only one, sort of comforting, you know. Not that . . . oh, I'm not saying this right."

Brianna gave the girl an impulsive hug. "Yes, you are. I know exactly what you mean. That's why I decided to talk to you. It feels good to me, too, knowing there's someone else who understands what I've been through."

"Oh, I do. It's awful, I feel . . . set apart from others, afraid they'll guess, you know?"

"Yes, I made myself into a hermit," Brianna said. "I realize now that Barret, that's my husband . . . was my husband . . . he encouraged my reclusive ways for his own reasons."

"Do you miss him?"

To say yes would make her sound insane, wouldn't it? But if Dulcie didn't understand, no one would. "I miss feeling that I belong to someone. I miss how important I felt when he needed me. And when he'd hold me, just hold me."

"I know."

The silence that fell between them was companionable, as though they no longer needed words to express their feelings, to share, to commiserate.

"Sometimes, when he's being mean—" Dulcie's voice was low and sorrowful. "—I wish a lightning bolt would smite him dead. But I don't really, you know. I can't imagine living without Punch."

The revelry had lost its appeal. Together, they wandered through the darkness beyond the firelight, dropping a word here and there to fill the silence.

"If it hadn't been for Col," Brianna said finally, "I would never have had the courage to come on this trip, to try starting over. But I'm so glad I did. When we reached the prairie and I looked out on all that open space, I felt a freedom I'd never known before. I still feel frightened sometimes, but I keep reminding myself I don't have to be, not ever again. And that's a good feeling."

Dulcie smiled wistfully. "I think I'd be afraid of so much freedom. I need someone to take care of me, you know?"

Brianna nodded. "I worry how I'll survive when we get to Oregon City and Col goes on his way. But I can't lean on him forever. I'll have to find a way to take care of myself."

"Aren't you tempted to . . . well, to latch onto the first decent man you come across and get married again?"

They found themselves beside Brianna's wagon. Nigh's dappled gray nickered a greeting and she caressed his soft nose. The thought of the man made her feel warm inside, yet hungry, in a way she didn't understand or know how to deal with.

"How can I be sure the next man won't be just like

Barret?" she said, though her mind refused to consider the idea that Col could turn out that way. "I think women like us have to be very careful to make sure we truly know a man before we give our hearts away. Col insists Barret couldn't love me and treat me as he did, and in theory it sounds true enough, but I think there's more to it than that. Sometimes it seemed as though there were two Barrets, the angry one and the kind one."

"That's exactly how Punch is! But I could never explain it to anyone else." Impulsively, Dulcie threw her arms about Brianna's neck, stretching on tiptoe to press their cheeks together. "Oh, Brianna, I'm so happy to know you. I don't feel so alone anymore."

"You're not." Brianna hugged her back. "And I'm equally as grateful to find you."

Crickets filled the silence as the music faded and the dancing feet grew still. People drifted wearily but happily toward their wagons, knowing that tomorrow the long, hard struggle to reach their Eden would begin anew.

"I'd better get back," Dulcie said.

"I'll walk with you. Punch may wonder where you've been."

Dulcie hesitated. "He won't like it if he knows I've been talking about him."

"Then we won't let him find out."

Alone on the hillock where he'd spent the evening on guard duty, Columbus Nigh had listened to the music and wondered if Brianna had joined the dancing. The image of her dancing in another man's arms, laughing up at him, flirting, nearly drove Col mad. By the time he was finally relieved of duty, he was ready to storm into the midst of the dancers, throw Brianna over his shoulder and haul her off into the darkness where he could make love to her until she knew she would never belong to anyone but him.

The sight of her walking with Dulcie Moulton instead of dancing failed to completely ease his frustration. Her face haunted him every day, no matter how far he roamed from camp in an effort to keep from touching her. At night he dreamed about her and it was almost more than he could do to keep himself from leaving his rain-soaked bed to sneak into the wagon with her. The only thing that could put him out of his misery would be to feel her under him, to feel himself inside her, to possess her mind, body, and soul. Yet he knew that to give in to his need would be about as smart as confronting a grizzly in its own den. One of them would not come out whole.

The women had reached the Moulton wagon. Nigh saw Punch Moulton's fists clench at the sight of his wife with the squawman's "sister," and felt his own muscles tense. Nigh couldn't hear what was said, but he knew Brianna was doing most of the talking. When the man's fists loosened and Nigh could see there would be no trouble, he shook his head in bemusement. If Brianna could handle a hunk of meanness like Punch, why had she allowed her own husband to mistreat her so badly?

Brianna waved goodnight and turned to follow her tracks back to her own wagon. Fifty feet away from her a man in a tall hat ducked between two wagons. The butt of a cigar glowed red in the darkness, then faded. The cigar's familiar scent drifted out to Nigh as he moved to intercept Brianna. Smiling, he stepped into the lantern light that spilled between the wagons.

"Enjoy the party?" he asked.

Brianna's hand flew to her heart. "Col! I wish you wouldn't sneak up on me like that."

"Sorry. Dark enough out here to hide a polecat, if it weren't for their stink. Mind if I walk along?"

"Of course not. You are my brother, after all," she teased.

Nigh could almost hear Magrudge curse as they passed.

"I didn't see you at the dance," she said after awhile.

So she'd noticed, he thought, aware that his pulse had just picked up. *Easy, squawman, don't get carried away.* "Guard duty," he said.

"Oh."

"Ain't much on big doin's, anyhow."

"Oh." *Idiot! Can't you think of something more intelligent to say than "Oh"?*

Out on the prairie a coyote yipped at a lopsided moon that reminded her of Col's odd little half-smile. She breathed in the sweet smell of applewood that clung to his clothes from the figures he whittled and wished she knew more about his life.

"Noticed you made a friend," Nigh said.

His voice was like the moan of the wind in the trees, soft, shivery, sensuous.

"Dulcie and I have a lot in common."

"She could use a friend. Moulton hassle you any?"

"No, he doesn't like me, but he was civil enough."

Nigh spit out the spent toothpick. She wondered if his lips would taste like the applewood he'd made the tooth-pick from. Making friends with Dulcie felt good, but watching couples dancing and having fun had left her feeling a different kind of loneliness.

A pack of dogs darted out from under a wagon. She stumbled, trying to get out of the way. Nigh reached to steady her and shockwaves zinged though his body from fingertips to groin. His hands clamped onto her arms and he pulled her close. She looked up at him, her lips parted in surprise. Her eyes were as big as the tin plates they used for supper. Her breath wafted over his face, sweet and seductive.

His heart felt like a slough full of frogs jumping every which way. He bit his tongue to keep from licking his lips at the thought of kissing her. He was no better than Magrudge, he thought, and let her go.

"Dogs seem to've caught the festive mood," he said.

"Yes, silly things."

Not as silly as you, she scolded herself. *The man has a wife, and even if he didn't, he wouldn't be interested in a big, old ugly thing like you.* The thought of Little Beaver was like a rose thorn in her finger. Impulsively, she said, "Col, why is it you've never mentioned your wife to me?"

He stopped and turned toward her. "My having an Indian wife make a difference to you?"

She heard the pain in his voice and wished she could honestly say "No," but the truth was that it did bother her to think of him with one of the pathetic, filthy squaws she'd seen in St. Louis and on the trail, so she hedged. "Only . . . well, because I consider you a man of principle, yet . . . you kissed me."

And I want to kiss you again, he thought. Now, and tomorrow and next year. "What's my kissin' you got to do with my wife?"

"A married man shouldn't kiss other women. Not the way you kissed me."

His hand lifted to her face and his fingers lightly traced the contour of her cheekbone, then swept over her hair before dropping back to his side. At the time, the story of

Little Beaver's death had spread through the mountains like dandelion seed on the wind. But Nigh had never told the tale himself. He couldn't tell it now. Not all of it, anyway.

"She was a Snake, what some call Shoshone. Her people found me with a Blackfoot arrow in my side and winter breathing down my neck. She nursed me. When spring came, I took her with me."

"Just like that?"

"Indian marriages are pretty simple. If a man and woman agree to live together, they're married. If she grows unhappy, she puts his things outside the tipi and he goes away. If he decides he don't want her, he sends her back to her family."

"Are you happy with her?"

"She died."

"I'm so sorry."

He shrugged.

They reached the wagon and stood in silence, locked in their own thoughts. Brianna was ashamed of the joy she felt at knowing he was no longer married. Yet she couldn't help crying out to him silently: Hold me.

Nor could she hear his own wordless plea: Touch me.

I need you.

I want you.

They never had a chance. Lilith and Marc burst out of the darkness. "We thought we heard you two out here. Where did you disappear to, Brianna? Did you know this lovely sister of yours doesn't remember how to dance, Mr. Nigh?"

"I'm not surprised."

"Well, you must do something about it. Why, I'd simply die if I had to sit in the background and miss out on all that fun." Lilith held out her hand, palm up and gazed up at the dark sky. "I thought I felt something wet."

Without warning, the sky opened up, pelting them with raindrops the size of rabbit droppings.

"Run for cover," Marc yelled.

Brianna scrambled into her wagon while Lilith raced off to her own next door. Nigh was rolling out his blankets on the India rubber mat underneath the wagon when Marc crouched down to peer at him. "Have you slept under here every night? Why don't you sleep in the wagon?"

"Brianna needs her privacy."

"But surely, once she's in bed . . ." Marc let the words trail off. He stood up and called through the canvas cover, "Brianna! Col's getting soaked under this wagon. Isn't there some way he could sleep in there?"

Her voice came to them, hesitant and uncertain. "I-I thought it would be considered improper. Is he truly getting wet?"

"Drenched," Marc said. "The wind whips the rain right under there. I see nothing wrong with a brother and sister sharing the same wagon, not under these circumstances, and I'm sure everyone would agree with me."

"I'm fine under here," Nigh called out loud enough for her to hear. "Old mountain man like me is used to sleeping wet."

"Nonsense. Brianna, do invite him inside, will you?"

"Of course, he must come in if he's getting wet. Help him with his things, will you, Marc?"

Nigh cursed under his breath as Marc snatched a heavy buffalo robe from him and dashed for the end of the wagon.

"Come on, man, I'm getting wet too, you know," Marc yelled.

Grumbling, Nigh took up his blanket and the bundle of clothes he used as a pillow and heaved himself inside the wagon. Marc said goodnight and made for his tent. Nigh stood there, hunched over, his wet hair brushing the coarse canvas ceiling. Holding his bedding in his arms, he stared at Brianna in the lantern light. She was fully dressed.

"I didn't have time to get into my . . . night things," she said, as his gaze roamed from her flushed face down over her body to her stockinged feet. Her shoes were all she'd had time to remove. Her arms were loaded with goods she had taken off the storage box so he could make his bed there. She was close enough to touch. Close enough to kiss.

"Soon as camp quiets down, I'll slip back outside."

"Don't be silly." Brianna blushed at her hasty words. The thought of him sleeping right there in the wagon with her sent her head reeling, yet she knew it was exactly where she wanted him to be. "Marc's right, you can't sleep in the rain. You should have told me the wagon wasn't protecting you enough."

A drop of water ran from his hair onto his forehead. She caught it with her finger before it could reach his eye. Heat flooded Nigh's veins at her touch. Without thinking he captured her hand in his and slowly raised it to his mouth. Their eyes met as his lips closed over the finger and gently sucked it dry. Then he dropped her hand and looked away.

"This won't work," he said in a low, husky voice.

Brianna shook off the tingling tremor that had started in her breast and worked its way to her lower abdomen. "We'll simply have to make it work. I can't let you go back out there. I'm ashamed to have been so thoughtless and selfish. You could have caught pneumonia."

She pulled her hand away, took the buffalo robe from him, folded it in half, and laid it on the narrow bench. He yearned to wrap his arms around her and draw her tight against him so she could feel what it did to him, simply to be in those cramped quarters with her, her bed so close and convenient and suggestive. How could he possibly spend an entire night there? He would never get any sleep. She finished making up his bed and glanced at him timidly before moving to the other end of the wagon where the lantern hung.

"If you're ready, I'll put out the light and you can turn around while I get . . . into bed."

Frozen with indecision, wanting to stay, needing to go, Nigh said nothing. He heard the whoosh of her breath as she blew out the flame. After a moment his eyes adjusted to the darkness and he could see her black-clad form against the white wagon cover. There was a whisper of fabric as she unbuttoned her dress, then a rustling as she whisked it off over her head. Now she was white on white and more difficult to make out, but his imagination filled in the gaps as he envisioned her removing her chemise and drawers. Blood rushed to his loins and he thought he would explode. It was more than he could bear.

He turned around and reached for the ties that held the wagon cover tightly closed above the tailgate.

"Get into bed, Columbus. What would Marc think if he saw you forsake a dry bed in here to crawl back under the wagon?"

Her breathy voice seemed to caress him. He was shaking inside, his head pounding in rhythm with his thundering heartbeat. But he could not move.

"Please, Col."

Releasing the breath he had not realized he had been

holding, Nigh swallowed. His mouth was as dry as summer sand. He forced his body to relax, telling himself this was no worse than hiding, stone still, while Piegan or Bannock warriors hunted him in the bushes.

Except that facing an Indian fight didn't cause his loins to ache or his blood to heat with desire. Bit by bit, through sheer force of will, he gained control. It was the most difficult thing he had ever done. Finally he lay down on top of the bed, fully dressed; he didn't dare do anything even remotely sensual such as removing his clothes. It would be some time yet before he would need the warmth of a covering.

Outside, several yards away, Edward Magrudge wiped the rain from his thin, ferretlike face and cursed. It was an interesting little scene he had witnessed before the Beaudouins barged in. If he hadn't known better, he would have thought the couple to be lovers rather than brother and sister. Thinking about it, he realized part of Brianna Villard's appeal lay in the fact that she was Columbus Nigh's sister. It added a delicious bit of irony to the situation and made him all the more eager to get his hands on her.

Nigh had fouled things up tonight moving into the wagon with her, but Magrudge knew there would be other opportunities. He had time to wait. It would heighten the anticipation and make the victory all the sweeter.

Chapter Fourteen

Columbus Nigh awoke to the blast of the sentinel's rifle at four the next morning. Keeping his eyes closed, he rolled onto his back and stretched. The first thing he felt with his toes was cold air. Then they brushed against something warm, firm, and soft, something that moved. He sat straight up the same moment Brianna did. Shakespeare rose from beside her, leaped from the bed and ducked outside.

Brianna's hair hung in a long braid over her shoulder, dark against the virginal white of her nightdress. As he stared at her, gathering his wits and stifling the surge of desire that lanced through him, she pulled the quilt up to her chin. Silently he cursed at the fear in her eyes.

"I'll get out of here so you can have some privacy." He swung his legs out from under the blanket he must have pulled over himself during the night. Since he was still dressed, all he had to put on was his moccasins. Then he was gone.

Brianna yawned and wished she could burrow back under the covers. What sleep she had gotten had been light and restless, as though she had been waiting for something to happen. What for, she didn't know. For Col to sneak into her bed?

A quiver raced down her back at the thought, leaving her tingling deep inside. She tried to shake off the sensation. Although she longed to be loved, the idea of sleeping with a man brought her only fear and disgust. The pleasure she experienced when Col kissed her didn't count; kisses were one thing, sex another. She crawled from the bed and dressed, scolding herself for thinking of Columbus Nigh at the same time she was thinking of sex. For all that she was running away from her husband, she was still a married woman. And Col had made it clear the night Dulcie Moulton was beaten that he wanted nothing more from Brianna than friendship. If that fact hurt, she chose to ignore the pain.

Lavinia and Lucy Decker were talking with Nigh when Brianna emerged from the wagon. Francois and Jean Louis were tossing a rawhide thong for Shakespeare to fetch. Next door, smoke billowed out from under the rubber tarp the men had rigged up over Lilith's stove as she tried, with her usual lack of success, to start a fire in the firebox.

"Good mornin'," Lavinia's voice could be heard clear to Independence. "Lucy was up early this morning baking her special scones. Expected to find Mr. Nigh here half drowned under the wagon after that storm last night. Glad to see you let him get in out of it."

Brianna ducked her head, pretending to pet Shakespeare in order to hide her blush. She glanced at Col from under the cover of her thick lashes, but he appeared engrossed in the scone he was eating.

"Have one, Missus Villard." Steam rose from the plate

of hot, fried bread Lucy offered Brianna. "Ma always said I made the best scones in Indiana, didn't you, Ma?"

As the girl darted a look at Nigh, Brianna was tempted to dump the whole plate into the fire. Why did being called "Missus Villard" make her feel so old all of a sudden? Saying that he had to go catch up to the oxen, Col took another scone from the plate and walked away. Lucy's gaze followed him until he was out of sight. When the girl turned back and saw Brianna looking at her, she said, "Doesn't he have the most masculine way of walking?" Then Lucy blushed. " 'Course, I reckon you don't look at him that way, you being his sister and all."

Lavinia bellowed out a deep laugh. "Come on, girl, we got our own wagon to get loaded."

A few minutes later, when Col returned with the oxen, Brianna studied the way he walked and decided Lucy was right. He moved with an easy rolling gait that was both graceful and ruggedly masculine.

Col glanced up from the yoke he was fastening around the thick necks of the lead pair of oxen and gave her a slow, crooked smile. Blushing, she looked up at the dark sky as a faint rumble sounded overhead. "Looks like more rain," she mumbled. Then she hurried to help Lilith get breakfast going.

Ellis and Tobias Woody glanced uncertainly at each other as they listened to their father give them their orders for the day. The Big Blue had receded little during the night. The storm that had threatened earlier had passed on by, but another one was expected that night or the next day. The men had decided to start fording the swollen river at once.

"Listen, Pa," Tobias said, "Ellis is better with livestock than Lyle. Let the boy stay here and help get the wagon across."

"It's time Lyle learned how to handle the beasts," Taswell Woody answered. "Ain't so hard, you know."

Of all his brothers, Lyle was Tobias's favorite. Perhaps because as the eldest, he'd had the greatest share in raising this youngest boy. Perhaps because Lyle—with his carrot hair and impish ways—was a male duplicate of Mary, their one and only sister who had died before Lyle was born. For the first time Tobias regretted having spoiled the boy. He didn't try to vindicate himself by remembering that he wasn't the only guilty party; as the oldest of the brothers he was the most responsible for not having forced Lyle to learn to swim. But it was too late for recriminations now. Short of confessing Lyle's inability to swim, there was nothing he could do.

Lyle was eighteen and capable of standing up for himself. No one would blame the boy for refusing to go in the water if he confessed he couldn't swim. There were others who could swim the stock across. But it had to be Lyle's decision.

Without a word, Lyle walked to his horse. Tobias fell in place beside him. He patted Lyle's shoulder and gave him a confidant smile as though what they were about to do was as commonplace as scything ripe wheat in the warmth of an autumn sun.

"You take the upstream side, Lyle. I'll take the downstream. Pretend you're herding on the open plain. You know, croon a little, whistle a little, keep them calm. When you feel Old Charley start to swim, take your feet out of the stirrups and slide backwards off his rump. If you don't, your weight will push him deeper underwater and cramp his movements. You could both drown, then. Just slide off and hang onto his tail and he'll tow you across slick as a whistle. When he gets his feet on the ground again, haul yourself back into the saddle. Nothing to it, little brother."

Lyle sat his horse as stiff as the planks they'd fastened to the dugouts for ferrying the wagons over. He knew what his brother was trying to do and fought a wild urge to steer Old Charley closer to Tobias's chestnut so he could grab a last hug. Only a thin line of whiteness circling his lips revealed his fear.

"I'll be the one doing the hard work." Tobias's tone was a bit too hearty. "All you gotta do is give the cows reassurance. I have to keep them from getting washed away. Guess that's what I get for being born first, huh, Lyle?"

Lyle forced a smile, but he couldn't meet Tobias's gaze. *Be with me today, Lord*, he prayed silently. *Show me I'm wrong for feeling like this is the last time Toby and I will work together.*

Columbus Nigh and a few others were waiting to herd the livestock across when Tobias urged his mount close to the mountain man. "Listen, Col, the folks don't know it, but Lyle, well, he don't know how to swim."

Nigh turned to stare at the man as though he'd just confessed to wetting his trousers.

"It's a matter of pride," Tobias said. "The boy's scared of the water, but I got to let him face this out on his own, if that's what he chooses to do."

Nigh pursed his lips thoughtfully as he watched Lyle Woody take up his position on the far side of the herd. Lyle's sorrel was skittish, no doubt picking up on the boy's fear. At eighteen a man's pride was a fragile thing. Hell, it was fragile no matter the age. Nigh wasn't sure it was worth risking a life over, but he reckoned that was up to Lyle. "I'll keep an eye out."

"Thanks." Tobias smiled.

Everyone was in place, each riding his most trusted mount. Nigh took up front position on the dangerous downstream side, Tobias behind him. When all was ready, he gave the signal and started the cattle, horses and spare oxen into the rushing river. Upstream, the raft, loaded with the Ferguson wagon, also started across, the long ropes attached to each end being guided hand over hand against the swift current by the men's brute strength.

Tobias saw Nigh slip off his horse's rump and latch onto his tail. Then Tobias felt his own mount begin to swim, and he too slid off. He tried to keep his eye on Lyle, but once in the water, it was impossible. *God, get him across safe and I'll start going to church with Ma again, I promise.*

They were nearly across. The dappled gray regained his feet and Nigh dragged himself back into the saddle. He turned to count the heads bobbing at the ends of tightly held horses' tails. On the far side of the herd, Amos Shorthill was pulling himself up onto his horse's rump. Behind him came Jim Lyon. Closer to Nigh was Tobias, his horse barely gaining its feet. Nigh looked to the other side again, searching for Lyle Woody in the bright red shirt that was as good a match to his carrot red hair as a buffalo is to a jackrabbit. About the time Nigh caught sight of the Woody boy he heard shouting further upstream.

The raft had safely reached the far shore and the Ferguson wagon was half unloaded. But the dugout on this side had swamped. The wagon lurched precariously. A bundle bound in Indian rubber fell from the back and was rapidly washed downstream. Nigh watched the men struggle to lever the wagon back up onto the plank, forgetting the floating bundle until he heard Tobias Woody scream his brother's name.

"Lyle! Watch out!"

Nigh brought his gaze down the course of the surging water and saw what had Tobias in a panic.

"Oh God!" Tobias screamed again. "Don't let go, Lyle. No matter what, don't let go!"

The rubber-wrapped bundle headed straight for Lyle's sorrel. The animal had scarcely gained its footing on the river bottom. Shore and safety were still a few yards distant. Lyle had felt the horse gain ground the way Tobias said he would. I'm going to make it, he shouted in his head. *Can you see me, Toby? I'm going to make it.*

Old Charley lurched as something slammed into his side. Lyle barely glimpsed the black object as it dodged around the horse's rump and banged into Lyle's head. The thick, coarse strands of the horse's tail slid from his grasp. Water rushed into Lyle's nostrils. He gasped for air and tasted the turbid water of the Big Blue.

Toby, oh Toby. This is what I was afraid of. This is what I knew would happen. . . .

Lyle flailed at the water, felt his toe touch ground, and fought his way back to the surface. He caught a watery glimpse of blue sky before the current dragged him back under and filled his lungs. His strength ebbed. There were no more thoughts now, no prayers, nothing.

Nigh wheeled his horse and forced the tired gelding back into the river. Frantically he searched for the boy, vaguely aware that Tobias was behind him. The rubber-wrapped bundle washed past. There was no sign of the boy. Nigh slipped from the saddle and dove under, hands stroking smoothly through the water as he searched. And prayed.

A hand came into view. Nigh lunged for it and felt limp fingers caress his. Before he could get a grip on it, the hand vanished. Feeling as though his lungs were about to burst, Nigh fought his way to the surface. He sucked in air and went back under, while the river carried him farther and farther downstream, away from the herd that was clambering onto the high bank, away from the men and the wagons where Brianna waited, unaware of his fate.

Brianna was with the Beaudouins as they awaited their turn to be rafted across the river when Francois raced up in a panic.

"Mama, Papa! Did you hear?" The boy skidded to a halt in front of them, panting. "Mr. Nigh got washed away down the river. He and Tobias were trying to save Lyle and they all got washed away."

The color fled Brianna's face.

"Oh, dear," said Lilith. "That's what comes from working on Sunday, I suppose."

Marc grabbed Francois and knelt to look into the boy's eyes. "Are you sure of this, son?"

"Yes, Papa. I heard Mr. Magrudge yelling for all the men to come double-quick, so they could search the shore for the—" he paused as though just realizing the import of his message, "—for the bodies."

"Oh God." Marc dropped his hands and bowed his head.

"Oh, Marc," Lilith said, "this is a terrible tragedy, I know, but I doubt the Lord forgives profanity under any circumstances."

Marc didn't bother answering. He surged to his feet and made for the river, Francois at his heels. Without thinking, Brianna dashed after them. She heard Lilith call to her, but only ran faster.

Not Col, she prayed. *Please don't take Col.*

Columbus Nigh thought he was a goner, sure. No matter how he tried, he couldn't make it to shore. The wild, swirling current seemed bent on sucking him under. Never had he felt so helpless. It wasn't the same frustrating sense of futility he'd felt when he'd returned to the tipi and found Little Beaver dead. There was no anger this time, no guilt.

Nigh had little strength left. He knew he couldn't fight the river much longer. Concentrating on keeping his head above water, he let the current take him, batting him this way and that like a stuffed buffalo testicle ball in a squaw's game of shinny. He bobbed to the surface and caught a glimpse of something red stuck on a log stretched across the water. Then he was sucked under again.

He clawed his way back to the surface and gasped for air. He paddled his arms, fighting to keep his head above water, and blinked to clear his vision. Then he saw it—the log, splashed with red like fresh drawn blood.

With his final ounce of strength, Nigh lunged for the log. The rough bark scraped his hands as the river tried to pull him under. He tasted the muddy river water as his fingers closed over a wrist-sized branch and clung. There wasn't time to wonder if he could hang on long enough. The muscles of his arms and chest burned as he strained to draw himself along the fragile branch until he reached the main trunk. With both arms wrapped securely over the log, Nigh coughed to clear his lungs of water.

"Nigh! Mr. Nigh!"

Col blinked and tried to focus. A swath of red swam before him. Then his vision cleared and he saw the boy clinging to the log half a dozen feet away.

"Nigh . . . thank God!" Lyle lifted his head from the log and struggled to smile while water splashed over him and streamed down his tired face. "Can't . . . hang on . . . much longer."

"You hurt?" Nigh asked.

Lyle spit out a mouthful of water. "My shoulder. Something hit me."

Nigh took in their situation and figured their chances of making it to shore were better than fifty-fifty. The tree from which they dangled was still anchored to the east bank where it had been uprooted by the storm. He worked his way close to the boy and tried to shout above the roar of the water. "Grab hold on the other side of the fork in the tree. Put your good arm around my neck. We'll duck under that limb and work our way to shore."

Lyle took a deep breath and did as he was told. For a moment, as they submerged themselves under the water to clear the branch, he feared the current would rip them apart and wash them down to the Big Vermillion. Then his head cleared water, and he knew they would make it.

Neither of them saw the second log coming. It struck Nigh in the side only an instant after he'd boosted the boy onto the bank. Lyle clambered onto the muddy shore and turned in time to see Nigh's head slammed against the thick trunk which had guided them to safety. Nigh's eyes closed as he lost consciousness.

Lyle threw himself onto the tree and latched onto

Nigh's wrist as the man went under. Lyle didn't know how long he clung to Nigh's hand. Moments passed like hours before his brother found him. But Lyle was certain he'd never been so glad to see Toby in his life.

Together they hauled Nigh on shore, then attempted to pump the water from his lungs. They were still at it when Magrudge's rescue party reached them. Hovering in the background, Brianna put her clenched fists to her mouth and watched silently as the men struggled to save Columbus Nigh's life.

Nigh never regained consciousness while he was carried back to camp, nor as he was stripped naked, dried off, and tucked into Brianna's bed.

By the next morning he had a lump the size of a duck egg behind his ear. When Brianna couldn't wake him, she went to find Lavinia Becker.

"Slap his face, pour cold water on him, whatever you have to do." Lavinia handed an iron cook pot up to her daughter in the wagon as they prepared to cross the river. "Ain't a good sign for him to be sleepin' so heavy still. Wish we had ice to put on that bump. If he don't want to wake up or if he seems odd in any way, you keep a close watch. If he's concussed, he may start vomiting."

It took a pailful of cold water to rouse Nigh. His eyes scrunched up with pain and he looked up at his tormentors in utter confusion.

"Col?" Marc moved close, edging Brianna aside. "I apologize for waking you in such a heartless manner, but we have to ascertain the seriousness of your condition. How do you feel, does your head hurt?"

"Hurts bad," Nigh answered. "What happened?"

"You rescued Lyle Woody from the river and in the process your head was slammed rather badly against a tree when a bit of flotsam struck you. You don't recall?"

Nigh shook his head, then grimaced at the pain.

"What *do* you remember?"

Nigh squeezed his eyes tight against the pain. "Lyle Woody?" His head lolled to the side and he was out again.

Marc turned to Brianna. "Best tell Francois to run and see if the Deckers have crossed yet. I'm afraid Col's hurt worse than we expected."

Three hours passed before the Villard wagon, with an unconscious Columbus Nigh aboard, was ferried across the Big Blue so Lavinia Decker could visit her patient.

"Concussion," she announced. "Has he been coughing?"

"Yes," Brianna said. "He sounds congested."

Lavinia nodded soberly and the fear Brianna had tried to contain rushed into her throat. Her voice caught as she strove to put it into words. "Is it pneumonia?"

"More likely he swallowed some of that muddy river water." Lavinia put her thick, stubby hand to Nigh's brow. "He's powerful warm, got a fever, I reckon."

"What do we do?"

"I seen some wild onions earlier. I'll send Lucy to fetch 'em and you can make a poultice for his chest. You bathe him with vinegar and cold water to bring down that fever, but be careful he don't catch no draft."

Lavinia was about to climb down from the wagon when Brianna, an attractive blush coloring her cheeks, asked, "How . . . much of him do I need to bathe?"

"All but the best part, dearie." Lavinia bellowed out a laugh. "All but the best part. Wish I could stay and help, but little Gordy Fairman tangled with a water snake and got bit. Melissa ran over to say they couldn't stop the bleeding. That's where I was headed when Francois found me." She patted Brianna once more and turned to go. "I know what you're thinking, water snakes ain't poisonous. Seen something like it once back home, though. Something in this particular water snake thins the blood out so it won't clot."

Marc helped Lavinia heft her bulk down from the wagon.

"I'll come back soon as I can." Lavinia straightened her skirts. "You send Francois after me if Mr. Nigh takes a turn for the worst. We may have to do something a little more drastic to clear out his lungs."

Nigh muttered something unintelligible, capturing Brianna's attention. She bent to feel his cheek and he caught her hand and brought it to his lips. "Don't go," he mumbled.

Brianna extricated her hand and went to get the bucket of water Marc left in the rear of the wagon. Francois peeped inside, his young eyes full of concern.

"Is Col gonna be all right?"

She didn't have the heart to tell him she simply didn't know, so she mussed the boy's hair and said, "Of course, he will. Go on now, but stay within shouting distance in case I need you to fetch Mrs. Decker again."

Turning back to her patient, she rubbed her hands down the front of her skirt and thought about the irony behind what she was about to do. By the time Columbus Nigh was well—if he survived at all—she would know his body as intimately as she did her own. Better than he would ever know hers.

Chapter Fifteen

Columbus Nigh moaned, drawing Brianna's attention away from her needlepoint. For three days he had been out of his head with concussion and the fever caused by swallowing the turbid river water. Lilith had offered to help nurse the man, but Brianna couldn't envision her fastidious friend bathing a naked man, and knew she had been right to refuse when she saw the look of relief on the woman's face. Now as Brianna bent over him, he thrashed in the bed, flung an arm over his eyes as though to shield himself from some awful sight and cried out, "Oh God, Little Beaver!"

She knelt beside the bed and murmured reassurances as she stroked his shoulder and arm. He was reliving his wife's death again, she thought. Little Beaver must have died an awful death.

Nigh calmed. He moved his arm to his side and opened his eyes, but his gaze was filled with pain. He uttered something in a soft, almost lyrical language and put his hand to Brianna's face. His thumb stroked the softness of her cheek. He was speaking to her in the Shoshone tongue, thinking she was Little Beaver, no doubt. Brianna wasn't sure what to do. Touching her seemed to soothe him. How he must have loved his Indian wife. Envy stabbed Brianna's heart. He closed his eyes. The hand dropped from her cheek and he slept.

Brianna force-fed him water and broth. She applied a fresh poultice to his chest of onions, turpentine, and goose grease to break up the congestion brought on by the river water in his lungs. Shakespeare wrinkled his nose at the stink of the poultice and fled the wagon.

She had sponged Nigh's body, watching the hair on his chest spring into tight little ringlets that loosened as they dried. She had felt the hardness of the muscles, saw the cold shrivel his nipples. With her finger she traced a jagged white scar on his abdomen where the line of hair dipped from his navel out of sight below the towel she kept across his loins. There were other scars, and she had come to know them all. The pale birthmark on his inner thigh was as familiar to her as the lines of her own face. She knew the thick coarseness of his hair, the sound of his sleeping breath, the smell of his skin, the shape of his bare feet.

And possessiveness had taken root in her soul.

Every time Lucy Decker came by to ask after Col, or to offer to sit with him, Brianna's reply became more and more abrupt and ill-tempered.

Brianna might have sympathized with Lucy's supposed fear of becoming a spinster, if it weren't for the young men who lined up at the girl's cookfire every evening with hunger in their eyes for more than Lucy's scones. To Brianna's mind, any one of them would make Lucy a more suitable husband than Columbus Nigh.

To hear Lilith, however, Lucy Decker would be the perfect match for Columbus; a practical down-to-earth woman who could sew his shirts, cook him a hot meal and balance his baby on one hip, all at the same time. As for the age difference, Lilith insisted that such a spirited girl as Lucy needed an older man to guide her. That argument made Brianna's blood boil, since it was that same old wife's tale about age differences, along with the fear of spinsterhood, that had put Brianna in Barret Wight's bed. But she couldn't tell Lilith that. Instead she sent Lucy away.

In the wee hours of the night, as Brianna sipped tea and watched Col sleep peacefully again, she studied the streaks of blond in the pale brown of his mustache. The feel of the mustache against her lips when he kissed her intrigued her. She couldn't resist running the backs of her fingers over it to see if it were truly as soft as she remembered.

His eyes opened. They were glazed but looked straight at her. When she set her tea aside and knelt by the bed to test his brow for fever, he captured her hand in his and cupped her cheek with his other palm. "Beautiful." His voice was hoarse and raspy.

Brianna stiffened, then relaxed as she realized he had mistaken her for his wife again.

Then his hand slipped behind her neck and pulled her toward him. "Want you . . . so much," he said as her lips neared his.

Brianna's heart danced along her ribs. Of their own volition, her lips parted. She moistened them with the tip of her tongue. His eyes followed the action. "Come here," he said, his tone so inviting she felt her body turn to liquid, thick and sweet and slow like syrup. A sweet ache began in her innermost depths.

Nigh's mouth was firm, his lips satiny as they skimmed

across hers, once, twice. She tried to tell herself it was wrong to take advantage like this. The man thought he was kissing his wife, not her. But she let her eyes close and gave in to her curiosity, needing to learn his taste, his texture, his scent. To explore the unbelievable sensations he aroused in her.

Brianna laid her hand on his chest and let the springy curls entwine about her fingers. The pressure he exerted at the back of her head increased. His other hand stroked her back. She let her own hand glide further up his chest, feeling the soft prickle of the hair, the firm nub of a nipple, the smooth, taut muscles of his shoulder. Her fingers tangled in his thick coarse hair and silvered shivers whispered down her spine.

The mustache tickled slightly, intensifying the shivers that set her nerve endings on edge. How could a kiss feel this good? She felt as though she had been lifted into a dream, all sensation and rapturous bliss. She never wanted it to end.

He nipped her lip lightly with his teeth, then suckled gently, first the upper lip, then the lower. The feel of his tongue grazing the sensitive insides of her mouth created a wildness in her. She answered in kind, finding herself as eager to give as to take. Their tongues met and formed a sensuous dance that sent her pulse soaring. She explored his mouth as he explored hers and found an unbelievable rightness to it all that amazed her as much as it enthralled her.

Then his hand moved from her back to cup the fullness of her breast. Burned by his heat and shocked by the wild surge of hunger that racked her body, Brianna gasped. She pulled away and his eyes opened. In their depths she saw passion and intense need. She also saw that they were every bit as clear and lucid as her own.

Dazed, she rose to her feet and turned away. "You . . . you must be thirsty. I'll get you some water."

"Bri," he whispered.

She ignored the plea in his low, husky voice. What had gotten into her? She'd acted like a wanton, believing him delirious. Had he been fully conscious all that time? Had he known he was kissing her and not Little Beaver?

With her back still turned to him, she pressed the cup of cold water to her breasts as though to cool their heat. *You've made a fool of yourself, Brianna Wight, and you deserve what you have coming. Face it, then crawl back inside your shell where you belong.*

When she turned, he was asleep. One hand lay curled above his heart as though still holding hers. His face looked peaceful, the color normal. Slowly she reached out to feel his forehead. It was moist with sweat.

The fever had broken. He would be all right now.

But would she? How would she ever face him again after the way she'd reacted to his kiss? After the way he had touched her so intimately. Wrapping her shawl about her, she drew back the wagon cover and climbed out. Then she walked into the pre-dawn darkness. And wept.

Columbus Nigh slept most of the next day. Each time he woke up, he found Lilith sitting next to him. Once he found Shakespeare pawing at his shoulder, a dead mouse dangling from the cat's mouth.

Lilith assured Nigh that Brianna was fine, but he remembered the shock in her eyes after they had kissed in the night. The thought that she might be running away from him now because of that kiss infuriated him. The exquisite rapture of waking to find her in his arms, of feeling her respond to him, had erased his own doubts. She belonged to him. Her marriage to Wight had been nothing more than a disastrous mistake. Surely she knew that now.

By evening, when Marc brought him a cup of broth along with the news of the day's events, and Brianna still had not come, Nigh knew she was avoiding him. The fool woman had allowed herself to be overcome with guilt. Or fear.

"It took two days to ferry all the wagons across the Big Blue. The Shorthill's dog was the only casualty, thank the Lord." Marc sat down and rested his elbows on his knees. "We've made good time. The weather's let up a bit and we've suffered no mishaps. In fact we managed to get ahead of that California company that squeezed us out at the Kaw. Looks like they've been struck by cholera. They were digging graves when we rolled past."

"Don't sound like I missed anything to worry about."

Marc chuckled. "Except for Lucy Decker's constant visits. I think that girl's got her cap set for you. You could do worse, you know."

Could do better, too, Nigh thought.

"We're camped in a pretty little valley tonight, and it's dry out for a change," Marc went on. "There's a fair stream here and quite a bit of timber, some of it good oak."

Nigh didn't hear. Thinking about Lucy had brought Brianna back to mind. She'd changed from the skinny, frightened widow he'd led out of St. Louis, so prim and proper and clinging to that cat as though it was all she had in the world. Now she could light a fire in a prairie wind, snap a whip and drive a team of oxen as competently as any man. She had the strength of an oak tree, inside and out. Lilith, by comparison, was a hot house flower. He glanced at Marc, wondering how the man would handle it if his flower wilted and died along the trail.

"Jeb Hanks came in with two fat bull elk," Marc was saying now. "Had three Shawnee with him. They've been all over camp trading moccasins, dried buffalo tongues, and jerked meat. Zeke Knowls seems to think it a good enough reason to break out his fiddle. So we'll be having a bit of a celebration after awhile."

Nigh sipped his broth and wondered when he had started thinking of Brianna as "his." Before or after last night's kiss? He wanted to ask Marc to send her in to him, but a fit of coughing took him before he could get out the words.

Marc took Nigh's cup and listened with concern as his friend hacked. Outside, pots clanged as the women prepared supper. Francois was begging for a bucket for catching tadpoles. Marc frowned when Lilith turned the boy down, saying tadpoles were dirty and might make him ill if he handled them.

"Sorry, Marc." Nigh had himself under control now.

Marc gave him a reassuring smile. "You know, Col, I don't mind telling you, you gave us one hell of a scare." Marc peeked under the wagon cover, as if worried his wife might have heard him curse.

Nigh's mouth quirked up. "Bit scared myself, thought I was headed for the spirit world."

Marc chuckled. "Couldn't have been too frightened. You managed to get Lyle Woody safe on shore before knocking yourself out on that log."

"Who rescued who, though? Somebody must've pulled me out."

"Lyle hung onto you until Tobias came along. The current had tossed Tobias into some calmer water where he was able to swim to shore. I guess you could say he got there in the nick of time."

Marc looked at Nigh's cup as he rose to go. "You didn't eat much. Shall I tell Brianna you're hungry for something other than onion plasters and broth?"

Nigh smiled. "Can't think of anything I'd like more."

"Tom Coover, you stop that." Betsy giggled as she tried to push her young husband away. His hands burrowed beneath her shawl to tickle her again, while she squirmed and squealed.

Then the game changed. His hands slipped around to cup her breasts while he nibbled her ear. She ceased her squirming and cradled his hands with her own, turning her face up to accept his kiss. His hand slid down her still-slim waist to the belly that had yet to show sign of the burgeoning life within. Betsy smiled and closed her eyes while he tested the roundness of her tummy with his hand, as though eager to feel some sign of the life they had created together.

On the windswept bluff above, Brianna dropped her gaze from the young couple and turned away. She knelt to admire brilliant pink prickly-pear blossoms, while the Coovers' youthful laughter floated up to her. Had she ever been that young? Certainly she'd never been that happy. Was it the child Betsy was expecting that filled them with such joy? Or the love so evident on their young faces? Brianna sighed. If only she had conceived. Perhaps a child would have changed Barret. Except that Barret had not wanted children.

She touched a finger to the silky pink petals and marvelled that such a spiny, unpleasant plant could produce a blossom so lovely. Sharp spines and dazzling beauty. Like sorrow and joy; can't have one without the other, her father had told her once. But it seemed to Brianna that it had been all too long since she'd had anything but spines.

Footsteps sounded behind her. She rose, turning at the same time. "Dulcie."

"Hu'lo, Brianna. You looked so deep in thought I wasn't sure I should bother you."

Brianna took the girl's hands in hers and smiled. "Of course, you should. I've missed you. I wasn't sure if I should come to your wagon, knowing how your husband feels about me, but I was hoping you'd come to see me."

"Punch don't dislike you, Brianna. It's just . . ."

"I know, it's Col. Never mind. We'll find a way to visit each other without upsetting Punch."

Dulcie drew a piece of paper from her pocket. "I was hoping I could ask you a favor."

"You can ask anything you like."

"I asked Lucy Decker how to make her soda bread, but she wrote it down instead of telling me." Dulcie blushed. "I can't read, you see."

"And you didn't want Lucy to know."

Dulcie made a face. "That Lucy, she's such a know-it-all. You should hear the way she talks about your brother."

Brianna frowned. "Yes, he has a wonderfully masculine walk, right?"

"Huh! If only that were all. She's determined to get him to marry her. You should warn Columbus. Lucy told me the reason her folks decided to go to Oregon was because She'd caused a scandal back home. She had an affair with a married man and when he refused to leave his wife for her, she raised a real stink, even went to see his wife and asked her to give him up. Lucy bragged how she got that man to bed her. I don't think she'd hesitate to use the same tactics on your brother."

"Thank you for telling me. I promise, Lucy Decker won't get her hands on my . . . brother, if I can help it." Brianna smiled. "Now, Dulcie, I've decided I won't read your recipe to you."

The light left the girl's eyes. "You won't?"

"No. I'm going to teach you how to read it yourself."

Dulcie eyes widened. "You mean, you'll teach me how to read? To read anything I want?"

"That's exactly what I mean. Lilith has some primers she brought along for her boys. I'm sure she'll let us use them if I offer to help Francois and Jean Louis with their lessons. Maybe some of the other children would like to come too."

"Oh, I'm sure they would, and the mothers would be thrilled."

"Fine." Brianna gave a brisk nod of her head. "It's settled then. Come to my wagon whenever you have time."

Clutching Brianna's hands, Dulcie fairly bounced with excitement. "I can't wait. Oh, Brianna, you've no idea what this means to me."

With that, the girl raced off. Smiling, Brianna turned and headed for camp. She'd gone only a few feet before she rounded a clump of bushes and walked straight into Edward Magrudge.

His arms closed around her before she could back away. His dark ferret eyes glittered like black ice.

"Well, this is a pleasant surprise, real pleasant." He pulled her tight against his thin body. The top of his head only came to her eyebrows, but that didn't bother him any.

"Excuse me, Mr. Magrudge, I didn't mean to run you over." Her arms were trapped against his chest. She tried to push him away but he was like a rock.

"You can run me over anytime." He licked his lips, his gaze on her mouth. She felt so good. This was what he'd wanted since the first time he'd seen her. The only way it could get better is to get the clothes out from between them so he could feel her bare breasts against his chest. Even if she weren't Columbus Nigh's sister, he'd still want her.

"Why don't I just show you there are no hard feelings between us." As his mouth moved closer to hers, he slid one hand down to her buttocks and ground his hips against hers so she could feel the hardness of him.

Brianna turned her face so his kiss landed on her ear. He laughed, but there was something ominous in the sound. Letting go of her buttocks he held her head still with his hand and put his mouth on hers. It was wet and tasted of tobacco spit. She held herself still, letting him think he'd won. When she felt him relax and give himself over to his passion, she brought her knee up between his legs.

"Damn . . . you," he gasped as he clutched at himself.

"Something wrong, Magrudge?"

Brianna whirled at the sound of Marc's voice, coming from behind her.

Magrudge tried to stand upright. His face was the color

of bread dough, his voice hoarse with pain. "Just teasing Missus Villard. Reckon she got the wrong idea."

"You all right?" Marc asked her after the wagon master hobbled away.

"Yes, I'm fine. How long were you standing there?"

"Long enough to see you give him what he deserved." He chuckled. "I knew your brother didn't like the man. Now I know why."

"Don't say anything to Col, please, Marc. It was a very . . . unpleasant experience, I'd like to simply forget about it."

"I'm not sure that's a good idea," he began. At the look on her face he shrugged. "All right, if it's what you want. Come on, I'll walk you back to camp. Col's awake and seems to feel much better. I believe he wants to see you."

Brianna dragged her feet as she followed Marc to the wagon. Being kissed by Edward Magrudge was as pleasant as jumping into a cactus patch, but facing Col wasn't going to be easy either, not after what had happened between them last night. Still, she longed to see him. The mere thought of it had her heart pounding. Was there no way to control her feelings for this man? A man she could never have. More spines, she thought. Nothing but spines.

Chapter Sixteen

The following day Nigh insisted on getting up. He was weak but the headache and congestion were nearly gone. He rode the dappled gray the better part of the morning, determined to regain his strength. While he rode, he admired Brianna's proficiency with the whip as she walked beside the rumbling wagon and directed the oxen.

He had been asleep when she finally came to see him the night before, and when he awoke this morning, she was already up and out helping Lilith. All day long Brianna had kept the woman at her side. Like a damned chastity belt, he thought, cursing.

About mid-morning he gave up and climbed into the wagon to rest. When the train halted for the noon meal and Brianna climbed inside to fetch the food, she found him asleep, lying on his back, his head pillowed on one arm, the other curled around Shakespeare's small body. The cat lifted his head, gave her a sleepy glance, then nestled down again and closed his eyes. She reached down to pet Shakespeare's head, and found her slender hand clamped inside Col's big callused one.

"Did you come to surrender?" His mouth quirked up on one side.

"Surrender what?"

"You. To me."

Frowning, she tried to free her hand. "I don't know what you're talking about."

"Don't you?"

The harder she tugged, the harder he pulled, until she found herself kneeling beside the bed. Finally she ceased struggling and looked him in the eye. He was grinning.

"I was just laying here thinking that you and me are a lot like the sun and the moon."

Her brow furrowed as she tried to make sense of that. His grin faded and his expression became solemn, his voice soft and deep and so sensuous she felt it vibrate deep inside her own body. With his free hand, he loosened the knot of her shawl over her breasts and slowly drew it off of her, letting it fall where it may.

"One guards the day, the other guards the night, and without both of them, the world would shrivel up and die," he whispered, drawing her closer. "The sun and the moon belong to each other. The way you and me belong together."

Her eyes widened. Her mouth opened, then closed, and she gave her head an almost imperceptible shake. "You're insane."

"Yeah?" He grinned. "Best humor me then. Never know what a crazy man might do."

He looked so handsome smiling at her like that, all clean and freshly shaved. His gaze was so intense she felt the heat of it penetrate her skin. It flowed like lava through her veins, and into her soul. Breathless with anticipation, she said, "Humor you? How?"

He untied her bonnet and tossed it aside. "Kiss me."

It was absurd, she thought. She was a married woman. What if Lilith were to come to check on her and see Brianna's brother kissing her the way no brother kisses a sister? The image of Lilith's shocked face made her laugh.

"Think it's funny, do you?" Putting a hand under each armpit he dragged her onto the bed, nearly squashing Shakespeare. With an indignant howl, the cat flew off the bed. Brianna laughed harder.

"I said humor me, not laugh at me." He feathered his lips across hers, brushed his thumbs against the sides of her breasts. Her flesh ignited and her laughter ebbed away. "Time I taught you respect, woman."

The world outside the wagon ceased to exist as his mouth claimed hers, taking, inciting, absorbing. Together they soared into the sky, the sun and the moon melded one to the other by a fire greater than either could resist. Nigh's mouth worked magic on hers, teasing and tantalizing. Nibbling, until they parted for him. He delved inside with his tongue, savoring her flavor. His kisses went from feather soft to hard and demanding, then back to satiny soft.

Snared in a web of sensation, she could do nothing but respond as her body demanded.

"You taste like the moon," he murmured against her lips while his fingers tangled in her hair.

Her laugh was brief and throaty. "How does the moon taste?"

"Soft, mysterious, elusive." His tongue traced the outline of her ear. Then he grazed her lobe with his teeth, smiling when she shivered.

"And you are hot, burning, consuming. Like the sun."

"You're learning, woman. Hang with me while the sun takes you a little higher."

His mouth blazed a trail along the sensitive skin under her jaw, then down the slender column of her neck where he dipped his tongue into the fragrant hollow at the base of her throat. She'd had no idea her skin could be so sensitive, or that lips could create such havoc. Then she became aware of his hand on her breast.

She froze, waiting for the cruel gripping pressure, waiting for the pain.

"The sun has more than one way to give pleasure," Col whispered against her lips, sensing her fear. "And he never gives pain. Not to the moon. His own sweet moon."

All she felt was the gentleness of his fingers as they moved lightly over her breast, circling, caressing, arousing. And then the pleasure.

She moaned and he took the sound into his mouth, as he longed to take her breast. Ignoring the aching need of his own body as he strove to gentle her. To teach her to trust. To give. To love.

"Brianna?" Lilith called.

Brianna gasped and leaped to her feet. She stood in the middle of the wagon, her breasts rising and falling rapidly as she struggled for control.

"Can't you find the food, Brianna? Is Col all right? He is in there with you, isn't he?"

Brianna gulped and took a deep breath. "Yes, we were just . . . talking. I'll be right out."

Nigh swung his feet off the bed and sat up. His own breathing was still ragged. She snatched up the carefully wrapped food, cooked that morning, and started past him.

"Whoa." He caught her arm, drew her face down to his and kissed her. Her lips were moist and puffy and incredibly sweet. "You're the moon, remember that. You've nothing to be ashamed of and no one to answer to."

"Not even the sun?"

"Not even the sun."

He released her then. She stared at him for one long moment, her hair loosened by his hands, her face flushed and so alive with passion it was all he could do not to strip off her clothes and take her. Then she hastened outside. Several minutes passed before he was able to follow and join the others. Brianna avoided his gaze, busying herself dishing up cold beans and cornbread while Lilith filled mugs with lukewarm buttermilk. Sitting down next to Marc, he accepted the plate Brianna handed him, wondering if she was as eager for bedtime as he.

The Beaudouin boys rushed up, panting, their clothes covered with filth.

"Jean Louie, you must stop racing around like a wild Indian," Lilith scolded. "You've got sweat running down your face." She brushed at his shirt and trousers. "And what is this . . . powdered substance all over your clothes? Oh, even in your hair!"

"We was having a snowball fight, Mama."

"Were having . . . a snowball fight? How silly, now tell me the truth."

The boy glanced at his older brother who suddenly became very interested in the food.

Nigh chuckled. "Couldn't be buffalo dung, could it, boys?"

Francois looked up, wide-eyed. "How'd you know?"

"You aren't the first boys who figured out dung made good pelting material."

"Buffalo . . ." Lilith's mouth fell open. "That is the most revolting thing I have ever heard." She leaped to her feet, grabbed each boy by an ear and yanked them toward their wagon where she fished out a clothes brush.

"What would Master Genot think if he could see the two of you?" Whisk, whisk. "Filth all over you. And talking like . . . like illiterate farm boys. You are Beaudouins, never forget that."

"No, ma'am."

"A Beaudouin only says ma'am when addressing a woman other than his mama." Whisk, whisk.

"Yes, Mama."

Lilith finished with Jean Louis and started on Francois. Jean Louis ran to sit beside his father while Brianna dished up his food. "Papa, Nate Goodman got to go hunting with his pa today. Will you take us hunting?"

"Yes, Papa," Francois said over his shoulder while he scrubbed his face with the wet cloth his mother gave him. "Tommy Shorthill's been out hunting with his father, too. He even has his own gun."

Marc ruffled Jean Louis's dark hair and smiled at his older son as the boy came to sit on his other side. "You can't have a gun, but we might try hunting tomorrow, if Col feels up to it. We need him to keep us from getting lost."

"Now, Marc, do you think it wise, taking the boys on such a dangerous errand? They're so young." Lilith tucked napkins into each boy's lap.

Marc winked at Nigh. "How do you expect them to grow up, Lilith, if you keep them pinned to your apron all the time? Francois is ten, after all. Col, how old were you the first time you went hunting?"

"Don't reckon I'm too good an example," Nigh said. "Lost my pa when I was about Jean Louie's age. Took me till I was thirteen to get enough money for a gun, and then it was only a rusty old musket. But there's a lot to learn about hunting besides shooting a gun."

"Like what?" Francois gave Shakespeare a bite of buttered cornbread.

"Tracking and setting traps. How to keep downwind and how to figure the most likely spot to find game."

Jean Louis's eyes grew large. "You mean tracking, like Indians do?"

Nigh's mouth quirked up. "Yep, like Indians do."

Francois turned to his mother. "Please, Mama, say we can go tomorrow. I promise to be good and mind Papa and Mr. Nigh."

Lilith frowned. She looked to Brianna for support, but Brianna was gathering up the empty dishes and seemed unaware of the conversation going on around her. "Oh, my, I truly don't know. I suppose, since Mr. Nigh will be along as well, it should be safe enough."

The boys shouted jubilantly. Gobbling down their food, they finished their meal and hurried off to tell the other boys. Then the report of rifle fire split the air, signalling the end of the noon break and time to get the wagons underway again.

Brianna and Lilith put the dirty dishes in the wagon to wash later. Nigh mounted up and rode off toward the rear of the train without a word. As she watched him go, Brianna snapped her whip over the oxens' lumbering backs and thought about the night to come.

The mere thought of being in Columbus's arms once more made her tingle deep inside. She had come to care for him, she could not deny that. Nor could she deny that she liked his kisses. But the thought of lying with him, of letting him do to her the same painful, degrading things Barret had done, filled her with terror. It would be dreadfully wrong, anyway, she told herself. To lie with Columbus Nigh would be a sin. She was a married woman and

could never belong to him. She should encourage him to
court Lucy Decker. At least Lucy could be a wife to him,
could give him children.

Brianna's heart squeezed painfully. Her hand moved to
the flat surface of her stomach as she wondered how a
child would look, a child fathered by Columbus Nigh. In
her mind she saw a boy Francois's age, tall and rangy and
loose-jointed, his light brown hair sun bleached, his eyes
like a summer storm. She shoved the image away. Don't
be a fool. *You can't have any man's child, least of all, Columbus
Nigh's.*

Nigh spent the afternoon visiting the wagon companies
behind the Magrudge train. Some consisted of no more
than two or three wagons, others of more than sixty.
There were even small parties of men traveling only with
packhorses or mules. He shared rumors, gave advice,
swapped tall tales and asked for news from the States. And
he watched, and listened.

Sundown found him squatting in the tall grass and
scrubby bushes beside a stream, watching two men make
camp. One of the men was small and wiry with a scraggly
beard. The other was bigger, though several inches
shorter than Nigh, and built like a bull, thick and chunky.
Nigh had recognized him immediately.

Barret Wight had a heavy hand with his animals. Just as
heavy, Nigh figured, as he'd had with his wife. Nigh
watched the man beat his mules and remembered the sight
of that thick, fleshy body lying on top of Brianna. He
remembered her bruises and her terror. His nostrils flared
and his mouth became a hard, straight line as rage tangled
his guts and knotted his fists. His gray eyes narrowed. He

should have killed the bastard when he had the chance that day on the prairie. He should have cut off the man's stinking privates and made the sonofabitch eat them.

The thought of his Brianna belonging to that animal, while Nigh himself could never claim her, burned into his heart like a brand. Had the country been less populated with emigrants, he would have been sorely tempted to kill the man.

"Oh my." Lilith's hand fluttered above her heart. "How exciting! New faces and a chance to dance. Brianna, we must get out our best dresses for the occasion."

"I only have two, Lilith, and they're nearly alike." Fiddle music sawed into the night air as Brianna finished putting away the supper dishes. Lilith draped her drying cloth over the tailgate to dry.

"Oh, bother those old black rags. Can't you wear something bright and cheerful for once?"

"You forget I'm in mourning, Lilith. Besides, I can't wear what I don't possess."

Lilith pouted, but said nothing more. She couldn't loan Brianna a dress; the woman was much taller and bigger breasted. Even if they had been the same size, Lilith would never embarrass her friend by making her more aware of the penurious state widowhood had imposed on her.

"Well, ladies, are you ready?" Marc came from the tent, dressed in a wrinkled frock coat.

"Oh my, no. Where are the children?"

Marc smiled at his wife indulgently. "You told them they could eat with the Goodman family tonight."

"Oh yes, of course. Well, I'll only be a moment." Lilith scurried off to change.

"Are you coming with us?" Marc asked Brianna.

"No, Marc, I really don't care for parties."

He smiled. "You're worried about Col, aren't you?"

"Yes." She reminded herself it was all right to let Marc know she was worried; Col was her "brother," after all.

To distract herself after the Beaudouins left, Brianna straightened up the camp, then climbed into the wagon to fetch her needlepoint. Shakespeare was asleep on Col's bed. She petted the cat and tried to ignore the warmth that flowed through her body as she thought of the man who would lie there later that night.

She was becoming used to his kisses. Addicted. Like a drunk to whiskey. It would not do, she reminded herself. She was not free to love any man. For a moment she let her hand linger in the depression left by his head in the bundle of clothes he used as a pillow. Even if she were free, she had barely begun to know herself, to be herself. It would be foolish to give herself over to another man, be someone else's property again, with no say in her life. She'd tasted freedom and was reluctant to give it up.

Outside, Edward Magrudge took one of his short cigars from the beaded pouch hidden inside his shirt. What luck for the widow to retire to her bed so early. He would have plenty of time to enjoy himself before the Beaudouin couple returned from the dance. As he lit the cigar, he wondered where her brother had gone off to. It didn't matter. The man wouldn't come back this late. Undoubtedly he had run into friends and decided to stay there until morning. Maybe he was off getting the same thing Magrudge wanted from his sister.

The widow would probably resist at first. Women always did, rich or poor. Made them feel more virtuous, he reckoned. He didn't mind. A slap or two and she'd give up her pretenses like all the others. Truth was, he liked them to fight a little. He enjoyed their screams and the way they rubbed themselves against him, pretending to struggle. Whores at heart, all of them. Columbus Nigh's fancy sister would be no different.

While he waited, he smoked his cigar and licked his lips, imagining her taking off each garment. Maybe he should sneak closer so he could watch beneath the wagon cover. Then he could climb in and catch her stark naked before she put on her nightclothes. Those plump breasts, bare and eager for his touch. Nipples tastier than buffalo tongue. And those long, lanky legs. Soft, smooth, supple. God, he couldn't wait to feel them wrapped around his hips. Merely thinking about it had him hot, hard, and pulsing.

Magrudge stole closer to the wagon. There was no end to his luck this night; the tailgate was still down and the wagon cover gaped open. But clouds covered the moon and it was too dark to see inside. He stubbed out his cigar on the iron tire of a wheel and hoisted himself onto the tailgate, too impatient to wait.

Brianna was sitting on her bed, her back to the rear of the wagon as she fished inside her valise for the needle-point supplies she'd purchased in Independence. She wished she'd brought the lantern in with her. A sound came to her from outside. Her hands froze and she cocked her head to listen. "Col?"

The wagon lurched beneath the weight of a hard, heavy body. Brianna turned and peered through the darkness at the form crouched on the tailgate.

"Col? Is that you? Don't play games with me."

The figure crept inside. A voice screamed inside her

head, "Barret! Barret!" But the rank odor of cheap cigar smoke told her it wasn't her husband. Before she could move to snatch out the caplock pistol she kept tucked into a pocket sewn inside the cover, Shakespeare rose up from Nigh's bed. The cat arched its back, laid back its ears, and let out a hiss that sounded like the air rushing from Marc's India rubber mattress when the plug was pulled.

The man straightened abruptly and let out a startled yelp as the cat swiped at his face with spread claws, barely missing the man's nose. Shakespeare snarled and slashed out again. The man cursed and fell backward onto the tailgate. Boots scraped and scuffled against wood, a heel caught and tore loose, then he was gone.

Brianna reached the tailgate in time to see the man pick himself up off the ground. She recognized his battered top hat in the faint light from the fire.

"Edward Magrudge, what do you think you're doing, trying to sneak into my wagon?"

His voice was free of its usual insolence. He sounded instead like a peevish child. "Thought you and me could get to know one another better. Why don't you call off that blasted animal of yours and we'll have us a little fun while everybody's at the dance."

"I'll do no such thing. You get out of here or I'll put a load of buckshot in your tail, that's what I'll do."

"Dammit, I can't do no fancy wooin' from out here. Can't you just forget about playing coy and invite me in?"

"You must be out of your mind. Col isn't going to like finding out what you tried to do while he was gone. Now move, before I get my gun or I will shoot you."

"All right, all right. Uppity woman and her cussed cat . . . be damned sorry. . . ." His voice trailed off as he hobbled away.

Brianna collapsed on Col's bed. She hadn't realized she was trembling until Shakespeare butted his head against her arm and she reached to pet him. "Who needs a dirty old dog around when they've got you?" she whispered. The cat answered with a purr.

It was several minutes before she could get hold of herself. Finally she found her needlework bag. She climbed from the wagon and lugged a camp stool into the brightest spot of lantern glare she could find next to the fire. She wished she had some of Marc's good wine to soothe her frazzled nerves. Forcing herself to relax, she took out her needle, threaded it with a strand of bright red wool yarn and set to work.

The hour grew late. Tomorrow was Sunday and Magrudge had agreed to make it a day of rest. The train had made good time so far. Thanks to the wagon captain's strict rules about the condition of wagons and the carrying of extra wagon parts, they had not suffered the lengthy delays some companies had. Nor had they been struck by illness. Cholera. The dread of it never left her. Every day there were new graves along the road to drive the fear deeper into her brain.

Col blamed the cholera on water fouled by too many animals and by people being careless where they dumped their garbage or defecated. He always insisted she use only the water from the barrel strapped to the side of the wagon and he was choosy about where he refilled the barrel. Warmth seared her heart as she thought about him.

After what had happened between them in the wagon that day she was a little afraid of what night would bring when he came back. But the fear didn't stop her from yearning for his presence, for the safety he had come to mean to her, for the secret joy that came from knowing he wanted her.

She cut off her line of thinking; it was treading on dangerous ground. There could never be anything between them. She belonged to someone else. She would never be free to be Columbus Nigh's woman.

It was nearly midnight when the music faded away with the wind and the Beaudouins returned. Jean Louis was asleep in Marc's arms and Francois's eyelids were drooping. Lilith said a weary but happy goodnight and vanished inside her wagon. Francois crawled inside the tent he shared with his father.

"The party was wonderful, Brianna," Marc said after he had helped tuck the younger boy in bed. "Good music and interesting people to talk with. Jeb Hanks said there must be almost a thousand people camped here along the river. Boggles the mind, doesn't it?"

"Yes, I never expected to see so many emigrating to California. The idea of picking up gold nuggets like pebbles from a stream sounds like a fairy tale to me. I can't believe it could be that easy."

"Nor I. But we're going to Oregon because we want something more substantial than instant wealth. The future lies in the land, an old fellow told me tonight. I must agree." Marc crouched to poke at the dying embers of the fire. Sparks spiraled through the air as they were caught by a gust of wind. "Col return yet?"

"No, he must have found friends somewhere and decided to stay the night."

"Quite likely. Hanks was telling me that Col is well liked among the mountain men, and much respected for his skill at staying alive and dealing with Indians as well. It must be difficult for a man like Col to be held back by a slow-moving caravan like this when he's used to going where he wants whenever he chooses."

Marc was right; Col was a little like the hawks that soared over the prairie, wild and free. He wasn't meant to be tied down. Perhaps that was why he had chosen a married woman to offer his affection to, a woman who could never ask anything of him.

"Want me to wait up with you awhile?" Marc asked.

Thunder pealed across the sky and they both looked up at the low, starless depths. There was no sign of the moon that had been so round and yellow only a few nights before. The moon Col had likened her to.

"No, we'd best get inside." The wind loosened a lock of her hair. She tucked it behind her ear.

"Storm's far away yet."

"I know. Thank you for your concern, Marc. I'll see you in the morning."

The wind nearly tore the small skeins of yarn from her hands as she gathered up her needlework, pausing only a moment when she heard his soft goodnight and his footsteps walking away. How lucky Lilith was, she thought, to have such a good man and know he would always be with her. Brianna set the lantern inside, then climbed into the wagon. She tried to school herself against being nervous, but after what Edward Magrudge had done, she couldn't help herself. The howling wind and approaching storm didn't help. She put the lantern on top of a flour barrel and turned it down as low as it would go. After putting away her needlework, she tucked the edges of a quilt under the wooden bow at the head of the wagon to keep out the draft. Then she undressed, put on her nightdress and crawled into bed. Sleep seemed far away.

For an hour she tossed and turned, tortured by the fear

of losing Col, of him growing tired and disgusted by the swarms of people hurrying west to crowd out the wild animals and the Indians and the freedom he loved. Of him abandoning her. Finally, in the lull that preceded the rain, she dozed, only to dream of driving the wagon on and on across an empty prairie, with not another soul in sight. When she heard hoofbeats approaching she ran to meet him, her heart full of joy. But it wasn't Columbus.

It was Barret.

Chapter Seventeen

Rain pelted Nigh's head and shoulders as he unsaddled the gelding and hobbled him. Brilliant shafts of lightning lit up the sky like a sunny afternoon, then plunged the world in darkness again.

But the man's attention was on the faint glow of lantern light that penetrated the wagon cover. He smiled, thinking maybe she had waited up for him. Waited for him to come home. A warmth filled him that had nothing to do with heat, or desire. When he reached the wagon he heard her cry out his name. Heard her fear. And the warmth vanished.

Another nightmare. Quickly, he hoisted himself into the wagon. As he had expected, she lay in bed, asleep.

Lantern light limned her cheekbone, firm chin, slightly up-tilted nose, and gracefully arched brow. It secreted her long neck in subtle, seductive shadows that invited his kiss. The single brown braid that lay on the quilt jerked as she tossed her head from side to side. Her breathing was ragged. The cat, disturbed as much by the storm as by Brianna's agitation, opened slitted yellow eyes and moved to Nigh's bed. Beneath the rumble of thunder and the

Wish You Were Here?

You can be, every month, with Zebra Historical Romance Novels.

AND TO GET YOU STARTED, ALLOW US TO SEND YOU

4 Historical Romances Free

AN $18.00 VALUE!

With absolutely no obligation to buy anything.

YOU'RE GOING TO LOVE GETTING
4 FREE BOOKS

These books worth $18, are yours without cost or obligation
when you fill out and mail this certificate.
*(If the certificate is missing below, write to: Zebra Home Subscription Service, Inc.,
120 Brighton Road, P.O. Box 5214, Clifton, New Jersey 07015-5214*

Complete and mail this card to receive 4 Free books!

Yes! Please send me 4 Zebra Historical Romances without cost or obligation. I understand that each month thereafter I will be able to preview 4 new Zebra Historical Romances FREE for 10 days. Then, if I should decide to keep them, I will pay the money-saving preferred publisher's price of just $3.75 each...a total of $15. That's $3 less than the publisher's price. (A nominal shipping and handling charge of $1.50 per shipment will be added.) I may return any shipment within 10 days and owe nothing, and I may cancel this subscription at any time. The 4 FREE books will be mine to keep in any case.

Name _____

Address _____ Apt. _____

City _____ State _____ Zip _____

Telephone ( ) _____

Signature _____
(If under 18, parent or guardian must sign.)

LP1294

Terms, offer and prices subject to change without notice. Subscription subject to acceptance by Zebra Books. Zebra Books reserves the right to reject any order or cancel any subscription.

TREAT YOURSELF TO 4 FREE BOOKS.

An $18 value.
FREE!

No obligation
to buy
anything, ever.

furious tattoo of rain overhead, Nigh heard her whimper. "No, Barret. Don't—"

Laying down beside her, Col slipped one arm under her shoulders and drew her close, murmuring as she struggled against him, "Easy, sweetheart. It's just me." Then he lapsed into the more musical sounds of the Shoshone tongue and pressed his lips to her moist temple. Gradually she calmed. Then her eyes opened.

"Col?"

"Yeah, you were dreaming."

Outside, the rain became hail the size of bullets that ricocheted inside the water bucket and hammered the wooden body of the wagon. The temperature fell. Brianna barely noticed. She was lost in the feel of his arms around her, so good, so warm, so right. She longed to keep him there beside her. All night. Forever. But she knew what he would want from her and the thought filled her with fear.

"You left the light on for me." He smoothed a strand of hair from her face.

"I . . . yes, it was so late."

She couldn't tell him it was more out of fear of Edward Magrudge. Col might kill the man, or get hurt trying.

Aware that she had not asked where he'd been, Nigh stared at her a moment longer. All the way back to camp he had debated whether or not to tell her what he had learned. Would the fact that her husband was still out there hunting for her come between them? How could it not? She was too good a woman to give her love to one man while she legally belonged to another. Nigh should be a good enough man not to ask it of her. But the truth was that he didn't care who she was legally bound to, as long as it was him she wanted. They were the sun and the moon. They belonged together.

Brianna couldn't see the expression in his eyes. The lantern behind him cast his face in shadow. Yet she sensed his mounting desire in the tightening of his arms about her, in the quickening of his breath. Equal amounts of dread and longing tormented her.

"You'd best go to bed, Col. You must be tired."

Only if I can share your bed, he wanted to say. *Only if I can at least kiss you first.*

His gaze dropped to her lips and, as if hearing his silent words, they parted.

She knew what was coming. As if with a mind of its own, her body pressed closer until she felt crushed in his embrace. His lips edged nearer. Silently she willed them to hurry.

The first kiss was light, a mere brushing of lips, dry, soft, testing. She let her eyes ease shut, let one hand slide up to his chest. Her fingers absorbed the soft feel of well-worked leather before moving higher, to the low vee of the shirt's opening—and his naked skin. Nigh moaned at her touch. Her lips parted and their breaths mingled in hot gusts as their tongues entwined. Knowingly, familiarly, his lips moved over hers, as though he'd kissed her a thousand times before. As though his only purpose in life was to kiss her, love her.

Oh God, she thought, *this is wrong. I can't let this happen.* But she was helpless to stop the inferno blazing between them. What power did he possess that he could so easily control her emotions? And her body?

Columbus lifted her hand from his chest and placed it on his shoulder. Instantly her fingers tangled in his thick hair. She didn't feel him draw away the quilt, didn't know when he began unbuttoning her nightgown. Maybe she didn't want to know. But when he reached inside to cup her breast she arched toward him, filling his eager palm with firm hot flesh. He swallowed her gasp of pleasure and moaned at the exquisite feel of her response.

While his lips rained kisses on her eyes, her temples, her cheeks, his hand moved to the other breast, gently squeezing and teasing until her nipple thrust forward, proud and hot, with a hunger she could not name.

She felt his breath, warm and tantalizing, in her ear as he worked his lips down to the sensitive spot below her ear lobe, then down her neck to the hollow at the base of her throat. And lower.

The fear and hunger that tore through her as his mouth closed over a nipple brought a whimper from deep inside. An ache began in her lower abdomen so fierce she thought she would die of it. An ache of exquisite pleasure she had never known before.

His mouth moved to her other breast while his hands continued to stroke, to caress, to arouse. Brianna felt as though he had set off firecrackers within her body as wild sensations rocketed inside her. Strange, wonderful, primitive sensations that frightened and enraptured her at the same time.

"Oh Lord, what are you doing to me?" she cried.

He lifted his head and gave a soft, throaty chuckle. "I'm making love to you, woman. Don't you recognize it?"

"No." She shook her head. "I-I've never known anything like this."

"I've barely begun to show you all there is to loving. Do you like it so far?"

"Oh yes."

"Then relax and let me show you more."

He kissed her and she wrapped her arms around him and kissed him back for all she was worth. But when his hand stroked down her side, then glided back up along her bare thigh, she tensed.

Nigh felt her stiffen, heard her breath catch in her throat and cursed silently. He had allowed his own desperate need to rush him and Brianna was paying for it. "Don't be scared, sweet woman. I don't have to show you everything now. We're the sun and the moon, remember? We have all the time in the world."

He took his hand from the smooth warm flesh of her thigh. Frustration filled him as he felt her relax. They lay staring at each other, eyes full of need, full of want. He felt each heave of her breasts against his chest as her breathing eased. Felt it within his heart, within his soul, a liquid pulsing clear to his loins. He would not push her, would not risk terrorizing her as her husband had. But he wouldn't give up on her either.

"Bri," he murmured, as though that one word voiced all he felt, all he desired. "It's all right, I won't take advantage. I won't ever do anything you don't want me to. Just let me stay—"

"It . . . it isn't right. I. . . ." she began. The sound of her name, so brief and achingly sweet on his lips, had thrilled her. She didn't want to send him back out into the rain.

"I'll sleep in my own bed. I won't touch you, unless you ask me to."

"All right."

His eyes closed and his chest rose and fell on a sigh. Sleeping so close to her would be hell. But no matter where he slept he'd still feel the warmth of her skin on his hands, taste her on his lips, smell her heady scent of roses and passion. Staying would keep open the door and give him the chance to show her she had no need to fear him.

Silently he rose and jerked his shirt off over his head. It wouldn't hurt to get her accustomed to the sight of him partially naked. He'd gentle her slowly the way he had the filly he had bought to keep it from being further mistreated. One day she would give herself to him, freely, joyfully, and it would well be worth the wait. When he reached for the ties to his leggings, the lantern light went out and his mouth quirked up in a sad smile, knowing she had doused the flame so she wouldn't be able to see him.

In spite of the darkness, however, Brianna could still see Columbus strip off his leggings. She told herself to close her eyes, but couldn't. As if the lightning were his ally, the sky brightened again and again, giving her an even better view of his broad chest and muscled thighs. It also showed her the evidence of his desire, still swollen and rigid beneath the breechclout he left on.

He was the sun, and she—? Could the moon be as frigid as she must seem to him right now? A feeling of great tenderness filled her heart at the thought of how difficult it must have been for him to stop when he did, and how easily he could have taken her against her will. As Barret would have.

It was at this point in her thinking that Brianna realized how much she had come to care for this man who had so riled and ridiculed her the first days of their journey together.

Knowing how hopeless their relationship was made it a bittersweet discovery.

*   *   *

Sunday having been declared a day of rest, there were no wake-up shots fired at four the next morning. But Nigh needed no signal. He awoke to the warmth and softness of Brianna's backside. Smiling into the pre-dawn darkness, he nestled closer and became painfully aware that his body was already fully aroused. He also sensed that Brianna, too, was awake, and afraid to move.

Lifting himself onto his elbow, he leaned over to kiss her ear. "Where's my coffee, woman?" he whispered. "I'm hungry as a spring bear, and parched to boot."

Then he forced himself to roll out of the bed, pull on his leggings, shirt, and moccasins, and quit the wagon. The ground was wet beneath his feet, though the storm had passed. Quietly he stoked up the fire, added wood, and prepared the coffee.

Brianna emerged from the wagon a few minutes later. At the sight of him crouched over the fire, she lowered her gaze to her feet like a bashful maiden. Her cheeks reflected the vermillion clouds in the eastern sky.

"Have you seen Shakespeare?" she asked.

"Likely caught him a fat mouse and is taking a snooze somewhere. He'll show up."

The silence between them was rich with tension as Nigh watched her slice bacon, set it on the fire to cook, then mix a batch of biscuits. Before she could go off to start another chore, he put his arm around her and hugged her to his side. When she glanced up in surprise, he winked at her.

"Woman—" His lips quirked up on one side. "—I'm starved. You burn my bacon this morning and I'm gonna take you off in them trees over there, hike up your skirt, and wallop you."

The words were so totally different from what she'd

expected that she burst into laughter. "You do, Columbus Nigh, and I'll make sure your bacon gets burned all the way to Oregon."

"Is that any way to talk to the head of the family?"

"Oh, Col." She put a hand to his cheek and he turned his head to plant a kiss in her palm.

Marc's voice came from behind them as he emerged from his tent. "Morning, Col. Glad to see you're back."

Blushing, Brianna scurried off to the wagon. Nigh turned to greet Marc.

"You and the boys ready to go hunting?"

"I am." Then Marc raised his voice. "But if the boys don't get a move on, we'll leave them behind in their beds."

Francois's answer was frantic. "I'm coming, Papa. Don't leave without me."

"Me, too." Jean Louis leaped down from the Beaudouin wagon, followed by Lilith who was shaking her head.

"You'd think killing animals was the only way to have fun, listening to those two," she muttered.

Nigh chuckled.

"They're boys, Lilith," said Marc.

Lilith pouted. "That doesn't stop me from worrying about them. They could get hurt out there."

"We'll take good care of them," Nigh assured her.

While they waited for breakfast, Marc sent Francois and Jean Louis to water the stock at the river. Chickens scattered as the boys raced off.

Brianna came from the wagon with a jar of gooseberry jam and a dish of butter. "Did the boys find any eggs today?"

Lilith looked at Marc with dismay.

"Oh, oh." Marc winked at Nigh. "Looks like I get the honors."

Nigh gave an exaggerated groan. "Reckon that means I get to milk the cow. Thought this was supposed to be a day of rest."

"What are you complaining about?" Brianna said. "We women get to spend the day washing clothes, baking, cooking beans, mending, separating the cream off the milk—"

Nigh surrendered, hands up. "Whoa, woman. Won't hear another complaint from me."

He took a toothpick from his pocket and stared thoughtfully at the ground. " 'Course, I ought to check the horse's shoes. Got to clean my rifle 'fore I go hunting. When we get back, there'll be butchering to do, and a hide to cure." He held up one foot, his big toe peeking through a hole. "Moccasins need patching, too."

Arms akimbo, Brianna faced him. "Then we all have too much work to do to stand around. Get going."

Grinning, he sauntered off to milk the cow picketed near the Beaudouin wagon. He'd barely gotten the stool and the pail in place when he saw Francois racing toward the wagons, Jean Louis on his heels.

"Brianna! Brianna!"

Brianna and Lilith came from the campfire as the boys skidded to a halt in front of their father and Columbus Nigh. Moisture beaded the boys' lashes and their mouths quivered.

"What is it, boys?" Marc hurried to intercept them.

Tears raining down his cheeks, Jean Louis launched himself at his mother. "Somebody killed him, Mama. Somebody hung him in a tree."

"Killed who, Jean Louie?"

The boy looked up at Brianna. He pointed toward the river. "Shakespeare."

Brianna went ice cold. For a second she was too shocked to move. Then her hands flew to her mouth. She let out a muffled cry and bolted for the river. No, she prayed silently as she ran. *Not Shakespeare. Please, not my Shakespeare.*

Several children were gathered around a bent old cottonwood tree on the bank, staring upward. Brianna ran toward them. The children all knew Shakespeare. A few had been coming for reading and writing lessons. Others came only to play with the cat, sometimes telling Brianna of pets of their own they'd had to leave behind. The Goodman girl, Fannie, started toward her, calling her name. The girl was sobbing.

"Missus Villard. Oh, Missus Villard, it's awful. Why would anybody do such an awful thing?"

Brianna felt Fannie's hands catch at her skirt and reached instinctively to hug the girl. Brianna's feet were barely moving her forward now. Her eyes were riveted to a gray object dangling from a dead branch of the tree, too heavy to do more than sway gently in the wind.

The children parted silently, creating a mournful corridor that led Brianna to the base of the tree. There she looked directly up at Shakespeare's lifeless body. The cat's eyes were open, but they seemed colorless now. His tail hung limp, his little paws turned toward the ground. She could easily have reached out to touch him, yet could not make herself move.

Without a word, Columbus cut Shakespeare down and placed the small, cold body in Brianna's arms. She buried her face in the soft fur as Nigh had seen her do a hundred times before. Then, slowly, she sank to the ground. With her head on her knees, she rocked back and forth on her heels, the cat's body clasped to her breast while wild sobs tore from her throat.

Fannie and Jean Louis wailed beside her. Francois sniffed and wiped at his eyes. Nigh swallowed. After a moment he asked one of the children to find something to wrap the cat in so they could bury him. Marc offered to fetch a shovel.

When the hole was ready, Nigh lifted Brianna to her feet and gently eased the body from her grip. He wrapped it in a ragged piece of toweling someone brought, then placed it in the hole. Brianna tossed in a handful of soil. When she straightened, Lilith's arms came around her, holding her while they watched Nigh shovel in the dirt and tamp it down. Marc found a large rock to place on top so the wolves couldn't destroy the grave and the children decorated the sight with wildflowers.

Gradually the others drifted away. The Beaudouins rounded up their boys and walked back to camp. Only Nigh was left to watch Brianna stare down at the lonely grave.

Cold anger raged inside him. The cat had been a nuisance but Nigh had gotten used to him. He'd even come to enjoy the animal. What mattered, though, was that Brianna had loved Shakespeare as if the cat had been her child and her dearest friend. Someone would pay for this piece of work, Nigh swore silently. He would see to it.

After Brianna and Col returned to camp and everyone had eaten, Lilith suggested Brianna take a nap.

"Good idea." Nigh needed to talk to her, privately. "You didn't get much sleep last night, what with the storm and worrying about me and all. Marc and me'll help Lilith with the dishes."

Brianna looked at the Beaudouin boys, sitting on the wagon tongue, kicking at pebbles in the grass and looking almost as forlorn as she felt.

"All right. But please take the boys hunting like you planned. It'll distract them, and we do need the meat."

"If that's what you want." He led her to the wagon. "I'll fetch my rifle and tuck you in."

Brianna climbed inside and sat down on her bed. Nigh knelt in front of her and pulled off her shoes. She was too quiet. Something was eating at her, something more than the death of her cat. It worried him. He didn't want to leave her alone like this.

When she spoke her voice was low and full of loathing. "It was Barret, Col. I wish I could kill him. I want to put a noose around his neck and hang him the way he—" her voice broke, "—the way he did my Shakespeare."

"Ah, Bri." He gathered her into his arms. "Don't, please. It wasn't Barret."

She looked at him, her eyes full of questions and pain.

"That's where I went yesterday," Nigh explained. "I found him. From what I could gather, he'd gotten healthy enough to molest the daughter of the poor fool who'd hauled him home after that storm. Barret had hightailed it out of there and was camped with another man some distance off the trail, likely so they wouldn't be noticed too easy."

"But, maybe they followed you here." She took hold of the front of his shirt. "Oh, Col, I'm scared. Barret had other ways of punishing me besides hitting me. He was always threatening me, telling me what he would do to me if I tried to run away again. It must have been him. Who else would have done such an awful thing just to hurt me?"

Nigh shook his head. "I don't know, but after he and his friend went to sleep, I pulled the picket pins on their mules. Even if they woke up when I left, it would have taken awhile before they could go anywhere. Those mules didn't waste any time heading back home."

She looked at him a long moment, then reached out to brush a finger along the fringe of his mustache. "Thank you. I don't know what I did right to deserve such a wonderful friend as you."

He kissed her finger. "You deserve a lot more'n me, just by being you. And I'm more than a friend, whether you want it or not."

Her hand dropped into her lap. "It's not that I don't want. . . . Please understand. My father was the only good man I'd ever known. I didn't know there were others. Like you. But . . ."

"But you're married."

Wearily, he moved to sit beside her.

"It's more than that. I'm scared. I don't want to be hurt anymore. And I don't want you or anyone else hurt because of me. You don't know Barret."

"I know all I need to know about that bastard. He's vermin of the lowest sort. And he'll have to kill me before he can ever get to you again. Just the thought of him touching you—"

"No!" She spun to face him. "Don't you see? I don't want you near him. I'll go back to him willingly, if it will keep him from hurting anyone else, especially you."

Rage darkened his eyes. "Like hell you will!"

Brianna cringed. Nigh lurched off the bed and stormed to the other end of the wagon. For some time he stood there staring down at nothing while he fought for control. When he turned back to her, his voice was calm. "Barret

Wight didn't kill your cat. Either Shakespeare did some-thing to get somebody else's back up, or you did, without knowing it. You sure nobody's given you a bad time about anything lately? Punch Moulton, maybe?"

Edward Magrudge! The name burst into her brain with the force of a bullet. Shakespeare had attacked the man last night and Magrudge had mumbled something about getting even. It had to be him. But she didn't dare tell Col. She would do anything to avoid a confrontation between the two men that might get Col hurt. Somehow she'd find a way to deal with Magrudge herself. She glanced up at Col and saw him studying her.

Slowly he walked back to the bed. He sat down beside her, cupped her face in his hands and forced her to look at him. His eyes were hard and as cold as a pond in January.

"What happened?"

She knew that deceptively calm tone he used to hide his anger. She wanted to deny that anything had happened, but the intensity of his gaze told her he wouldn't believe her.

"Someone . . . a man . . . came to the wagon last night while you were gone. Marc and Lilith were at the dance and I was alone. When he climbed inside the wagon, Shakespeare was on your bed. He started hissing and growling. Then he attacked the man and—"

"Who? Give me the bastard's name and I'll—"

"No! You can't. I mean . . . I don't know who it was. It was dark."

All he could see in her eyes now was terror. Of him? Of the man? Nigh wasn't sure, but he'd find out. "Did he touch you? Did he—"

"No, I promise, he never had a chance to touch me.

Shakespeare was all over him. The man fell out of the wagon trying to get away, and he . . . he swore at Shakespeare, but he didn't try to hurt him. He just went away."

"You're sure you didn't recognize him?"

She buried her face against his chest so he couldn't see the lie in her eyes. "I'm sure."

"All right." Col wrapped his arms around her and held her close. "Don't fret any more about it now."

When Nigh stepped down from the wagon after making sure she was in bed, he felt something hard through the soft sole of his moccasin. Bending over, he picked up the heel off a boot. Full of thought, he joined Marc at the fire.

"You lose a heel off your boot, Marc?"

Marc lifted each foot and glanced at the soles. "No, you find an extra?"

Yeah, he'd found one. And he had a hunch how it had come to be there. All he needed was a name to go with it. He went back to the wagon and searched the ground for clues. For anything out of place, anything that didn't belong there. Then he smiled and picked up a soggy cigar butt.

Edward Magrudge!

Chapter Eighteen

The dead antelope attracted a crowd. Since they were shy and exceedingly swift, few of the emigrants had seen one up close.

"Curiosity killed this one," Francois bragged as the men watched Nigh skin the carcass. "While we hid in the grass, Mr. Nigh waved a kerchief from the muzzle of his rifle. The antelope came closer and closer to see what it was—"

"Yeah," Jean Louis added. "Then Mr. Nigh shot it. Papa says it's a pronghorn, but Mr. Nigh calls it a prairie goat."

Abner Goodman scratched his paunch and said, "Meat any good?"

"Col says it's coarser than venison," Marc said, "but juicier and more tender."

Nigh let the talk drift over his head as he skinned the pronghorn and eyed the assortment of boots shuffling around him. None were missing a heel. He laid out the hide and started the butchering. The best cuts he put in one pile on the hide. In another he placed smaller cuts.

"Hey, squawman, ain't you ashamed to be seen doing

women's work? Where's your squaw, anyway? Off pleasurin' some buck for a few beads maybe?"

The air tensed. The men fell silent.

Nigh looked up to see a new set of boots. Complete with heels, he was disappointed to note. Slowly he got to his feet, pulled out his kerchief and swiped at the blood staining his arms from elbows to fingertips. "My pa used to say you could calculate a man's age and the level of his smarts by the size of his mouth." Nigh looked directly at the owner of the boots, Punch Moulton. "Reckon he'd a changed his mind about that, though, if he'd ever met you, Punch, 'cause he'd a figured you for a twelve-year-old moron, and you must be at least eighteen."

Whispers turned to chuckles.

Punch bristled. His face turned red and his chest began to swell the way Marc's rubber air mattress did when he blew into the air valve. Punch looked about to explode when Jeb Hanks joined the throng and stepped between the two men. Behind Hanks was Edward Magrudge.

"Ya asked for that one, Punch," Hanks said, laughing. "Wal, lookee here at this fine buck. Oughta be a tender one, Col."

"Take a piece, Jeb." Nigh's eyes, as he stared Punch down, were as cold as death and as sharp-edged as the blade he'd used on the meat.

Unaware of the tension, young Nate Goodman piped up with, "Whatcha gonna do with the horns, Mr. Nigh?"

Nigh could see Punch wasn't up to starting anything in front of a crowd. Nothing physical anyway. Punch's type preferred dark alleys and uneven odds—in his favor. Smiling at the Goodman boy, Nigh picked up the antelope's liver and held it out. "Figured to give them horns to the first boy brave enough to take a bite of this liver."

"Raw?"

"That's the way the Indians do it. They believe it gives them a bit of the animal's strength. Prairie goats run real fast. If you ate this liver, you just might end up being the fastest runner in the whole company."

Nate stared at the bloody organ. It was slick and shiny and jiggled on Nigh's bloody palm. Bile rushed into the boy's throat. Grimacing, one hand over his mouth, he raced away.

The men laughed.

"Listen to the damn squawman," Punch sneered. "He's trying to teach your young'uns Injun religion. And you just stand there laughin' with him."

"Why don't you go pick on something the size of your brain, Punch?" said Taswell Woody.

"Yeah," added Tom Coover. "Get rid of some of these confounded skeeters. They've nearly et me alive."

Punch Moulton's dark eyes narrowed to the size of raisins. His hands fisted.

Edward Magrudge stepped up beside Punch. "You're first on guard duty tonight, Moulton, and it's getting dark."

Glaring at the wagon captain, Punch walked over to Dulcie. "You comin' with me?"

"To stand guard?" Dulcie said with raised brows.

A few of the men snickered.

For a moment it appeared as though Punch might hit his wife. Then he mumbled something ugly and stomped off. The other men began to wander away.

As the wagon captain joined them, Nigh noticed the

man's gait was a bit off, the way it might be if one leg were shorter than the other.

Or if one boot were missing a heel.

Lilith bundled her boys off for a good scrubbing. As Brianna and Dulcie climbed into Brianna's wagon for a reading lesson they heard Jean Louis say, "I would've taken a bite of that old liver, Mama, only Papa was hanging onto my hand and wouldn't let go. You reckon it would work the same way if it was cooked just a little?"

Halfway through Dulcie's reading lesson, Nigh came in looking for a clean shirt. Dulcie had already learned her alphabet and was trying to sound out the small, three-letter words in the Bible Brianna was teaching her from. Noticing Columbus's interest, Brianna maneuvered the slate she had borrowed from Francois so Col could study the alphabet she'd printed on it. A sudden movement brought all three pairs of eyes to the rear of the wagon. Dulcie's hand flew to her throat.

Punch Moulton was peering inside. "What's going on in there, sugar?"

With pride and defiance, Dulcie said, "Brianna is teaching me to read."

"Yeah? I suppose you're gonna tell me her squaw-lovin' brother's helpin' to teach ya, too."

"Your brain's showing again, Punch," Nigh growled as he climbed out of the wagon.

To prevent a fight Dulcie clambered down from the wagon and dragged her husband home. Alone, Brianna leaned back against the side of the wagon and wondered if her teaching career was over already. After a time she took out writing paper, fitted the penholder with a fine steel point, opened the ink vial and began to write.

20 May 1849

Dear Mrs. O'Casey;

Today is Sunday and a day of rest. Tomorrow we reach the Platte and the day after that, Fort Kearny.

Everyone is in good health. Nearly every other wagon company has someone sick with cholera, and we see new graves every day. Lilith is terrified. Being buried in an unmarked grave in the middle of nowhere, her body perhaps unearthed and devoured by wolves, is the most horrible fate she can imagine.

This rough life is very difficult for someone as fastidious and delicate as Lilith. There never seems enough time to bathe properly—even if one could find the privacy. Usually, we are too tired at the end of the day to care about cleanliness.

My hands are rough and callused now. My hair is dull and lifeless and since I rarely have time to rebraid it, wisps have broken off around my face which blow continually into my eyes. And my feet are always tired and sore.

Barret has discovered my whereabouts, but Mr. Nigh sees to it that I am protected, so do not worry about me.

I am suffering greatly from grief, however, as someone has murdered my sweet little Shakespeare. Everyone I have ever loved has been taken from me. I feel more alone than ever, and in a land where fear and danger seem constantly to hover over us. Thank goodness for Mr. Nigh. At times he makes me so angry I want to throttle him, yet he is good to me, too. He is like good French bread, so hard and crusty on the outside you wonder how you could ever bite into it, then on the inside, soft and warm and nourishing.

My eyes grow heavy with sleep, so I will close here. I will write again from Fort Laramie. Until then, I remain your faithful friend,

Brianna Villard

Nigh found Edward Magrudge alone, sitting on the tongue of his wagon trying to nail several thicknesses of rawhide to the bottom of his boot. Leaning indolently against the wagon, Nigh watched, a toothpick hanging from his mouth. "Lose the heel off your boot?"

Magrudge glanced up, then went on struggling to keep the assorted scraps of rawhide in place long enough to drive a nail through them and into the sole of his boot. Nigh tossed him the heel he had found by Brianna's wagon.

"Here," he said, "maybe this'll help."

Magrudge looked down at the heel, then up at Nigh. "Sure. Thanks."

Nigh took out his knife and a half carved piece of wood and began to whittle. "Funny thing about that heel. Found it by my sister's wagon. Seems someone tried to sneak into her bed a couple nights ago and lost that heel in the process. Wouldn't know anything about that, would you, Magrudge?"

"I lost my heel today. Got it caught in some rocks down by the river. When I broke it lose, the heel tore free and fell in the water."

Nigh nodded and kept on whittling. After a time, while Magrudge fidgeted with his boot, his fingers seeming to grow more clumsy by the minute, Nigh said, "That was the night somebody hung Brianna's cat from a tree. I figure it to be the same man since it was the cat kept him from getting to Brianna. Kinda humorous, don't you think? Cat defeating a full grown man that way?"

"Christ, man, why the hell are you asking me?"

Nigh blew the fine shavings from his carving, then pocketed it and the knife. " 'Cause if I could prove who did it, I'd cut the bastard's balls off and make him eat them. You being captain of this outfit, though, I know you'll see to it my sister isn't bothered again."

Magrudge rose to his feet and watched Nigh walk back to the Villard wagon. His hands trembled. He itched to throw the hammer he held at Nigh's head and see the man's brains splatter from the Little Blue all the way to the Missouri. "We'll see who ends up without his balls, Columbus Nigh. I'll bed that snippy sister of yours yet. She won't be so high and mighty by the time I get through with her."

Nigh was never so glad to hear thunder in his life. The first patter of rain on the wagon had him gathering up his bedding. He grinned as he climbed inside the wagon. Brianna watched silently from her bed as he dumped the bedding onto the supply box, then stripped off his shirt.

Brianna tried not to watch him undress. She forced herself to look away. Her gaze passed over the smoke-stained canvas roof with its wooden hoops, the caplock pistol in its pocket, complete with powder and patching. She studied the barrels of flour, dried beans and hardtack, and sacks of salt, sugar, rice, and corn meal. Finally she shut her eyes.

As each moccasin hit the floor, her pulse accelerated. The soft rustle as his leggings fell set her insides awhirl like leaves in a dust devil. She held her breath, waiting to hear him climb into bed. When the silence became unbearable, she opened her eyes to find him standing next to her bed staring down at her.

Without a word he laid down beside her and gathered her into his arms.

"Col, what are you—?"

He silenced her with a kiss. When he lifted his head and she could breathe again, she whispered, "This is wrong, Col. I don't belong to you."

"No, you belong to yourself. No one else. Remember that."

Then he kissed her again. Her disappointment when he got up and went to his own bed was a physical ache, in her heart and deep in the pit of her abdomen.

The last thing Nigh wanted to do was sleep. His whole body throbbed with need. Give it time, he told himself. Give it time. Let her get used to him, learn to trust him. Eventually she would learn to love him, want him. But, damn! To lie there so close and be unable to touch her, had to be worse than getting his hide peeled off, bit by bit, by a hoard of bloodthirsty Blackfoot squaws.

The Platte River was everything Columbus Nigh had said it would be, sluggish and turbid, rolling in eddies, yet no where more than four feet deep. The day's heat had lost some of its bluster by the time the Villard and Beaudouin wagons reached the top of the long ridge of sand hills that bordered the Platte River valley. Arm in arm, Brianna and Lilith gazed out over the dun-colored expanse of water, elated to have reached this milestone without the breakdowns and illnesses others had suffered.

"River's high." Nigh stood beside Brianna, his hand on her shoulder.

"It looks like a great inland sea," Brianna said, "wider even than the Mississippi, only without trees."

"My Lord, look at the people." Marc pointed to the wagons and herds of oxen, horses and mules dotting the south bank. "No wonder we haven't seen any buffalo."

Nigh said nothing. He thought about the wagons scarring the beautiful wild country he loved to roam. He envisioned the trees cut down and smoky cabins cluttering every valley. Where once he had traveled weeks without catching sight of another human being, there would soon be masses of people, killing off the game and throwing their trash everywhere. Their guns would make such a racket Nigh figured a man could never again hope to hear the proud cry of an eagle or the bugle of a mating elk.

Sensing his distress, Brianna put her hand on his where it lay on her shoulder. "Nearly all of them are going to California, Col."

He looked down and saw the understanding in her eyes. God, how he loved her. There wasn't another like her. It seemed the most natural thing in the world to pull her close and kiss her temple. He might have moved on to her sweet mouth if she hadn't warned him away with a frown.

"Is that snow down there, Papa?" Jean Louis pointed to the splashes of white that streaked the sandy earth below.

"Alkali," Nigh said. "Poison to animals. Not too healthy for people, either. Be seeing plenty of it for the next few hundred miles. Flavors the grass as well as the water. Milch cows generally dry up on the Platte and stay that way till they reach Oregon."

"Well, at least there'll be plenty of water," Marc said, noticing the rainwater that stood in every buffalo wallow and swale. The air, hazy from cookfires, hummed with the noise of insects hatching in the stagnant pools.

"Not good water, though," Nigh said. "Looks like them pilgrims have been digging wells, trying for better water. If they're smart, they'll let it sit for a few hours with a little bran or cornmeal on top to help it settle, then scoop off the wiggle-tails. River water's not much better. Both can bring on the flux."

Reaching the valley floor, the wagons turned west to follow the river bank. As usual, Lilith and Brianna walked together sharing their thoughts and keeping watch over the children, while Nigh, Marc, and Tobias drove the wagons.

Camp that night was opposite Grand Island, which sat one hundred and fifty yards from the south bank and blocked the emigrants' vision of the north bank, almost two miles away. The men waded across to raid the island for wood. Since the road from here on would be sandy and difficult to maneuver, Magrudge ordered emigrants with overburdened wagons to lighten their loads. Those with extra bacon used it as cooking fuel rather than throw it away.

At bedtime, Col made a show of studying the sky where clouds had obliterated the moon and stars. "Gonna rain," he said. Brianna busied herself with the dishes and said nothing.

After she had retired, Col climbed into the wagon and repeated the routine of the night before. Lying on Brianna's bed with her snuggled in his arms, he told her what to expect when they reached the fort, and described the trail they would follow for the next few weeks.

"Worst thing about the trail along the Platte is that it doesn't rain much," he said, smiling down at her. "Think folks would notice if I just kept on sleeping in here?"

"I'm not sure that would be a good idea, Col."

He tipped her face up to his with his hand and peered into her blue-green eyes. "Why not? You don't want me in here with you?"

She lowered her lashes to hide her expression. "What I want has nothing to do with it. I'm a—"

"It has everything to do with it, Bri. Fact is, what the two of us want is all there is to the matter. I want you and I think you want me. Am I wrong?"

She looked him in the eye. "But all you really want is my body, Col. Even if I could get past the fact that I'm married and that letting you touch me would be a mortal sin, I can't give myself to someone who's going to go off and leave me once we get to Oregon."

It was Nigh's turn to mask his feelings. He wanted her body, that was true. But he wanted more. Her love, her respect. Her.

Yet he wasn't certain he could truly settle down, never to roam his beloved mountains again, to laze away the summer on a river bank doing little more than witnessing the life going on around him. To live the Indian life, close to the earth and the spirits. To sleep when he chose, eat when he chose. Make love when he chose. A piece of paper and a few words spoken by a preacher meant nothing to him. Only Brianna had the right to give herself to him and if that's what she chose to do, what business was it to anyone but him?

But if she thought she needed the paper and the words, what then? He was sure he loved her enough to do it up legal, the white man's way. It was the forever part that scared him. If he found the need to roam too strong to ignore, would she go with him? Would she wait?

With a silent snort, he told himself he was likely getting way ahead of himself. Brianna Villard Wight had never given him any indication that she would want to tie the knot with him. With an uneducated squawman. When he thought about it, there didn't seem much chance she would want anything permanent with him. Or even temporary.

Gazing at her, he ran his thumb along her lower lip. "I want more than your body, that much I can tell you. But only you know what's in your heart, and only you can decide in who's hand you want to place that heart." He bent and kissed her. "As for the future, that'll just have to take care of itself when the time comes. In the meantime, I'll be waiting."

Then he rose and went to his own bed, leaving her with the echo of his words to keep sleep at bay throughout the long, stormy night.

Eight miles of travel the next day brought them to the upper end of Grand Island and Fort Kearny. Situated on swampy bottomland south of the river, the fort was made up of sod-roofed adobe buildings, tents, and sod huts. Vegetables struggled to grow in the deep sod of one roof. The soldiers were unshaven with patched uniforms and shaggy hair. As the wagons passed, several ran alongside asking for whiskey. A small cluster of Indian tipis stood nearby, the dark-skinned inhabitants lounging in their shade.

Magrudge led the company a half mile beyond the fort and signalled a halt. Time would be allowed for trading at the sutler's store and posting letters, as well as for the noon meal.

Lilith was appalled by the crude structures of the fort. The muddy grounds were so churned up by wagon wheels and livestock it was impossible to tell whether they were walking in mud or animal manure. Naked Indians with blankets draped casually about them lounged against the walls outside the store. Lilith kept a hankie soaked in French perfume to her nose to fend off the odor and gathered her skirts close about her to keep from brushing against the savages as she passed inside.

The sutler's store was a shabby affair with a muddy, dirt floor and a roof of poles, brush, and sod. Compared to Beaudouin's Mercantile in Bowling Green, Kentucky, the goods were shockingly expensive. Rope was four dollars a pound; salt, ten cents; kettles, fifty cents; whiskey, fifty cents a pint. Only staples like flour and bacon, bought by the sutler from overstocked emigrants, were cheap.

Lilith bought a few tins of sardines, baking powder, soda, coffee, and syrup. Marc bartered with the sutler's assistant for a 1839 Walker Model Colt revolver that could be loaded without removing the cylinder. Nigh traded two of his carved figures for horehound candy for the children and Brianna posted her letter to Mrs. O'Casey.

As they left the store, three carts loaded with furs and drawn by mules pulled to a stop in front of them. One of the drivers leaped down and hitched up his greasy leggings. He wore a patch over one eye and a beaver skin hat dangling with shells and feathers. Telling Brianna to go on with Lilith and Marc, Nigh walked over to the man and slapped him on the back.

"Wal, dog my ears if'n it ain't old Columbus Nigh," the man said. "Hey, Pappin, lookee-here who I found."

A dark man swung himself down off a short sturdy pinto pony. "Columbus, it is good to see you, *mon ami*. You are headed for the mountains, no? You want a job? The Company could always use a good man such as you."

Brianna stopped, holding her breath for Columbus's

answer. The small Frenchman noticed her watching from the front of the store.

"Ah, the beautiful woman," Pappin said, leaning closer to Nigh. "She is yours, *oui?*"

Nigh looked at her over his shoulder and his mouth quirked up in a smile. "Let's just say she's not available to any of you buffler-witted jackasses."

"Ah, I do not blame you, she is *magnifique.*"

Embarrassed, Brianna ducked her head and hurried to catch up with Lilith and Marc. The three of them hadn't gone far before they were stopped by a young hunter in buckskins, accompanied by an Indian.

" 'Scuse me, ya all know that tall man over there with them traders?" the young hunter asked Marc.

"Columbus Nigh? Yes, he's a friend."

"Nigh, I thought so." The hunter spoke then to the Indian: "He's the one we heard Hatchet Face palaverin' about up at Wind River. Five Piegan warriors jumped Nigh once. He kilt 'em all with nothing but a knife."

The Indian only grunted but his expressionless eyes lit up with interest as he stared at the man in question.

The young hunter turned back to Marc. "Thank ya, mister. My friend here and me, we been hopin' to meet up with this Nigh feller. Up in the mountains the Injuns and old trappers call him Grizzly Heart cause he's kilt more white b'ars than anybody and never got more'n a scratch on his belly. They say he's about the bravest of the mountain men left now. Ya must be right proud to call him friend. He's some, he is."

Marc laughed. "Well, yes, he is 'some,' isn't he? This is his sister, Brianna Villard."

The young man whipped off his skin hat and nodded to her. "Proud to meet ya, ma'am."

Still nodding, he took several steps backward, staring at her as though he'd never seen anything like her. Then he turned, slapped his hat back on his head and scurried over to join the men at the carts, the Indian behind him.

When the trumpet sounded for the wagons to start the afternoon's journey, Nigh still had not returned. Brianna couldn't help but worry. His words from the night before were still going round and round inside her head. Had she pushed him too far? Had he decided to accept Pappin's job and leave the wagon train here instead of going on to Oregon? Would he have left her if she had given herself to him as he wanted?

If she could only know that he loved her, nothing else would matter. But he had never said those words, and she could only assume that it was because all he felt for her was lust. Why was it that lust from Nigh suddenly seemed more attractive than love from any other man she knew?

As the thoughts tumbled in her mind, she barely noticed the acres of prairie dog towns they passed, humped with mounded burrows where the small rodents stood on hind feet, watching for predators. On one mound several tiny burrowing owls lined up at the mouth of the hole and stared at the passing wagons with round eyes.

"Look, Mama," Francois called. "They look like old men with skinny legs and brown coats like Papa wears."

Francois and Jean Louis raced out into the prairie dog village, laughing as they tried in vain to catch the owls and rodents before they could dive into their burrows.

Three miles west of the fort they passed a squalid assembly of mud huts called Dobytown. Several of the town's residents stepped from their doors to watch the wagons pass. Lilith, walking beside Brianna, frowned and said, "Goodness, there are a great many women here, aren't there? But they haven't a decent dress among them, the poor things. Why, they're half naked."

Brianna smiled. "I believe those are 'ladies of pleasure,' Lilith, and they dress that way on purpose."

Lilith's eyes widened. "Oh, my. Francois, Jean Louie, come here at once." Hustling the children into the wagon, Lilith tied the covers tightly closed, refusing to let them out until the wagon was well past the town.

Hearing horses approaching from behind, Brianna turned, her heart leaping into her throat at the thought that it might be Columbus. Then he was there, tying the reins to the back of the wagon.

"Col," she said. "I-I was worried."

"Were you?" He glanced around, then gave her a quick kiss. "I like the idea of you worrying about me. Here." Nigh handed her a bundle wrapped in the stained brown paper used by the fort sutler. "Open it."

She plucked at the string and ripped the paper in her eagerness to see what he had brought her. The package fell open, revealing a straw hat with a wide brim trimmed with ribbons the same blue as her eyes. There was also a tin of English tea.

"Oh, Col, it's beautiful." She whipped off her old black bonnet and placed the straw hat on her head. "But you shouldn't be buying me gifts. I'm—"

"Nothing wrong in a brother buying his sister a hat. Now you can throw away that ugly black thing you been wearing."

He was right; no one would think the gift unseemly at all. She smiled. "Yes, thank you. And for the tea, as well. We've been out so long, I can't wait for supper so I can brew us a cup."

A soft mewing sound came from the bundle Nigh still

held. Her questioning eyes met his. Grinning, he folded back the worn leather.

"Oh, oh!" she cried, reaching for the tiny kitten. "Where on earth did you find him?"

"The sutler had a whole passel of 'em someone had traded for goods."

The cat was black except for one white patch over its eye and four white paws. "He's adorable. I'll name him Patch. Oh, I love him, and the hat, too, but you really shouldn't have spent your money on me."

"Didn't. The sutler sold my carvings right off, and asked if I had more."

"That's wonderful. Still, you should have gotten yourself something, instead of me. Like trousers that would cover your . . . well, all of you. I do appreciate your thoughtfulness, though." Standing on her toes, she kissed him. The kitten, crushed between them, yowled and climbed onto her shoulder. Brianna laughed. "He's feisty, isn't he?"

"It's a she, not a he." Nigh caught her around the waist to keep her from moving away, whispering, "I'll go back and get the whole litter if you'll give me a kiss for each one."

Brianna colored and slapped away his hand. "Behave yourself, Columbus Nigh. You're my brother, remember?"

He gave her a ferocious scowl. "Yeah, and finding it damned inconvenient, too."

"Here, you need something to occupy your hands as well as your time." She handed him the whip. "I haven't seen Dulcie since last night, so I'm going to see her and show off my new hat, and my new kitten."

"Take a burlap sack with you and pick up any buffalo chips you find. We'll need them for the fire tonight."

"Buffalo chips?"

"Droppings," he said with a grin. "The dry ones make a passable fire."

She grimaced. "Are you serious?"

"Dead serious. Won't find much else to burn along the Platte, might as well get used to 'em." He poked his face close to hers, still grinning. "You tell the fresh ones from the dry ones by the flies crawling on 'em."

"I have tried to tell you before, Mr. Nigh, I am not stupid. Nor am I possessed of a weak stomach. I'll find your chips and bring them back."

While he searched for a burlap sack in the back of the wagon, Brianna began searching for "chips," determined to show him she was no longer a "greenhand." When he caught up with her, she was daintily holding up a large, grayish disk-shaped object with her forefinger and thumb.

"Look, I've found one already." Patch was chasing a tumblebug that had escaped from the dung.

"Sure did." Nigh held open the sack and she dropped the treasure inside. "Found you a nice little spider, too. Glad to see you made peace with the critters."

She looked down to see the spider crawling up the long sleeve of her dress. Screaming, she flapped her arm, trying to shake the spider loose.

"Whoa." Nigh grabbed her arm. He let the spider walk onto his finger, then hunkered down to set it gently on the ground. "Gotta treat every critter with respect. Could be a relative, you know."

Brianna shuddered and skipped away as the spider started toward her. "What do you mean, a relative?"

"Some Injuns believe they'll come back in their next life as an animal or an insect. Even a tree."

"Reincarnation? Is that what you believe?"

Nigh shrugged. The spider scurried off and Nigh pushed himself to his feet. "Injuns do. Every critter, even skeeters, have spirits." He flicked a mosquito off her cheek with the tip of a finger, then brought the back of the finger down her skin in a soft caress.

"Did your wife believe that?" It had been a long time since she'd allowed herself to think about his Indian wife. Now, after all that had happened between them, she found that it bothered her even more to know he had shared a bed with one of those dark, dirty creatures.

Nigh held her chin with his palm, his intense gaze gathering warmth while her skin and blood burned with a heat that had nothing to do with embarrassment.

"Learned it before I ever met her. Indians respect everything God put on this earth. They study the animals and the rocks and the trees, every side of nature, to figure out where they fit in themselves, the way some folks study the Bible. The earth is their mother and they revere her, sorta like Catholics revere the Virgin Mary."

He tucked his hands into his belt and watched a hawk rise on an updraft, lazily circling higher and higher. "Most whites see Injuns as nothing but heathen savages, but—" he returned his gaze to her and bathed her in its warmth, "—to my mind, they got more religion than most of them preachers, with their starched collars an' their starched souls, who come out here looking down their noses at a people they don't even try to understand."

"You love them, don't you?" She was looking at him as though she'd never truly seen him before, and realized that in some ways, she probably hadn't. "Not just . . . her, Little Beaver, but all her people."

Nigh's eyes lifted again to the hawk while he pulled out one of his wooden picks and stuck it between his even white teeth. "Reckon so."

He was something, she thought, truly something. A man who loved Indians and respected the spirits of spiders. He hid so much behind those granite eyes of his. What else would she learn about him before the journey was over? He could teach her a great deal. And suddenly, she knew she wanted to learn it all, every wonderful piece of earthy wisdom stored in that unassuming head of his. She wanted to know his history. She wanted to know him.

The hawk spotted something for his supper. He dove toward the earth and vanished beyond the bluff. Nigh dropped his gaze to her face. "Best get going, sun's about to set and I want you back afore dark."

She glanced at the sun standing on the rim of the earth like a gold coin balanced on its edge. The wagons rolled steadily on, vanishing into the orange glow as though the sun were gobbling them up. "Does the sun have a spirit too?" she asked, reluctant to leave.

"Yep, it's the big spirit, the Grandfather. Indians pray to the sun the way whites pray to Jesus. In my mind, they're one and the same. Reckon there's a bit of God in everything." He looked at Brianna as he added, "Sun, rocks, cows, birds, man . . . woman."

The breath caught in her throat at the sensual way he said the last word while he stared deep into her eyes, his very gaze a caress, a tribute, a benediction. Something clicked inside her, like a key turning a lock. She knew it was her heart he had opened and that she would never be able to evict him from its depths.

* * *

Darkness fell. Up on the bluffs, prairie wolves yipped and howled. Lilith stuck her head out the back of the wagon every few minutes to see if Brianna had returned. Seeing her, Nigh shook his head. He, too, was worried.

Finally, Magrudge gave the signal to corral. Being near the head of the train, Nigh was among the first to get his wagon in position. The rear of the train, and Punch Moulton's wagon, trailed nearly two miles behind. Lilith was fussing at Nigh to go look for Brianna so Tobias Woody, who had been driving the second Beaudouin wagon, offered to unhitch Nigh's oxen as well as Marc's.

Nigh found Brianna a quarter of a mile back, the burlap sack slung over her shoulder as she trudged along, Fannie Goodman at her side, carrying Patch.

"Confound it, woman. Told you to get back afore dark."

Fannie gave the kitten back to Brianna. "I'd best get back, Missus Villard. Mama will need help with supper."

"That's fine, Fannie, thank you for keeping me company." When the child was out of earshot, Brianna turned on Nigh. "You've no right to talk to me that way, Columbus Nigh. I'm not your wife. Or even your sister. In fact, if my memory serves me correctly, I am still your employer. I'll ask you to remember that, in future." Then she stomped past him toward the wagon.

Cursing, Nigh followed on his horse. When he reached her, he leaned over and jerked the sack from her hand. He tied it to the back of his saddle, then caught up with her again and scooped her up into his lap. The high pommel of his Mexican saddle cut into her bottom; she squirmed in discomfort, the kitten clutched to her breast. Nigh gritted his teeth at the reaction her wiggling aroused in his groin and held onto her. "Told you if I brought you on this trip I'd have to be in charge. Either you do as I say, or I'll damn well tie you in the wagon."

"You wouldn't dare!"

"Wouldn't I?"

Even in the darkness she could see the steel glint of his hard-edged eyes, and knew he would do exactly as he'd said. Lifting her chin stubbornly, she said, "Dulcie has another black eye and was terribly upset. She's afraid to come for any more reading lessons for fear Punch will hit her again and hurt the baby."

"Somebody needs to show that bastard how it feels to get his face bashed in."

When they got back to the wagon, they found Lilith in tears as she struggled to light the lantern. She burned her finger and cursed daintily. When she saw Brianna and Col, she leaped to her feet. "Where have you been? I couldn't find any wood and Marc's still off with Jeb Hanks. I sent the boys out hours ago to find something to burn and they're not back yet. I simply can't do all this by myself."

Brianna stared at her in shock. "Lilith! You're not acting like yourself at all. Are you all right?"

Lilith moaned, grabbed at her stomach and bolted into the darkness.

"Lilith?" Brianna put Patch in the wagon and stepped into the darkness. "Are you ill, Lilith?"

There was no answer.

Nigh dug a shallow pit for the fire while Brianna got coffee ready to boil, using water from her own barrel. Lilith returned, looking weak and unsteady. Then she turned abruptly and ran back out into the night.

"Something's wrong, I'd better go after her," Brianna said and hurried off.

Francois and Jean Louis came back toting a few sticks good only for kindling. Nigh placed the sticks on top of the buffalo chips and set the boys to work finding stones to line the fire pit. By the time Marc appeared, the coffee was ready and meat was boiling in a pot suspended from a tripod over the fire. Nigh stood at the edge of the lantern light, his thumbs hooked in the back of his beaded belt as he peered pensively into the darkness beyond camp. The boys sat beside the fire, unusually quiet.

"Where's Lilith and Brianna?" Marc said.

"Out there somewhere."

Nigh walked over to Beaudouin's wagon and took off the lid to the water barrel. "Where'd you get this water?"

Marc looked inside the barrel. It was half full. "I don't know. It was nearly empty this morning but I was hoping to reach a good spring before filling it again."

"Mama filled it from a well we passed," Francois said, his dark eyes round with concern. "Is Mama real sick?"

"Sick?" Marc felt the hairs on his neck rise. Like everyone else, he had noticed the increasing number of new graves along the road. Eddies of fear washed over him. He grabbed Nigh's arm. His voice was only a whisper.

"Cholera?"

Nigh shrugged. "Could just be alkali water."

But when Lilith returned, leaning heavily on Brianna, her eyes sunk in her pinched face and her skin cold and clammy, Nigh knew Marc's guess had been correct. Lilith Beaudouin had contracted cholera.

4
3 ◦ — ASH HOLLOW

NORTH PLATTE RV.

SOUTH PLATTE RV.

2

N →

FORKS OF THE PLATTE

PLATTE RIVER

1. Cholera camp
2. Lower California crossing
3. Windlass Hill
4. 500 mile point

1

FORT KEARNY ◦

Chapter Nineteen

By bedtime two more cases of cholera were reported, Amos Shorthill and Abner Goodman's elderly mother, Sara. A meeting was called. The people were frightened. They had all seen what cholera could do back in Independence and had counted heavily on the hope that they would be able to leave the epidemic behind in the settled regions of the States.

"Well, I for one, ain't sticking 'round here waitin' to catch the cholera from them who's already got it," Punch Moulton shouted. "I'm gettin' the hell out of here."

"Punch's right," someone yelled.

Columbus Nigh raised his hands until the crowd quieted to let him speak. "Cholera isn't spread by touch or contaminated air. It's fouled water and food. Why else would only a few people get sick out of a whole company?"

Everyone tried to speak at once. Arguments erupted on all sides. Magrudge and Jeb Hanks hollered for everyone to quiet down and discuss things reasonably. Finally Jeb fired a shot into the air.

"Lookee here, folks," Jeb said. "I got to agree with Col.

Cholera's worse on the Platte 'cause water here ain't fit to drink, never has been. That's what's made the sickness worse."

Heads nodded but not everyone was convinced.

"I still say it'd be safer to keep those who're sick away from the rest of us," a woman shouted.

"Do what ya want," hollered Punch, "but I ain't sticking 'round here to see if I can catch it."

In the end it was decided that isolating the victims couldn't hurt and might help. A few like Punch intended to set out then and there, darkness or no. Others chose to wait until daylight. Tom Coover and Lyle Woody volunteered to ride back to the fort and fetch the military doctor.

The thought of getting Lilith professional medical help from the fort gave Marc some hope. Still, he and Nigh walked back to their wagons in silence, their shoulders weighted with despair.

Lilith lay in her bed in a fetal position, hugging her abdomen while Brianna bathed her face with cool water.

"I'm going to die," Lilith cried. "I know it."

"Don't think that way. You must have courage and fight this. Here, I want you to swallow this. It's chamomile tea and milk thickened with tapioca to give you sustenance."

Lilith pushed the cup away. "It's no use. I'm dying. I'll be left all alone here and the wolves will dig me up and—"

"Hush, you're not dying. I won't let you die." Brianna couldn't say any more, the tears were too close. Never had she felt so inadequate and frightened. Going outside, she asked Nigh to ask Lavinia Decker what else could be done.

Marc put Francois and Jean Louis to bed in the tent.

Following Nigh's suggestion, Marc dumped his water barrel. The thud of the axe and the splintering of wood came to Brianna through the wagon cover as Marc took out his fear and frustration on the hapless barrel.

Nigh returned from the Becker wagon to find Marc pacing and wringing his hands.

"Lavinia wrote out some things to try, plasters and the like." Nigh handed Brianna a slip of paper. "How is she?"

Brianna crouched on the tailgate and whispered, "Oh, Col, I'm scared. She's so thirsty, but water makes the cramps worse, and she immediately passes everything I give her. She's too weak to get up, so I'm going to need clean sheets and someone to lift her while I change the bed."

"I'll get Marc, he needs something useful to do."

Nigh boiled water and insisted they scrub their hands with lye soap after handling Lilith. Following Lavinia's instructions, Brianna bathed Lilith's icy feet in hot salt water. She mixed spirits of camphor and tincture of rhubarb with laudanum, applied thirty drops to a spoonful of sugar and made Lilith suck on it to fight the diarrhea. It came back up almost as fast as it went down. Brianna fed her salt in brandy to ease the vomiting and when that stayed down she tried the sugar mixture again. The cramps spread to Lilith's legs. Brianna rubbed them with cayenne pepper in vinegar, then applied a hot mustard plaster.

"Water, please. Water," Lilith begged continually.

Brianna gave in, adding a drop of laudanum to ease the pain. Lilith's sunken eyes were so dark with unhealthy shadows she almost looked as though she'd been beaten. Her skin was wrinkled and cracked like an old woman's. Brianna bathed the sweat from the cold, blue-tinged flesh and prayed. Why Lilith? she asked, thinking of her friend's horror every time they passed a new grave. Why ₋ilith?

"I want to die," Lilith whispered, feeling her bowels release again, with nothing she could do to stop it. "So humiliating. Just let me die and get it over with."

"Shh." Brianna's throat constricted as she held in her sobs. "You will get well, I won't let you die."

When Lilith finally dozed off, Brianna slipped outside. Flies buzzed around her head as she dropped the washrag in a pan and sucked in fresh air. No matter how she worked to keep everything clean, the stench from the fouled linen was overwhelming.

Marc came instantly to his feet from his seat by the fire when he saw her. "Is she . . . ?"

"She's the same. I simply need a few moments rest."

"Of course. I'll sit with her." He started toward the wagon, then turned. "I'm extremely grateful for your help, Brianna. You've been a good friend to Lilith."

"I love her, Marc. She's closer to me than my own sister was." *My own sister whom I also lost to cholera.*

Marc nodded and climbed inside the wagon.

Brianna heard him murmur softly to his wife while she washed her hands. Brianna flexed her stiff shoulders and rubbed her aching back. Inside the wagon Lilith retched and groaned, and retched again. Brianna squeezed her eyes shut but the tears slipped out from under her lashes and trailed down her cheek.

It was a nightmare. Would she truly lose Lilith, too? Was God punishing her for leaving Barret by striking down first her sister and now her dearest friend? If it would keep Lilith alive, Brianna would go back to Barret, no matter what he did to her. But deep inside, she feared it was too late. Lilith was too weak. If she survived the night it would be a miracle.

Brianna would sicken next if she didn't take care, Nigh figured, watching her. She didn't even look like herself. Her dress was wrinkled and stained. Loose wisps of hair curled about her drawn face. He had done what he could to protect her, but he knew it wasn't enough. Helplessness didn't sit well with him. He jabbed his knife into the earth and rose to his feet.

Her voice, tight and thick with emotion, came to him through the darkness, telling him she knew he was there: "I keep remembering Julia. And that poor couple in that wagon, dead while their little girl—"

"This won't help Lilith none. Or you." He drew her away from the wagon to keep Marc from overhearing.

"I know," she said. "It's just that I never really had a chance to know Julia, and now. . . . Even Shakespeare's gone. I can't bear to think of losing Lilith, too." She forced back the tears that crowded her throat. "I'm beginning to wonder if Barret made a pact with the devil to deprive me of everyone I love, everyone I get close to or care about."

"That's foolishness and you know it."

She swung about to face him, her eyes wild with fear and grief and anger. "Then why, Col? Why did my mother and father have to die so young? Why Julia? Why Lilith?"

Nigh tried to pull her close and stop her painful flow of words. She jerked from his grasp and glared at him, one fist pounding her chest. "I'm the common denominator here, don't you see? I must be some sort of hex. It should be me in there instead of Lilith. She has a man who loves her. And two children. It isn't fair, Col, it isn't fair."

"Stop it!" He took hold of her wrists and held her still. "Don't you go feeling guilty 'cause it's not you in there. The goddamn well water made her sick, not you. How do you think Lilith would feel if you were the one dying in there? Think it'd be any easier for her to watch you die?"

Brianna could no more look away from him than jump the moon. His gaze speared her with its intensity, but his voice was whisper-soft. "Think it'd be easy for me?"

She collapsed against him and the tears spilled onto her cheeks. "Oh, Col, I'm so scared."

He brushed the hair from her brow and put his lips to her warm skin, drinking in her scent, locking it within his heart along with the memory of how she felt in his arms. Just in case. "We're all scared," he whispered.

She wrapped her arms about his waist and tucked her head in the warm hollow of his neck beneath his ear. Her body convulsed against him as she sobbed quietly, her tears soaking his shirt, and his own throat grew tight.

Gradually, she became aware of his hands stroking her hair, her back, the sensitive curve of her neck. He made shushing noises in her ear and rocked her from side to side. She wiped the tears from her eyes but made no move to leave. It felt so safe, so comforting in his arms, she wanted to stay there forever. Here she could find love, she thought. Here she could find everything she'd ever wanted—if she didn't belong to someone else. She pulled herself away.

"I'd better go back in to her."

He nodded and forced himself to let her go.

Lilith was vomiting when the doctor from the fort arrived. When the spasm passed, he checked the faintness of her pulse and studied her glassy eyes. He felt her skin and pinched the back of her hand. He shook his head.

Brianna and Marc followed him from the wagon and waited tensely for him to speak.

"She's badly dehydrated—" He paused as he tied his bag back on his saddle, "—and suffering shock. Keep her warm. Try laudanum mixed with pepper or camphor, any stimulant, even peppermint. Repeat the dose hourly and keep up the mustard plaster. But I must be honest with you, I've yet to see a patient recover once they start vomiting."

"Surely there's something you can do," Marc pleaded.

"I'm very sorry. Her case has advanced very fast. If I could've gotten to her sooner." He shrugged. "As it is. . . ."

Nigh took him to see Amos Shorthill and Sara Goodman.

"She won't die, Marc." Brianna squeezed Marc's hand. "I won't let her."

"I know you've done all you could."

"Get some rest. You can use my bed, I'll call you if there's any change. You have the boys to worry about, Marc. Stay strong for them."

He went off toward her wagon and Brianna went back to Lilith.

An eternity passed before Brianna heard the sentries fire their rifles to wake the train. Chains rattled and oxen lowed as people got ready to move out. Dogs barked and a baby cried. There was no smell of food cooking. Those who were well were too anxious to get away from the sick to bother with breakfast. The racket increased as the wagons got underway. Most were gone before the sky grew light.

Brianna heard Nigh call her. Outside she found Clive

Decker maneuvering his wagon into place next to Marc's while Clive's son Jonathan shouted directions. Elwin and Cedric Decker waited to unyoke the oxen. There was no sign of the oldest boy, Samuel, and his family.

"Lucy's sick. Reckon Lavinia's inside with her," Nigh told Brianna. "Clive sent Sam and his family on with the others, but he and the boys chose to stay."

Another wagon rumbled into view.

"That's Tom Coover, bringing Betsy."

"No, not Betsy. She's so young. And she's breeding."

"Gonna be hard for Tom to take care of her alone. Reckon him and the Deckers'll need help."

Brianna straightened her shoulders and tucked a wisp of hair behind her ear. "I'll do all I can."

"The Shorthills and Goodmans are coming, too."

"I'll start with Betsy."

Nigh stopped her with a hand on her arm. "Just don't forget to take care of yourself. Can't do anybody any good if you get sick yourself."

She tried to smile. "I know. I promise to rest after I see Betsy. She must be so frightened."

We all are, Nigh thought as he watched her walk away.

"Missus Villard, I'm sorry," Betsy said, taking Brianna's hand. "I tried to tell Tom it's that bad alkali water, but he won't listen. He's being over-cautious 'cause of the baby, is all."

"He's right, Betsy, it's best to make sure."

"You think my baby will be all right?" The girl's eyes were big and full of fear.

"Of course. We'll take good care of both of you." *Oh, please, God, not Betsy and her baby. Two lives, so young, so innocent.*

While Brianna doused Betsy Coover with pepper-laced

laudanum, Jeb Hanks rode in. Nigh went to meet him. The weathered old wagon pilot rested his arms on the pommel of his saddle and looked around. "How many so far?"

"Five, not counting Mrs. Beaudouin."

"How's she?"

Nigh shook his head.

Jeb stared off into the distance where the rest of the Magrudge Company was kicking up dust as it hurried away. The Decker's brown and white mongrel sniffed a wagon wheel, lifted his leg, then moved on. "Miz Beaudouin won't be the only one to go, I'm thinkin'."

Nigh took out his knife and began whittling. Sitting idle never had sat well with him.

"Why're you here, Col?" Jeb asked. "Your sister sick?"

"No. She and Lilith Beaudouin got to be mighty close. Brianna won't leave till Lilith recovers or. . . ." He let the rest of the sentence hang.

Jeb straightened and tipped his hat further back on his bald head. "Strong woman, your sister. Good'un, too, I'm thinking. Well, best get going. Lemme know if there's anythin' I can do."

Marc and Tom joined Nigh as Jeb trotted from the camp. Overhead a turkey buzzard circled as if he could already smell death in the air, its broad wings black against the weak morning sunlight. Nigh watched the bird, his hand itching to take out his gun and blast the buzzard to hell. "Don't sit well with Jeb, leaving us like this."

Tom nodded. "Good man, Hanks. Hell of a sight better than Magrudge."

"The Lord will settle with Magrudge some day," Marc said. "And Punch Moulton, as well."

Nigh grunted. "The Lord may have to stand in line."

Brianna did not rest after leaving Betsy Coover. She visited the Decker wagon, offering Lavinia her help. Then she went to see Sara Goodman and Amelia Shorthill. On her way back to Lilith, she stopped to try to cheer up Francois and Jean Louis. They were sitting by the fire, ignoring the kitten that was chewing on their dusty pant legs. The sight of those small, drawn faces tugged at her heart.

Children shouldn't have to be sad and scared, she thought. They shouldn't have to lose their mothers the way she had when she was little older than Jean Louis.

"Brianna?" Lilith reached out a hand as Brianna returned to her seat beside the bed. The woman was a shriveled up imitation of her original self. Brianna swallowed to keep from gagging at the smell of vomit and reached for a clean rag to wipe Lilith's chin.

"Brianna, listen, please," Lilith whispered hoarsely, pushing away Brianna's hand. "Keep an eye on my boys. Marc's a good father, but children need a woman's care."

"Hush, Lilith." Brianna stroked the stiff, sweat-soaked hair from Lilith's blue-tinged face. "Don't worry about any of us, just concentrate on getting well."

Love shown from Lilith's sunken eyes as she reached to touch Brianna's face. "You've become so dear and . . . and Col. Without you, I couldn't have stood this trip."

"Shh, save your strength, Lilith."

"No, we both know better. Let me speak while I can." She licked her dry lips. "Why is it I can see it all so clearly now? The selfishness, the shallowness, of my life. Thought I was so clever. Huh! Wasn't smart enough to be clever." She moaned, then said, "Don't . . . don't let them leave me in the dirt. Make Marc put me in a box. Can't bear the idea of . . . of wolves digging me up."

Lilith's voice was growing weaker. Brianna struggled to force words up past the knot in her throat. "You can't give in like this. Think of Marc, and the boys. They need you. I need you. Please, Lilith, fight!"

Lilith didn't seem to hear. "Don't waste yourself. You get . . . get married, have children. Don't be afraid. Sometimes . . . have to take happiness when and where . . . never look back. Life's too precious. . . ."

Her voice faded. Her eyes eased shut and her features went slack, except for a tiny smile on her bluish lips that remained even after she'd slipped away.

"Lilith?" Brianna picked up Lilith's limp lifeless hand and a wail of grief tore from her throat.

"Lilith!"

Chapter Twenty

Coyotes howled and fought among themselves, excited by the scent of death. Brianna shuddered at the sound and looked out from the bluff over the treeless Platte River Valley below. Off in the distance smoke spiraled into the sky from Fort Kearny. She wondered if Dr. Fullwood would take any satisfaction in knowing he had been right about Lilith, and decided that no one in the business of saving lives could take satisfaction in that.

Jean Louis wiggled his sweaty little hand in hers and she glanced down at the boy. He had Lilith's straight thick hair and patrician nose and her restless, impatient nature as well. On the other side of the boy, Marc, holding Jean Louis's other hand, gave it a tug to make the boy settle down.

Pain and suffering and death were something Lilith had had little experience with. Though she was sympathetic to the pain of others, she was at a loss in dealing with her own. Joy was her element, not grief. So Lilith did not encourage painful confidences from friends or relations. Understanding this, Brianna thought it ironic that Lilith had been forced to endure so much the last hours of her life.

The steady scrape and thrust of shovels were the only sounds in the warm afternoon air, except for the distant shouting of people and lowing of oxen in the valley below. On the bluff there were only the shovels, the wind in the grass, and the coyotes on the next hill. The eye could see for miles, but something about the endless rolling hills kept sound locked in the swales and hollows, the way Brianna hid her pain in the emptiness of her heart.

Lilith's coffin had been put together from odd pieces of lumber scrounged from the leavings of others, and from the folding table she had insisted on bringing so as to enjoy some measure of comfort on the trip. Brianna wondered if Lilith would have felt so keenly about her table and crisp white linen cloths, if she'd known to what use they would eventually be put. While the men worked on the coffin the women had washed Lilith's still-plump body and dressed it in her fanciest ball gown. Wherever Lilith was now, Brianna hoped she was dancing and laughing, her pain forgotten.

There had been a time when Brianna believed in God and heaven and hell, a time when she had knelt next to Julia and their father in the grand St. Louis Cathedral, and felt comforted by the pomp and ceremony. It was during her marriage she began to question the religious teachings of her childhood. Now, watching the men pile rocks on Lilith's grave to deter the waiting coyotes, she found herself questioning a good deal more.

On top of the rock pile Jonathan Decker and Columbus Nigh set a larger stone on which Marc had carved, "Lilith Ann Beaudouin, 1817-1849. She was loved." Now, as though born to the pulpit, Clive Decker's crisp tenor voice sliced through the air with the Forty-ninth Psalm, inciting a ripple of movement through the small group of mourners. As the last words fell away, Amelia Shorthill's soft soprano voice took up the first verse of "Nearer My God to Thee," and was quickly drowned out by Lavinia Decker's booming alto. Beneath the rise and fall of the melody Brianna heard Marc's choked sobs and wished she could let go of her own grief as easily.

Brianna knelt to place a bouquet of white larkspur by the headstone. Columbus offered a hand to help her up. Hesitantly, she put her hand in his. If she were to love this man, would he be taken from her too? As her eyes met his, she thought it was just as well she was married to someone else. Otherwise she would be sorely tempted, and she would do anything rather than risk Col's life.

Somewhere behind them, Barret was doing all he could to overtake her, but she no longer felt afraid. She had no tears left, no emotions, nothing. Her heart had shriveled like the dried apples in the pies she and Lilith had often made together.

All the way back to camp, down the ravine that led from the bluff, her hand in Nigh's sure grip as though he feared letting go of her, the last line of Lilith's epitaph taunted her: She was loved, she was loved, she was loved.

Glancing at Marc's haggard face and the boys' tearful ones, Brianna knew it was true. Lilith had been loved, and Brianna felt ashamed of the envy she felt. She desperately wanted what Lilith had known with Marc. A real marriage. Love. Children. Would she have to pay for the mistake of marrying Barret for the rest of her life?

Lilith's voice came to Brianna as clearly as the howls of the coyotes back up on the bluff. "Sometimes you have to take your happiness when and where it offers, and never look back."

Barret Wight wiped the dust out of his eyes with his shirt sleeve and peered harder at the scribbled notes pinned to the wall outside the sutler's store. Notices of lost cattle, messages left by emigrants for friends following behind. Letters to families with coins and notes attached, begging east-bound travelers to take the missives to the States and mail them. Even a list of those who'd died along the way. Nothing that hinted of Brianna having passed that way.

Beside Barret, Stinky Harris stuffed his mouth with horehound candy and grinned. "Um, that soothes my sweet tooth. It'll feel good to sleep in a real bed tonight, too. Captain Ruff was friendly, wasn't he?"

"Who cares?" Barret growled. "All I want to do is find someone who can tell me something about my wife. What did you say her sister's name was again?"

"Didn't get her first name, husband's name is John Somerville." Or something like that, he added silently.

Two soldiers came out of the store. Barret put out a hand to stop them, holding up the daguerreotype for them to see. "Afternoon. Trying to catch up with my wife. Either of you seen her, by any chance?"

The first soldier glanced quickly at the picture, shook his head and walked on. The second soldier said, "She's a looker, isn't she?"

Barret glared at the man. "Have you seen her or not?"

"Listen, mister, the captain's been keeping count and he says there's been at least four thousand wagons through here this spring. That's enough to make even a looker like your wife hard to remember." The soldier walked off.

"Damn! You'd think somebody'd remember her." Barret stuffed the photograph back into his pocket.

"Told you it was going to be like looking for a needle in a haystack." Stinky popped another candy in his mouth.

Barret's fist caught Stinky square in the jaw. "Blast you to hell, Harris. If you'd done your job right, I wouldn't have to be making a fool of myself, asking every jackass soldier where my wife is. I'd already know."

Stinky picked himself up and rubbed his sore jaw, but said nothing. He'd seen enough examples of Barret's temper to know when to keep his mouth shut.

Barret massaged his knuckles. "Get out of here. Go see what kind of deal you can get trading our horses for fresh ones."

"Made me swallow my candy," Stinky whined as he stalked away.

Over by the blacksmith shop a tall man in buckskins sat on a barrel, whittling while he listened to Stinky Harris make arrangements with the blacksmith to get horses shod and packmules traded for fresh ones. After Harris left to join Wight for supper at a boarding house run by a Mormon family, Columbus Nigh got up and stepped inside the shop. A barefoot boy was working the bellows while the smith fired up a horseshoe. The smith had arms like boulders and a bulldog face covered with black stubble. A large number of horses and mules waited outside for the blacksmith's attention.

"Got more'n you can handle, looks like." Nigh gnawed on his toothpick. "How 'bout I pick out some mules for that last fellow, save you the trouble?"

The smith wiped his sweating brow with the back of his hand as he studied Nigh, leaving a streak of soot behind. He was naked from the waist up except for his leather apron and a thick matt of black hair. "You're Columbus Nigh, ain't ya?"

Instead of answering, Nigh made a few last cuts with his knife on the carved eagle he held. "Got young'uns?"

"Two, why?"

Nigh handed him the eagle. He fished another chunk of wood out of a pouch slung from his belt and started a new carving. "Got it in my mind to make sure the owner of them mules has a real leisurely trip."

The smithy grinned. Here was a good story to share with the boys over the whiskey barrel that night. "Fine with me." He pointed to a pair of mules snubbed to the rail inside the corral. "Jest don't be lettin' them two loose." He winked. "Bad medicine, them two. Ain't a picket or hobble been made can keep 'em in camp. Don't take to packsaddles, anyhow."

"Thanks for the advice." Nigh finished up the simplified carving of a mule deer lying down and handed it to the man. Then he headed for the corral and the two snubbed mules.

That evening Punch Moulton and a few men from the Magrudge Company appeared on horseback outside the cholera camp. They were on their way to the fort, they explained, but couldn't pass by without inquiring how things were going. After expressing their sorrow about those who had succumbed to the illness, they went on their way. An hour later they met Columbus Nigh on the trail.

"Why ain't you back with the others, squawman?" Punch asked.

Nigh ignored the Kentuckian. He nodded to the rest of the men. "Problems up ahead?"

"Yeah, goddamn buffalo," Ben Crater said. "Stampeded through camp last night and took half our oxen with them. We spent most of the night trying to round them up."

" 'Cept we never found 'em all," another man added. "Got to buy more at the fort before we can travel on."

"Anyone hurt?"

"No, just got the shit scared out of us is all."

"You been to the fort, spreading the cholera around?" Punch asked Nigh.

Nigh chewed on his toothpick a moment. "Reckon if I could infect anybody, I'd start with you, Moulton. Can't think of anybody deserves it more."

The other men chuckled as they watched Nigh urge the dappled gray past them.

"Goddamned squawman!" Punch Moulton muttered. One of these days, if he had his way, he'd get even with Columbus Nigh.

Punch and his party reached the fort well before noon. They dismounted near the blacksmith shop where the corrals were situated and walked over to check out the stock that was for sale. Punch's horse had picked up a stone in its left rear hoof. He had the hoof propped on his bent knee and was trying to pry out the stone with his knife when he heard someone come up behind him.

"Punch Moulton! What the hell are you doing here?"

Punch looked up to see Barret Wight and Stinky Harris. He continued prodding at the stone. "Tolt you I was headed for Oregon. How come you're here? You cain't be headed for the goldfields. I already made you rich in that poker game at your tavern."

Wight had no wish to admit his wife had run away from him. "I'm looking for someone, favor for a friend." He sent Stinky a look, warning him to keep his mouth shut, then brought out the daguerreotype. "His wife ran out on him. Have you seen her?"

The sight of Brianna Villard dressed in a fancy dress, looking all high-toned and proper, nearly caused Punch to swallow the chunk of tobacco he had tucked in his cheek. "Yeah, I know her all right. She's with the same wagon company as me. Says she's a widow."

Wight tried to sound aloof to hide his excitement. "That doesn't surprise me. Tell me, is she with anyone?"

"A filthy squawman, that's who. Columbus Nigh. Says he's her brother."

"Damn the bitch! She hasn't got a brother." Wight's jaw twitched as his teeth ground together. "Harris, get over to that fool smithy and tell him to get a move on."

"I already did everything but threaten to shoot him, Barret. He won't budge, says we have to take our turn like everyone else and it may be tomorrow before he gets to us."

"Your friend's 'wife' ain't goin' far," Punch said, with a knowing smile. "She's nursin' a bunch of folk sick with cholera, 'bout twelve, thirteen miles up the road. Don't guess they'll be ready to pull out for a couple days at least."

Wight nodded. "Well, finally, something's going right for us. You sure she isn't sick, too?"

"Looked fit enough when we passed this evening. Nigh musta jest left here, passed him on the trail."

"Columbus Nigh? He was here? At the fort?"

Punch nodded. The rock flipped out and he let go of the hoof. Straightening, he pocketed his knife. Barret put his arm around the Kentuckian's shoulders. "Punch, I've got a proposition for you. How would you like to earn some money?"

"Col, where have you been?"

Columbus Nigh studied Brianna as he slipped from the gelding's back. It pained him to see her looking so tired and bleak. Her grief over Lilith and all the sleepless hours of nursing had taken their toll on her.

She had not cried when Lilith died or anytime since. It seemed to Col that she was trying to vent her grief by working herself to death, and he didn't figure it was a very healthy way to go about it. Days had passed since he'd last seen even the smallest smile on her face.

"Been to the fort."

"I knew that much. Why did you go there?"

The idea that she might have missed and worried about him pleased him. Hoping to get a smile out of her, he said, "If you knew where I was, why'd you ask?"

Brianna groaned with frustration. "Never mind." She whirled and started to flounce off. He stopped her with a hand on her arm.

"Wait a minute. How're things going here?" His eyes had lost the lightness of a moment before. There was a gravity to them now that told her something was going on.

"Amos Shorthill and Sara Goodman are gone. They could have used you to help with the burying."

Irked that he'd ignored her question, she followed him

to the cookfire where he crouched to pour himself a cup of coffee.

When he rose to his feet, the steaming tin cup in his hand, he wasn't more than a foot away from her. If he leaned a bit closer he could kiss her, but he was entirely too conscious of the Woody boys greasing the hubs of their wagon wheels a dozen yards away, and Fannie Goodman seated on the ground reading to the smaller children. Next door, Marc was clumsily patching a tear in his wagon cover. He settled for teasing her some more instead: "Maybe someday you'll find I'm good for more than digging graves."

She colored and, in her embarrassment, spoke without thinking. "I've always known that. You're kind and warm and thoughtful . . ." Her voice trailed off as he grinned at her. The rose of her cheeks deepened as she realized he had duped her into exposing some of her feelings for him.

"How 'bout kissing?" He leaned closer, his eyes on her lips. "Am I good for kissing?"

With both hands she shoved him away, causing him to spill coffee down his shirt. "You're incorrigible, Columbus Nigh."

He chuckled as she stomped off, then cursed himself for letting his lust for her wipe more important matters from his mind. "Hold on there, woman."

"What now?" she growled as he caught up with her.

He glanced around and lowered his voice as he spoke. "Barret Wight's at the fort. Been showing around a photograph of you. Did what I could to slow him down, but I'd feel a sight better if we could put some distance between us and him. Fast."

"The daguerreotype! I never thought of him using that to track me down." She gnawed her lower lip as she tried to think what to do. "The men have been fretting about the others getting so far ahead of us. With more wagons passing us every day, it's going to be difficult to catch up. If they're willing, I believe we could make those that are still sick comfortable enough to travel without suffering any harm."

"I'll talk to them. Stick close to camp. Use the chamber pot in the wagon if you have to, but don't step foot outside the corral."

Silent as a cat, he was gone. Brianna stayed where she was, working to control her mounting panic. The fort was only twelve and a half miles away, according to Marc's viameter. Twelve and a half miles was all that separated her from Barret's temper, Barret's retribution. Would he lock her in the fruit cellar once he had her home? Would he destroy her clothes and make her go naked again? Or offer the use of her body to his friends as he'd threatened so often?

Her gaze strayed to Col's tall, muscular figure, highlighted by the fire as he talked with Marc and the other men, his thumbs tucked in back of his wide beaded belt. She smiled, knowing without seeing it, that a toothpick dangled from between his lips. Gentle, demanding lips that haunted her nights. If Barret caught her, she would never see Columbus Nigh again. Suddenly she realized that none of Barret's promised punishments could compare to the pain of that.

The night aged quickly while Brianna tended to Violet and Taswell Woody, then Lucy and Lavinia Decker. The decision had been made. They would break camp at dawn—not far away now—and travel as fast as the crowded road would allow, in order to reunite with the rest of the Magrudge Company as soon as possible.

"Missus Villard?" Lucy Decker's voice broke into Brianna's thoughts. "Why hasn't Col been in to see me? Is he afraid of getting sick?"

"Lucy!" her mother admonished. "It wouldn't be proper for him to visit you in bed. You forget, young lady, the two of you aren't engaged yet."

"But we will be real soon, Mother. He wants to marry me, he as much as told me so."

Brianna tried to scold herself for wishing Lucy had died instead of Lilith or Betsy, but the thought persisted. When she left the Decker wagon, her thoughts and emotions were so jumbled she forgot Col's warning to stay in camp. She needed to be alone and think. It wasn't until a hand snaked out of the darkness and clamped onto her arm that she realized her error.

Panicked, she struggled, tearing at the viselike grip with her fingers and digging her heels into the ground as the man dragged her farther from the camp. He cursed and yanked hard. She stumbled to her knees. He grabbed both her wrists and jerked her back up. His features were mere shadows in the darkness, yet she knew it wasn't Barret; the fingers wrapped around her wrists weren't stubby enough. The knowledge gave her courage. She sank her teeth into one of his hands and tasted dirt.

"Damn you, you filthy slut!" He let go to backhand her across the face.

Brianna staggered backward from the blow, but her mind was working enough to know that she was free. She caught herself, turned and ran. Through a gap between the wagons she saw Col standing with the other men. So close, so close. She opened her mouth to scream, but the sound came out a strangled gasp as her assailant tackled her, throwing her to the ground.

He landed on top of her, his arms around her middle. One hand cradled a breast. Panting, he chuckled harshly in her ear as he squeezed her rounded flesh. "Didn't expect no benefits like this when I promised your old man I'd bring you his message."

Punch Moulton! Her stomach turned at the thought of having his hands on her. She could still see his fist slamming into Dulcie's bruised face. He was nothing more than a younger version of Barret.

The instincts born of a hundred beatings took over. *Keep quiet. Don't goad him. Show enough fear to placate. Don't cry, don't beg. Be invisible, a mere pebble in the grass. He can't hurt a pebble.*

"Hey, whaddya say, *widow* woman?" he breathed sarcastically in her ear. "You likely been lettin' that squaw-man diddle you, I know he ain't your brother. So why not me, too?"

He was grinding his pelvis into her buttocks and Brianna found suddenly that she couldn't simply lay there and let him have his way as she would have Barret. She wasn't the same woman she'd been the day she ran from St. Louis. And Punch Moulton wasn't her husband.

If she could get him to let go of her for a moment, lull him into trusting her . . . Before he could do what he was proposing, he would have to let her turn over, and there were clothes to be gotten out of the way. Swallowing her revulsion, she said, "Like this?"

"Why not? Ain't you never done it like a bitch in heat?"

He lifted himself off of her enough to pull up her skirt. Taking advantage, Brianna swung back with her elbow as hard as she could and screamed.

His arm deflected the blow from her elbow as he fell, pinning her again beneath her. She bucked to throw him off. He wrapped his hand in the long tresses that had come loose from the knot at the back of her head and yanked hard. She screamed again.

From the circle of wagons came the sound of running feet. Brianna could see Col peering out into the darkness, Marc and the Woody boys behind him.

"You cussed bitch, you keep your mouth shut if you want to live." Punch's cheek lay against hers. The stale whiskey odor of his breath filled her nostrils. The stubble on his jaw scraped her tender flesh. Panting, she lay still beneath him.

Nigh said something to the others, then stepped over the wagon tongue and vanished into the shadows.

"Damn," Punch muttered, searching the darkness. Keeping his grip on her hair, he scrambled to his feet, drawing her up with him. His head jerked from side to side as he tried to pinpoint Nigh's location. The click of Nigh's pistol being cocked somewhere close by—too close—brought him to a halt. But he wasn't ready to give in.

"Listen good," he whispered. "Barret's coming for you and if that squaw-screwing lover of yours is anywhere around when he gets here, Barret's gonna put a bullet in him. Maybe you, too."

Then he was gone.

A moment later Nigh was beside her, the pistol in his hand. "What happened? Was it Barret?"

She shook her head, unable to trust her voice yet.

"Where did he go?"

"I-I don't know, it's too dark to see."

He picked her up and carried her to the wagon, his eyes still searching the dark night. "Who was it?"

She didn't dare tell him. Nigh would kill Punch and

then go after Barret. She couldn't risk Col getting killed, too. "A friend of Barret's."

"What'd he want?"

"He said Barret was coming for me, and . . . and I'd best be ready. You frightened him away." The rest of Barret's message would have to remain her secret. And, no matter how much it hurt, she would have to find a way to make Col stay away from her.

For his sake.

Chapter Twenty-one

Almost as soon as she had settled herself in bed that night and put out the lantern, Brianna felt the wagon lurch as someone climbed inside. She knew it was Col, yet a part of her froze, terrorized by the thought that it might be her husband. Her arm curved protectively around the small cat beside her while she held her breath and waited. As though Nigh sensed her fear, he said, "It's me, Bri."

She closed her eyes, dreading what she must do. "What are you doing in here? It's not raining."

"Rain or not, I'm bunking in here. Ain't taking no chances on anyone sneaking past me to get to you while I sleep."

Her eyes had adjusted to the dark, allowing her to make out the movement as he pulled his buckskin shirt off over his head and hung it on a nail in one of the wooden hoops. What the shadows hid, she saw clearly in her mind: The dusting of hair that angled down over his flat stomach, the clearly defined muscles of arms and shoulders, the narrow hips and corded legs. He sat down to remove his moccasins, then stood again to take off his leggings. It came to her that she was holding her breath and she forced herself to exhale.

She was growing hot and tingly in her most private places. Somehow she had to get her mind on something else. Had to find a way to make him leave her alone.

"You agreed to sleep under the wagon in good weather. And stop saying 'ain't.' There is no such word."

"Huh! Coulda swore I've heard it before." One legging slid to the floor. Her stomach clinched.

"Could *have sworn* you heard it before—but only by ignorant people."

"You sayin' I'm stupid?" The second legging dropped and her bones dissolved.

"No, only ignorant of good English."

"Can't read neither. That bother you?"

She bit her lip to keep from telling him how she truly felt. "Of course, it bothers me, I—"

"You could teach me to read. I already learned the alphabet." He moved the kitten out of the way and sat on the bed facing her, one hand braced on either side of her. Then he bent and kissed her. His voice was low and husky. "You never answered my question earlier tonight. Am I good for kissing?"

Honeyed sensations jolted through her body as he kissed her again. She felt like the brandy she had mixed with sugar and mutton tallow to dose her patients with: smooth, liquid, fiery hot, and potent. His mouth moved to her temple, then worked its way downward. Her limbs refused to obey when she ordered them to push him away. Panic washed over her. Was Barret outside somewhere, watching her wagon? She had to make Columbus leave.

"Col, I'm so tired and I can't sleep when you're in here. Why don't you go sleep by the fire?"

Nigh stared at her a long time. He could hear the fear in her voice. "Something wrong?"

"Yes, something's wrong. I want to sleep and to do that, I need to have the wagon to myself."

He got up but didn't leave. To her dismay, he lifted her blankets and crawled in beside her.

"Col! What are you doing?"

"Should be obvious."

He leaned his powerful shoulders against the wagon and drew her close so her head lay on his naked chest. His scent washed over her, threatening to destroy what control she had left. She forced herself to pull away. "Columbus Nigh, you get out of this bed right now."

"I'm staying where I know no one can get to you without going through me first."

"All right, then I'll leave."

"The hell you will! What's the matter with you, woman?"

He snared her as she tried to climb over him. She found herself lying partly on top of him, held there by strong arms she could not fight. His warmth branded her through her muslin gown. His springy chest hairs poked through the thin fabric to tickle her breasts.

Nigh lost all perspective as her nipples hardened against him. He forgot he was there only to protect her. He forgot everything except his burning need for her. Threading his fingers through her thick hair, he drew her face down to his. The touch of his lips on hers was like lightning, leaving him scorched and trembling.

After the first moment of struggle, Brianna lost herself to the demands of her body, to the ache and the need she didn't understand. Here was Columbus holding her close as she had so desperately wanted all those long awful hours she had fought to keep Lilith alive. Here was the man she could not bear to be away from, whose very life had somehow become more important than her own. The life Barret Wight was threatening to take.

But Barret wasn't here.

It came to her in a flash; if Barret could have come for her himself, he would have. Something had held him up somewhere behind them, so he had sent Punch to let her know she could not escape. How long she had before Nigh's presence near her put him in danger, she didn't know. But surely they had tonight.

One night to enjoy each other. One night in which to steal a life's worth of memories to survive on, once she was back in St. Louis. And under Barret's thumb.

Her arms entwined around Col's neck. "Kiss me. Oh, please, kiss me and never stop."

Nigh frowned at the desperation in her voice. One moment she was trying to make him leave, and the next, she was demanding he kiss her. Was it fear? It hadn't taken much for him to figure out that her sexual experience with her husband had given her more pain than pleasure. He had hoped to show her sex didn't need to be that way. Now she was offering him the opportunity to do just that and, although his instincts told him there was more to her sudden reversal, his own needs refused to allow him to examine the matter too closely.

"I'll kiss you all you want," he whispered as blood surged through his body to engorge him with a passion more compelling than any he had ever known before. "Anywhere you want," he added, merging his mouth with hers.

His tongue traced the outline of her lips, than ran along the seam until it parted, letting him dip inside to explore the textures of her teeth, her tongue, every sensitive surface of her mouth. Brianna was powerless beneath the onslaught of his passion. She could do no more than allow, accept, accede. His taste intoxicated her. It inflamed her senses and numbed her brain. She couldn't think. Didn't want to think. Only to feel.

Nigh spread kisses over her face. He nibbled her ear lobe, traced the petaled curves with the tip of his tongue and breathed his warm breath inside until she shuddered.

"Should I kiss you here?" he murmured beneath her jaw. "Or here?" He nipped her chin with his teeth and worked his way down the smooth white column of her neck, giving her tiny, sensuous bites until he reached the base which he laved with his tongue.

Brianna moaned and writhed against him. "How do you do that?" she whispered brokenly. "How can you make a bite set fire to my insides that way?"

Col chuckled. "Do I?"

"Yes. It makes me feel wild and . . . and hungry."

"Where else would you like to be kissed, woman?" He worked a hand between them to cup her breast. "Here? Would you like the feel of my mouth on your breast? Would you like me to suckle you like a babe?"

His words were like flames licking along her nerves. The heat and moisture gathered between her legs where a pleasurable ache throbbed. For an instant the image of Barret, grabbing and clawing at her, intruded, and she started to draw away.

Thinking she was making room for him to touch her more freely, Col began to caress her rounded flesh and lightly circle her nipple with his thumb. At once the small nub tightened and thrust forward.

"You feel so good," he murmured, his lips on hers. "I want to touch every inch of you, with my hands and my mouth. It's right between us. You know that, don't you? We belong together."

The sun and the moon, she thought. Was he right? Did they belong together?

His hand was creating heaven with her breast. In spite of her fear, she found herself unable to move away. Unable, or unwilling, to stop him.

With his free hand Col slipped the ribbon from her thick braid. His fingers worked the strands loose, then fanned the mass out so that it covered them like a blanket of shredded satin. He gloried its texture and inhaled its scent. Roses. The fragrance mingled with the clean woman smell of her. The slightly musky, sensuous essence of her growing passion was driving him wild.

Rolling them onto their sides, he slid the top button of her nightdress from its hole. Her whimper and the hand that fluttered above his forced him to rise above the volcano of his own raging need and recognize that the tenseness in her body was fear, not desire. Slow down, he told himself. He was pushing her too fast. He slid his hand back down to her breast. Her hand followed and hovered there. Barely cupping her rounded flesh, he held his hand still and concentrated on kissing her, until he felt her relax.

He suckled her lower lip, tickled the sensitive inner surfaces of her mouth with his tongue, then suckled her upper lip, subtly preparing her for the feel of his mouth on her breasts.

Brianna's hand fell aside and she returned his kiss, gladly allowing herself to get lost in the heat and the pleasure he gave her. When his mouth left hers and began its moist, nibbling voyage down her neck, she did not object. He kissed her collarbone through the muslin of her nightdress and she gasped. His breath warmed her skin. When his lips moved lower, the coolness of the damp fabric against her flesh added to the new flood of sensations he created.

Then she felt his mouth on her breast and froze. The exquisiteness of his touch there was like a flower bursting through the snow after a hard winter, to bask in the rays of the sun. In the heat of the sun. The burning, blazing heat. Her entire body seemed to draw inward on itself, tensed as though waiting for some fantastic explosion, a volcanic eruption that would rock her being and change her forever. It frightened and enthralled her at the same time. She thought there could be no greater pleasure.

Then his lips surrounded the pebbled peak of her breast. She sucked in air and steeled herself, knowing something was about to rupture deep inside her, down low in her abdomen near the apex of her legs where the throbbing pitch of need was most extreme. She hung there in suspension, while he gently licked her breast, caught her nipple between his teeth and let it slide free between his teeth, then suckled lustily.

"You're burning me up," she murmured as she arched against him. "The sun . . . the rays of the sun . . . scalding me."

"Not yet," he whispered against her breast. "I can make you hotter, take you higher."

His hand moved back to the buttons of her gown, working quickly now, deftly, as he slipped one after another free. His lips found the exposed flesh and suddenly she knew he had been right. This was even better, bare flesh to bare flesh. She marvelled that it could feel so good, so right. She had felt Barret's mouth on her breasts, Barret's teeth. It had hurt her, sickened her. But this was Columbus and every touch of his hands, his lips, was heaven.

Brianna moaned and arched higher as his mouth

closed over her naked breast. She tasted like nectar and felt like the finest velvet. He ran his tongue around the rosy circle of her areola and gloried in the satiny texture. Her hands were in his hair, holding him tightly to her. The little whimpers coming from her throat were tearing at his control. He desperately wanted to rip away her gown, wrap her thighs around him and plunge deep inside. The thought of how it would feel to be sheathed in her moist heat had him hurting so badly he knew he would die if he couldn't have her.

He moved to her other breast and heard the thunder of her heartbeat match his own. He laved and worshipped her with his lips, his tongue while his hand inched down her rib cage to the graceful curve of her waist and hip. He smoothed his palm across her flat stomach, then fanned out to caress her thigh.

When Brianna felt his hand dip between her legs, she stiffened and waited for the pain.

Col's head lifted, his hand stilled. "You're so beautiful, so perfect," he whispered. Then his mouth reclaimed her breast and his kiss was almost reverent in its tenderness. For the first time in her life Brianna felt beautiful. She tried to relax. This was Col. He wouldn't hurt her.

But she found herself waiting for him to roll her onto her stomach, waiting for the pain, for the humiliation. Passion gave way to fear.

Nigh felt her emotional withdraw and cursed silently. He lifted himself on one elbow and looked down at her. She turned her face away. Cupping her cheek with his hand, he felt the wetness. "What is it? You know I won't hurt you."

"I-I know. I just can't. . . . Barret keeps intruding. I keep waiting for the pain."

"Blast his infernal hide! I could kill him for what he's done to you."

"No!" She looked at him then and put her hand to his face. "Please, I couldn't bear it if you were hurt."

His anger melted at the urgency in her voice. She cared for him. Only love could cause such fear. His heart soared. "Shh. I won't be the one to get hurt. Don't worry about me, sweet woman. I didn't know anything could be as good as it is with you. I'm not about to give you up now."

The words were what she had longed to hear. Yet they struck terror in her heart as she remembered the message Punch Moulton had given her. The words burst from her without warning: "You have to give me up, Col. Barret will kill you if he finds you anywhere near me."

He chuckled but it was a grim sound. "No, he's the one who's likely to die if we meet up again. Forget about it, Bri. All that matters is what's between you and me."

"The sun and the moon?"

"Yeah, the sun and the moon. I haven't even begun to show you the pleasure my hands can bring you."

"To-tonight?"

"No, it's late now. You need rest. We have lots of nights ahead of us, and more joy than you can imagine." He settled onto his back and brought her close against his side, her head on his shoulder.

"But, Barret—"

"Forget him, Bri. I won't let him ruin what's between us. Just leave it to me, I'll take care of Barret. Now sleep."

She lay there for a long time before he felt her relax. Damn that rotten husband of hers! What had he done to her to create such fear of what should be all beauty and pleasure? In that instant Nigh knew with every fiber of his being that one of them would die, Barret Wight or Columbus Nigh. It was inevitable.

He felt the slight tremors of her body before he became aware of the dampness against his skin. "Bri? What's wrong now? Are you still afraid?"

"No," she sobbed. "I-I feel so . . . so empty."

He couldn't help chuckling. "So do I, sweet woman. Your body wants loving now, not sleep. I can give you the release you need, if you'll trust me."

"I trust you. It-it's not that." Her voice broke as she cried harder, her hands over her face. "It's Lilith. It's everyone, everything I ever loved. Julia, Shakespeare."

He murmured something soothing in a foreign tongue and pulled her closer. What had happened was obvious to him now. The unsatisfied passion on top of all the emotions she had kept bottled inside her for so long had finally snapped her control. Her grief over Lilith's death and the horror of the cholera epidemic had freed itself. The tightness in his own throat as he listened to her sobs was thankfulness and relief.

"I'm sorry. I'm sorry. I can't seem to stop."

"You don't need to," he said. "Let it all out. Everything will be fine now, I promise."

Brianna wanted to believe him. With all her heart. But he didn't know Barret as she did. And Barret had help, Punch Moulton and the other man Barret had been travelling with. She had botched things tonight, letting herself fall under the spell of Col's kisses, his caresses. Did she dare do as he wanted and leave everything to him? How could he when he didn't even know who all his enemies were? Should she tell him about Punch?

No, she had to find a way to solve this herself. A way that wouldn't endanger Columbus.

Chapter Twenty-two

Brianna yawned and thought longingly of the wagon seat in the shade of the canvas cover. But she knew she would fall asleep the moment she was seated. Without her whip cracking over their heads to keep them going, the oxen would halt in their tracks and slumber on their feet.

The day before, Arthur Hickum decided to sit on the wagon tongue while he drove. No one knew whether he fell asleep or merely lost his balance. Two wheels rolled over his legs, crushing them, before help reached him. Both legs were cut off and still the man died. Brianna had no intention of making the same mistake, so she kept walking. Her feet sank in the deep sandy soil of the churned-up road and she stumbled.

"Bri, you all right?"

She looked up to see Col riding up beside her on the dappled gray, and she smiled at him. "I'm fine. How much further is it to the crossing?"

"Couple of miles."

He dismounted to walk beside her, his gaze beneath the wide brim of his hat warm and soft as he studied her. Sweat dripped down his temples, leaving tracks on his dust-covered face. His hat, hair, buckskins, and every inch of visible skin were white with dust. She grimaced at the thought that she must be every bit as dirty as he was.

The wind had been unrelenting the past few days, kicking the fine white dust of the trammeled road into clouds that made it difficult to see more than a few hundred yards. The only good the wind brought was in sweeping away the hoards of mosquitoes and buffalo gnats that usually hovered over animals and people alike. When it was calm the insects got into mouths, nostrils, eyes, and ears. They clustered in stinging masses on the tender skin below the oxens' dewclaws, and in the horses' nostrils, until the animals became unmanageable. Smudge fires of green sage helped at night, though even the smoke did little to deter the grasshoppers that invaded cookpots, water buckets, and skillets.

"Saw Punch Moulton talking to you," Nigh said. "Just passing the time? Or was he being his usual mouthy self?"

"Passing the time."

Brianna wanted to tell him the truth. She wanted him to make Punch leave her alone. She wanted to be able to sleep at night and to stop looking over her shoulder during the day. Her nerves were stretched as tight as a rawhide knot dunked in water and heat-dried. But getting Punch off her back would necessitate admitting that it was he who had attacked her the evening before they left to catch up with the train. She'd also have to repeat Punch's warning to stay away from Columbus if she wanted him to stay alive.

A warning Col himself made impossible for her to heed.

Ever since Brianna and her small party of recovering cholera victims had rejoined the wagon train, Punch made a point of wandering past with a threatening glance that made her skin crawl.

She glanced up now and saw the hunger in Col's eyes and her insides quickened in response, making her blush.

His gentleness and the passion he was able to elicit from her with a single touch astounded her. Though it had been days since the last rain and he had gone back to sleeping under the wagon, he still managed to find moments to hold her, to kiss and caress. She knew he was growing impatient and that he couldn't understand her reasons for keeping him at arm's length. Whenever she saw him coming, she tried to make sure she wasn't alone. Always he knew and reacted with anger. At times the tension between them was like quicksand, deep, inconstant, and deadly.

If only Barret could disappear off the face of the earth, if she could forget she was married, if Col could—or would—offer her a future. If, if, if.

Every day her guilt and fear convinced her she should put Columbus Nigh from her heart. And each night, when she crawled into her bed, her fickle heart and her wanton body ached for him to sneak inside and show her more of the joy he had promised her.

Angling a glance at him she saw that he was studying the sky. He looked down at her and grinned. "Storm clouds in the west. Might rain tonight."

Before she could reply, there was a blast of gunfire. Brianna jumped, let out a frightened cry and instantly found herself in his arms.

"It's only the men shooting at a herd of buffalo up ahead," he assured her, his lips tasting the salty sweat on her temple. "Want to go watch?"

Gently, she disentangled herself. Was he hoping to get

her off to himself again? "I'd better not. The oxen won't move one foot in this heat without the whip cracking constantly over their backs."

"We won't be far. Tobias will keep a watch on them."

He lifted her into his saddle, then leaped up behind. After riding a quarter of a mile away from the caravan, he steered the gray into thick shrubs growing along a dry creek bed and reined in. When he jumped down and reached up for her, she said, "What about the buffalo, Col? Why are we stopping here?"

"To hell with the buffalo." He lifted her down and pulled her close against him. "I'm starving."

She wedged her arms between them. "Starving for what?"

"What do you think?" he said before his lips claimed hers. After a long time he lifted his head and grinned. "Lord, woman, if we don't shake loose from this train, I'm gonna dry up and die for wanting you."

"Oh, Col, you're so silly." But she couldn't stop herself from smiling with pleasure at his words.

Very deliberately he took her hands from his chest and forced her arms to circle his waist. "You're still fighting me. Why?"

She rested her head against his chest to hide her face. "You know why. I'm married."

"Your husband threw away his right to claim you the first time he hit you. You don't owe him anything, Bri. Especially loyalty. You think he never cheated on you, a man like him?"

"Oh, I know he cheated. He had a mistress in town that he was supporting. He even bought her a house. Glory was her name. She was a prostitute when he met her."

"Knowing that, how could you feel guilty for loving me?"

"His sins can't erase mine, Col."

He sighed and moved away from her. "Does the man have to die for you to feel free of him?"

"No." She grabbed his arm and turned him back to face her. "You can't kill him. I could never live with myself, let alone you, if you had his blood on your hands."

"Damnation, woman. You sure know how to make it difficult for a man."

"I don't mean to."

He framed her face with his hands and gazed down at her. "I don't know how this is all gonna end, Bri, but one thing I'm certain of: You belong to me. No one else. You hear?"

She put her hands on his and tried to smile, though she knew their relationship was hopeless. Barret would come for her and someone would die. They would all be better off if she simply turned around and went back where she belonged, with her husband. At least then she could be sure that Col would be safe. The thought of leaving him shredded her heart. Yet she knew there was no other answer. Tonight, after everyone slept she would find the courage to steal a horse from the communal herd and ride away. In the meantime, they had today and she had a sudden need to spend as much of it with him as she could. "Can we go see the buffalo now?"

When they caught up with the hunters, they saw a dozen men on horseback in a ragged circle around a single buffalo bull. Several men were firing at the bull. It retaliated by charging first one, then another, its massive head shaking, flinging mucus and blood everywhere. The horses dodged the bull's pointed horns easily. It was exhausted and badly wounded. Runnels of blood poured down its sides from a dozen wounds, matting the thick winter hair that still clung in tattered patches. The bull's tongue lolled from its mouth as it panted and snorted at its assailants. Ruddy foam flecked its sides.

"Oh, Col," Brianna cried. "It's awful. Why doesn't the poor thing die?"

"Can't throw a buffalo in his tracks with a shotgun. Even with a good rifle, man's gotta know where to aim."

She saw what he meant. Punch Moulton's buckshot was having about as much effect as a tossed handful of pebbles. He gave up firing at the huge body and aimed instead at the animal's shaggy face. The bull bellowed in anger and pain, but stood its ground.

"Why is Punch doing that?" she asked.

"He's trying to blind it so they can move in close enough to slit its throat."

"Oh, Col, it . . . it's inhuman. Please, you know how to do it, put the poor thing out of its misery."

She appealed to him with her dazzling blue topaz eyes that were filled with pain and revulsion, and he couldn't deny her. He had a hunch he'd never be able to deny her anything. Not when she looked at him like that. Pushing himself off the gray's rump, he took his Hawken from its scabbard.

Punch was still firing at the bull's head. The horses pranced nervously at the scent of blood and death. With his long-legged gait, Nigh strode past the mounted men where he had a clear shot, then raised the Hawken to his shoulder.

"Hey!" Punch shouted. "This is our kill. Whaddya think you're doing, squawman?"

Nigh ignored the man. The bull faced him silently, head bowed as though it knew its time was over and the pain would soon end. Nigh took careful aim and fired.

The bull staggered. It tried to plant its feet farther apart to keep its balance but its knees buckled. It bellowed, swaying from side to side, the one eye still in its head rolling and glazed as death claimed the shaggy beast. For a moment the enormous body became rigid. A tremor convulsed its heaving sides, then it went down. Nigh lowered the rifle, turned and faced the ring of men.

"Sorry, boys. Don't go along with torturing critters. You want to hunt buffalo, use a weapon that'll do some good. And aim for his lights, just above the brisket behind the shoulder."

Nigh glanced back at the buffalo. It was old, eight years by his guess, and weighed a ton. He shook his head at the waste. "Take the tongue and some humpribs, if you want," he told the hunters. "Rest'll be too tough to eat."

"You sonuvabitch!" Punch raged at Nigh's back.

Nigh mounted the dappled gray with a running leap, as graceful as the antelope that had danced in the distance throughout the morning as the train rumbled past. Nigh reached around Brianna for the reins, turned the horse, and headed for the wagon.

The South Platte was rising, due to distant storms. Likely it would take the rest of the afternoon to get the wagons across, but no one wanted to wait. If the water rose too high, they would be stuck there for days until it subsided again. The beds of the wagons were raised and the teams doubled. As each wagon reached the other side, the extra oxen would be driven back across so they could be added on to other teams.

Nigh refused to let Brianna drive their wagon across, taking the whip himself while she sat beside him hanging on to the edges of the hard wooden seat. The river here was more than a thousand yards wide and, although the water was never more than three feet deep, the current was deceptively swift.

"We're lucky to be near the head of the train," Nigh told Brianna. "The more that cross over, the more the sand's likely to shift and create deep pockets for the cattle to flounder in or bust the wheels."

She glanced at him with surprise. "Why did you have them run the stock across first, then?"

"Gettin' trampled makes the river bed more stable. Don't guarantee the quicksand won't shift, though."

The wagon creaked and lurched as they started down the bank into the water. Nigh steered the team in a diagonal, downstream course for an easier crossing, giving most of his attention to keeping them moving. All went well until Marc's team, ahead of them, balked and came to a halt. Brianna gasped as Marc's wagon began to sink heavily on one side. The men stationed at strategic points across the river to watch out for such instances, shouted and rushed in to help. Nigh kept going.

"Stop, Col!" Brianna cried. "We've got to help Marc."

"We'd only get stuck, too." Nigh whipped up his team and moved them around the sinking wagon. Brianna scooted to the side of the seat and peered around the wagon cover to watch as they passed Marc. Tobias and Jeb Hanks had unhitched Marc's team and was driving it to a nearby sand bar. Marc stood in the wagon bed, handing out goods for others to carry over. When the wagon bed was empty, they took off the wheels, floated the box to the sand bar and began to put it all back together again. She breathed a sigh of relief when her own wagon lumbered up onto solid ground again.

The crossing took the remainder of the day. Camp was made on the north bank. Along about bedtime Brianna found Columbus Nigh standing between the wagons staring up at the moonless sky, his thumbs in his belt. Lucy Decker had left only moments before. Her girlish chatter had dominated the evening—and Col's attention—until Brianna was ready to scream. And knowing that she must leave during the night to make her way back to her husband did nothing to ease the pain of wondering if the flighty young miss would end up getting the man Brianna loved, once she was gone.

"What are you doing?" she asked, stepping up beside him.

He smiled down at her. "Praying for rain."

If Brianna shared his prayer, she pretended otherwise. Yet it did rain. Grinning, Col climbed into the wagon. He didn't bother making his bed, but stripped down to his breechclout and crawled in with her. She hadn't the strength to make him leave.

Long into the night he held her close, kissing and caressing her until she thought she would die of the strange, frenzied sensations he aroused in her. He was suckling her breast, one hand lazily stroking her stomach below her navel when she took his head in her hands and cried out, "Col, I can't bear any more. I ache so. Please, I think I'm going to explode."

"I ache, too, sweet woman. Sometimes I ache just looking at you. Let me love you, let me end this torture for both of us."

"I can't. It's adultery, and that's a sin."

"I told you, that bastard you're married to forfeited his rights."

"God didn't."

Col groaned. How could he argue with her when she brought God into it? To his way of thinking, the Lord had to be more understanding than that . . . and more forgiving. But he couldn't seem to convince her. "Then let me give you a release you can't dispute."

"How?"

"By touching you. That's all, just touching you." He moved his hand to the inviting valley between her legs. "Here, where you most need it."

"I-I don't know. I—"

He silenced her with a kiss. Slowly, with his hands and his lips, he brought her back to fever pitch. His body screamed for its own release, but he ignored its needs. When she was once again writhing beneath his hands and moaning with the agony of withheld satisfaction, he slipped his hand beneath her gown and gently caressed her thigh. Gradually, he worked his hand higher until he reached the moist heat he sought.

Groaning at the ecstasy of feeling her like that, so hot and eager for him, he took her nipple between his teeth, let it slide free, then suckled it hard while his fingers delved for the sweet secret recess his body so longed to plunder.

Brianna moaned as her body carried her to a higher plane of sensation. She was a star soaring through the sky, taking her to the very peak of existence. Her legs opened to him of their own accord. She arched and stiffened, expecting pain and finding only rapture. Her nails bit into his shoulders and her hips met the timeless rhythm of his caressing hand.

Col felt her shudder as the spasms of release took her over the edge into Eden. His lips stretched taut against his clamped teeth as he fought to maintain control over his own body. The need to take her was so strong, it was all he could do to keep from stripping off the confining clout and driving into her until he could find his own peace, his own Eden.

As their pulses slowed he cradled her in his arms, kissing her face and murmuring to her in Shoshone. Her eyes looking up at him were dazed yet with passion.

"Is . . . is what I felt. . . . Is that what happens when a man—?"

He laid his palm against her cheek and smiled down at her. "If the man knows what he's doing and cares for the woman, it is."

She turned her face into his palm and kissed the callused flesh. Then her fine brows drew together. "But you didn't. . . . Do you hurt now the way I did before . . . ?"

He closed his eyes and nodded. "But what you felt is better, more intense, when a man and woman are joined as they should be."

That was something too difficult to imagine. What concerned her more was knowing that he was in pain. "I-I don't want you to hurt, Col."

He opened his eyes and tipped up her chin so he could see into her heart. "Do you trust me enough to let me show you how much better it can be?"

How many times had her trust been violated? Even though—or perhaps because—her mother had died giving her life, she had trusted her father never to leave her the same way. Yet he had. She had trusted the man who offered her his name, his fortune, and his love. Only to learn that the Wight fortune had suffered greatly at Barret's hands. All he wanted was her inheritance to refinance the Wight Brewery, and all he gave in return was pain and terror. She had even trusted. . . . Who? God?

Fate? There, too, she had been let down when the child she'd prayed so hard for never came.

But she knew now that she didn't deserve anything good in life. Hadn't Barret told her that often enough? She was nothing but a big, ugly woman no one else wanted, a woman even life had seen fit to deny the normal feminine joys.

Well, if there was one thing she could handle in life it was pain. So what did she have to lose?

Brianna gazed up at Columbus Nigh's handsome face. For once the expression in his gray eyes was as clear and open as a summer sky. In their depths she saw need, but she also saw honesty and caring. Swallowing the sudden lump in her throat, she summoned up her courage and nodded.

Totally aware—even if she was not—of the priceless gift she offered, Col's heart squeezed, and he felt a tenderness for this woman deeper and stronger than he had believed possible.

He used that tenderness to make love to her, with his lips, his hands, and every fiber of his heart. Carefully, he stoked the fires still smoldering within their bodies, taking his time and feeding the flames bit by bit until they raged and leaped and roared.

Only when she whimpered and begged did he move over her, nudging her thighs apart with his knees. Then he took her hand and placed it on the rawhide thong that kept his clout tied about his hips.

Her eyes full of torment, she stared up at him. She knew what he was asking of her. He wanted her to prove her trust by releasing that thong.

Only Col knew that more would be bared than his masculine flesh. To do this would bare her soul, leave her wide open for all the pain she had come to expect from life. But only by forcing it to stand naked in the sun's burning rays could her fear be seared from her heart and the door be opened to the love and joy she sought.

Brianna felt for the end of the tie, and pulled.

Quickly Nigh swept the clout away. Then she felt the hot prod of his flesh between her legs. Supporting himself on his wrists he lifted himself above her and let his eyes take their fill of her. He bent and kissed each breast, the pulse in her throat as rapid and fragile as hummingbird wings, her eyes, her cheeks, her mouth.

With the care and ease of that same hummer, seeking nectar from the ruby throat of a Rocky Mountain rocket-flower, he entered her. He smiled at her gasp of pleasure. Smiled wider at her whimpered protest as he withdrew.

Teasing her with the tip of his tumescence, he whispered, "This is the only key that can open your door to heaven, woman." Then, baring his teeth in an expression of sweet agony, he threw back his head and plunged, crying out as he did so, "And I own it!"

Instinctively, Brianna met his thrusts with thrusts of her own. She wrapped her legs about his hips and her head thrashed from side to side on her pillow, moans issuing from deep inside her chest as time and again she was impaled on a burning shaft of the sun. When, teetering on the brink of the sun's inferno, she opened her mouth to scream, Col swallowed the sound with his mouth.

"Go on," he urged hoarsely. "The door to heaven is open. Escape. Now, woman! Now!"

Together they burst free.

When the spasms finally began to fade, he collapsed on her, burying his face in her hair. His heart pounded against her breast. He breathed in shuddering gasps. "Now, woman," he ground out, "even you can't argue that you belong to me. And I'll kill *any* man who touches you."

The next morning the wagons started up the high point of land called Windlass Hill which separated the South Platte from the North Platte. Sweeps of flowering blue lupine tinted the rolling land, complimenting the purple clouds scudding across the sky.

Nigh smiled lopsidedly and winked at Brianna. He laughed when she blushed, knowing she was remembering the pleasure he had given her the night before.

Ahead, at the summit, Jeb Hanks, Edward Magrudge, and others from the lead wagons were staring out across the vast plain, visible for the first time since they had left the valley of the South Platte.

It was like staring into the onslaught of night.

Col rode up to join the men, leaving Brianna behind. Overhead the light took on a dirty-yellow cast. The wind whipped Brianna's skirts about her legs in spite of the buckshot sewn in her hems. She laughed as she fought to hold them down.

In the distance, dark clouds rushed in wild confusion toward the hill where the emigrants stood watching. At the heart of the storm, lightning stabbed through the air, followed immediately by the loud crackle of thunder. Brianna gasped at the sight. The display was magnificent, savage and frenzied, like nothing she had ever seen before. The wind increased, tearing away her bonnet and loosening the hair from its knot at the back of her head. The roar grew in pitch until she thought she would go deaf. Then the rain began.

At the head of the wagon train, a few hundred yards

from Brianna, Col pointed to a whirling funnel, black as ink, at the heart of the storm, the small end pointed at the earth. "Tornado!" he shouted in Jeb's ear.

"Best get the folks to shelter," Jeb shouted back. "We're sitting ducks on this hilltop."

"There isn't time to get the wagons down off of here," Magrudge said.

Nigh was already heading for his horse. "I'm going after Brianna. Ride down the line fast as you can and tell everybody to get down to those trees in Ash Hollow. It's their only chance."

The unleashed power of the storm was awesome. Brianna watched, mesmerized by the grand display. Electric fire rent the air in jagged bolts with such ferocity it ricocheted from cloud to cloud and earth to sky and back again in vivid zigzag patterns against the dark background. Thunder splintered the air and rumbled with a force that shook the ground beneath her feet, while the wind drove the rain against her in horizontal sheets. The snapping of the wagon covers over their heads added to the din.

Pangs of fear licked at Brianna's nerves as she judged the power of the storm. She looked around to see the other people plastered to the sides of their wagons as she was. The storm was like nothing she had ever seen, but she knew it carried danger and death in its midst. The others were every bit as hypnotized by it as she had been. If they didn't find shelter, they would surely all be carried off by that swirling black funnel. The noise was too great to make herself heard. She would have to go to the next wagon to deliver her warning.

She was working her way toward the back of her wagon, hanging on as best she could, when suddenly Col was beside her on the gray.

"Gotta get off of here," he shouted as he reached for her.

"Tie the horse on the other side of the wagon," she yelled back. "We can get underneath or inside."

"That twister will blow these wagons to kingdom come. Give me your arm. We're getting out of here."

She was trying to climb inside the wagon. "I have to get Patch."

He spurred the gray around the corner of the wagon, not about to risk losing her now that he had finally won her. "Forget the damn cat. There's no time."

At the same moment that his arm came around her waist to lift her from the tailgate, she spied the kitten lying in Col's bedding and she scooped it up. In the next heartbeat she was seated in Col's lap, the cat nestled against her breast.

Col bent forward, forcing her down, too, as he whipped the horse into a gallop. Wagons flew past in a blur as they rode hard for the valley below. By the time they reached the crest of the hill both their voices were hoarse from screaming for the people to get down into the trees. Then they themselves were plunging down, the gray sliding, stumbling, in desperate haste to reach bottom.

They made it into a thick copse and skidded to a halt. Col leaped down and lifted Brianna to the ground. They flattened themselves against the earth among rose bushes and chokecherries. Patch cried and struggled to get free but Brianna clung to her.

Finally the wind and rain eased. The noise dimmed. Col raised himself up enough to see through the trees. "Tornado never even came near the hill. We're safe."

He lifted her back onto the horse and they headed back to the wagon. The roar of the wind sounded more distant now. Brianna felt something hard strike her arm. "It must be hailing."

"Black hail," Col said. "Come on."

Brianna bent her head to shield her face as they raced back to the trees. The hail hit with a force that stung their skin right through their clothes. Then Brianna screamed and began to flail at the biting pellets. It wasn't hail at all, but thousands of grasshoppers falling out of the clouds in the wake of the tornado. They clung to her dress and tangled in her hair. A live one slid beneath her neckline into the valley between her breasts. Frantically she clawed at her bodice, trying to get it off so she could get to the insect.

"Hold still," Col demanded. Quickly he tore the buttons from their holes and peeled the dress down. The hopper jumped free. "What's this?" he lifted a large button that hung on a bit of yarn around her neck.

"It-it's a button from Barret's nightshirt. I found it in my hand the morning I left St. Louis. It came off while he was hitting me and I kept it to remind myself of all I was running away from."

"Good idea." He replaced it where it had lain against her camisole. "Why haven't I seen it before?"

"I take it off at night when I wash up before bed."

He nodded. "Look at it a lot, Bri. I don't want you ever forgetting what that bastard did to you."

Another grasshopper struck her bare shoulder and bounced onto her breast. Col disengaged the insect from her camisole and pulled her dress back into place.

Within an hour the sky cleared, the air became still and the sun shone brightly, quickly drying what the rain had dampened. People emerged from their wagons, shaking their heads, muttering or chuckling about the strangeness of the storm. As they walked, dead grasshoppers crunched beneath their boots.

Brianna and Col made their way with the others, back up the hill to the crest where the land dropped nearly five hundred feet at a forty-five degree angle to the wooded glade below.

"Oh Col, how will we ever get the wagons down without losing them?"

"Probably will lose one or two."

"Gawdamighty, Magrudge!" bellowed Jim Lyon when he saw the drop-off. "Why didn't you find us a better route? Somebody's bound to lose everything they own tryin' to go down this hell-ride."

Magrudge glared at the man. Jim Lyon had done nothing but complain all the way from Independence. "You think you can find a better goddamn route, you're welcome to try."

The people gathered together around Magrudge and Hanks as the two men explained how they would lock the wheels with chains attached to the wagon boxes, then slowly lower the wagons down the hill on ropes. Everyone was ordered out of the wagons. There was too much chance of passengers being killed or badly maimed if a wagon broke loose.

Brianna stood to the side, chewing her lip as they got ready to take the first wagon down. Dulcie came to stand beside her. The two women held hands and prayed while the men, hanging onto the ropes holding the wagon, grunted and swore and sweated until the wagon had safely reached the bottom. The work was made all the more difficult and dangerous for the layer of slippery grasshopper bodies that covered the road. The owner drove off to the selected campsite and the men trudged back up the hill to do it all again. But before they began, the women hustled out with their brooms and swept the road clean.

Jim Lyon insisted on unloading a few of the family's more valuable possessions, while his wife, with her bulbous nose and flat chest, screeched and threatened and wailed dire predictions. The Lyons were impoverished "crackers" from southern Missouri and had barely met the requirements for inclusion in the train. They were short on food, cash, and common sense, Nigh had said on meeting them.

The Lyon wagon had skidded halfway down, the men hanging onto the ropes attached to the rear wheels, when a loud cracking sound was heard. The wagon lurched as the rear axle broke. The tail end dropped to the ground with a thud and scraped along fifty feet or more before one of the front wheels gave. Then the wagon tilted onto its side and rolled into a ravine. Bits and pieces splintered and flew off in every direction. Wind sailed scraps of clothes and bedding over the trees. A flour barrel bounced crazily over the rough ground until it crashed against a tree, spewing the white powder everywhere. The wagon came to rest upside down in the bottom of the wash in a cloud of dust and scattered goods.

Most of the members of the Magrudge Company considered it ironic that the Lyon wagon was the only one lost. Had the tragedy happened to any other family, the celebration that took place that night might not have been as gay. But each family loaned or donated goods to replace those that were destroyed. Then they sang and danced the night away, grateful to have survived the tornado and the harrowing rigors of Windlass Hill.

Edward Magrudge, standing with Punch Moulton,

watched Brianna laugh as Columbus Nigh attempted to teach her to dance. It seemed to Magrudge that the widow got prettier every day, especially smiling as she was right now. She had shed her widow's weeds and wore a dress of blue calico she had sewn herself. The scooped neckline and the shirring that began below her full breasts and ended at the pointed waistline, emphasized the perfection of her figure. She was no longer gaunt, but deliciously voluptuous. His loins ached, just looking at her.

Punch elbowed him in the side, grinning. "Hey, got a hankerin' fer a piece of that widow, have ya?"

Magrudge glowered at the man. "Naw, ain't my type."

"Whoo! That high-class bitch snubbed you, did she? Hell, you shoulda expected that, Magrudge."

"Can't be too high class and have Nigh for a brother."

For some reason Magrudge couldn't understand, Punch thought that particularly funny. Incensed, Magrudge stomped away. Punch would stop laughing when he saw the uppity Widow Villard beg for Magrudge's favors. And that's just what she'd do once he showed her what a real man like himself could do for her. Her late husband had likely been a milksop who'd let her run things. What she needed was a real man, and Magrudge was the one.

He'd noticed the way Nigh had taken to slipping from camp at night, not returning till morning. Maybe he'd found himself a woman in another train. That suited Magrudge fine. He'd be watching. Next time Nigh went courting, Magrudge would pay the widow a visit. And this time there'd be no goldarned cat to louse things up. Not a full-grown one, anyway.

Chapter Twenty-three

Brianna fanned her hot face with her hand. "Please, can we sit this one out? I'm exhausted."

Col led her out of the twirling throng and seated her on a flour barrel. "You were just getting the hang of it."

"Maybe, but I'll never dance as well as Lucy Decker."

He turned to watch the Decker girl dance with her brother. Her flying skirts offered a glimpse of slim ankles and firm calves. Brianna frowned, scolding herself for opening her big mouth.

As if feeling Col's eyes on her, Lucy glanced over. Instantly she broke from her brother's grasp and pranced over to them. "Come on." She took Col's hands in hers and pulled him toward the other dancers. "You haven't danced with me once tonight."

Giving Brianna a helpless shrug, he let the girl drag him away.

Brianna couldn't bear watching them. She sauntered over to the table the ladies had loaded down with pots of coffee, roast beef from a cow someone butchered when it broke its leg coming down off Windlass Hill, rabbit stew, golden brown biscuits, corn bread, jam and preserves, salad made with dandelion leaves, lamb's quarter, and dock, baked beans, vinegar pies, rough-and-ready cake, and pitchers of sorghum.

Someone had flavored the water with a precious supply of honey, she discovered when she helped herself to a glass. But it failed to dispel the bitterness of seeing Col leave the dancers and disappear into the darkness with young, pretty Lucy Decker.

Brianna left the party behind and wandered toward her wagon, wondering if she could steal some of the food and hide it to take with her when she snuck away that night after everyone was asleep.

What were Col and Lucy doing alone out in the trees? Was he kissing her as he had kissed Brianna last night?

When she reached the wagon, she found she was too restless to go to bed. She sat on a stump and stared at the smoldering remains of the cookfire, wondering how the tangle of her life would ever unsnarl itself.

She had been a fool to give in to Col. Unless he had already tired of her, unless someone like Lucy stole him away from her, he would never let Brianna go now. Someday Barret would catch up with her and then there would be hell to pay. Someone, she greatly feared, would die. The thought that it could be Col sent her abruptly to her feet.

Just as gunfire exploded in her ear.

"This is far enough, Lucy. Go ahead, talk."

Nigh watched the girl fidget with the tips of the shawl she had draped over her shoulders as they stepped beyond the wagons and away from the heat of the bonfire.

Lucy turned to the side so he could see her blond hair

tumbling down her back. She had learned long ago that men found it difficult to resist her hair. She gave her head a slight shake so that her curls bounced. "I only wanted to be alone with you."

He stuck his thumbs in the back of his belt and shifted his weight to his left foot. "What for?"

She turned to face him then. "You've been nice to me, and . . . and I wanted to tell you how much it's meant to me." She moved closer, letting her shawl slip from her shoulders as she reached up to put her hands on his chest. "I like you, Col, I like you a lot. Don't you like me a little?"

"What exactly do you want, Lucy?"

On tiptoes she kissed him square on the mouth.

He shoved her away. "You little fool, you got the slightest idea what you're doing?"

Anger flashed through her eyes, so brief he wondered if he truly saw it. Then her expression filled with pain.

"No, I don't," she said, her voice choking slightly. "I love you so much I don't know what to do, but you obviously don't care 'bout me at all. Go back to the party, Col, go back and forget the fool I've made of myself over you."

Sobbing, she rushed off into the darkness.

Nigh cursed. He'd had no idea she had taken such a notion about him. She was too young to even know what love was. Damn! He couldn't simply go off and leave her hurting the way she was; no figuring what she'd do. With a sigh, he started after her.

Then he heard the distant shot.

* * *

Lucy was panting by the time she reached the stream. She stopped and listened, then smiled at the sound of footsteps hurrying in her direction. Col had followed as she had prayed he would. She ripped her dress off over her head, stripped off her petticoats and was lifting her chemise when a man burst from the bushes and came to a dead stop in front of her, a rifle in his hand.

Punch Moulton looked quickly about. The girl was practically naked. And alone. "Well, well, what you doin' out here, sugar? You waitin' fer me?"

Lucy smiled, her mind working quickly. He wasn't Columbus Nigh but he could give her the means to get her the man she wanted. All she had to do was get herself pregnant and name Col as the father. Her parents would see to it he did right by her.

When Nigh reached Brianna's wagon, he found Lavinia Decker fussing over her while Dulcie Moulton brought her a cup of tea thick with cream. Several men stood about, guns in their hands, staring out into the night.

"What happened?" Nigh demanded.

"Somebody almost shot your sister."

Nigh's gaze met Brianna's over the steaming cup.

Tobias Woody emerged out of the darkness. "Didn't see nobody. Hanks is still looking. Don't imagine it was nothing more than an accident. Heck, there's been plenty of folks shot accidentally the last few months, and there's no sign of Injuns."

"Huh!" muttered Jim Lyon. "How can he be certain in the dark and all? Sure as shootin' we're gonna get scalped in our beds tonight."

Abner Goodman hawked and spat. "I say we post guards. Maybe a few of us should fan out and search a bit farther."

"Yeah, where's Punch? He'll wanna be in on this."

Hanks, with Magrudge close behind, pushed his way through the crowd. "No need to panic. Varmint's gone now, but it weren't no Injun, that I gar-an-tee."

"How in thunder can you do that?"

Hanks raised his hand for silence. "You hear any dogs yapping? If thar was Injuns yonder, ever' hound in camp'd be raising a ruckus fit to wake the dead. Dogs cain't stand Injun stink."

The men listened and glanced around. An owl hooted upriver. From across the murmuring river came a faint reply. Crickets chirped. A burning log popped and crackled. All else was silence. Reluctantly they tucked their pistols back into their belts.

"Go on about yer business," Hanks said. "Gonna lay over tomorry so's the women kin wash n' such, this bein' the first good water we've come acrossed in days. Enjoy the rest."

"Praise the Lord!" Lavinia Decker bellowed.

The others muttered agreement and began to wander off.

"What happened?" Nigh asked Brianna when they were alone.

She stared at him, her eyes large and luminous in the lantern light.

"Like Tobias said, someone accidentally fired their gun and it just happened I was nearly in the way." She shuddered, remembering the rush of air on her ear as the bullet sped past.

He stared at her as though he didn't quite swallow her

story. Angry that she should feel guilty for not telling him about Barret's threat after the way Col had gone off with Lucy Decker she glared at him. "I'm fine. Why don't you go back to your new little plaything and leave me alone."

"What are you talking about?"

His eyes were blazing. A voice in the back of her head told her here was her chance to keep him safe. By keeping him away from her. That shot in the dark had shown her how foolish it would be to try going anywhere alone. Swollen rivers, tornados, wolves. How could she possibly protect herself from all the danger waiting out there?

"Keep away from me, Col. I-I'm ashamed of what happened last night. I feel dirty, as though I was one of your squaws."

She knew the words would hurt him. But the pain so clear in his face was like a lance in her heart. She wanted desperately to take the words back.

Col stared at her, seeing the mortification and the regret in her eyes. Regret that she had let a squawman touch her.

"Please," she begged, closing her heart to his pain. "I can't bear being around you after . . . after. . . . Just go, please."

She jerked herself from his grasp and climbed into the wagon, tying the cover tightly closed behind her.

Nigh kicked viciously at the wagon wheel. Cursing, he stomped off to find Jeb Hanks. The old mountain man would have a jug of whiskey hidden somewhere in his plunder, and Nigh felt a powerful thirst coming on.

The next day dawned bright and clear. The smell of lye soap pervaded the camp as women scrubbed several days worth of grime from clothes and bedding. Those who had space to carry it loaded up on firewood. Men repaired tack, tarred their hubs, rearranged loads, mended ropes. Children squealed as they played, dogs yapped. A high, sweet voice sang "Maryland, My Maryland." A rich, low voice countered with "My Old Kentucky Home."

Nigh woke with an aching head and a parched tongue. His mouth tasted like old Hanks had fed him horse droppings with his liquor the night before. Nigh opened his eyes to find the grizzled old man peering at him from across a small fire. Hanks chuckled at the expression on Nigh's face. He poured coffee into a tin cup, added a dollop of whiskey, and brought it to Nigh.

"Lookee here, old hoss, best get some hair o' the dog in ya 'fore ya crawl away t' lick yer wounds."

Nigh accepted the coffee and blew on the dark, steamy liquid to cool it. Hanks sat back down across the fire, his legs crossed Indian style.

"Wanna talk 'bout it?" Hanks asked.

Nigh lifted a questioning eyebrow at the old man.

"I know, it's a unwritten law in the mountains that a man don't ask personal questions. But when ya been around long as I have, there's things ya figure out." Hanks swilled the last of his coffee and set down the cup. He picked up his rifle and proceeded to swab the barrel with a cleaning rag and his wiping stick. "Ain't got no sister, have ya?"

Two girls raced past, screaming. Behind them came Tommy Shorthill waving a fat frog. Nigh sipped his coffee and kept quiet. Hanks saw the twitch in Nigh's jaw and knew his words had rekindled the anger the man had come to him with the night before. Hanks also knew Nigh wanted to hear what else he had to say.

"Had me a wife once. Didn't know that, did ya?"

"She was a Crow and a damned good lookin' one, if I remember right," Nigh said in hard, tight voice.

"Naw, before that. 'Fore I come to the mountains. Her name was Mary. Pretty as a sunrise over the Wind Rivers, she was. Sweet, too." Hanks shook his head and Nigh saw the wistfulness in the rheumy old eyes. "Mary died birthin' me a son. Boy died too. Point is, this old coon knows whut it's like to have a good woman. Knows a good 'un when he sees it, too. You're a dang fool, if you let that widder get away."

"Don't reckon to let her get away."

"Then whut in thunder ya doin' spending the night drinkin' trade whiskey with an old man like me fer?"

Nigh lumbered to his feet. If that was all the snoopy old buzzard had to say, he'd heard enough. He needed to dunk his head in cold spring water and clear the fog out of his thinker. Somehow he had to make Brianna see sense before it was too late. "There's more to this than you know, Jeb."

"Ya mean like the fact she's still got a husband, an' that the husband's been followin' us fer days now?"

Nigh stared at the man, then snorted. "You worthless old crow bait, shoulda known better'n to try to fool you."

Hanks kept on swabbing out his rifle. "If that big German keeps shootin' like he did last night, you'll likely be safe, but I wouldn't count on it. Best you go plug his lights fer 'im or you'll find yerself sleepin' with me the rest of the trip."

"The hell I will! Besides, I'm not sure it was the German last night. Figure he's got help right here in camp."

"Yeah, Punch Moulton. Now there's a polecat fer ya. Weren't fer him, might could smell the roses round here."

Nigh chuckled. Hanks might be getting old, but he

hadn't lost any of his Indian sense yet. No one would ever put anything over on Jeb Hanks. "I'm not sure he's the only polecat on this train. Keep an eye on him, though, and I'll take care of Brianna."

"I jest bet you will."

Nigh headed for the wagon. Hanks was right, there were wild roses blooming along the creek bed and around the springs, as well as currents and chokecherries. The scent of the roses reminded him of Brianna and his feet picked up speed.

When he spied her, he had to swallow disappointment. She was surrounded by a dozen women, washing clothes in boiling pots over fires built along the creek. He stopped to watch and she looked up after a moment. Her chin came up, her back stiffened and her eyes darkened to sapphire. He went on to the wagon and set about seeing to his own chores while he waited for a chance to talk with her.

It wasn't until after the noon meal that Nigh managed to get Brianna alone. She'd been as cold as Patch's nose toward him all morning and he was losing patience. After all, she was the one who refused to cooperate and do what was necessary to get free of the bastard she was married to. She had a bee up her bottom, that was sure, but he had a hunch it had nothing to do with his previous wife, and he was determined to find out what had brought on her temper.

Brianna had lain awake most of the night, crying and waiting for him to come back. More than once she had gotten up and started to dress so she could go find him. The fear that he was with Lucy kept her in the wagon. Over and over she assured herself she had done the right thing to protect him from Barret.

How she wished she knew exactly how Col felt about her. More than anything in the world, she wanted his love. And he had acted as though he did love her, when he looked at her, when he touched her.

Yet he'd gone off into the dark with that Lucy Decker. What had they been doing when the shot was fired? Why had it taken so long for him to reach the wagon? Had he been touching Lucy's young body the way he'd touched hers? Had he been making love to Lucy?

Brianna had tried to push away such thoughts when they came to her in the wee hours of the morning. But she knew he had not come back. Where had he slept? The question haunted her all morning. Then she had seen him. Bits of dirt and grass clung to his rumpled buckskins as though he'd slept on bare ground. His hair was disheveled, his eyes bloodshot and tired. He looked like he hadn't slept either. In fact, if she didn't know better she might think he'd been drinking all night. Had he been drunk on something other than alcohol? Like Lucy Decker's love?

Now he stood before her, his big hands tucked into the back of his belt, his weight on his left leg, the way he always stood when facing down trouble.

"You ready to talk sense to me?" he asked.

She poured hot water from the fire into her dishpan and added cold till it was cool enough to use. Then she slid the dirty tin plates and silver into the pan. "I told you how I felt last night. What else is there to say?"

"Dammit, woman, there's something going on here you're not telling me about. Now put those dishes down and talk to me."

She scrubbed a plate clean and set it aside. "Did you enjoy yourself last night?"

He looked at her, dumfounded. "Yeah, till the damn trouble started. What's that got to do with anything?"

"You're never going to learn to speak without cursing, are you?"

Nigh lifted his arms and his eyes to the heavens. What was he to do with her? Striving for control, he put his hands on her shoulders and turned her to face him. "Bri, what are you afraid of? What hold has Wight got over you? Please, talk to me."

"I don't know what you're talking about." She pulled from his grasp, picked up the wash pan and dumped the soapy water on the ground, nearly soaking his moccasins. "I asked you last night to stay away from me. Perhaps I should make it more clear. You're fired, Mr. Nigh. I'll get you your pay and you can go on your way."

She headed for the wagon, but he didn't wait to see what she would do. He had to get away from her or they were both likely to be sorry for what he might do.

Brianna watched him stalk off to his horse and gallop away. Then she climbed into the wagon, lay down on the bed, and cried.

"Goddamn no-good mules!"

Up one hill after another, Barret Wight trotted his sorrel, then stopped to scan the horizon for sign of his pack mules. When he heard the sound of hoofbeats in the next draw, he hurried that direction, hoping it would be one of the stubborn blasted animals.

"Hou!"

The stranger approaching on a dappled gray gelding was tall and lean with a body that had known hard work, and was as strong and tough and supple as old rawhide.

He wore a pistol in his belt and carried a rifle in a scabbard made of leather with bead work along the opening and fringe a foot long.

Barret eyed the handsome scabbard and wondered if the man could be parted from it without bloodshed. Then he looked into the man's eyes, as gray and ominous as the clouds scudding across the western sky. Hard and sharp, like tempered steel. The man's mouth was a grim slash in his weathered face. A sliver of wood protruded from one corner.

A mountain man, Barret thought. He had seen men like him before in the public room of his brewery, men who had survived years of dealing with savages and grizzly bears in what they called The Shining Mountains where few civilized men had set foot and lived to tell about it. Dangerous men only a fool would cross. Barret decided the scabbard wasn't so handsome after all.

"Lost?" the stranger asked.

"No, my mules ran off. Haven't seen them, have you?"

The man shook his shaggy head. "Seen Injuns, though. Ain't wise, you bein' out here alone."

Barret looked about nervously. He'd had all the run-ins he wanted with Indians. "I've got a partner around here somewhere. He's looking, too. If we don't find our mules, we'll be stranded."

"You got a horse and a rifle. Hang onto your hair and you'll be all right." The man nodded curtly and rode off.

"Yeah, sure." Barret gave a disgruntled snort. Easy enough for a man like that to say all he needed was a horse and rifle. Probably wouldn't know what to do with a bed or a chair if he had one. Barret didn't try to fool himself into thinking he was as tough as the stranger, or that it would be as easy for him to survive, living off this empty land.

Columbus Nigh allowed himself to snicker at the bumbling greenhorn he'd just left, once he was out of earshot.

When he'd set out that morning, Col had had it in his head to kill the man. But every mile he rode, he heard Brianna's voice telling him she'd never be able to live with him if he killed her husband. It was looking less and less like she would ever live with him anyway, after last night. Unfortunately, that didn't stop him from wanting her. And no matter how much he bounced the matter around inside his head, he couldn't convince himself to give up his dream of making her his wife.

Still, on first sight of the man, the need to feel his hands around Wight's throat and see the life fade from his sadistic eyes, was almost too strong to resist.

To see Wight roaming the plain in search of the mules Nigh himself had picked out for him back at Fort Kearny, helped ease the disappointment of not being able to kill the man.

Wight had already fallen a good distance behind the Magrudge wagon train and there was more than an even chance that the mules he sought were being roasted over some Indian's fire at that very moment. By the same token, it wouldn't hurt any to drop by Wight's camp to make sure things were in order.

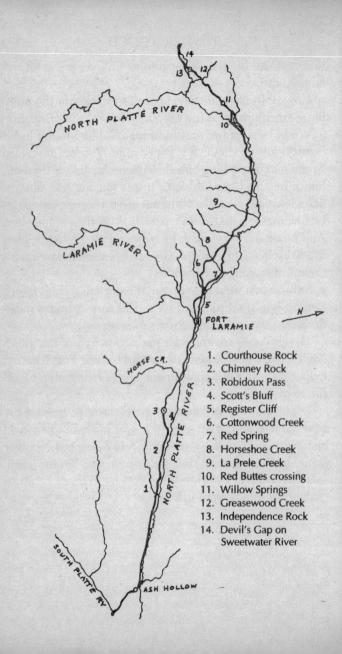

1. Courthouse Rock
2. Chimney Rock
3. Robidoux Pass
4. Scott's Bluff
5. Register Cliff
6. Cottonwood Creek
7. Red Spring
8. Horseshoe Creek
9. La Prele Creek
10. Red Buttes crossing
11. Willow Springs
12. Greasewood Creek
13. Independence Rock
14. Devil's Gap on
    Sweetwater River

Chapter Twenty-four

After Columbus rode off, Brianna spent the day helping Marc sort out Lilith's things. Until Brianna pointed out that the Lyon family, who had lost their wagon on Windlass Hill, could use the extra Beaudouin wagon, Marc hadn't been able to bring himself to even look at his wife's personal belongings.

Marc insisted Brianna keep anything she wanted. She chose a bonnet, a few pieces of jewelry and Lilith's embroidery basket. Lilith's clothes were divided among the women on the train who were closer to her size. When that was done, the loads in Marc's two wagons were rearranged and the empty one driven over to the Lyon camp.

The noon meal passed without any sign of Nigh. Lavinia Decker dropped by, complaining that her daughter had stayed out until the wee hours of the morning and refused to say where she had been. Brianna couldn't help wondering if the fact that both Col and Lucy were missing most of the night could be a coincidence. Brianna's anger toward him turned to despair. How could she fight Lucy's youth, her pretty looks, and her availability?

Weary and dispirited, Brianna spent an hour playing with Patch and fighting off her fear. Only last evening, the world had seemed so sunny. She had shed her somber widow's weeds and worn the new dress she'd made to please Col. His eyes on her had been warm and tender. She looked more beautiful than ever, he'd told her. But he hadn't said he loved her. Not once had he ever said that. It should tell her something, she supposed.

Restless, she wandered the camp, sharing a cup of coffee and bit of gossip here and there. She couldn't say how she ended up in Jeb Hanks camp.

"Hou, ma'am." The old mountain man stood before her, bow-legged and bent. "Do sumpthin' fer ya?"

She smiled. Jeb Hanks and Col had ridden together back in their beaver-trapping days. Perhaps she could get him to tell her what he knew about Col, and about Little Beaver, too.

"You got sumpthin' on your mind, 'pears to me," Hanks said when she remained silent. "Whyn't you jest spit it out?"

She blushed. "Am I that transparent?"

"Not to most, I reckon. But most ain't been knockin' round this old world as long as me."

"I see." She couldn't help smiling. Hanks was unique and she liked him. "Maybe . . . well, could you tell me about Col's life in the mountains? He isn't fond of talking about himself and. . . ."

Hanks gave her a knowing smile that had nothing to do with his reply. "Most o' the men I've knowed since leaving the States behind are reluctant to talk 'bout their pasts fer one reason or t'other. Some's running from the law, some jest like being alone. Reckon Col's like that, don't take t' crowds much."

"Did you know his wife?"

"Little Beaver? Purdy little thing, she was. Young, too. They wasn't together long."

"Did he love her a great deal?"

"Have t' ask him that. Col saved her pappy's life in a Blackfoot raid, took an arrow in his side doin' it. Old Chief Yeller Feather took Col back to his lodge an' Little Beaver nursed him back to health. When Col was ready to leave, the chief give 'im the girl as his wife. Wouldn't a done fer Col to refuse, you know. Bad manners. Took good care of her, though, an' he felt powerful bad when she was kilt."

"How did she die?"

Hanks gave her a long, searching look as though trying to make up his mind about something, then wagged his grizzled head. "Reckon knowin' that'd go a long ways in helpin' ya understand the man, but ya oughta ask 'im yerself. Ask 'im how he lost his little finger, that'll get 'im started."

The little finger with the missing joint! Those first few weeks on the trail, Brianna had wondered how Col had lost the joint. She hadn't had the nerve to ask then. Later, she became so used to it she didn't even notice it anymore. Now she realized, from Jeb Hanks suggestion, that the missing joint had something to do with Little Beaver's death, and she was more curious than ever.

Brianna was preparing for bed when she heard someone call out a greeting to Col. Quickly, she snatched his bedding out of the wagon and stuffed it underneath. Then she climbed inside. She put out the lantern and tied both ends of the wagon cover tightly closed. After what seemed forever, Nigh came to the foot of the wagon and called out

to her. Only Patch mewed in answer. Brianna pretended
to be asleep.

Col cursed and crawled under the wagon, bumping his
head on the wagon hounds. More cursing followed, two
thuds as his boots hit the ground, the rustle of bedding,
and finally silence. With a sigh that was half-relief, half-
regret, Brianna rolled onto her side and pounded her
pillow into a more comfortable lump.

"Don't know what nonsense you got in your craw,
woman," he muttered through the floor of the wagon.
"But you best be ready to talk about it tomorrow."

Talk about it? Confess that she was trying to save his
life? Or ask him outright if he spent last night making love
to Lucy Decker? Never.

To end her relationship with Col might kill her. But
that would be better than seeing him murdered by her
husband. Even losing him to Lucy would be easier to take
than his death. No matter how it all ended, Brianna felt
as though her own life was already over.

At midnight a light rain began to fall. Lying awake in
her bed, Brianna heard Nigh curse and turn over in his
bed. Turning her face into her pillow, she cried.

Barret returned from his mule hunt weary and irate, to
find his camp a shambles. It appeared as though it had
been torn apart by a pack of wolves. Goods lay scattered
for fifty yards in every direction. The bacon and dried
meat was gone. Flour whitened the earth like deposits of
alkali and coffee lay in small dark heaps like deer pellets.
There was no sign of the mules, or of Stinky.

Without pack mules or goods, there was nothing he
could do but wait for morning and try to buy supplies

from passing emigrants. His empty stomach grumbled as
he wrapped himself in his blankets and tried to sleep.

The Magrudge Company's wagons were ferried across
the Laramie River for two dollars per wagon. From there
they travelled barren hills and sandy ravines until they
reached the high plain where the long, upward haul
began that would lead them to the famed Rocky Mountains.

At Cottonwood Creek, heavy rain drove them into an
early camp. Ravines, dry minutes before, ran high with
floodwater. Cook pots and saddles shielded the emigrants
from a barrage of hail the size of horse dung. By nightfall
the sky cleared and the air became pleasant.

The next morning Brianna placed a few twigs on last
night's coals and blew hard until a tiny flame shot up. The
flame was as weak and tepid as she felt.

Hot days, cold nights, wind, dust, insects, and tension
had taken their toll. Like most of the other emigrants, her
face was so lumpy with gnat bites she looked as though
she had smallpox. She tongued grit from one side of her
mouth to the other and thought longingly of a hot bath.
Last evening's rain had not lasted long enough to lay the
dust, meaning that today would be as miserable as yesterday.

As the fire caught, she added buffalo chips, then prepared coffee. Col was nowhere to be seen. He'd spent the
past week driving stock or scouting with Jeb Hanks. Even
when he was in camp, he barely spoke to her. It had been
that way since Ash Hollow when she locked him out of the
wagon.

Lucy Decker was more cheerful than ever. Even Dulcie

seemed happier, confiding to Brianna that Punch had been leaving her alone more lately, even in bed.

If Col was suffering the same agony as Brianna, he gave no clue, while she rode a teeter-totter of anger and despair. There had been no sign of Barret and no more "accidental" shots in her direction. Her determination to protect Col by keeping him away from her was waning. She missed him. And she needed him.

As though summoned by her thoughts, she saw him driving their oxen toward camp. Marc, Francois, and Jean Louis were close behind with their own oxen.

"Breakfast will be ready soon," she told them as she set bacon to frying.

"Ate with the Deckers." Nigh positioned the first pair of oxen and placed the yoke across their necks.

"The boys and I didn't," Marc put in cheerfully.

Brianna ignored Marc. She rounded on Nigh, hands fisted on her hips. "Ate with the Deckers? Or just Lucy? Why don't you eat supper with her as well. Sleep with her, too, if you haven't already. And while you're at it, you can just. . . . Oh, just get out of here! And take these blasted insects with you!" She flapped her hands at the cloud of mosquitoes hovering around her and stomped off.

"Papa?" Jean Louis tugged at his father's hand. "Is Brianna angry about something?"

"Uh, why don't we go visit the Woodys?" Marc took the boy's hand and motioned for Francois to come along. "We don't see Tobias much now that we don't need him to drive the extra wagon."

"But, Papa—"

After they were gone, Nigh dug into his possibles bag and pulled out a small pouch. He walked down to the creek and found Brianna on the damp grass along the bank, sobbing into her hands. Hunkering beside her, he took off his kerchief and held it out. She turned her back to him, sniffed, sniffed again, and took the kerchief. When she had blown her nose, he handed her the pouch.

"What's this?" she asked.

"It'll keep the insects away."

"But what is it?"

"Bear grease."

"It smells awful."

"Works, though."

"Did you smear some on your precious Lucy?"

"You angry because I ate with the Deckers?"

"Should I be?"

She got up and marched back to camp. Muttering about the contrariness of females, Nigh followed. Ignoring him, Brianna took a sack of flour from the wagon. She set it on the table, reached inside and made a depression in the white powder with her fist. Then she poured in a little water and mixed up a batch of biscuit dough right there in the sack—a trick she learned from Lavinia to save time and dirty dishes.

"You're the one made it plain I wasn't wanted round here." He poured himself some coffee and sat down.

The words stung. She longed to tell him it wasn't because that was how she wanted it. Instead, she tore off a small chunk of dough and gave it a vicious squeeze, as though it were his neck. "Didn't hear you complain."

"Do any good if I did?"

In answer, she kneaded the dough viciously. Then she cut and slapped biscuits onto a pan and shoved the pan into the reflector oven.

Col rose and took her by the arms, forcing her to face him. "You gonna tell me what this is really all about?"

"I thought I fired you. Why are you hanging around here, pestering me?"

His hands fell from her arms as though he'd been stung. "All right, woman. You want to get rid of me? Fine. I'm gone."

With that he stormed off.

A minute later, Marc came from his wagon next door. He shuffled his feet, shoved his hands in his pockets and took them out again. "Brianna, you were Lilith's best friend," he said finally. "You did all you could to keep her alive. I'll be grateful to you for the rest of my life for that. Now something is dreadfully wrong between you and another very good friend of mine. I know it's none of my business, but I'd like to help, if I can."

She looked at his kind face, and the temptation to confide in him was strong. He was a good man and meant well, but she wasn't sure she could trust him not to repeat her every word to Columbus. That was something she could not risk. It would only send him after Barret, possibly to his death.

"I appreciate your concern, Marc. But, as you said, it's none of your business." She heaved a sigh and added softly, "There's nothing you can do, anyway. There's nothing anyone can do."

Not long after the wagon train got underway that day, Tobias Woody showed up, telling Brianna that Nigh had sent him to relieve her from driving.

"Did he say why?" she asked.

"No, and I didn't ask."

It was obvious she wasn't going to get any answers from the young man. Angry and frustrated, she tied on her bonnet, settled Patch inside the wagon and started walking while Tobias cracked the whip over the oxens' backs and drove the wagon. In a few minutes Nigh rode up on the dappled gray. He had a black gelding in tow. "Climb on, we're going for a ride."

His tone warned against arguing with him, but she thrust out her chin and said, "Where?"

"You'll find out. Just get on the horse or I'll put you on, and let me warn you, woman, I'm not feeling very gentle at the moment."

"No, Col. I can't go off with you. Someone might see, might. . . ."

"Might what? Who?"

She blinked back the tears that threatened. "Don't you understand, he . . . you. . . . Oh, damn!"

Furious and frustrated, knowing he'd do as he promised, Brianna threw herself onto the black, not caring that her skirts were hiked up and her stockinged calves showed. He stared at her only a moment, then turned and kicked the gray into a trot.

They soon left the train behind, heading north. He led her through a maze of small hills and ravines, then into a deep valley entirely surrounded by towering perpendicular rocks. High overhead a family of hawks soared in wide, lazy circles. Brianna tipped back her head, her eyes shielded by her hand as she watched them.

Nigh followed no trail, yet he seemed to know exactly where he was going. Finally, they entered a small canyon. A spring gushed out of the rock to form a deep pool and a narrow stream that emptied eventually into the North Platte. The floor of the canyon was carpeted in rich green. Ground squirrels scampered through the grass, stopping now and then to stand on their hind legs and stare at the intruders. Yellow warblers sang from the willows and robins stalked fat worms along the bank. White yarrow and yellow cinqfoil bloomed in the meadow. It was like a private, hidden heaven.

"Oh, Col, it's wonderful," Brianna cried, jumping down from her horse, her anger forgotten in her enthusiasm. "How did you find it?"

He watched her turn in a full circle, taking in everything, the high rock walls embracing the green meadow, the bright flowers bending with the breeze, the birds and rodents. Her smile was as big as the moon still riding the western sky. In spite of the dust and insect bites covering her face, he thought her the most beautiful sight of all. An ache started in his heart and worked its way to his groin.

The days since their last night together on the South Platte had become a torture he endured only by staying where he couldn't see her. The nights, even though he had worn himself ragged, were impossible. Only stubborn pride kept him from sneaking into her wagon after the others had gone to bed. All he had to do was close his eyes and he could feel her silky flesh beneath his hand. He could taste her, smell her.

At odd times of the day and night he would remember the delicate arch of her brows, the tiny mole on her neck at the collar line, the way the loose hair at her nape and temples curled as sweat dampened them, the graceful, loose-wristed way she fanned the flames when she started a fire, or the shy, hungry glances she sent his way when she thought he wasn't looking.

The idea that she might want him, love him, as much as he wanted her, seemed as far-fetched as Jim Bridger's yarn of petrified birds singing in petrified trees on the lower Yellowstone River. He hadn't opened his heart to her because he thought she could learn to love him, but because he'd had no choice.

She had become like air to him, like food and water and sleep. And he'd be damned if he'd let her drive him away for no good reason.

But he'd have to handle her exactly right. It would be like gentling her all over again. He didn't mind. Especially when she smiled at him the way she was smiling at him now.

"Stumbled onto this place some years back." His low drawl hid the racing, thudding ache in his chest, and the desire that sent blood rushing to his groin. "Thought you might like a bath."

"A bath, oh, yes." She hurried over to the pool and knelt to test the water. After the hot days they'd been suffering, it felt deliciously cool to her fingers.

Nigh dismounted and left the horses to graze on the lush grass. She was trying to reach the buttons on the back of her dress when she felt him brush away her hands and undo the top button himself. She jerked away and turned to eye him warily.

"Wait a minute. Why are you being so considerate of me all of a sudden?"

"Ain't treating you no differently than I ever have."

She couldn't argue that. "All right. Why are you being nice after how rotten I've been to you lately?"

His mouth quirked. "Have you been rotten?"

"You know I have. Now what are you up to?" She glanced at the pool and back at him. "You brought me here so you could get me naked and seduce me, didn't you?"

"Sounds like a right good idea," he said, grinning.

He looked so handsome, it was impossible to hang onto her anger. She closed her eyes and dredged up the vision of him dancing with Lucy. "If you wanted sex, you should have brought Lucy instead of me."

"Dammit, woman, I don't want Lucy." He started toward her, his hands fisted. "I want you and I damn well intend to have you."

She backed up, holding up a hand to fend him off. "Lucy was good enough for you in Ash Hollow. You can't have her and then come running back to me just because you got tired of her."

His words seethed from between his clenched teeth. "I never had Lucy. Not that night, nor any other night."

Her foot sank into water as she reached the edge of the pool. He had her trapped. There was nowhere to go. With both arms out-held in entreaty, she cried, "Col? Col, what are you going to do?"

He stopped two arms lengths away. "I'm going to give you a choice. You can take your clothes off and start bathing. Or I'll rip your clothes off and have you as you are right here on the ground."

"What . . . what are you going to do while I bathe?"

"Take my own bath."

"No! I-I want you to go away."

He shook his head, kicked off one moccasin, then the other.

"But. . . ." She crossed her arms over her breasts in a gesture of such maidenly modesty that he laughed.

"Seen you naked before, woman." He took his gun from his waistband and set it on the grass. Then flipped off his possibles bag. His slow drawl and sleepy, slitted eyes were so sultry and sensual, she felt her blood heat and her pulse quicken.

"I've had my hands on nearly every inch of your body." His belt dropped and he reached for the hem of his shirt. "I've tasted your mouth, your ears, your neck."

The shirt hit the ground and he stepped closer. Her knees turned to pudding. "I've touched you where no man will ever touch you again."

He yanked on the thong that held up his leggings, let them fall, then stepped out of them as gracefully as a cat in a puddle. "I've suckled your breasts, woman, and I intend to suckle them again. Here. Now."

One more step brought him up against her hands, naked except for his clout. Her head shook back and forth as she tried to deny the power in his gaze, in the muscles bulging from his chest, shoulders and arms, in his very stance.

Reaching out he took her hand and guided it to the tie on his clout.

She stared at him, her brow furrowed as though she couldn't believe what he expected of her.

"Do it," he said in that quiet, dangerous voice that told her he'd reached the limit of his patience.

Taking the thong in her hand, her gaze held by the turbulent storm in his, she yanked. The clout slipped, hung for a moment on his swollen member, then fell.

"Now turn around," he told her.

She turned and felt his hands on the buttons down her back. He parted the fabric as he went and placed his warm, moist mouth on her bared skin. She sucked in her breath and bit her lip to keep from moaning with the pleasure of his touch.

When the last button had been freed, he peeled the dress down over her shoulders and arms, his mouth following in its wake. The dress caught on her hips. He pushed it off and let it fall. Then he brought her around

to face him again and started on the buttons of her camisole.

Brianna's lips parted. Once more holding her gaze with
his, he bent and kissed her. Her eyes closed. Inch by inch
she felt her upper body bared to the breeze, his hungry
gaze and searching mouth. Adrenalin roared in her ears.
It speared through her veins, sending her blood and her
heart racing. A sweet ache started between her legs and
her hands itched to feel his body beneath them.

When his lips closed over a nipple, she could no longer
stay silent. She moaned. She wound her fingers in his hair
and held him to her, lost in the pleasure he gave her. She
barely even noticed when he freed her of her drawers. But
when he left her breast and knelt to remove her shoes, she
cried out in protest.

"Don't fret, sweet woman," he murmured, standing
again. "I'll give you everything you want. In time." Then
he picked her up and carried her into the pool. At waist
depth, he let go of her legs and let her body slide down
along his until her feet touched bottom.

Common sense fled. Need overcame fear.

"Col," she whispered as his mouth tried to claim hers.
"I've missed you so much I thought I would die, but this
is so wrong, so dangerous."

He nuzzled her chin, her ear and her neck. "Dangerous, how?"

"Barret. He . . . he might be close. He might have
followed us. He'll kill you. I-I couldn't bear it if he killed
you."

"Is that what this nonsense has been about the last
week?"

She nodded, her brow furrowed with anxiety.

"Barret's nowhere near here. I've been visiting his

camp, destroying his supplies, setting his mules free. He's been too busy chasing them to worry about us."

"But there's. . . ."

"What? Or is it who?" He stepped back, his eyes as dark and fierce as the tornado they'd survived at Windlass Hill.

She closed her eyes and shook her head. "I can't tell you. I *won't* tell you. You'll kill him and—"

"Punch Moulton!"

Her eyes flew open.

"I'm right, aren't I? That bastard's been threatening you, scaring you so bad you've been afraid even to talk to me. You're right, I ought to kill him."

Her fingers dug into his arms. "No! Please, Col. Think of Dulcie. Think of her baby."

He stared at her a long time before the tension in his muscles eased under her hands. His mouth was a hard, straight line beneath the sweep of his sun-bleached mustache. His hand came up to poke one finger between her breasts. "All right. But if that belly-crawling son of a snake comes anywhere near you, he's gonna have a run-in with my fist, understand?"

She nodded and let out the breath she had been holding.

"Now come here." He put his hands on her waist and drew her against him. "I've missed you and before we leave this valley, you're gonna know exactly how much."

Then he brought his lips fiercely down on hers. When he lifted his head, words poured out of him like sugar from a torn sack.

"Lord, but I want you, woman. I want you so damn bad I don't know if I can hold off until you're ready for me."

He kissed her nose, her chin, her cheeks.

"Got to tell everyone I'm not your brother, to hell with what they think."

He kissed her ear and the sensitive spot at the hinge of her jaw.

"You're mine. Can't let you go, never let you go."

He angled his way down to her neck, tasting the dust and the salty sweat and wanting nothing more than to taste every inch of her. Putting his hands under her armpits, he lifted her until his mouth could take its fill of her breasts.

Brianna braced her arms on his shoulders, her fingers digging in to the hard muscles. A sob clawed its way up from her chest, through her throat, to burst from her lips. "Oh Col, I thought I'd lost you. . . ."

He lifted his head to look up at her. The sun behind her cast a halo of light around her head. She gazed down at him, tears tracking her cheeks. Slowly he lowered her to the sandy bottom of the pool.

"You'll never lose me, Bri. Can't you see I love you?"

A light entered her eyes, making them shine. "But, I'm not young like Lucy. I'm not pretty either, just big and—"

He gave her a shake. His eyes that had been so soft a moment before, turned hard again. "Don't say that. You're the most beautiful woman in the world to me and that's all that matters."

Her lips curved in a coy smile. "But I am big."

"You're perfect." He drew her into his arms, crushing her breasts against his chest and cradling her hips against his. "You fit me like you were made for me. What more could a man want?"

She laughed, then sobered. "I've been so scared

and. . . ." As if embarrassed, she buried her face against his neck. "Col, I-I hurt."

"You hurt!" He rubbed against her to let her feel the hardness of his need. Her shyness and her vulnerability touched him and made him want her all the more. "Woman, you don't know what hurt is."

With soap he produced from the pocket of his shirt, he lathered her entire body, lingering at her breasts and the juncture of her legs until she moaned and squirmed against him. Then, his lips quirked up in a smile, he dunked her.

She came up spluttering, but she was laughing, too.

Happy to take her turn, she lathered her hands and smeared him with white suds. The hairs on his chest sprang back up after her hand passed over them, each rimmed with white like hoarfrost. She turned him around and soaped his back, glorying in the firm ridges of muscles and the texture of his skin, rough compared to her own. As her hand dipped below his waist, she noticed how his skin smoothed out where his buttocks began. A sudden fit of shyness took her and she stopped. He turned to face her. Without meaning to, she let her gaze drop and her face grew red. He was fully aroused.

"Aren't you going to finish?" he said, grinning.

The words were a dare. She pushed aside the ghost of her old familiar fear. Firming her chin, she took the soap and lathered her hands again.

Col watched her conquer her shyness and fear. Her touch when it came was all the more incredible, knowing what it cost her. She dabbed a dollop of suds in his navel, smiled up at him, then blew it away. Her warm breath on his wet skin made him tremble. When her hand moved below the water and found him, he groaned. She reached between his legs, cupping him gently, washing, caressing, exploring, until he thought he would have to order her to stop. Then she moved on, crouching with only her head above water as she washed his hairy legs.

Slowly she worked her way back up and found, to her surprise, that she no longer wanted to skip over that part of him that made her truly his, that bound them together. Sex with him was not the ugly, painful, degrading act she had been forced to submit to with Barret.

Touching Col, joining with him was right and beautiful. It made her feel beautiful, loved, cherished. She wanted to make him feel that way too.

So she took him in her hand and tested the varying textures, the firmness, the pulsing throb, and marvelled that she could bring that look of tortured bliss to his face.

Col groaned and pulled from her grasp. He was on fire, his patience gone. He dunked himself to rinse away the soap.

When he came back up, he crushed her to him and took her lips in a savage kiss. Then he gentled it, feathering his mouth over hers. She responded with a whisper of her lips on his. Growling with pleasure at her response, he deepened the kiss. She mimicked his every move.

If he devoured, she consumed.

If his tongue dipped into her mouth, to taste, to tempt, to tantalize, hers tiptoed to dance coyly with his.

If he suckled her lower lip, she suckled his upper one. If he nipped, she nibbled.

Finally he tore his mouth from hers and moved to her breasts. Each nipple in turn he laved and sucked while she tangled her fingers in his wet hair and moaned. He couldn't get enough of her. His hands travelled every curve, every plane, every hollow and dip. And his lips followed, down lower and lower, until the water blocked his way.

Cupping her buttocks with his hands, he lifted her, then slowly eased her back down until his hardness found the soft heated portal he sought. Before his lips claimed hers, he saw her shock turn to purring contentment as she closed tightly around him, sheathing him in hot ecstasy.

He took her like that, in a ride more wild than she'd ever imagined. To a height she could not believe.

When it was over, he bathed her again. Then he carried her from the water and laid her on the grass. With the sun warming and drying them, they curled up together and dozed the morning away.

Brianna was the last to awaken. She opened her eyes to find Col braced on one elbow, looking down at her. He was smiling crookedly. She stretched and smiled back.

"I wish we didn't have to go back," she said. "I wish we could stay here forever and forget all about. . . ." Her voice trailed off and he knew it was her husband's name she hadn't been able to say.

He leaned down to kiss her. "We don't have to go back yet."

His mouth moved to her breast, his hand to her thigh. The next hour he spent fulfilling a dream that had pestered him for weeks. He kissed every inch of her body.

When he moved between her legs, she tried to pull him away. A shaft of blistering heat dissolved her objections as his tongue found her. Lost in rapture, Brianna closed her eyes and surrendered to the warm seduction of the sun's fiery rays.

Chapter Twenty-five

The afternoon was gone by the time Nigh and Brianna rejoined the wagon train that wound snakelike along the trail below them. The sun had barely begun to rouge the western skyline. Grabbing Brianna's reins, Nigh brought them both to a halt.

"Gonna leave you here," he said.

"Why? Where are you going?"

"I want you to go back to the train. I'll be back sometime before morning."

Her eyes narrowed accusingly. "You're going after Barret, aren't you?"

When he didn't answer she urged her horse closer so she could take hold of his arm. "Please, Col, if he's as far back as you said he is, there's no need. You'll only be putting yourself in danger for nothing."

His eyes softened as he gazed at her. His mouth quirked. "Sure like having you fretting over me, instead of mad at me."

"If you go, I'll be furious with you."

He grinned and ran a finger over her succulent lower lip. "Yeah, but I think I know how to soften you up now."

From a rise a few hundred yards farther up the trail, Edward Magrudge smirked as he watched the touching farewell. No doubt they'd snuck off somewhere to roll in the grass together. Huh! Punch Moulton had told him the truth. Columbus Nigh and Brianna Villard were not brother and sister. The high-toned "widow" who thought she was too good for Edward Magrudge, had been rutting like any other whore with a filthy squawman.

She would pay for that.

And soon, Magrudge thought, pleased to see Nigh ride off in the direction of Fort Laramie. Thanks to Punch, Magrudge knew where Nigh was probably headed. More importantly, the wagon captain knew that it meant Brianna would be sleeping alone and unprotected tonight.

At least she would be until Magrudge joined her.

His body stiffened and began to throb with need at the thought. He rubbed the growing bulge in his crotch and whispered, "Soon, old friend, real soon."

One by one the lanterns winked out. The wagons grew dark and the night became silent, except for the roar of the creek, the "Whoo! Whoo!" of an owl, and a coyote yipping in the hills somewhere.

The road had taken the train away from the North Platte. Ever since Fort Laramie, high rocky cliffs and broken ground had hidden the North Platte from view. Tonight they'd found a fine camp on Horseshoe Creek, with good wood, clean water, and the best grass in weeks. Fifteen miles wasn't anything to crow about, but they'd had worse days, Brianna thought. Tomorrow they'd try for LaPrele Creek. She punched her pillow and lay back down, too worried about Col to sleep.

Patch curled up beside her, her ears perked at the yapping of the coyote. Brianna stroked the kitten and murmured to reassure her she was safe. Patch rewarded her with the low rumble of a contented purr.

Where was Col?

Anytime now she expected to hear rain on the canvas roof. But the day had been glorious. She didn't want to go to sleep and lose the glow her day with Col had given her. Tomorrow the guilt would come, and the fear. Tonight she wanted to wallow like a buffalo in the memory of his touch and his sweet words. He loved her. She wasn't sure she'd ever be able to believe it. With all her heart, she wished he were here with her now to prove it to her, over and over, the way he had in the hidden canyon.

It was close to midnight now. Surely he would be back soon.

If only Barret would give up and go home. For Col to die trying to guard her freedom would be too cruel, too unfair. He shouldn't be fighting her battles for her. She shouldn't *allow* him to fight them.

She sat up as realization struck home with the impact of a two thousand pound buffalo impaling her on his horns. Why hadn't she thought of it before? The answer was so simple. Hadn't she wanted to see it?

The likelihood that she had indeed been avoiding the reality of her situation was not pleasant to accept. But there it was.

She had the means to make Barret give her a divorce. Not here with her on the Oregon Trail. No, it was back in St. Louis buried under a rose bush. But she was the only one who knew the location and she was the only one who could wield the power that the knowledge gave her.

Power. What a sweet word, she thought as she lay down again and snuggled into her bed.

Tonight was the last time Columbus Nigh would play knight in shining armor for her, the last time he would endanger his precious life for her sake. She'd make sure of that.

A whisper of sound from outside caught her attention. Wind. Or footsteps in the grass. Patch sat up, her sharp golden eyes and pointy ears directed toward the rear of the wagon. When the sound came again, Brianna, too, sat up.

"Col?"

Silence.

"Col? Is that you out there?"

This time she heard a muffled response, a weary, indistinct grunt so like Col, her heart leaped. The wagon lurched beneath his weight. She grinned. It wasn't raining yet, and she didn't care whether it did or not. Wanting to be ready for him, she yanked off her nightdress, pulled the quilt up to her nose and waited.

Columbus Nigh sat motionless on the dappled gray's back and watched the doe lower her head to the slow-moving backwash at the edge of Horse Creek. The deer was so close, Nigh could hear her lap up the water. He'd seen hundreds of scenes like it, a wild animal going about its business, unaware of danger because the danger was downwind.

A few more days would bring them to the Sweetwater River. His gaze wandered toward Laramie Peak. Before dark, the peak had been hidden by dark angry clouds heading this way. It was still hidden. Stars and a partial moon told him the storm was a few hours away yet, even though midnight must be close now.

Once they hit the Sweetwater he'd be able to see the towering, snowy peaks of the Wind River Mountains in the distance. The mere thought warmed his heart. For seventeen years, the Western mountains had been "home" to Nigh. The Wind River Valley in particular.

A notion had niggled at the back of his mind all day. He wanted to show Brianna the beauty of the Wind River and his special valley. They could visit the Gros Ventre Range as well, then angle north to the lower Yellowstone with its geysers and stinking mud pots. The need to share his world with her, see if it gave her the same thrill it gave him, grew stronger with every minute.

Brianna had her heart set on Oregon. Not Nigh. But wherever he went, he wanted her beside him. He wanted to marry her, to bind her to him forever. The idea astounded him. The only kind of marriage he'd ever imagined was the one-day-at-a-time Indian kind, all he had thought a man like him could hope for.

But Brianna had given him hope for more. And that was the most amazing notion of all. That he, Columbus Nigh, a crude, illiterate squawman, might actually win a woman as beautiful and fine as Brianna Villard.

Of course, thanks to her, he wasn't as uneducated as he used to be. Still, for her to love him was almost impossible to be believable. Yet he had only to remember back a few hours to their time by the spring to know it had to be true, whether she admitted it or not.

For his part, Nigh would take her on any terms, whether it meant running the rest of their lives to avoid Barret Wight, or facing the man now.

If killing Wight was what it would take to make Brianna his for the rest of his life, Nigh would do it. He'd shoot Wight down in cold blood, the same way he would a rabid wolf.

The doe lifted her head, ears pricked. The gelding, too, was listening. Then Nigh heard it—hoofbeats. Slow, hesitant hoofbeats.

The doe bolted.

Nigh stayed where he was.

A few seconds later, the rider emerged in a patch of moonlight. The horse, a bay gelding, nickered a greeting to the dappled gray. Even in the dim light, Nigh recognized the man, and had a hunch what he was up to.

"Looking for me?" Nigh drawled.

Stinky Harris whirled in his saddle and cursed as his gaze found Nigh, silhouetted against the silver wash of the creek.

Barret had sent Stinky to rendezvous with Punch and learn what was happening. As Stinky was preparing to ride back, Nigh and Brianna had showed up and Punch had pointed the man out. When Nigh rode off alone, the two men decided it might be an excellent time to ambush the pain in the butt.

Stinky had meant to be invisible. But it wasn't too late to rectify matters. He had the element of surprise on his side; Columbus Nigh didn't know he was about to die.

If Nigh hadn't been the man he was, he might not have caught the glint of metal near the man's hip. As it was, instinct sent him flying off the gray's back a fraction of a second before a pistol shot ripped the air. He rolled as he struck ground and dug for the pistol tucked in his belt.

A second shot shattered the night. Then silence.

                    * * *

The hand over Brianna's mouth tasted like manure
and smelled like sweaty tobacco as she bit into the thick
fleshy palm. Magrudge cursed. He jerked his hand away
for only a fraction of a second, but it was long enough for
her to manage a strangled scream before the hand
slapped back down over her mouth.

"Quit fighting me, you slut."

Magrudge's breath was as foul as his hand. He lay on
top of her, pinning her legs with his. Her arms were
pinned, too, but she had hold of the quilt and wouldn't let
go. With his free hand he struggled to tear the quilt from
her death grip. "You're gonna like what I got better than
what that stinking Nigh gave you today."

He laughed at her muffled curse.

"Nothing I like better'n a beautiful woman with spirit.
Like Little Beaver. You know who she was?"

She tried to bite his hand again. He slapped her hard
and had the hand back over her mouth before she could
do more than yelp. His grip was so tight her teeth cut into
her lips and she tasted blood.

"Little Beaver fought, too," he whispered, while his
hand snaked under the quilt to find warm, naked flesh. He
wormed his way under her arm and captured a breast.
"Ah, that's nice, bigger'n Little Beaver's."

Brianna choked on the bile her revulsion brought up
from her stomach. She let go of the quilt to push his hand
away. In the tussle that followed, Magrudge managed to
pull the quilt to her waist. His legs kept him from getting
it all the way off.

Magrudge found it awkward, trying to get her uncov-
ered and fend her off at the same time. The bitch was

stronger than he'd expected. But that only added to the challenge, and the excitement.

Her left arm was still locked beneath him, but she was belting him with her right for all she was worth. His ear rang from the resounding blow she struck on the side of his face. Growling, he cuffed her a good one.

Blackness swirled inside Brianna's head. The world retreated. She fought to remain conscious. Magrudge had managed to work his trousers part-way off and was yanking again on the quilt.

Neither of them heard the approaching hoofbeats outside. Suddenly Magrudge's heavy body was hauled off her.

The wagon rocked from side to side as Columbus Nigh yanked Magrudge up by the shirt collar and threw him from Brianna. One glimpse told him she was alive. He didn't take time to ask questions. He dragged Magrudge to his feet and punched the man in the stomach with a force that slammed him into the tailgate. Nigh smashed his right fist into Magrudge's nose, then his left into the wagon captain's jaw.

Marc Beaudouin's face appeared above the tailgate. "I've got him, see to Brianna." Magrudge disappeared as Marc grabbed hold of the man and hauled him out of the wagon.

Nigh turned to see Brianna huddled in the far corner, the quilt drawn up to her chin. Without a word he sat on the bed and pulled her into his arms. She was trembling, her breasts heaving as she fought back tears. Gently, he held her, one hand stroking her bare back, his lips against her hair.

"It's all right," he murmured. "You're safe now, he won't touch you again."

An image came to his mind: Magrudge lying on top of her, his hands grabbing at the sweet flesh Nigh had so tenderly loved earlier that day. Rage roared in his ears, shutting out all other sounds. It took every ounce of his strength not to leave her there, frightened and alone, while he tore Magrudge apart, limb by limb. Never had he felt such fury. Even finding Little Beaver battered and bloody had not effected him like this.

"Col, he . . . he . . . Little Beaver."

Thinking she was trying to assure him that, unlike Little Beaver, she was alive, he murmured, "I know. Thank God."

Brianna hiccuped and tried again. "No. Magrudge . . . he said Little Beaver fought. I think he . . . he's the one—"

Nigh pulled back and stared at her. Her words sank through the fog of his mind, like rocks in a misty pool. "Are you all right?"

She nodded.

"Don't worry," he said.

Then he was gone.

When Nigh leaped down from the tailgate, he saw Magrudge sitting on the tongue of the next wagon. The man's pants were in place and he was sucking on the side of his palm. His nose angled crosswise on his face. Blood trailed down around his mouth and dripped off his chin. Jeb Hanks stood nearby, feet spread, a pistol trained on Magrudge.

Marc Beaudouin put his hand to Nigh's shoulder. "Is she all right?"

Nigh didn't answer. He barely noticed the people who had been brought from their beds by the ruckus. All he saw was Edward Magrudge. And Little Beaver's torn body.

With the quickness and precision that had kept him alive this long, Nigh's brain sorted facts and memories: Magrudge beating and raping a Snake squaw during a fur trapper's rendezvous. Magrudge—one day before Little Beaver died—stopping at Nigh's camp to tell him hunters were needed at the fort. Magrudge leering at Little Beaver that same day. The pieces fit.

In a haze of pain and rage, Nigh walked to Magrudge. At his sides Nigh's fingers slowly clenched and un-clenched. No expression showed on his face. His eyes were blank and deadly calm. But it didn't deceive Edward Magrudge.

"Don't you be giving me that look," the wagon captain sneered. "I only wanted what you been getting all along. You ain't her brother and you ain't got no more right to her than me."

A muscle in Nigh's jaw jumped. "Tell me about Little Beaver."

Taken aback, Magrudge said, "Don't know what you're talking about."

Nigh took hold of Magrudge's collar with both hands and hauled the man to his feet. With their noses inches apart, Magrudge's squashed and smelling of blood, Nigh repeated his question in a low toneless voice. Magrudge saw murder in the cool gray eyes. He tried to laugh off his fear, but the sound caught in his throat.

"Spill it, you murdering bastard." When Magrudge didn't answer, Nigh drew back his fist and rammed it into the man's belly.

Magrudge doubled over. His tunic, still clutched in Nigh's hand, tore from neck to waist. Nigh jerked him back upright. He was about to hit Magrudge again when he spied a small beaded pouch partially hidden by the torn edge of the man's shirt. The pouch hung on a rawhide thong. Something about it struck Nigh as familiar. He took out his knife and cut the pouch free. The moment his fingers closed around the beaded leather, Nigh knew where he'd seen it before.

"Little Beaver. This was hers. You killed her, didn't you?"

Magrudge gave a snort that was half-laugh, half-terror. "You're crazy."

"Am I?" Nigh's voice was as cold as a glacier. "Tell me."

Magrudge froze beneath Nigh's penetrating gray gaze.

"Tell me!" Nigh rammed his knee into Magrudge's groin for emphasis. The man gasped, his eyeballs nearly popping from his head as he clutched himself. Nigh opened his fingers and let him slide bonelessly to the ground, like a snake. But Nigh wasn't finished. The pebbled texture of the beaded pouch in his hand spoke to him. The voice was female. Little Beaver's or Brianna's, he wasn't sure. But the voice was loud and insistent. "Revenge," it said. "Revenge, revenge, revenge!"

Nigh watched Magrudge slither over the ground in his pain and knew he had to kill him.

His aim was swift and sure as Nigh kicked Magrudge in the back. When the man arched against the pain, Nigh kicked him in the ribs, sending Magrudge over onto his back.

In desperation, Magrudge drew a knife. Nigh kicked it away. He straddled the man and struck him again and again, oblivious to the alarmed shouts as Jeb Hanks and Marc tried to pull him off.

His hands felt good, felt right, as they closed around Magrudge's throat. Lips flattened against his teeth, drawn back in a savage growl, Nigh watched through a haze of red as Magrudge's eyes rolled up in their sockets. The man's mouth worked silently trying to suck in air.

Then he went still.

A voice penetrated the red haze. "Don't, Col. He isn't worth it. Oh, please, Col. . . ."

Nigh tried to let go. His fingers refused to work. He concentrated on the panic in Brianna's voice. She was alive, and that was all that mattered. She was alive and she was his.

Then he heard the click of a pistol being cocked somewhere behind him.

Instinct sent Nigh rolling over the ground. A split instant before he came up with his gun drawn, he heard the crack of gunfire, followed by a second crack.

Ten feet away Punch Moulton clutched at his chest. His face contorted. Then he crumpled to the ground. A woman screamed.

Nigh looked down at the gun in his hand. It was still cold. He hadn't fired a shot.

Turning, he saw Jeb Hanks, his pistol still pointed at Punch. Beside him lay Edward Magrudge, a bullet hole square center in his forehead.

Brianna's arms enclosed Nigh. He clung to her, his eyes still on the wagon captain's inert form. "He's dead."

"Punch meant the bullet for you," she said, holding him tighter.

Together they turned to look at Punch Moulton. Marc was kneeling beside the body feeling for a pulse. He glanced up and shook his head. Dulcie clapped her hands over her mouth and began to wail.

Standing, Marc said, "We all saw it. Punch meant to kill Col. Jeb had to shoot."

"We also heard what Edward Magrudge said," someone spoke up. "Columbus Nigh isn't Brianna Villard's brother."

At the words, Brianna buried her face in Col's neck. He rose, drawing her up with him. His voice was as hard as the iron rims on the wagon wheels. "What's between Brianna and me is nobody's business but ours. We aren't going to explain, and we aren't going to apologize."

"Good for you!" Lavinia Decker stepped forward, hands on her hips. "It's about time you admitted what we been seeing on your face for weeks now, every time you looked at her."

Brianna's head came up. Red-faced, she stared at the crowd of people, many of whom she had come to love.

Someone chuckled, breaking the tension. A moment later everyone was laughing. Brianna wrapped her arms about Col's waist and smiled.

"Now, Columbus," Lavinia went on, her finger wagging in front of Nigh's face. "We'll expect you to take over as wagon captain."

Col pursed his lips. He glanced at Brianna, then lifted his gaze to Laramie Peak. "No. Don't reckon I'm your man."

"Why not?"

Again his eyes sought Brianna's. "Let's just say I've got other bacon to fry."

"Well, somebody's got to take the job."

"There's plenty of good men in the company." Col put his hand on Marc Beaudouin's shoulder. "Like Marc here."

"Suits me."

"Me, too. Anyone object?"

"Motion's carried then. Marc Beaudouin's our new wagon captain."

Marc chuckled and held up a hand. "Don't I have anything to say about this?"

"Sure do," Lavinia said. "You're the one who has to make sure Columbus Nigh there treats Missus Villard with respect. That means no hanky-panky before he finds a preacher to make everything legal and right."

"Now wait a minute——" Nigh began.

Grinning, Marc wagged his head. "Lavinia's got a point, Col. We're God-fearing, law-abiding folks in this company. If you'll recall, there was a law passed among us at the beginning of this journey, that any man caught seducing or otherwise taking sexual advantage of female members be tried by his peers and if found guilty, be given a choice of firing squad or hangman's noose."

" 'Course——" Lavinia frowned, "—may take till we get to Oregon City to find a preacher man."

Col looked to Brianna as though expecting her to straighten the matter out. At once, she lowered her eyes to her feet, her cheeks as pink and maidenly as the rose-buds back in Ash Hollow.

"Good hell!" Col spluttered.

Chapter Twenty-six

For the third time, the mule sidestepped, thwarting Barret's attempt to put the packsaddle on its back. Twice Barret had set the awkward wooden saddle down and whipped the animal. This time he kicked it instead, shouting every profanity he could think of in the tall furry ears. Whether it was the kick or his deafening curses that got the mule to stand still, he didn't know. Nor did he care. He got the packsaddle in place, lashed on the packs, then looked about to make sure he hadn't forgotten anything.

His eyes strayed to the bluffs north of the trading post where the trader's halfbreed daughter had disappeared up a draw, carrying a pail and a digging stick. Her ma must have sent her after wild onions or some other kind of roots.

Robidoux and Barret had sat up most of the night gambling and passing a jug of trade whiskey back and forth. Barret liked the French-Canadian trader, even considered the man a friend. But damn! Sure would have been fine crawling between the slender young thighs of Robidoux's pretty daughter. Old Adam had been a rock in the front of his pants since Barret first laid eyes on her.

If he'd had time to spare, he'd have found a way to get to the girl. The Magrudge train was almost a week ahead of him. Impatience made him feel edgy and mean. A roll in the grass would have calmed him, but he didn't have the time. He shook his head again, trying to ignore the ache in his groin thinking about the girl brought on.

Going into the log cabin that housed the trading post, he said his thanks and his goodbyes. When he came back out he gave the bluff where the girl had disappeared a final, regretful glance. Then he mounted his horse and started up the steep hill that led out of the small valley and on to Fort Laramie.

He'd gone no farther than the other side of the bluff when his horse began to limp. Cussing, he stopped and dug a pebble out of the horse's left rear shoe. It was when he went to remount that he spotted the girl.

Grinning, he picketed the animals where they would be hidden from the road. He found her squatted on the ground, scraping spines off hunks of prickly pear cactus. She looked up, saw her father's new friend, and smiled.

Barret admired the fat cactus leaves she showed him, moving slowly but steadily closer until he was able to crouch next to her. The sight of the high, firm mounds in the front of her doeskin dress made his mouth salivate. He babbled something about how pretty she was and put his hand on her thigh. This time when she looked at him, her eyes filled with uncertainty. Barret knew he had to move fast. He shoved her onto the ground, threw his thick body on top of her, and stifled her cry with his mouth.

She fought like a cougar. Barret had to hit her several times before she lay still, whimpering while he yanked up her dress and thrust himself inside her.

A virgin. Young, incredibly tight, and forbidden. Delicious. It occurred to him, as he refastened his trousers and gazed down on the sobbing girl, that rape offered a thrill no willing woman could.

There they were. The Wind River Mountains.

Columbus Nigh sat on the dappled gray and gazed across the spurs that formed Sweetwater Valley, to the higher peaks in the distance. Tomorrow they would camp at Greasewood Creek and the next day he would once again taste the cold, pure water of the Sweetwater River, born in the mountains he had never been able to get out of his heart.

Alone there on the sagebrush-covered hilltop, lost in memories of his Wind River Valley, he didn't feel the icy chill of wind blowing off the snow-capped peaks he loved. The notion absorbing his mind was too loud to be called an echo, and yet it wasn't new. It was the same notion he'd had at Horse Creek, just before Stinky Harris tried to kill him and wound up dead instead.

Would Brianna leave the train and go with him, if he asked? Oregon had meant no more to her at the beginning of their trek than a haven from Barret. In spite of her determination to get there, Oregon had no ties for her, no future that awaited her arrival. If she would let him, he would give her his own valley as her haven. And himself for her future.

They would be safer in the Wind River Valley. Barret would never expect them to leave the train and go off into the wilderness. Greenhorn that Barret was, he would find it difficult, if not impossible, to follow them.

It was a good plan. Brianna was no squaw, but he knew she could handle the rugged life he had in mind. Yellow

Feather's village would be there somewhere. He could trade for a tipi and an extra packhorse. At summer's end, after he had shown her why he loved this country, they could return to the Wind River Valley where he would build them a cabin, a home.

Home. Lord, but that sounded good. He chuckled, surprised and pleased. Life was looking better than he could ever remember, better even than sharing a pile of roasted humpribs on a summer evening with friends around the campfire.

He tongued his toothpick to the corner of his mouth and thought of the wonders he could show her. His certainty that they would affect her the same way they had him turned his craving into need. His eagerness churned in his gut and filled him with restless energy. He turned the gray and headed back down the long hill, determined to convince her of his plan.

They had crossed the North Platte on rafts at Red Buttes the night before and camped at Willow Springs. Storms had swollen the river. It was four hundred yards wide and very fast. Hardly anyone made it across without losing part of his load and two men had died. Today was a recuperation day.

Game would be scarce in the barren country ahead of them. It was a country of alkali ponds, sagebrush, and very little grass. Even the springs tasted like stove coal. Dead cattle poisoned by alkali already littered the trail. One entire team had been found, still yoked. The water at Willow Springs was cold and pure, but had to be shared with several other companies.

All about him as he wove his way through the camps, rose the companionable sounds of talk, mixed with laughter and snatches of song. Children chased lizards. Men repaired wagons and gear. Women spread freshly scrubbed sheets and garments over the sagebrush. The air was redolent with the good smells of fresh-baked bread, beans, pies, and the fragrant smoke of sagebrush fires.

He found Brianna sitting at their makeshift table, mending garments. After hearing him out, she cocked her head, a look of confusion on her face. "Col, are you asking me to be your squaw? To follow you around the mountains, caring for your lodge, cooking your food, and keeping your bed warm?"

Nigh blinked. Her eyes were like brittle shards of sky, intensely blue and frigidly cold. He hunkered down beside her, spit the pick from his mouth and studied her while she threaded a needle and bent to mend one of her dresses.

"Something eating at you, Bri?"

Brianna let out a long sigh. She set aside her mending and folded her hands in her lap. In her eyes he saw pain, doubt, and regret. He glanced around. There was no sign of Marc or his boys. For the first time in days, both Dulcie and Lavinia weren't hovering over them.

"Been a long time since we been allowed more than a second of privacy, hasn't it?" he said.

"Not since the night you tried to choke Edward Magrudge to death for killing Little Beaver."

Col nodded. "Is that what this is all about?"

She pushed to her feet and walked away from the wagon to stare at the countryside, much as he had done earlier. "It occurred to me that night that you must have loved her a great deal to still feel so much rage over her death. I admit that part of my pain is because I'm jealous."

He held out his hand and surveyed the stub of his little

finger on his left hand. Maybe it was time he told the story of that day when he had found Little Beaver dead. "Will you take a ride with me?"

She allowed him to lift her onto the gray, then mount behind her. He took her to the top of Prospect Hill where he had sat minutes before, mapping a future he had hoped she would want to share with him.

"Little Beaver wasn't much more'n a child by your standards. Indian women grow up fast." He shrugged, wondering why he had bothered to tell her that. Then he dismounted and lifted her down.

"It was late fall. We were camped on the Ham's Fork when Magrudge stopped by to tell me they needed meat over to Fort Bridger. I never saw him again until I took you to find your sister outside Independence.

"I spent two days in the mountains hunting meat for the fort. Little Beaver stayed in camp. She was used to fending for herself. Indian women can take care of themselves nearly as well as a man."

He gave a snort and shook his head. "Reckon I'm still trying to justify leaving her alone." He was silent some minutes before he went on. "I went back to take her with me to deliver the meat. She loved to look at all the foofuraw the store offered and visit any of her kin who might be there. Reckon women are alike in some ways, red or white."

Eyes dark and somber, he gazed toward the snowy peaks. Brianna's heart ached for him. She longed to tell him none of this mattered. She had gotten over her revulsion for Indians somewhere along the trail. At Fort Laramie, she thought. The Sioux and Cheyenne there were nothing like the Kanza back home. Brianna had admired the beautifully quilled garments of the northern tribes, their proud stature and intelligence. Watching a mother bathe her child in the river had shown Brianna that women everywhere were indeed very much alike, as Col had just said.

"She was naked." His words and the hoarseness of his voice shocked her as Col continued his story.

"Naked and sprawled on the floor of the tipi, legs spread and bloodied. One arm broken. Her face so swollen and battered, I hardly recognized her."

There were other things he could not describe, things Brianna didn't need to know, but that would haunt him forever. "Never even knew her medicine pouch was missing, till I saw it hanging from Magrudge's filthy neck."

He turned toward her and she felt another jolt of shock at the lack of emotion in his eyes. "I took her as my woman so I wouldn't offend Yellow Feather." His eyes closed and he shook his head. When he opened them again, she glimpsed anguish and guilt before he looked away. "No, that's not entirely true. I wanted what she represented to me: home, family, all the things I'd never known, even when I was a little scrub."

He came to Brianna then. He took up her hand and rubbed her palm with his thumb while he stared her in the eye with an expression that begged for understanding.

"I was born in a shack, Bri. My father worked the docks, odd jobs when he could get them, picking pockets when he couldn't. My ma died before I learned to walk. Only women I knew after that were whores Pa dragged home. I was nine when he was killed in a brawl. You're right if you think I'm not good enough for you."

When she opened her mouth to object, he placed a finger over her lips. "I followed in my pa's footsteps, picking pockets till I was big enough to sweep floors in a brothel. When I was seventeen I signed on to trap beaver."

He pointed then to the snowy Wind River peaks, wreathed with clouds in the far distance. "Up there I found peace, found out who and what I was. Or thought I did. Since I met you I haven't been so sure." His mouth quirked in a smile that was meant to tease. But it didn't erase the sadness in his eyes.

"I never loved her, Bri." The words were so soft she might not have heard, had she not been so close. "Kept meat in her pot, supplied hides for her clothes, bought her foofuraw from the fort. I even. . . ."

His Adam's apple bobbed as he swallowed hard, and his gaze fell. The afternoon sun glinted on moisture in his eyes and she caught her breath. Tears. That a man of his strength, a man who had lived the roughest of lives, could be soft and vulnerable, touched her in a way his words could not. But his next words stopped her heart.

"She was carrying my child."

Such a simple statement, but, along with everything else he'd told her, it spoke volumes. He had taken a young girl, used her to his own ends, giving back only what his hands could provide, and when she was about to give him what he most wanted in the world—a family—he had let her down. He had worn the guilt of her death like a hair shirt, and in his mind, only avenging her death could absolve his sins.

Should she tell him what she suspected? No, it would be too cruel, not knowing how this mess would end. Brianna lifted the hand that held hers and looked at the little finger that was shorter than the one on his right hand.

"Indian tradition," he said in answer to her unasked

question. "A sacrifice to show grief when a . . . a loved one dies. Reckon I needed to make some sort of sacrifice at the time."

Slowly, while he watched, Brianna brought the severed finger to her lips and kissed it.

"Lord, but I love you, woman."

He pulled her to him and hugged her so tightly she thought her ribs would break. Against her hair, he said, "Saying her name, the name of one who's gone to the other side, is bad medicine to an Indian. Don't reckon her medicine coulda gotten any worse, marrying me. Before you decide whether or not you want to come with me, maybe you ought to think on that. I might be bad medicine for you, too."

"I don't need to think about it, Col. You've brought a gentleness into my life I've never known. You taught me to care about myself again, and to stand up for myself. That's not bad medicine. That's good, all good."

His Adam's apple bobbed again and he blinked back tears as he held his gaze on the snowy peaks so far away. Her own gaze lifted to the blue and white pinnacles.

He had not mentioned marriage between them, not once. She discovered that it didn't matter. Neither did Little Beaver. But there were other things that did. She drew herself from his embrace and turned back toward the wagon train. "Now there's something I have to make you understand, Col."

His heart sank to his toes at the gravity in her voice, knowing that he wasn't going to like what she was about to say.

"I'm not free to go with you, or with any man. That night, after you took me to the hidden canyon, before Edward Magrudge came to my wagon, I realized that I had been allowing you to fight my battles for me. I can't do that anymore."

"Bri—"

She whirled to face him. "No, Col. Let me finish. What kind of life would we have hiding out in the mountains, waiting for my husband to find me and maybe kill you, or kill us both? You asked me to trust you once, and I did. Now you have to trust me. I'm going to wait here for Barret—"

"Dammit, Bri, you can't mean that." Rage contorted his face. "Have you gone crazy?"

"No, I think I've merely grown up, finally. That's something Barret will have to accept, as he will have to accept the fact that I will never again allow him to strike me, torture me, or threaten me."

"He isn't going to accept anything except having you back under his thumb to pound on whenever it suits him, and you know it." Col grabbed her by the arms and shook her gently. "Don't do this, Bri. The bastard'll wind up killing you one day, if he doesn't do it the minute he gets hold of you again."

Her chin lifted and her spine was as stiff as a wagon tongue. No sign of emotion showed in her eyes. "I have to do it, Col. I'm sorry it hurts you. I never intended that, but you know as well as I do that it would never work between us as long as he's out there trying to track us down."

His hands slid from her arms. The gray eyes that had been so full of hope were now as barren and icy as the glaciers that slumbered on the highest peaks of the mountains Columbus Nigh so loved. "I won't stay to see him put back all the bruises I helped heal."

"I understand."

"Then I'll take you back to camp."

Neither of them spoke a word all the way to the camp. After he had lifted her off the horse, he fetched the few belongings he had stored in the wagon. Brianna watched silently as he helped himself to enough cold fried bacon, coffee, biscuits, and beans to see him to the Wind River Mountains.

"Tell Marc if he ever needs anything, he can find me in the Wind River Valley."

"I'll tell him."

He refastened the flaps on his saddlebags, tied on his bedding, and heaved himself into the saddle. He said no goodbye, nor even looked back.

Dry-eyed, Brianna watched him go. Like the china tea pot she had once broken to give herself a chance at a new life, her heart shattered.

Chapter Twenty-seven

"Bitch! Goddamn whore-bitch!"

The words burst out of the darkness like lightning from storm clouds. Barret poured water out of his boot and set the boot on the bank. He emptied the second boot and scowled at the sorrel grazing contentedly some feet away. Ought to shoot the confounded animal, Barret told himself.

"Throwing me just because a damn fish jumped after a fly!" He raised his voice and shook his fist at the mare. "Ought to make crow bait out of you. And them mules along with you."

The horse didn't so much as cock an ear. Barret had let go of the lead rope as he floundered in LaBonte Creek and the packmules had bolted. One had bucked its way out of the water. The packs it had carried now lay strewn for a good two hundred feet along the river bank. He didn't know where the blasted mules had gone and wasn't about to go searching in the dark.

It was the bitch he was married to he wanted most to shoot. If she had stayed home where she belonged, none of this would have happened. When he got her home he'd lock her in the fruit cellar until she was so spider-bitten and crazy, no one would listen if she did babble to someone about what she'd unearthed in the barn.

The thought of taking her home gave him an odd sense of comfort, as if the two—Brianna and home—were synonymous. With a shock, he realized he had barely even thought about Glory since leaving St. Louis. It was Brianna who filled his mind, Brianna he hungered for at night.

As Barret searched the scattered packs for coffee and a kettle, he wondered why Stinky Harris had not yet come back from checking in with Punch Moulton. Maybe the man would be more reliable if Barret blacked both his eyes for him when he got back.

Somewhere out in the darkness a mule brayed. It sounded close. Heaving a sigh, Barret put down the pot he'd found and tiptoed, barefoot, toward the sound. He didn't dare trust the contrary animal to stay put until morning.

Ten miles back, a Frenchman and two Indians settled in to a cold camp of their own. They gnawed jerky, passed a jug of whiskey, and cleaned their weapons while they chuckled over the incredible foolishness of the greenhorn they had tracked all day. A couple more days and they'd catch up to the bastard.

Then the fun would begin.

Nigh didn't even make it out of the Willow Springs encampment before he heard a woman screaming his name. Hope leaped into his throat. He wheeled the gray about, his eyes seeking Brianna's tall, lithe form. But it was Lucy Decker he saw running toward him, her skirts hiked up as she dodged the sagebrush in her path. Nigh's bowels squeezed up, knowing the girl was bringing trouble with her.

Lucy was out of breath when she reached him. "Where you going, Col? I need to talk to you."

"I'm leaving, Lucy."

"What do you mean, leaving?" She clutched at his knee, her green eyes wide with alarm.

"I mean I won't be back. Now let go." He pried her fingers loose only to have her latch onto his stirrup.

"But you can't go without me. I love you, Col."

Beyond patience, he snarled, "What are you up to, Lucy? You know I don't want you."

Lavinia Decker was coming toward them. In a move he was sure was calculated to get her mother's attention, Lucy wailed loudly, "I'm carrying your baby, Col. You can't go off and leave me."

Anger surged through him. "You may be carrying someone's baby, but it sure as hell ain't mine, and you know it."

"Lucy?" Lavinia said as she reached them.

Crying tears as big as buffalo chips, the girl turned to her mother. "He has to marry me, Mama, you have to make him marry me."

Lavinia looked as though she'd aged ten years. "You got yourself in a hole of your own digging, girl, and this time I'm not bailing you out." Turning to Nigh, Lavinia said, "Sorry 'bout this, Columbus. Girl's got herself in the family way, but I know you ain't the father."

"He is, Mama. He *is* the father. You have to make him marry me."

"No, Lucy. Ever since I noticed you ain't been washing out any monthly rags, I been askin' round. Didn't take me long to figure out who you been messing with. Another married man, only this one went and got hisself killed on you. And I ain't about to let you pass blame on an innocent man."

Her tears genuine now, Lucy backed away, her hands held out in supplication. "You don't understand, Mama. I just want to be loved, that's all. Why can't the men I want, want me?"

"You got to give love to get it back, honey, and I'm afraid that's something you don't seem to know how to do."

Putting her arms around the girl, Lavinia guided her back to their wagon.

Watching them walk away, Nigh felt as though he'd just battled three grizzlies and a pack of Blackfoot warriors—and lost. He felt older than Lavinia Decker looked, older than the mountains he was heading for. Then he saw Brianna, still standing where he left her. For several long moments she stared at him before turning her back and sitting down at the table to take up her mending as though nothing important had happened at all.

In that moment, Nigh knew he'd lost a bigger battle than any amount of grizzlies and Blackfeet could wage.

The moon was full, as round and pale as a woman's breast.

Brianna's breast.

Columbus Nigh stared at the shimmering trail cast across the rippled waters of the Sweetwater River by the silver magic of the moonlight. The trail beckoned to him. Beyond the Sweetwater Valley rose the Wind River Mountains, their snowy peaks like disembodied wisps of cloud in the night sky. Tomorrow would see him at Three Crossings and another day would put him in the foothills.

He could smell snow from the highest peaks on the icy gale buffeting his small fire. His eyes ached from the blowing sand and alkali. His heart ached as well, but he scorned the pain of it, the same way scorned its cause.

Brianna.

How could he feel so much pain when he had no heart left? She had ripped it from his body as carelessly as she would pluck the blossom of a rose.

Ruthlessly banishing her from his mind, he dug into his saddle bags for the leftover biscuits he had brought with him. Not because he was hungry, but because eating gave him something to do. And activity kept him from thinking. He stared at the pale, round biscuits in his hand, seeing only a woman's breasts.

Sweet, tender breasts, with tips as pink as a rosebud, as beckoning as the cry of the wilderness whispering in his ear.

Dropping the biscuits into his lap as though singed by long-dead heat rekindled by his errant thoughts, he reached for the jug stolen from Jeb Hanks on his way out of the Willow Springs camp. He yanked out the cork and put the cool ceramic to his lips. One deep gulp after another gurgled joyfully down his gullet. The firewater blurred the image of the woman that refused to leave his mind, and dulled the pain in his chest where his heart should be.

Relief without solace, rest without peace.

Again he drank, angry that his long, hard ride could deplete the strength of his body without touching the damnable workings of a brain filled with too many memories and too little sense.

A lull in the whining gale brought a snatch of music from an emigrant camp closer to the rock Father De Smet called the Register of the Desert. A pile of granite over a quarter of a mile long and bearing the inscriptions of fur trappers, explorers, and emigrants.

Nigh winced as a trickle of whiskey found the crack in his lip, chiseled by the dry, hot wind. Leaning his head back on his saddle, he closed his eyes and let the music mingle with the night sounds to lull him to sleep.

In the faint glow of early morning, clear and dry and deathly still, he awoke. The fire had been reduced to smoldering embers. His slitted, bloodshot eyes caught movement and he froze.

The coyote sat back on its rump, a pink crescent of tongue peeking from between its teeth. Canny golden eyes seemed to mock him with their soberness.

Disgruntled and out of sorts, Nigh inched his hand toward the gun in his belt, planning to shoot the annoying critter. Before reaching its goal, his hand encountered something dry and crumbly. He looked down to see the biscuits he had spurned the night before. When he picked them up he realized they weren't as dry as he'd thought.

The coyote appeared to grin at him. In the short whiskers around the canine mouth were a few white crumbs. The critter had been literally eating out of Nigh's hands. Or, to be more accurate, out of his lap.

With a snort, Nigh tossed the rest of the bread to the coyote. Within seconds both had disappeared.

Contenting himself with coffee and cold fried bacon, seasoned with alkali dust, Nigh saddled the dappled gray and turned his nose westward.

His head thudded dully in his ears like the stomp of dancing feet. His mouth tasted like fouled alkali water and his stomach roiled in reprisal at last night's harsh treatment. He dosed his stomach and mouth with sweet river water and ignored the headache.

A pair of antelope fawns leaped out of his path and bounded away as he continued his journey toward the Wind River Range. Farther on a bald eagle grudgingly abandoned the carcass of an ox that lay on the trail. Nigh's stomach heaved as he breathed in the stench.

Long about mid-morning he wasted half a dozen shots on a small bunch of mountain sheep high up the rocky cliffs. To soothe his sore temper, rather than his empty stomach, he shot the head off a rattler. He considered the idea of eating the snake but the effort of cooking it seemed too great. At Devil's Gap, he traded some of his carvings to emigrants for fresh-baked bread and cold beans instead.

Then he rode five miles off the trail into the Green Mountains to let the dappled gray feast on grass that hadn't already been chewed to the nub by the livestock of emigrants.

His own meal was as tasteless as the dust he'd been swallowing for days. If he'd stayed with the wagon train he'd have been eating dried apple pie and antelope stew. Brianna had become more than a passable cook.

Brianna.

There was no moon to remind him of her today. But he needed no reminders. She stuck in his brain like a well-burrowed tick. He glanced up at the sun that blazed down on him from a mercilessly clear sky, adding insult to injury with its blinding glare and suffocating heat.

The sun and the moon.

Did she miss him as much as he missed her? Nigh didn't think it was possible. She was so complex compared to Little Beaver. Indian women were experts at masking their emotions, but within their own lodge there was no need. From loved ones they hid nothing. He would never understand the way Brianna's mind worked.

Yesterday, when he told her about Little Beaver's death, she had been full of compassion and understanding. Even now, the memory of how she had kissed his butchered finger, tied his throat in knots. At that moment he had known he was loved. He had felt blessed.

Then she had banished it as though it were no more than a hoard of mosquitoes.

Dammit! They had made love. They had worshipped each other with their bodies.

Her voice came to him as though he were still there, facing her on Prospect Hill: *You've brought a gentleness into my life I've never known. You taught me to care about myself again, and to stand up for myself. That's not bad medicine. That's good, all good.*

He swallowed and blinked back sudden tears.

I realized that I had been allowing you to fight my battles for me. I can't do that anymore.

Didn't she know he wanted to protect her? To fight dragons and pursuing husbands and anything else that threatened her?

What kind of life would we have hiding out in the mountains, waiting for my husband to find me and maybe kill me, or kill us both?

The damn fool woman! She was trying to protect him!

Nigh sawed on the reins. The gray reared and pivoted at the same time, facing northeast when he came down on all fours. Sitting there, Nigh stared with narrowed eyes back the way he had come.

Brianna belonged to him and she knew it. Whatever

notion she'd had in her craw when she told him she was going back to Barret—

No, that wasn't right.

I'm going to wait here for Barret—

She'd said wait, not go back! What else would she have said if he hadn't interrupted? Why had he let his bruised ego blind him to what she was doing?

Digging his heels into the dappled gray's sides, he turned his back on the snow white peaks of the Wind River Mountains and headed east.

He'd fought Pawnee, Arapaho, Blackfeet, and Bannock. He'd killed more grizzlies than most and set his foot where no other man had ever trod. Every part of his anatomy bore scars that said he was no coward. Never before had he let another man walk off with what belonged to him, and he wasn't about to start now.

Brianna was his. He'd see Barret Wight dead before he'd let that yellow-bellied woman-beater touch one hair on her stubborn head.

Night was half over when Columbus Nigh found the Magrudge wagon company on Greasewood Creek. Only a scrappy yellow dog challenged him as he rode through the circle in search of Brianna's wagon.

It wasn't there.

Even Marc Beaudouin's was out of place. Nigh found it parked next to the Woody's. He dismounted and rapped his knuckles on the side of the wagon. "Marc?"

After a moment of silence, a voice came back: "That you, Col?"

"Yeah. What are you doing in Marc's wagon, Tobias?"

"Hang on. I'll be right out."

Tobias emerged barefoot and shirtless, still buttoning up his trousers. "Glad to see you, Col. Been a mess o' strange doin's around here since you left."

There was only one "doin's" Nigh wanted to hear about. "Where's Brianna?"

"That's what I'm talking about." Tobias finger-plowed his hair, leaving it standing straight as a row of corn stalks. "After you left, we held a powwow. You know, to set new rules and such, what with Marc being the new wagon captain. We figured—"

"What about Bri?" Col interrupted.

"That's what I'm getting to. All of a sudden she says she ain't going on with us. Says she's going to camp at the Mormon ferry till her husband catches up with her." Tobias let out a low whistle. "Whew! If you don't think that didn't set up a ruckus. Musta been five minutes 'fore we could hear her explain that—"

Again, Nigh interrupted. "Is that where she is? The Mormon ferry on the North Platte?"

Tobias nodded. "Marc insisted on taking her. I'm driving his wagon till he gets back, and Ma's taking care of his young'uns. Clive Decker's acting wagon captain."

"Damn! When did they leave?"

"Soon as she could get packed up, after you left."

Nigh was already swinging himself into his saddle. "Thanks, Tobias."

"Wait! You gonna take off after her on a played-out horse?"

Nigh looked down at the dappled gray's sagging head and heaving sides and cursed.

"Get your gear off," Tobias told him. "I'll fetch my buckskin. You can swap him back for the gray when you get Brianna back here where she belongs."

Without another word the two men went about their business. Twenty minutes later Nigh was once more on his way. He had forty miles to travel before reaching the Mormon ferry. But the buckskin could handle it.

Tobias had traded for the gelding from a French-Canadian at Fort Kearny. The "Canuck" was smaller than American horses raised in the east, but was stronger and had greater endurance. American horses faired poorly when deprived of the grain they had been raised on, while Canucks thrived on the short buffalo grass that was mostly all that was available this far west. If all went well, Nigh would reach the Mormon ferry by noon tomorrow.

Barret was feeling too good to bother getting riled at the dog that woke him. The mutt was probably only barking at the full moon riding high overhead. Barret pulled his blankets over his head and burrowed deeper into his bed.

Ever since the fiasco at LaBonte Creek when his horse had thrown him, things had gone smooth as a woman's tit. It was as though the mules knew he was at his breaking point and they'd best not test him again. And the sorrel had been good as mother's milk.

He'd made excellent time and figured he had a good chance of catching up to Brianna within the next couple of days. The only thing that still troubled him was not knowing what had happened to Stinky Harris. Barret had begun to think Indians must have gotten the fool.

Or Columbus Nigh.

But, in spite of the stories he'd been hearing about the fur trapper-turned-emigrant guide his wife had taken up with, Barret wasn't scared. The man would have to be a

magician to do all the feats he was credited with. And
Barret was no milksop. No, the man would have to get up
mighty early to beat him.

Tomorrow Barret would get an early start. Ten miles
would bring him to the Mormon ferry. Once he was
across the North Platte, the country was reputed to be
fairly wide open. A man on horseback could leave all
these two-bit farmers choking on his dust then.

Soon he would have the pleasure of once more feeling
his hands on his wife's skinny, deceitful body. The only
question was what to do with her first. Throw her on her
back and diddle her to death, or simply choke the life out
of her.

With hundreds of emigrants camping along the river,
waiting for a chance to cross, Barret had no way of knowing that only two miles back a halfbreed trader and two
Indians lay sleeping with their feet to the fire, like the
spokes of a wheel.

Each slept with one eye open, their weapons close to
hand and vengeance in their hearts.

Chapter Twenty-eight

With steady hands that belied the state of her nerves, Brianna rolled up the sides of the wagon cover and fastened them to allow a breeze to pass through.

"Really, Marc, there's no need for you to stay. I'll be fine."

Marc squinted into the sun to gaze at her where she stood on the wagon seat, folding back the front of the cover now. "You have any idea how long it'll take your husband to get here?"

Brianna disappeared inside the wagon. She squeezed her eyes shut and took three deep breaths to dispel the panic that seized her every time she thought of facing Barret again. Feeling better, she straightened her spine, picked up a quilt from her bed and stepped back into the open. "Col said he was about five days behind us. That was three days ago, though, and Col hadn't paid him any more visits, so it's possible Barret is closer now."

She gave the quilt a hard shake before flipping it on top of the wagon cover to air out. "I have my pistol, I'll be fine, really. You'll only make me feel more guilty if I detain you any longer. You are wagon captain now."

Marc kicked at a rock and pursed his lips. "I've seen that pistol, Brianna. It's an old caplock. You'll only get off one shot. What if you miss and don't have time to reload?" He shook his head. "There's just too much that could go wrong for me to feel comfortable leaving you here alone."

She laughed and waved an arm to take in the hoard of emigrants camped about them, but the sound was strained. "How can you call this 'alone'?"

He fanned his gaze over the motley gathering and allowed himself a smile. What she said had some merit. The only way Barret Wight might catch her completely alone was to hide near the sagebrush patch designated as the women's privy area. Marc wrinkled his nose, thinking how unpleasant that would be, considering how the place must smell. "Just the same, I think I'll stick around awhile. I have a good horse. It won't take me long to catch up with the wagons."

Brianna resisted the urge to throw herself in his arms and kiss him silly with gratitude. Since the moment she had known what she had to do, she had not allowed herself to contemplate other possible results besides the one she wanted. But deep inside, she was terrified.

At night, alone in her bed with nothing to keep her hands and mind occupied, she found herself haunted by memories tucked away in some furrow of her brain. Memories of life with Barret Wight. She hadn't fooled herself about the risk involved in confronting her husband. Even with all the people coming and going here, and in spite of what she called her "ace in the hole," she knew she could easily wind up dead. Or, at the very least, back in St. Louis under Barret's sadistic thumb.

Threatening him would only enrage him, unless she

handled it just right. And with Barret, enraged meant insane, murderous.

"Well," Marc said, shoving his hands in his pockets. "I believe I'll try to walk off that enormous breakfast you forced down me. Want to come along?"

"No, Marc. You go ahead. I have a few other things I want to get done here."

"All right." He gave her a wave of his hand and sauntered off toward the ferry where the men of the Mormon family who lived nearby were already at work rafting folks across the river.

As soon as he was out of sight, Brianna climbed down from the wagon. She called Patch. The cat was growing fast and had easily figured out how to get down from the wagon. It was getting back in Patch had a problem with. Cradling the animal to her breast, Brianna kissed the silky head. Patch was Brianna's only physical link now with the man she loved—the only one she could hug, anyway— which made the cat all the more precious.

After putting Patch in the wagon, Brianna fetched her pistol and tucked it into her pocket. Then she walked to a hill where she could sit and watch the comings and goings along the crowded river banks. In a few more days it wouldn't be safe to seek such solitude. Even now, if Marc knew where she was going, he would stop her.

But for days Brianna had lived with the tension of constantly hiding her feelings, of giving false impressions and feigning a confidence that didn't exist. She needed some quiet time alone. And she wanted to go over her plan, to map out every detail of what she would say, how she would say it, and to envision the countermoves Barret might make. As though they were playing chess, she thought with a grim smile.

Except for a few children playing tag among the sage-brush, Brianna passed few people on her walk. The adults were all too busy preparing their wagons for the crossing, or catching up on the chores that were so difficult to keep up with traveling day in and day out.

She made her way to a large outcropping of rock part-way up the hill. After checking for rattlesnakes she settled herself on a flat shelf of rock. She drew up her knees and spread her skirt to cover her feet.

A west wind cooled her back while the sun toasted her face and arms. It pleased her to think of the sun's warm caress as Col's love, guarding her. The wind carried away the shouts of the men working the rafts. Even the laughter of the children playing a hundred yards away sounded like whispers, giving her the illusion of total isolation.

Where was Col right now? she wondered, crossing her arms over her knees. Could he possibly miss her as much as she missed him? Soon, if everything worked out, they would be together again. He loved her. She had to believe that. It was all that gave her the courage to do what she had to.

As soon as she had convinced Barret to give her her freedom, she would climb back in her wagon, join an-other train—or go alone, if need be—until she reached the eastern tip of the Wind River Mountains. Col had pointed the range out and told her that his valley lay between the northeastern foothills and the river that bore the same name as the mountains. She would find him.

With the hot sun on her face, she closed her eyes, lay her head on her arms, and indulged herself in daydreams of Col's surprise and joy when he saw her.

They would build a cabin near the lake he had told her about. He would trap and hunt. She would plant a garden with seeds members of the wagon company had given her: English peas, sweet corn, turnips, cabbage, onions, beets, beans. They could go to Fort Bridger for the other supplies they'd need.

She made a mental note to search for canning jars. Maybe some of the emigrants here would sell or trade her a few. Paraffin, too, and cheesecloth. There would be berries in the mountains to gather and preserve. Col could show her herbs and roots to collect for food and medicine.

It would be a lonely life for a woman accustomed to the company of others. But Brianna had received few visitors during her three years of marriage. She was used to being alone.

Of course, that had been before she'd met Lilith and Marc and Dulcie. Brianna's dream faded as she remembered the pain of saying goodbye to Dulcie. The girl had cried. Then she had grown angry and called Brianna a fool. In the end Brianna had been forced to take the girl into her confidence. Dulcie hadn't been convinced that Brianna was doing the right thing, but she—better than anyone else—understood Brianna's need to make this bid for freedom.

Then Dulcie had confided to her of the growing friendship between her and Marc, a friendship Brianna had been too buried in her own problems to see. The thought of those two ending up together pleased her. She wanted Dulcie to find the same hope and joy Brianna had discovered with Col.

Col. How could she need anyone else when she would have him? Then there was the gift next year would bring. She smiled, thinking about it. Next year she and Col would have everything they could want. The Wind River

Valley would be their Eden. It was almost too good to be real.

The braying of a mule close by—too close—brought her abruptly from her fantasies. There was a movement to her right. Bushes rustled. The tangy scent of sagebrush filled her nostrils. Sagebrush and animal sweat and danger.

Something blocked out the sun. Something large and ominous.

Slowly, without changing position or moving her head or arms, Brianna eased open her eyes.

Limned by the saffron yellow glare of the sun was a man. A bulky man with splayed feet and blunt-fingered hands, his facial features concealed in shadow.

But she knew him.

For an instant she was back in the house on the Mississippi River. A storm lashed wildly at the windows, the thunder echoing inside her head. A draft gusted up her skirt. Did he know she had learned his secret?

So much had happened since the awful night of Barret's revealing nightmare. She wasn't the same woman now, but she knew instinctively that Barret was very much the same man.

This time he wouldn't be satisfied with beating her. No, this time, if he touched her at all, he would kill her.

"So, I've finally caught up with you." He shifted and his familiar face came into focus.

She lifted her head and steeled herself against the panic that made her limbs quake and her stomach knot.

"I'm glad to see you, Barret. I was afraid I would have to wait here another week before you caught up."

Harsh laughter broke from his chest. "You expect me to believe you were waiting for me?"

"Yes, I was—"

"No more lies, you conniving bitch. You've put me through enough. You framed me for your own murder. Hell, I wish I had killed you." He moved closer. "I've let my business go to hell, running after you. I've been beaten, robbed, and left on the prairie to die, all thanks to you."

Brianna felt vulnerable huddled there on the rock. A feral gleam in his eye, a wildness, told her he was teetering on the edge of sanity. Slowly she sat up and lowered her legs until her toes touched ground. Then she braced herself.

"Remember Marve, my sorrel?" As though anticipating her next move, he stepped to the right, blocking her most direct route through the sagebrush to the safety of the crowd below. "A goddamn Indian stole him. I still have Maisy, though. If you're nice, I'll let you ride her home."

Brianna straightened and slipped her hand into her pocket. The cool grip of the pistol gave her a faint sense of security. Why had she never noticed the cruelty so plain in the hard line of her husband's mouth? The flicker of madness in his eyes? "I'm sorry you suffered because of me, Barret."

His thin lips stretched into a grisly caricature of a smile. "Not half as sorry as you're going to be."

His gaze touched every part of her, as if inspecting her for Col's fingerprints burned into her flesh. She blushed with shame, then scolded herself. What she and Col had done was not wrong. It was what Barret had done to her that was wrong. He was only trying to intimidate her as he used to, but she knew how to fight him now.

"You look good," he said. "Younger."

You look old, she thought.

It was true; there were new lines around his eyes, on his shallow forehead and around his mouth. The hair at his temples had grayed.

"Maybe it's because you've filled out," he said. "You look more like the girl I married."

Brianna stiffened at the way his gaze caressed her body. She knew that look. Being hit, she could handle. But she couldn't bear the thought of having his hands on her in a sexual way.

"Remember the cellar?" His smile was a sneer. "It's waiting for you. The spiders, all those wonderful little creatures with their wiggly little legs, are waiting for you. They're almost as hungry for you as I am."

She forced herself to smile, hiding the shudder that raced down her spine.

"Spiders are God's creations, did you know that?" She edged away from the rock, from him, hoping he wouldn't notice. "Col taught me to appreciate them. After all, they have their place in the world, just as we do. They keep the insects down and that's a good thing, isn't it? What good do you do for the world, Barret?"

His sneer turned to a scowl. "I could rid the world of the lying, adulterous whore you've become. That should be worth something."

"Truly? Do you recall the old saying about people in glass houses . . . how does it go? Oh, by the way, how is Glory? Does she still live in the place you bought her on Locust Street?"

"What do you know about Glory and the house on Locust?" His fists flexed as though itching to clamp around her neck.

"You told me."

A muscle jumped in his jaw. "I never told you anything."

She smiled. "You told me a lot of things, actually. In your sleep. Things about your mother, for example."

"What about my mother?"

Brianna swallowed. Her heart was slamming against her ribs like an axe on wood. His voice had been hard, threatening, but he hadn't cringed at her words, as she had expected he would do. Doubt spidered down her spine. She felt for the trigger on the old caplock in her pocket and kept the smile plastered on her face. "That she was in love with someone, a man she wanted to marry."

Barret paled. That he had been prepared to hear her words was confirmed by the next words he spoke.

"You made a grave mistake burying the silver where you did." He chuckled. "No pun intended."

He bowed, mocking her with his composure. His smile was as lethal as rattlesnake venom. "That's how I knew you weren't dead. You had me fooled until then, but I would have figured it out eventually. You can't outsmart me."

"I was smart enough to write down everything, including the new location of the skeletons, and leave it with someone who could turn it over to the sheriff if anything happened to me."

At last she had the pleasure of seeing his confidence shaken.

"Tell me," she asked, "am I correct in assuming that the second skeleton was your mother's lover? The one you caught doing to her what you so disgustingly yearned to do yourself?"

His hands balled into fists. "He had no right to touch her. I was the one who loved her most. I quit law school for her, even broke off my engagement to Cynthia Van de Brake so I could devote my life to taking care of Mother. She betrayed me. She was going to abandon me."

The madness in his eyes reminded Brianna of a rabid wolf she'd seen on the prairie. She almost expected to see froth appear at the corners of his mouth.

He moved closer, his nostrils flared like a predator catching scent of its prey. "But I taught her she couldn't treat me that way. I'll teach you, too. Maybe, if you beg me prettily enough, I'll let you live. But you'd better start now."

Brianna's heartbeat thrummed in her ears, as loud as the tornado she'd witnessed at Windlass Hill. It deafened her to everything except the rasp of his heavy breathing and the crunch of sagebrush under his feet as he advanced on her.

Resisting the urge to scream, she said, "I'm not going to beg you, Barret. Not now, not ever again. You can beat me all you like. You can even kill me. But if you do, Marshal Rainey and everyone else back home will know about your unhealthy affection for your mother and how you murdered her."

He moved so quick, she hadn't a chance to escape or to draw the gun from her pocket.

"You bitch!" The first blow connected to her jaw, knocking her to the ground. He snatched her back up by the arm and struck her again. "You great big traitorous bitch! You mailed that little story of yours to someone, didn't you?"

Her mouth opened but all she could get out was a squeak. Her head spun crazily and brilliant pinpoints of light blurred her vision.

"Who did you mail it to?" he screamed in her ear. "Tell me!"

Her head snapped as he slapped her. "Tell me!"

Everything had gone wrong. All she had accomplished was to trigger his madness by mentioning his mother; the two went together like thunder and lightning. Now he would kill her. With his bare hands, he would tear her apart until there was nothing left, not even enough to bury. Col would never even know she was gone. *Oh, Col, save me. I don't want to die.*

Columbus Nigh pulled on the reins, bringing Tobias's buckskin to a halt. Frantically he stood up in the stirrups and studied the terrain.

He had been so sure he had heard Brianna's voice calling him.

Was he too late? Had Barret already found her?

The North Platte was a silver ribbon in the morning sunlight. Wagons lumbered past him along the dusty trail, creating a cloud that nearly obliterated the distant landscape. All around him dogs were barking, men cursing, chains jangling. A woman called to her children.

But Brianna's voice was silent.

One more mile would bring him to the Mormon ferry. Dropping back into the saddle, he jabbed his heels into the horse's sides and bolted forward, praying that he hadn't failed Brianna the same way he had Little Beaver.

"No!" Brianna screamed silently in her head. She would not give in. Barret might kill her, but she would not make it easy for him.

Her hand tightened on the handle of the gun.

Barret laughed, the sound every bit as demented as his mind. "It doesn't really matter if you mailed it, does it? I don't have to go back to St. Louis. Shit, I'm halfway to Oregon, I might as well go the rest of the way."

His grip on her neck loosened as he considered his options. "No. I like the idea of going to California better. With all the people going there to hunt gold, no one would ever find me."

Gratefully, Brianna sucked in air as his thumbs eased up on her windpipe. Her head cleared. Bit by bit she edged the pistol out of her pocket, fighting for strength, praying for time.

Praying to see Col one more time before she died.

Barret's laughter sounded shrill and maniacal in her ear. "It doesn't matter what I do with you, either, bitch. I can kill you right here, right now. No one's paying us any attention. I'll just squeeze the life out of you, slowly, the way I've dreamed of doing so many nights on this filthy, murderous trail you dragged me over."

His fingers tightened once more on her neck. She nearly had the gun free. One more minute, she prayed. *Just give me one more minute.*

"By the time someone finds your body," he went on, "I can be well on my way. No one will ever be able to prove it was me."

He was cutting off her air again. She could feel her strength fading. Life was sliding away.

"Die, bitch," he whispered against her cheek. "Die."

The gun came free. It weighed more than the buffalo bull Col had shot on the South Platte. More than three loaded wagons. Fighting to keep her eyes open, to stay alive only a little longer, she struggled to raise the nose of the gun. Her finger closed over the trigger.

The blast rocked her body.

Surprise and confusion widened Barret's eyes. His hands slid from her neck, down her chest, over her breasts. Then he staggered back and let out a bellow of pain.

Brianna dropped the gun. She slumped to her knees, rubbing her neck and gasping for air as she watched him clutch at his leg. A bright red stain was spreading from his groin to his knee. She hadn't managed to hit anything vital.

"You shot me," he said, his voice childish now. The madness was fading from his eyes. "Why? Why did you—?"

Horses pounded up the hill toward them, but she didn't have enough stamina left to lift her head to see who was coming—until Col's name burst in her mind, as beautiful as the fireworks display she'd seen as a girl in St. Louis. She looked up, a smile already forming on her lips.

But there were three men coming toward them, not one.

And none of them were Col.

Two were naked except for breechclouts, their dark copper skin daubed with paint. Feathers fluttered from their ebony hair. They carried lances, bows, and quivers, and held short-barrel carbine rifles across their laps. As they grew closer she saw that the third man, dressed in fringed buckskins, was white, with dark brown hair rather than black.

All three came to a halt directly in front of them. Brianna held her breath, waiting for them to pin her to the ground with their lances. Never had she seen such savage-looking men, like demons from hell.

No one spoke. The entire world seemed to have come to a standstill. Dust puffed feebly about the horses' feet. Even the wind had stilled, as though afraid its bluster would pale in comparison to the furor these three ferocious men could unleash.

One of the horses pranced to the side and she heard the tinkle of tiny hawk bells attached to its mane. The sound seemed so out of place in the tense setting, it brought her perilously close to laughter.

Finally, as though just realizing they were no longer alone, Barret tore his gaze from the wound in his thigh and looked up. Surprise registered on his face, then pleasure as recognition set in. "Antoine. Look, she shot me. My own wife shot me."

She felt the man's fierce scrutiny on her face and neck where bruises had already begun to color and swell, and she shuddered. There was death in those eyes.

"Madame," he said with a strong French accent, and a polite nod. "I am Antoine Robidoux. To you I give my sympathy, and my heartfelt gratitude for your poor aim. It would have been a great *desappointement* to find our friend dead after we have traveled so far to find him."

"Good Christ, Antoine," Barret complained. "Get over here and help me. I'm bleeding to death here."

The Frenchman only looked at him, his eyes like agates of purest black. "You remember *mon jeune fille, monsieur?* My little daughter?"

The color fled Barret's face, leaving him as pale as Brianna's wet drawers. "Sure, I-I meant to say goodbye to her before I left, but she wasn't around."

"This is strange," Antoine said, rubbing his bristly

chin. "She say to her you give a very special farewell. Ah, but I am being rude. Allow me to introduce to you my companions." He gestured to the shorter of the two Indians. "This man is Runs the Buffalo, brother to my wife. The other is Yellow Fox. You remember, I mention him to you at my post, *oui?*"

Slowly, Barret shook his head. His eyes had grown so round Brianna could see white all around the pale irises.

"Yellow Fox is the best marksman of my wife's people," Antoine continued with a cold but proud smile. "It is said he can shoot the balls off a man running for his life. This fall Yellow Fox was to have taken my sweet daughter for his wife. You notice he has cropped his hair, eh? You know what this means?"

Again, Barret shook his head.

"It means that he is mourning the loss of a loved one. I, too, mourn this great loss. Do you know why, *monsieur* Wight?"

"It . . . it's nothing to do with me. Look, I've been shot. You have to get me some help, I—"

"My daughter's name can never be spoken again," Antoine interrupted.

Brianna gasped, remembering Col's words about the speaking of a dead one's name being bad luck.

Antoine glanced at her. "I see that you, *madame*, know the significance of this. My little one was shamed, you see, taken against her will, by a man she mistook as a friend.

"The Black Robes have spoken much with her about the sanctity of marriage and the importance of going to a husband with innocence intact. She think Yellow Fox will no longer want her, so she take her knife and plunged it into her heart. She is with her ancestors now, but my friend finds this small comfort. You are a *femme*, you have the tender heart, no? You will understand that we must avenge this wrong done my *petite fille.*"

"Wha . . . what are you talking about?" Barret blubbered. He began to back away, his bloodied hands held out in front of him. "Why is that . . . why is that savage looking at me like that?"

Antoine nodded at Yellow Fox. The Indian drew an arrow, nocked it and drew back the string of his bow.

"Wait . . . wait a minute," Barret screeched. "She came onto me. You know, she *wanted* me to—"

The sentence went unfinished. The lie was cut short by the twang of Yellow Fox's bowstring and the dull thwack as the arrow drove deep into Barret's thick chest.

Chapter Twenty-nine

With a strangled gasp, Barret staggered under the arrow's impact, then caught himself.

Brianna screamed. The sound seemed to bring the world alive again. She lurched to her feet and stumbled backward, away from the awful sight of her husband and the brightly painted feathers quivering at the end of the shaft protruding from his chest.

Beyond the grisly scene, the huge emigrant encampment also came alive like a hive of bees knocked awry; people raced everywhere, confused and alarmed. Men ran toward the hill where she stood, armed with rifles, shovels, and picks.

Barret's hands encircled the shaft. The disbelief in his eyes changed to horror as he watched the second Indian nock an arrow in his bow. "No . . . no!"

Antoine held up his hand. The Indian waited.

As the Frenchman dismounted and walked over to him, Barret fell to his knees. "God, Antoine, have . . . mercy. Don't . . . let them . . . hurt me anymore. I didn't. . . ."

His voice faded as Antoine drew a knife from his belt.

The Frenchman knotted his hand in Barret's hair. He shoved Barret face-down on the ground, ignoring the man's howl of pain as the arrow was driven through his body. The barbed steel tip with its grisly coating of blood emerged to point into the sky like a cockeyed road sign.

Brianna covered her face with her hands but she couldn't stop watching. Her breath came in terrified gasps and the roar in her ears blocked out all sound.

With the tip of his skinning knife, while Barret gasped for air and gurgled up bloody froth, Antoine carved a circle four inches in diameter in Barret's scalp. Then, his fingers tangled in Barret's pale yellow hair, Antoine braced his foot on the man's back and gave a hard yank. The round patch of scalp tore loose with a sickening, sucking sound. Blood splattered everywhere, catching Brianna.

Brianna gagged.

Nigh reined in his horse and gazed about him in confusion. Across the river the rafts used by the Mormons to ferry wagons and emigrants across the North Platte bobbed in the water, loaded and ready, but unattended. People were running toward the hill beyond the crudely built log building that housed the Mormons. Already a large crowd had gathered there. Then he noticed that even the people on this side of the river were frozen like statues, their eyes glued to the same hill.

As he rode down to the water he caught the word "Indians," then "She shot him." Foreboding lashed at his insides.

He didn't waste time asking himself what the Indians could have to do with Brianna. The other three words were enough to drive him into water, whipping his mount with his quirt as he forced the animal across the shallow but treacherous river.

The horse stumbled as quicksand sucked at its hooves. Nigh whipped him harder and screamed obscenities in his trembling ears. The horse jerked free and plunged forward.

Halfway across, they sank in one of the inexplicable holes the Platte was famous for. Before Nigh could slide off to allow the horse to swim, the buckskin found purchase on the shifting, sandy bottom and they were moving again.

Panic drove Nigh on.

Dripping wet, he raced toward the hill, his lips moving in silent prayer as his glance raked the crowd, searching, always searching, for Brianna.

"Naw, the Injuns are gone," he heard someone say as he worked his way through the throng.

His bowels knotted in figure eights as a woman, her hands clasped to her plump cheeks, said over and over, "The poor woman. The poor, poor woman."

Cursing and ordering people aside, he drove the buckskin deeper and deeper into the mob while fear ate at his innards like turkey vultures on a corpse.

The Indians put away their bows. Yellow Fox spoke to Antoine in a tongue much like Brianna had heard Col use, then tossed the Frenchman a rope. The arrow was carefully withdrawn, wiped clean on its victim's shirt, and returned to its owner. The rope was tied around Barret's chest and he was turned onto his back. His eyes, so like the color of the sky, stared sightlessly into the sun.

Falling to her knees, Brianna vomited.

Antoine swung himself into his saddle. He handed the scalp to Yellow Fox who quickly attached it to his lance. Antoine secured the rope to his saddle and, as one voice, the three men tipped back their heads, opened their mouths and let out a spine-tingling scream.

The horses reared and danced, kicking up dust. Then the men lashed the animals with their quirts and galloped away, dragging Barret's body behind them over rocks and sagebrush.

The last thing Brianna saw of her husband were the puffs of dust raised by his body as it bounced along, and the bloody patch of his scalp dangling from a lance. She retched and retched until there was nothing left in her stomach.

Suddenly Marc was there beside her.

"Brianna, are you all right?" He helped her to her feet. With her arms around his waist, she clung to him as tears escaped her eyes and ran down her cheeks.

People of all ages milled around them, stirring up the dust and the heat. Voices jangled. The smell of unwashed bodies crowded out the scent of sagebrush. Brianna held her attention on the familiar, comforting face of her friend.

"They killed him, Marc. Oh God, they killed him."

"I know. I saw them drag him away as I was running up the hill. The wind carried his howls of pain clear down to the water. Someone yelled 'Indians!' Then I heard you scream."

She laid her head on his shoulder and gave in to the tears that had simmered below the surface of her emotions for days. Awkwardly, Marc patted her back and murmured inanities in an effort to comfort her.

"Come on," he said when she began to calm down. "Let's get you back to the wagon where you can lie down."

She drew away and he handed her a handkerchief.

"My mouth," she said with a grimace. "Can you get me something I can rinse it with?"

He called out to one of the men watching with gruesome fascination as flies swarmed in the warm pool of blood on the ground, and asked to borrow the flask the man carried.

"Here." Marc held the flask to her lips. "It's whiskey. Just swish it around and spit it out."

After she had done as he told her, he held the flask to her mouth again. "Now take a swallow. It will calm you."

She choked and gasped as the fire burned its way down her throat into her stomach. Then the liquor's warmth spread through her veins and she felt a bit of the tension ease from her body.

Someone was shouting and shoving his way toward them. The crowd parted reluctantly before the mounted rider. Then she saw him.

"Col!"

He was there, staring at her as though he couldn't believe what he saw. His gaze dropped to her blood-stained clothes and the relief in his silver-gray eyes vanished. In a heartbeat he had dismounted and was facing her, his hands on her arms. Marc released her and stepped away.

"The blood, you're covered with blood," Col stammered hoarsely. "Where are you hurt? Is it bad?"

She glanced down at her dress, noticing for the first time the blood splattered on her from Barret's wounds. "It . . . it's Barret's blood, not mine."

He let out his breath and pulled her into his arms. The lower half of his body was soaking wet. She could feel it dampening her own clothes.

"Bri, oh God, Bri." He muttered her name over and over, holding her so tightly she could barely breathe. But she didn't care. This kind of breathlessness she could handle. Col was here. Her love was here. She drew back and smiled up at him. The water splashed on his face as he crossed the river and had turned the dust to muddy runnels that dripped from his chin. His eyes were rimmed with red. But he had never looked more handsome.

His long fingers on her bruised jaw and cheek were gentle. His voice was hard. "Did Barret do this? Where is he, I'll kill him—"

"You're too late. He's gone, Col. He'll never bother us again."

Again he heard the words, "She shot him." Over her shoulder Col questioned Marc with his eyes. Marc nodded. Looking back at Brianna, Col said, "I ought to paddle you. You made me so angry I couldn't think straight. When I realized what you intended to do, I nearly rode my horse to death trying to reach you."

"It wasn't necessary," she said. "But I'm so glad you did."

He frowned. "What do you mean, it wasn't necessary?"

She smiled at the fear in his eyes. "I mean that as soon as I convinced Barret to grant me a divorce, I was coming to find you. In our valley," she added softly.

"In our valley," he repeated, shaking his head. "You're crazy, you know that? The Indians would call you Woman Who Has Gone Out Of Her Head."

"No. They'll call me Woman Of Man Without Fear."

He kissed her then, so tenderly, so reverently, Brianna

felt her eyelids prick once more with tears. Swallowing them, she entwined her arms about his neck and kissed him back. He tasted of dirt and river water, but she barely noticed. Her lips moved over his, telling him with action what she hadn't been able to say in words until this moment.

"You're mine now," he whispered against her whiskey-flavored mouth. "As soon as we can find a man of the cloth, I'm going to make sure you can never leave me."

She cocked her head and gave him a coy smile. "You'd better. I'd hate to see the next generation of Nighs come into this world illegitimate."

He stepped back, staring at her as though she'd spoken in a strange language. Slowly his gaze swept down over her, lingering on her breasts and stomach, searching for evidence that what she hinted at was true.

Brianna blushed. "It won't be here till spring, Col. That's several months away yet."

First he smiled. He grinned. Then he let out a whoop every bit as loud as that the Indians had given before dragging off Barret Wight's body.

"Go find a preacher, Marc," he shouted. "We're having a wedding."

Col grabbed her about the waist and swung her in a circle, round and round. Abruptly he stopped and said, "I'm sorry, did I hurt you? Did I hurt the baby?"

She laughed and clung to him. "No, silly, we're not made of glass."

"No, you're moonshine, spun like a spider's web to snare me. You even taste like moonshine," he teased.

The joy in his eyes altered, grew serious and took on depth. He pressed his lips to her temple and his voice became hoarse and unsteady as he whispered, "Ah, Bri, I love you so much. You do know that, don't you?"

"Yes, although sometimes I can't believe I could be so lucky."

He looked at her in astonishment. "You know what I am and all that I'm not. Yet you can say that?"

"You're a gentle and caring man, Columbus Nigh. What more could any woman want? Knowing that you love me makes me feel more blessed than any woman alive."

She pulled back, took his hand and held it to her stomach. There was no denying the pride in her voice and her eyes when she spoke: "You gave me this child. Already I love him as much as I love his father. We're a family now, Col. A family."

He swallowed, his eyes suspiciously bright. "Told you we belonged together, didn't I?"

"Yes, Col. The sun and the moon. And next year a little star to add to our own special heaven."

About the Author

All my life I've dreamed of traveling the Oregon Trail. In spite of the hardships and danger, I yearn to go back and live just a little of that exciting, historic period. To truly see—instead of *imagining*—how the land looked. Without concrete. Without telephone poles. Without smog or crumpled Coke cans glinting from the weeds along the road.

In *TENDER TOUCH* I was able to see it through Brianna's eyes. To taste the dust. To feel the heat, the sore feet, the lack of privacy, the fear and exhaustion. To know the awe of new sights, the anticipation of beginning a new life, and the very special warmth of Columbus Nigh's smile.

TENDER TOUCH was a Golden Heart Finalist in 1991 under the title *BRIANNA*. I hope my readers enjoy reading it as much as I enjoyed writing it. I'd love to hear from them, at 1816 Tramway Drive, Sandy, UT 84092. Please send SASE for reply.

My first Zebra historical romance, *TAMING JENNA*, is available in bookstores and my newest historical romance, *FOREVER MINE*, will be published soon by Zebra Books.

Please turn the page for an exciting
sneak preview of
FOREVER MINE
Charlene Raddon's exciting new
historical romance
coming soon from Zebra Books

Chapter One

To Bartholomew Noon the unceasing rumble of the sea and the melancholy cry of gulls were the very embodiment of his loneliness. Constant. Never ending. But loneliness was not the cause of the heavy sense of foreboding that had come over him on awakening that morning. A warning he well knew better than to ignore.

In the hope of escaping the gloomy cloud hanging over him, he had hiked the steep trail down to the beach where a man could be alone. Here on the driftwood-littered strand, he could be himself. No one to placate. No one from whom he must hide his innermost feelings in order to keep from being manipulated or tormented. Here, he could ponder his unwonted presentiment without interruption.

Out where the water deepened, a wave of translucent jade crested, curled in upon itself, then broke in a boiling froth that tossed and fumed until its force ebbed. Then, indolently, it crept toward him until the foam-tipped water encircled his boots, as if to embrace him in empathy and compassion, before being sucked back into the gray Pacific Ocean, stealing the sand from under him as it went.

A derisive snort erupted from deep inside Bartholomew's chest as he shrugged off his imaginings. The sea neither embraced nor understood him. What it did do, a few grains at a time, was erode away the land, the same way life with Hester was eroding away his soul.

The sky darkened from gray to black as a storm drew near. Fog, pushed by the wind herding the storm inland, had already obliterated the headland to the south where Hester and the lighthouse awaited him. The air grew more chill. Soon the rain would begin. Resolutely, he thrust his icy fingers into his coat pockets and turned his back on his beloved sea. It was time to see to his responsibilities.

The thick February mist formed droplets on his lashes and the tip of his sturdy nose. Under his Keeper's cap, his damp sable hair formed a mass of loose curls.

"Come on, Harlequin," he called to a puffin feeding in the shallow water, "time to go."

The stubby bird scooped up a last mouthful of tiny mole crabs in its garish orange and red beak and waddled out of the surf toward the man, every bit as though it had understood the human command. Awkwardly, it flapped its raven wings, flying barely high enough to reach the man's broad shoulder, but it seemed content there. Bartholomew patted the sleek snowy feathers of its breast as he climbed the bluff that rose above the strand. The wing Bartholomew had mended was nearly as strong as ever. Any day now the bird would rejoin its own kind on the seastacks off the Oregon coast, leaving Bartholomew more alone than ever.

Evergreens draped in moss crowded close around him as he made his way up the trail, and added to the gloom of the foggy morn. Tree trunks, misshapened by ferns that rooted in every gnarl, appeared like phantoms in the drifting mist, writhing and moaning in the rising wind. It was when the track ran close enough to the cliff to offer a last view of the sea that Bartholomew saw the ship.

One second the vessel was there, the next it was gone. The fog congealed to the consistency of Hester's sausage gravy and lay every bit as heavily upon the sea as the gravy did in Bartholomew's stomach. His dark eyes strained to penetrate the ghostly vapor. If he was right, Pyramid Rock lay directly across the vessel's course.

Like a too-tight seam, the fog split apart. In the resultant window, he spotted the ship, heading straight for the hidden rock.

He screamed for the vessel to veer sharply portside, knowing in the more reasonable portion of his brain that he was much too far away to be heard.

The rising wind hurtled the ship closer to its destruction, as easily as a stone cast from a sling. To the man the scene played out in painful slow motion, grating on his nerves like wood beneath a rasp. People were on that ship, people who would die. He wanted to rage at the heavens for allowing such tragedy.

The thought that there might be survivors sent him racing back down toward the beach, until reality brought him to a halt.

At sea level the white-capped waves would hide the ship from him. Even if it did crash, there would be time to fetch horses from the lighthouse station and get back before the sea deposited its victims on the sand. Meanwhile, he could hope he was mistaken about the ship's danger.

Even as his mind formed the thought, he saw it happen. Ship and rock appeared to merge and become one as they collided. Then, as though to refuse such a marriage, the cold lifeless stone ejected the helpless mass of wood and sailcloth back out into the sea. Billowing white sails crumpled as the mast snapped and collapsed upon the heaving deck. The wind and the roar of the sea drowned out the splintering of wood and the screams of men, but Bartholomew heard them. In his heart.

For one more moment the ship bobbed uncertainly upon the waves, then sank from view. Bartholomew turned and raced up the steep forest trail. The puffin frantically flapped its wings to maintain balance on the man's broad shoulder, then plummeted unnoticed to the mossy earth.

Hester was coming from the garden when her husband sprinted out of the woods and around the fenced compound in which the houses stood. She crept along as though each step was an act of painful labor. With one hand she carried the freshly rinsed ceramic chamber pot she used at night instead of making the long walk down to the cold water closet off the kitchen.

"Where you going in such a hurry?" She waited for him to reach her, her shawl clutched over her flat, pious chest.

"Shipwreck," he said as he passed her. "Crashed into Pyramid Rock. I'm taking the horses down to the beach for survivors."

"What'll you do with 'em if you find any?" she called after him in the waspish voice she was careful never to use around others.

Bartholomew didn't bother to answer. He rushed into the barn, snatched bridles off the wall and went to work readying the four horses they kept for hauling supplies.

Hester was still standing on the path, her thin face scrunched with disapproval, when he led the horses out into the fog.

"Won't have no putrifying bodies stinking up my house," she said, following him to the back porch of their home.

"Don't worry, Hester, I'll put them in the barn."

He glanced up as a white beam cut weakly through the thickening fog, followed by a red flash. On a good day the beam could be seen twenty-one miles out to sea. But today wasn't a good day. At least Pritchard had not fallen asleep and allowed the light to go out.

"Have Seamus relieve Pritchard, Hester, and send the boy down to help me. Right now I need blankets, and that brandy we keep for emergencies . . . if you haven't drunk it."

Hester blanched, then colored. In her best imitation of refined gentility, which she usually saved for company, she said, "How dare you accuse me of drinking alcoholic beverages. You know I am a member in good standing of The Tillamook Women for Temperance Coalition . . . even if you have buried me here where I can't get to the meetings anymore."

Her husband tossed her a look of disgust, saying nothing about the bottle of Dr. Hamilton's Heavenly Elixir he had found that morning under the porch steps. The so-called tonic was mostly alcohol, but Hester had ignored his demand that she destroy her supply. She claimed it gave her strength and made her feel better. Bartholomew no longer cared. It made her easier to live with, if nothing else.

"Yes, Hester. Now get the blankets, please, I haven't time to argue."

"Get them yourself then. You can move faster than me."

The day was nearly gone before Bartholomew was able to head back to the lighthouse station, exhausted and gloomier than ever. Each time he had spotted a head bobbing on the waves, or a body clinging to a piece of flotsam, he had swum out to bring the victim ashore. He built a bonfire to guide survivors through the fog and warm them when they arrived. He emptied one woman's stomach of seawater and dealt with the deep gash her son had received on one leg. He carried or dragged lifeless bodies through the surf to dry land. He rubbed life into the frozen limbs of the living, doled out blood-warming doses of brandy, then loaded everyone—dead and alive—onto the horses for the ride over the headland.

Pritchard Monteer met the cavalcade halfway along the trail and took charge of the extra horse. Slung over its back were two wet, blanket-wrapped bodies, a bright-eyed black and white puffin perched irreverently on top.

"Are you all right, Uncle Bart? Seamus was out playing with those blasted goats again and Aunt Hester couldn't find him or I would have been here sooner."

Bartholomew had no strength to reply.

Across the rump of the bay mare he rode lay a small shrouded bundle, two dainty bare feet dangling limply from beneath the blanket. A third horse carried a young man in his teens, an unconscious woman cradled in his arms. Two more men rode double on a buckskin gelding, looking as weary as their dark-visaged rescuer.

At the back gate of the compound, Bartholomew dismounted and looped the reins around the rail. He took the woman from her son and carried her to the house while Pritchard helped the others alight. Before Bartholomew could open the door and usher his charges inside, Hester swung the portal wide and stood barring the entrance.

"Where do you think you're taking them?" she asked.

He stared at her with eyes like black ice until she backed away nervously. Then he motioned for the shipwreck victims to go on in and warm themselves at the kitchen stove. Turning to Pritchard, Bartholomew handed over the unconscious woman. The younger, smaller man staggered under the weight his uncle had so easily carried.

"Put the woman in Hester's room, and the boy in the garret. The men can share my room."

Pritchard waited until Hester gave a reluctant shrug before he carried out his uncle's orders. Bartholomew closed the door and pinned his wife to the wall with his harsh gaze. His voice was low and deadly calm. "Those people nearly died, Hester. They're exhausted, half-frozen and in shock. The boy lost a lot of blood. Would you truly deny them the comforts of a dry bed and some warm broth?"

"Why can't you put them next door? They'll track up my floors. I just—"

"Hester!" Bartholomew's large hands grasped her shoulders, dangerously close to her chicken-thin neck, and lightly squeezed. She squinted up at him, daring him, her thin lips so pinched they nearly disappeared. Slowly, he loosened his fingers and forced himself to relax.

"There's an extra bed over there," she said with a smug smile, knowing she'd won that last round.

"One bed. Where would the rest of them sleep?"

"The boy can sleep on the floor and Pritchard can share your room till they're gone."

To Bartholomew, Hester's brown-checked shirtwaist gave her complexion a sallow cast and deepened the blue stain beneath her dull, hazel eyes. She wore only dark, somber colors, considering anything brighter to be appropriate only for "loose" women. Yet she insisted on wearing ruffles and ruching and bows that made her look like a gift-wrapped prune. Her values were high, her rules strict, but she tended to twist them to suit her needs. Regarding her with a mixture of pity and exasperation, he said, "You won't mind running next door several times a day with hot broth and whatever else they'll need?"

Hester's eyes yawned wide in astonishment. "Let them make their own broth. Or let Seamus do it, Lord knows he's not worth much else. I'm no scullery maid, I'm your wife."

"Only when it suits you," he muttered.

"What?"

Ignoring her question, he said, "Do you truly think that would be the Christian thing to do, to leave them to shift for themselves in their condition? Or to push them off onto an old man?"

"I daresay a little rest is all they need. You know what the good book says: 'The Lord helps those who help themselves.'" She bobbed her beaklike chin as if dotting an exclamation point.

Bartholomew smiled sadly. "The Bible says no such

thing, Hester. But it does say 'Blessed are the merciful, for they shall obtain mercy.' "

Hester's mouth opened, closed, and opened again. "So I didn't say it exactly right, it still—"

"They stay, Hester." His voice was like cold granite. "I'll sleep with Pritchard. You can sleep down here on the sofa, or take the extra bed next door. I don't care. But those people *will* stay in this house, and you *will* care for them until I can get them to Tillamook. Is that clear?"

Her eyes filled with hatred as she glowered at him. Without another word, she stormed into the kitchen, slamming the door in his face. Alone, Bartholomew pressed the inner corners of his eyes with thumb and forefinger. The discreet clearing of a throat brought up his head. Pritchard stood in the doorway to the hall which opened onto the end of the porch.

"Excuse me, Uncle Bart. I had to move some books off your bed onto the floor. The shelves were full. But the folks are all settled in now."

Bartholomew gave a weary sigh. "Fine, Pritchard. Come on and help me with the bodies now."

"What'll we do with the others when they're feeling better?" the younger man asked as they led the horses to the barn.

"We'll drive them to Bigg's place and get him to take them in to Tillamook. From there they can catch a ride to Astoria and go on to San Francisco where they were headed in the first place."

"I think I'd be wanting to stay off ships if I was them." Pritchard shuddered. He wasn't very brave at the best of times, but the thought of having a deck break apart beneath his feet and chuck him into an icy ocean made him want to crawl under his bed and never look at the sea again.

In the barn, as they lowered the last of the victims to the floor, a blanket slipped, exposing the face of a young woman with russet hair and a freckled nose.

"Holy Hector," Pritchard muttered, staring at her.

Bartholomew flipped the blanket back over the girl's face and dragged himself to his feet.

"Pretty little thing, wasn't she?" The boy hop-stepped to keep up with his uncle's long loose stride as he went to tend the horses. "Married, too. At least I guess she was, she's wearing a gold band."

Bartholomew stopped and looked at his nephew. "The other day you were asking me if the Hopkins girl over on Trask River had married yet. What is this sudden interest in the marital state of young females, Pritchard?"

The boy colored. "I . . . well. . . . Holy Hector, Uncle Bart, I am a grown man. Why shouldn't I be interested in women? Maybe I'm tired of baching it with old Seamus while you go home to Aunt Hester every night."

"Good hell." *If the boy only knew.* Pritchard had turned twenty-two a month past. In truth, he wasn't a boy any longer, though he would always be one to Bartholomew. "So, you're thinking of getting married, are you?"

His cheeks bright rose, the young man shrugged and gave his uncle a shy smile. "Actually, I've been doing more than thinking about it. You see, I . . . well, I've been trying to find a way to talk to you and Aunt Hester about this for weeks. I contacted Pa's brother in Portland a while back, the one who's an attorney, and he placed an advertisement for me back East."

"What kind of advertisement?" Bartholomew asked as he turned the mare into her stall.

"For a bride."

Bartholomew stared at him in amazement, certain he had not heard right. "A bride? You advertised for a bride?"

Pritchard filled a bucket with grain. "Uncle Edward wrote to a lawyer friend of his in Cincinnati and asked him to screen applicants for me. It took three months, but now—" he grinned, "—she's on her way."

Bartholomew took the bucket and dumped the grain into the mare's feed bin. "Are you telling me they found you a bride, and she's already on her way here?"

"Kind of like getting hit by a wild pitch, isn't it? That's how I felt when I got the news."

Pritchard filled another bucket and took it into the buckskin's stall. Through the haze in his head, Bartholomew heard the grain strike the metal bottom of the bin. A thin cloud of chaff rose toward the loft.

"Uncle Edward's friend knows her and her family real well," the boy said over the partition. "In fact, he and her father are law partners. Her name is Ariah Scott and she'll be coming in on the train next week."

Bartholomew was still standing in the mare's stall, an expression of bewildered astonishment on his face when Pritchard emerged with the empty bucket.

Pritchard chuckled. "I'm getting married. Plumb throws you a curve ball, don't it?" His smile faded and his gaze fell. "I . . . uh, was hoping you might do me a favor, Uncle Bartholomew."

Bartholomew frowned. The boy only addressed him by his full given name when he was in trouble or wanted something outrageous. "I can't arrange a leave for you, if that's what you want. You know I have a shipment of pheasants to deliver in Portland next week. The buyers are expecting it and a delay could put us too close to nesting time. Frank Worden is coming to take my shifts, but he can't cover for both of us, and it's too late to change things anyway."

"I wasn't going to ask you to change anything. I was only hoping you could pick Ariah up for me at the Portland train station while you're there."

"Who? Oh no." Bartholomew shook his head, holding up a curry comb as if to fend off Pritchard with it. "There's no reason she can't take the train to Yamhill and then catch the stage like everybody else."

"But the worst part of the trip is between Yamhill and Tillamook. Especially in March. You know that ride over the Trask River toll road is pure hell at the best of times, let alone in spring when it's all muddy and everything."

"Then have her take a steamer up the Columbia and around to Tillamook Bay."

"I suggested that, but she's terrified of boats."

Bartholomew slung his arms across the mare's back, rested his forehead against her side, and groaned. "Can't you have her wait a month till the weather's better?"

"I don't want to wait another month. I'm a man, Uncle Bartholomew, and I'm looking forward to having a wife of my own. I have needs, like any other man. That's something you should understand, even if it has been a long time since you've had to worry about how to fill those needs."

Bartholomew stifled the bitter retort about the so-called pleasures of marriage that came to mind. He might have attempted to set the boy straight, except that Pritchard took after his aunt in one way—he saw only what he wanted to see, heard only what he wanted to hear. Clamping a commiserating hand on the young man's shoulder, he said instead, "I do understand. But don't you think the solution you've chosen is a bit drastic? You don't even know this woman. Lord only knows what she looks like."

"No, I don't think it's drastic." Pritchard shook his head so enthusiastically his baseball cap nearly flew off. "You know how lonely it is here. I want a family of my own, a wife I can share things with. And children, I want children." He grinned. "Nine boys. My own baseball team. Wouldn't that be grand, Uncle Bart?"

"Yes, Pritchard, that would be grand."

Suddenly, Bartholomew felt a hundred years old. A yearning so sharp it pierced his being, urged him to hurry back down to the beach where he could lose himself in the roar of the waves and the scream of the gulls overhead.

Loneliness and a man's needs. Had there ever been a day in his adult life when he hadn't suffered those needs?

Maybe one. The night his father died, when a prettier, more amiable Hester had come to his bed to comfort him. One brief moment when he thought he had found heaven.

But that had been a lifetime ago.

Chapter Two

The train was already standing on the track when Bartholomew parked his wagon and hurried to the loading platform. The engine puffed steam and noisily belched out black smoke while it disgorged its passengers. People rushed to greet relatives and friends, adding joyous shouts and laughter to the chug-chug of the idling train and the rumble of baggage carts on the wooden platform.

For several seconds Bartholomew stood breathing in the hot-metal smell of the engine, mixed with perfume, body sweat, and wood smoke. The air hummed with an excitement he did not share. Pritchard's request that he save the young man's bride from the hazards and discomfort of a stagecoach ride from Yamhill to Tillamook still nettled Bartholomew.

What on earth would he do with her on the long trip home? What could they talk about? Even if the weather remained fair and the road in good condition, they would still spend four interminable days together. Days when they would be entirely alone, for Hester had pleaded illness and opted to wait in Tillamook with friends until he returned.

Days of freedom from Hester and responsibility which Bartholomew would otherwise have looked forward to with the eagerness of a child at Christmas.

And what of the nights that went along with those days? Miss Ariah Scott was a city girl. From what Pritchard had learned of her—which wasn't much—she had never so much as stepped foot out of Cincinnati before. Often he stayed with friends when he traveled, the Olwells, the Uphams, and the Rhudes, but what if it became necessary to camp out? How would such an inexperienced miss handle sleeping on the road with a strange man? And what would his friends think about him traveling with a young, unmarried woman? He would soon find out.

Several women stood on the loading platform, trunks and satchels stacked at their feet as they waited to be met. Two were elderly. Another proved to have a child hiding behind her skirts.

Then he saw her. Miss Ariah Scott.

Three or four inches taller than Pritchard, her body had as much substance as a puff of air. In spite of the current popularity of the perfect, hour-glass shape, this woman obviously disdained the use of body padding such as Hester used in filling out her figure. Miss Scott's face was long enough to wear a halter and bound to curdle cream.

Bartholomew started forward, feeling both sympathy and irritation for his idiotic nephew. Before he half reached the horse-faced stick of a woman, she let out a screech and flew into the arms of a tall gentleman. Only partly relieved, Bartholomew went back to studying the crowd.

All the passengers had disembarked from the train, and most had already left the station. A young woman came from the station house and joined an elderly lady. He dismissed her at once as being too pretty to have to resort to an arranged marriage with a man she'd never met. She glanced around, and bounced up and down on her heels with glaring impatience. When she turned his way, affording him a full view of her face, he sucked in his breath at its delicate beauty.

Burrowing into the shadow of an overloaded baggage cart, Bartholomew drank in his fill of her, the way an old seaman would guzzle a tankard of ale after too many months at sea. Her hair was the ordinary brown of a walnut shell. Her form, in a well-made traveling suit the color of hot house orchids, hinted of fragility. Her face was less than perfect, its shape too symmetrical, the skin too flawless, without even a smidgeon of character. As for the features, the brows were too thick, the nose too small and straight. And the mouth. . . . Good hell, that well-defined mouth with its tiny mole perched so enticingly at the tip of one rounded peak fairly begged to be kissed.

But, except for her mouth and the fresh, innocent sort of sensuality he sensed about her, he was at a loss as to explain her appeal. Then he heard the trill of her laughter, like the song of a bird: clear, resonant, *alive,* and he knew. Her face was animated, her hands quick and graceful in their gestures. She was a living, breathing advertisement for youthful enthusiasm. For life.

Awed by her affect on him, Bartholomew forgot about Miss Ariah Scott. He forgot Hester and Pritchard and the lighthouse station where he was Head Keeper. Had something not burst him out of his trance, he would likely have been content to stand there forever, watching this entrancing creature in her fantastical orchid attire. But at that moment a gray-haired man appeared. With an exclamation of joy the girl rushed toward him. She made as if to hug the man, nearly losing her balance when he quickly backed away.

"Here, here, young woman," the man blurted. "What do you think you're about?"

An elderly lady hurried over to them. "Anthony, what is going on here? Who is this . . . this female? Tell me at once or you'll be sleeping on the summer porch for the rest of your deceitful life, along with that mutt of yours."

Anthony's hands went up in testimony to his innocence. His irate wife took hold of his ear and hauled him to the buggy, casting the girl a look of contempt as she went. Instinctively, Bartholomew's feet carried him toward the trio, his protective urges to the fore. But the girl was already scurrying back to her friend. He turned away so she wouldn't know he had witnessed the embarrassing scene.

"Oh, Mrs. Doughney," the girl wailed when she reached the old woman, "why can't I ever think before I act? My mother always told me I was too impulsive by far and that I hadn't a modicum of common sense in me."

"No harm done, my dear." The woman patted the girl's gloved hand. "You're a bit anxious, is all. Be patient, your gentleman will show up."

"I'm afraid patience is another of my failings. How am I ever to be a proper wife when . . ."

The girl looked up and caught Bartholomew staring at her. Hope blossomed in her eyes. They were so full of eagerness, those eyes, lively and optimistic and innocent. Stunning eyes the exact shade of forget-me-nots.

Abashed at being discovered spying on her, he stepped forward. "Forgive me, I didn't mean to stare. I'm—"

"Are you Mr. Noon?" she asked.

Taken aback, Bartholomew stammered, "Why, yes. That is . . . do you mean to tell me you are—"

"Oh, I knew you'd come." With that she threw herself into his arms.

Bartholomew stiffened with shock, then shut his eyes as his body succumbed to the soft warm feel of her. His arms closed about her. It was heaven. It was hell. His jaw clenched as he fought the urge to snatch her up and run away with her. Resolutely he moved his hands to her arms and set her away from him. Over the girl's shoulder, Mrs. Doughney winked at him. Flushing with embarrassment, he spoke with stiff formality.

"I take it you are Miss Ariah Scott from Cincinnati?"

She laughed gaily. "Of course I am. Who else . . . ?" Her voice faltered, her smile fled. "Gracious Sadie, I've done it again, haven't I?" Her hands flew to her face and she stared in dismay, first at Bartholomew, then at Mrs. Doughney. "I've made a fool of myself again. Oh, I am hopeless, aren't I?"

"No, my dear," Mrs. Doughney assured her. "I'm sure Mr. Noon finds you as refreshing a change from the usual stiff-necked young misses from back East as I do. Is that not so, sir?"

Bartholomew smiled, glad to be able to switch his attention away from the girl. "Indeed, ma'am. And I am doubly relieved to see that someone was able to convince her to bring along a chaperon for her journey." He awarded the older woman a deep bow. "Bartholomew Noon at your service."

Chuckling, Mrs. Doughney gave an old-fashioned curt-sey. "Utterly charming. If your nephew's manners are as gracious as yours, young man, I shall feel satisfied that my Miss Scott has found herself a good husband. I am not, however, her chaperon, but only an old woman lucky enough to have made her acquaintance when I boarded the train at Pendleton for my yearly visit to my son here in Portland."

"And what need do I have for a chaperon, I'd like to know?" Ariah Scott faced them, arms akimbo, a frown marring her pretty face. "It is nearly the twentieth century, after all, no longer the dark ages. Although one could hardly tell it from the way women are still being treated in some countries." Looking to Bartholomew she said, "Did you know that Greek women are cast from their homes and left to beg beside the road, or chased down and threatened with death, merely because some man got ahold of them? Even the savages here in the West are more humane to their women than that."

For the first time in longer than he cared to recall, Bartholomew found himself smiling with genuine pleasure. "The fact that a man was able to get his hands on your Greek woman proves the need for good chaperons."

Ariah glared at him. "All it proves is that she was foolish enough to let herself get into a situation she could not handle. Anyway, this is America, not Greece. Women here are taking charge of their own lives every day. Haven't you ever heard of Arizona Mary?"

He shook his head no, but he couldn't help smiling. Miss Ariah Scott was more than beautiful. She was unique, one of a kind. A fiery suffragette in nymph's clothing. And totally irresistible.

"Arizona Mary drove her own sixteen-yoke team of oxen and competed with other male freighters quite successfully," Miss Scott was saying. "Or what about Charlie Pankhurst who drove a stagecoach for years until she died and people discovered she was a female? And did you know there have been ten female mayors already in the state of Kansas?"

"No, I didn't know that," he said, struggling not to chuckle now. "Were any of them elected to a second term?"

Taken aback, Ariah dropped her hands from her hips and stared at him. "Why, I don't know. There wasn't anything in the article about that."

Mrs. Doughney politely cleared her throat. "Well, this is all terribly interesting, my dear, but now that your young man is here, I believe I shall hire myself a buggy and go on to my son's house. The trip was the most enjoyable I can remember in a long time, but I am quite tired now."

"No one is meeting you?" Bartholomew asked.

"No. My son is unmarried, Mr. Noon, and a very busy doctor. I discovered long ago that I was able to reach his home and kick off my city shoes much more quickly if I didn't rely on him to tear himself away from patients in time to pick me up. The arrangement pleases us both."

"May I offer you a ride, then?"

"What are you driving, if I may be so rude as to ask?"

"You may be as rude as you like, but I'm afraid I have only a farm wagon. Much more useful for hauling supplies than a buggy."

"Of course it is. Unfortunately, it also has only one seat and that one not too comfortable. In front of the station there are men sitting around in nice cushioned buggies, hoping to pick up a few coins by driving old ladies like me to hotels and such. You won't mind, I'm sure, if I give my business to one of them and let the two of you get on your way."

Sudden panic at the thought of being alone with the

entrancing child standing next to him assailed him, but he managed a calm, "No, of course not."

"Oh, Mrs. Doughney." Ariah threw her arms about the old woman. "I shall miss you so. You've been so kind."

"Nonsense, child. Haven't enjoyed myself so much in years. Waiting with you until your fiancé's uncle came for you was the least I could do." Her eyes sought out Bartholomew and, once again, she winked. "And it was worth it. Mr. Noon is a handsome devil. Should give you an idea what you can expect in your own young man."

Ariah released her and looked back at him. "You're right, he is handsome. And I should have expected it, from the description Mr. Monteer wrote of him in his wire. In my excitement I had forgotten about it until now."

Her gamin smile made Bartholomew's chest tighten. Surely this had to be a mistake. An awkward, immature pup like Pritchard couldn't possibly be lucky enough to win a nymph as intriguing as the one who stood before Bartholomew now.

Bartholomew thought of Hester and tasted a bitterness so vile he closed his eyes to it, shocked and mortified by the vehemence of his emotions. He felt as though someone had pried open his soul and spewed its contents onto the muddy, horse-befouled street. Frantically, he snatched at his last remaining bit of self-control, at the precious indifference to life he had so painfully, conscientiously cultivated over the years in order to survive.

"Yes, well, I must apologize for leaving you standing so long." He forced a smile. "You're not quite what I expected either."

Mrs. Doughney chuckled and waved a finger at him. "I

know exactly what you were expecting, young man. A prune of an old maid with a bun so tight it could probably hold up her stockings. Am I right?"

The tightness in his chest loosened a fraction as he gazed at the wizened face with its lively, dancing eyes.

"I confess." He awarded Mrs. Doughney a gallant bow, but his gaze was on the girl. "That was exactly what I expected."

Miss Ariah Scott grinned.

Ariah. The name suited her. Light and airy. Perfect for a nymph. He struggled to regain his composure and remember what he was about.

All around them, passengers continuing on to Goble, where train and all would be ferried across the Columbia River before resuming the journey to Seattle, were boarding the train. Soon the platform would be empty except for porters and employees of the Union and Northern Pacific Railroads. And Bartholomew suddenly realized he too was eager to be away; he could not wait to have Miss Ariah Scott to himself.

"Actually," she was saying, "I never would have guessed you were Mr. Monteer's uncle. You seem much too young. How old are you anyway?"

Bartholomew burst into peals of deep masculine laughter that were rusty from lack of use, and which drowned out Mrs. Doughney's polite warning cough.

"Gracious Sadie!" Ariah blushed prettily. "I truly should have my mouth sewn shut. It's likely the only way I'll learn to stop shoving my foot in it."

Never, he wanted to say. Such delectable lips were meant to be used, though he did have a purpose other than conversation in mind. "I shall be thirty this year, eight years Pritchard's senior."

"An excellent age." Mrs. Doughney gave an approving nod of her gray head. "Old enough to have sown your oats, as they say, and to have made something of yourself, yet still young enough to adjust to the tricks fate plays on all of us, eh?"

Bartholomew glanced at Miss Scott, wondering if *she* could be one of fate's tricks. Something niggled at his memory. He shrugged it away.

"I'm sure you're right. Now, Miss Scott, if you'll point out the rest of your baggage, I'll get it loaded while you finish your goodbyes. We've a long way to go."

"Oh, yes, of course." She gestured to two small crates and a large trunk. "That's it there."

Bartholomew shouldered the trunk as though it contained nothing more than bird feathers, holding it in place with one arm while he squatted to pick up one of the crates.

As he put space between himself and the two women, he chuckled silently, remembering how he had wondered what he would do with the girl during the four long days of the journey home. There was no doubt about what he wanted to do. His hands ached with the need to stroke that smooth, velvet flesh, to explore and discover its secret contours. Thinking about it, four days no longer seemed enough.

He set the crate alongside the boxed-up fancy rosewood etagere Hester had insisted he buy her, then lowered the trunk onto the wagon bed.

Hester. Bartholomew's fantasy burst like the seed head of a giant dandelion, scattered by the wind.

Hester was his wife—till death do them part—no matter how much he might wish things were different. And Ariah Scott belonged to Pritchard.

His shoulders sagged under a weight of guilt as great as a steam engine. He rested his arms on the sideboard, braced his forehead on a fist, then shut his eyes and tried to banish the image of the girl's sweet tempting mouth, so lush, so—

A warm hand closed over his arm. "Are you all right, Mr. Noon? Is there anything I can do for you?"

Bartholomew looked down to see Ariah Scott standing only a kiss away, gazing up at him with those incredible forget-me-not blue eyes, her luscious lips moist and parted, her concerned expression sweetly, guilelessly intent.

And he plummeted into hell.

Taylor—made Romance From Zebra Books

WHISPERED KISSES (3830, $4.99/5.99)
Beautiful Texas heiress Laura Leigh Webster never imagined that her biggest worry on her African safari would be the handsome Jace Elliot, her tour guide. Laura's guardian, Lord Chadwick Hamilton, warns her of Jace's dangerous past; she simply cannot resist the lure of his strong arms and the passion of his *Whispered Kisses*.

KISS OF THE NIGHT WIND (3831, $4.99/$5.99)
Carrie Sue Strover thought she was leaving trouble behind her when she deserted her brother's outlaw gang to live her life as schoolmarm Carolyn Starns. On her journey, her stagecoach was attacked and she was rescued by handsome T.J. Rogue. T.J. plots to have Carrie lead him to her brother's cohorts who murdered his family. T.J., however, soon succumbs to the beautiful runaway's charms and loving caresses.

FORTUNE'S FLAMES (3825, $4.99/$5.99)
Impatient to begin her journey back home to New Orleans, beautiful Maren James was furious when Captain Hawk delayed the voyage by searching for stowaways. Impatience gave way to uncontrollable desire once the handsome captain searched *her* cabin. He was looking for illegal passengers; what he found was wild passion with a woman he knew was unlike all those he had known before!

PASSIONS WILD AND FREE (3828, $4.99/$5.99)
After seeing her family and home destroyed by the cruel and hateful Epson gang, Randee Hollis swore revenge. She knew she found the perfect man to help her—gunslinger Marsh Logan. Not only strong and brave, Marsh had the ebony hair and light blue eyes to make Randee forget her hate and seek the love and passion that only he could give her.

Available wherever paperbacks are sold, or order direct from the Publisher. Send cover price plus 50¢ per copy for mailing and handling to Penguin USA, P.O. Box 999, c/o Dept. 17109, Bergenfield, NJ 07621. Residents of New York and Tennessee must include sales tax. DO NOT SEND CASH.